GRAPHIC
NOVEL

GODDESS GIRLS

APHRODITE THE BEAUTY

CREATED BY
JOAN HOLUB &
SUZANNE WILLIAMS
ADAPTED BY DAVID CAMPITI

ILLUSTRATED BY EDUARDO GARCIA
AT GLASS HOUSE GRAPHICS

Aladdin
New York   London   Toronto   Sydney   New Delhi

ALADDIN
AN IMPRINT OF SIMON & SCHUSTER CHILDREN'S PUBLISHING DIVISION
1230 AVENUE OF THE AMERICAS, NEW YORK, NEW YORK 10020
FIRST ALADDIN EDITION AUGUST 2022
TEXT COPYRIGHT © 2022 BY JOAN HOLUB AND SUZANNE WILLIAMS
COVER ILLUSTRATION BY JOÃO ZOD
ILLUSTRATIONS COPYRIGHT © 2022 BY GLASS HOUSE GRAPHICS
ART BY EDUARDO GARCIA. ADDITIONAL ART BY JOÃO ZOD, MARCOS CORTEZ, AND NOZA.
LETTERING BY MARCOS INOUE. ART SERVICES BY GLASS HOUSE GRAPHICS.
ALL RIGHTS RESERVED, INCLUDING THE RIGHT OF REPRODUCTION IN WHOLE OR IN PART IN ANY
FORM. ALADDIN AND RELATED LOGO ARE REGISTERED TRADEMARKS OF SIMON & SCHUSTER, INC.
FOR INFORMATION ABOUT SPECIAL DISCOUNTS FOR BULK PURCHASES, PLEASE CONTACT
SIMON & SCHUSTER SPECIAL SALES AT 1-866-506-1949 OR BUSINESS@SIMONANDSCHUSTER.COM.
THE SIMON & SCHUSTER SPEAKERS BUREAU CAN BRING AUTHORS TO YOUR LIVE EVENT. FOR MORE
INFORMATION OR TO BOOK AN EVENT CONTACT THE SIMON & SCHUSTER SPEAKERS BUREAU AT
1-866-248-3049 OR VISIT OUR WEBSITE AT WWW.SIMONSPEAKERS.COM.
THE ILLUSTRATIONS FOR THIS BOOK WERE RENDERED DIGITALLY.
THE TEXT OF THIS BOOK WAS SET IN FONT ANIME ACE 2.0 BB AT 6.5 POINTS OVER
7.5 POINT LEADING AND STEINANTIK AT 10 POINTS OVER 11 POINT LEADING.
MANUFACTURED IN CHINA 0522 SCP
2 4 6 8 10 9 7 5 3 1
LIBRARY OF CONGRESS CONTROL NUMBER 2021945035
ISBN 978-1-5344-7393-5 (HC)
ISBN 978-1-5344-7392-8 (PBK)
ISBN 978-1-5344-7394-2 (EBOOK)

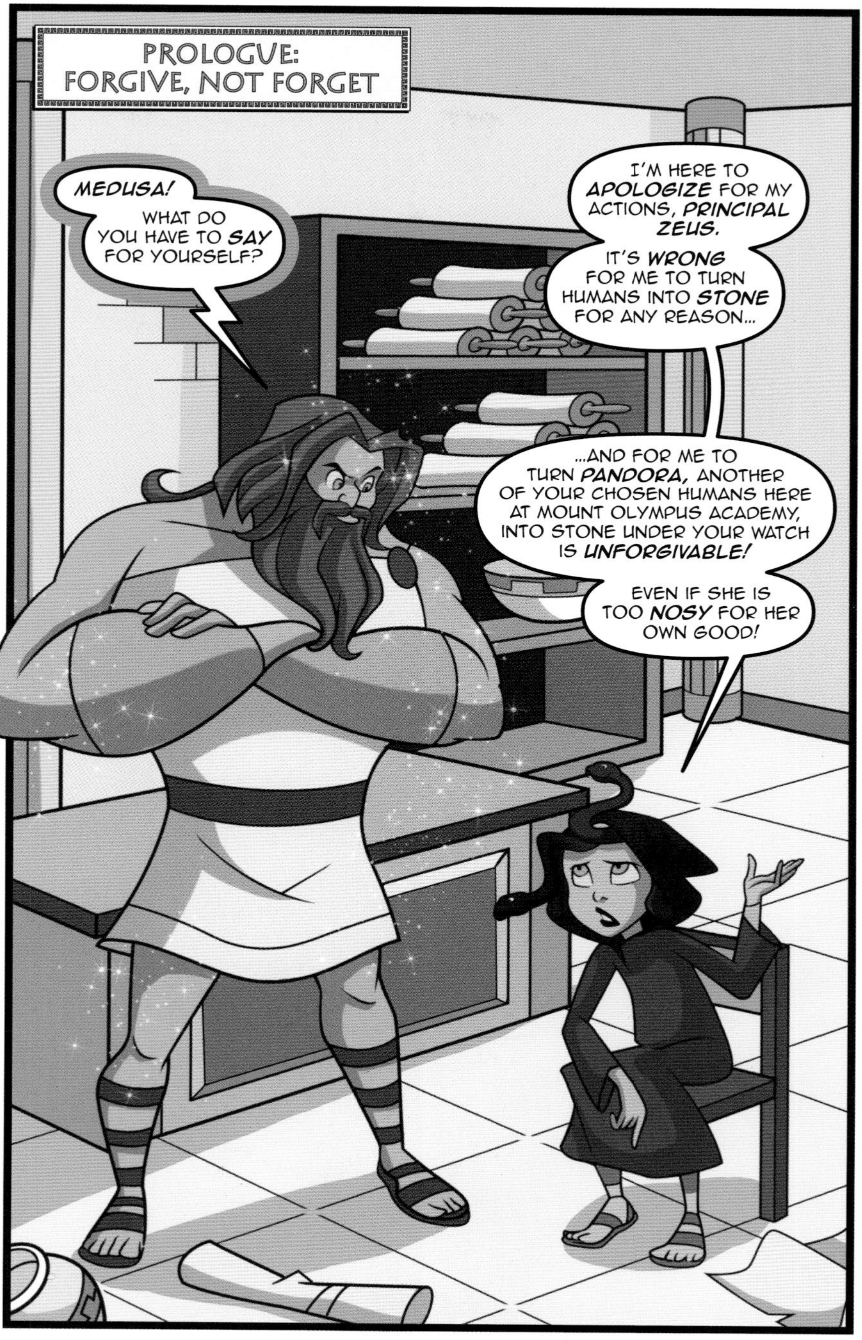
PROLOGUE:
FORGIVE, NOT FORGET
MEDUSA! WHAT DO YOU HAVE TO SAY FOR YOURSELF?
I'M HERE TO APOLOGIZE FOR MY ACTIONS, PRINCIPAL ZEUS.
IT'S WRONG FOR ME TO TURN HUMANS INTO STONE FOR ANY REASON...
...AND FOR ME TO TURN PANDORA, ANOTHER OF YOUR CHOSEN HUMANS HERE AT MOUNT OLYMPUS ACADEMY, INTO STONE UNDER YOUR WATCH IS UNFORGIVABLE!
EVEN IF SHE IS TOO NOSY FOR HER OWN GOOD!

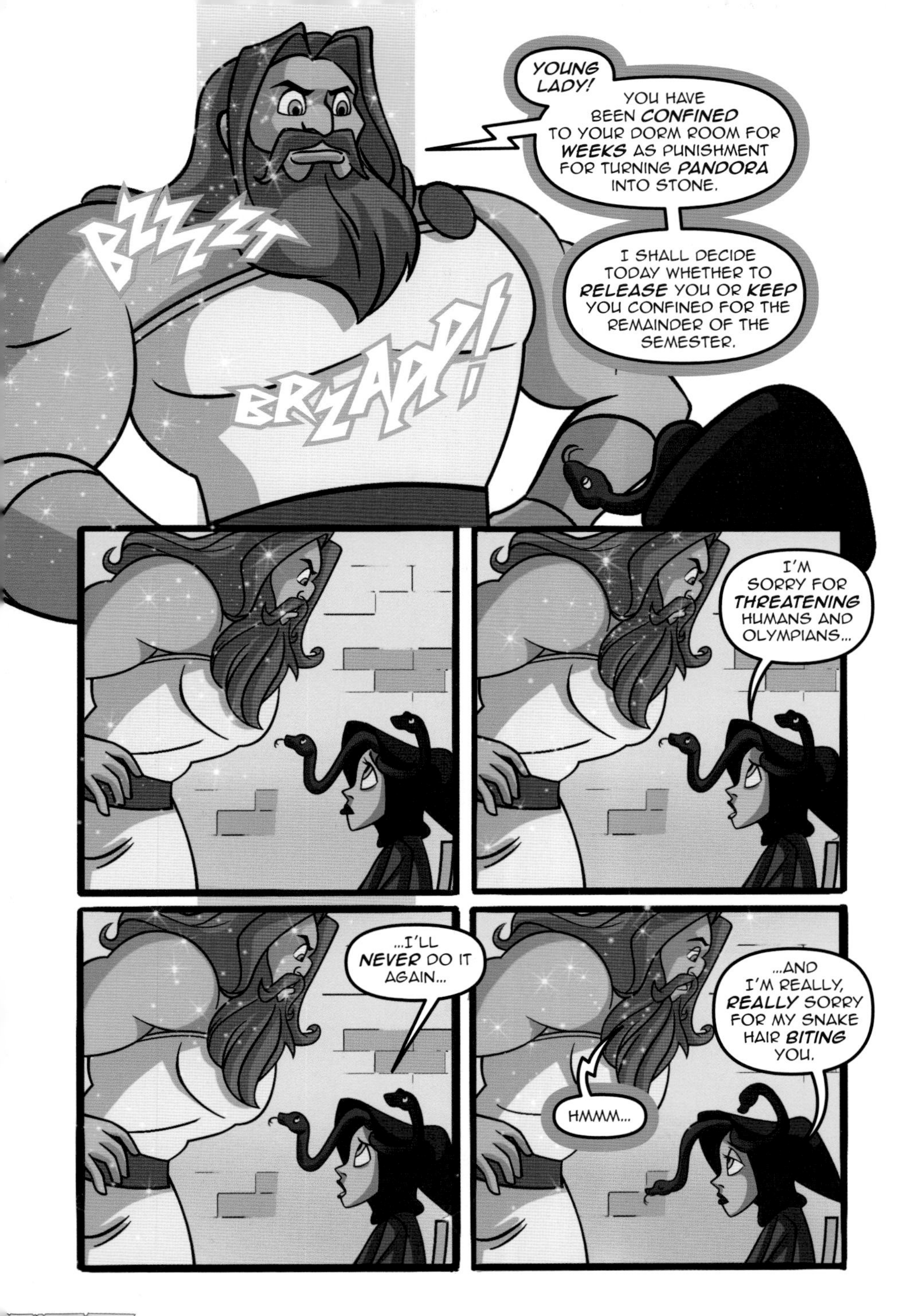
YOUNG LADY!
YOU HAVE BEEN CONFINED TO YOUR DORM ROOM FOR WEEKS AS PUNISHMENT FOR TURNING PANDORA INTO STONE.
I SHALL DECIDE TODAY WHETHER TO RELEASE YOU OR KEEP YOU CONFINED FOR THE REMAINDER OF THE SEMESTER.
BZZZZT
BRZAPP!
I'M SORRY FOR THREATENING HUMANS AND OLYMPIANS...
...I'LL NEVER DO IT AGAIN...
...AND I'M REALLY, REALLY SORRY FOR MY SNAKE HAIR BITING YOU.
HMMM...

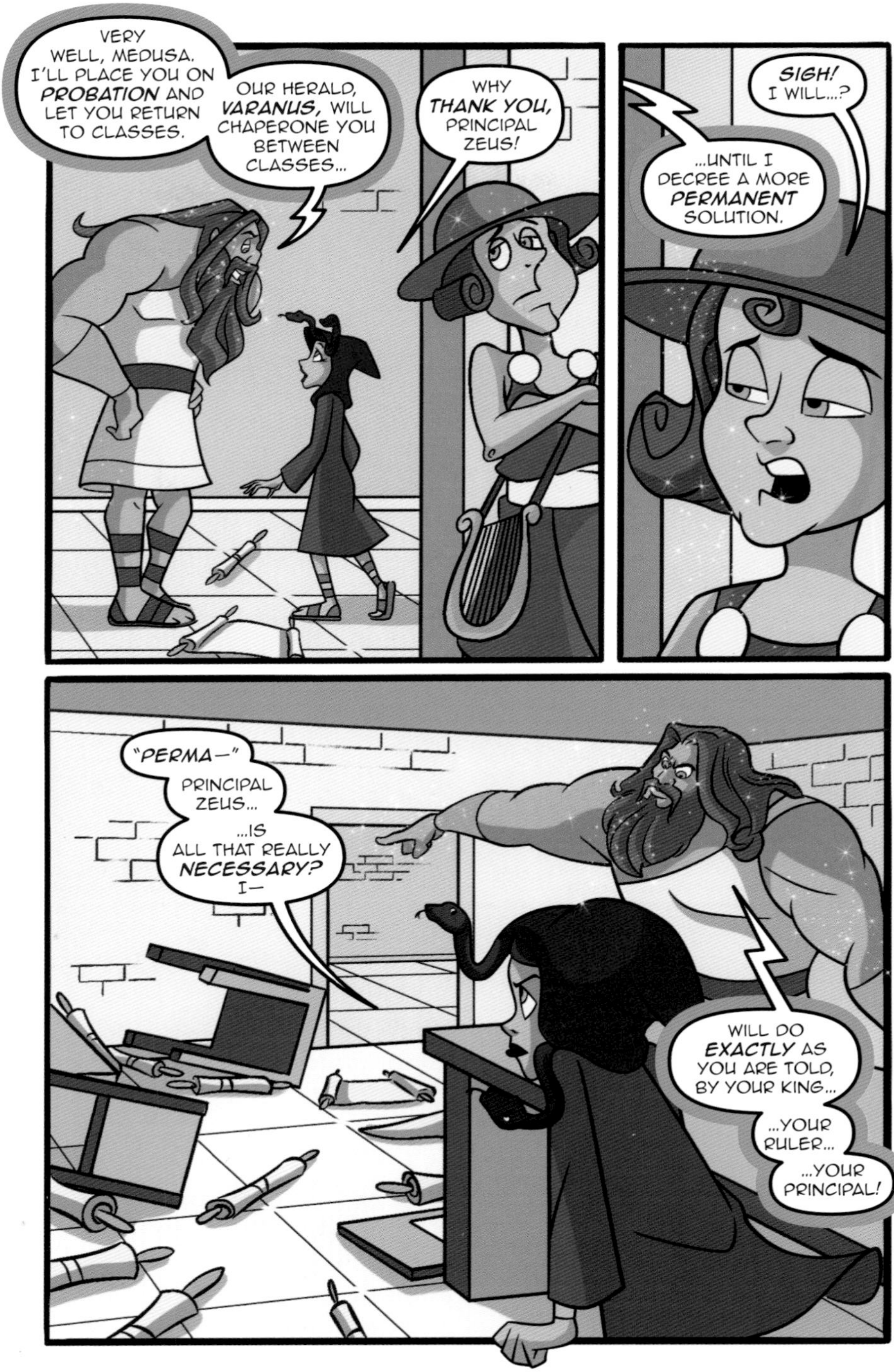
VERY WELL, MEDUSA. I'LL PLACE YOU ON PROBATION AND LET YOU RETURN TO CLASSES.
OUR HERALD, VARANUS, WILL CHAPERONE YOU BETWEEN CLASSES...
WHY THANK YOU, PRINCIPAL ZEUS!
...UNTIL I DECREE A MORE PERMANENT SOLUTION.
SIGH! I WILL...?
"PERMA—" PRINCIPAL ZEUS...
...IS ALL THAT REALLY NECESSARY? I—
WILL DO EXACTLY AS YOU ARE TOLD, BY YOUR KING...
...YOUR RULER...
...YOUR PRINCIPAL!

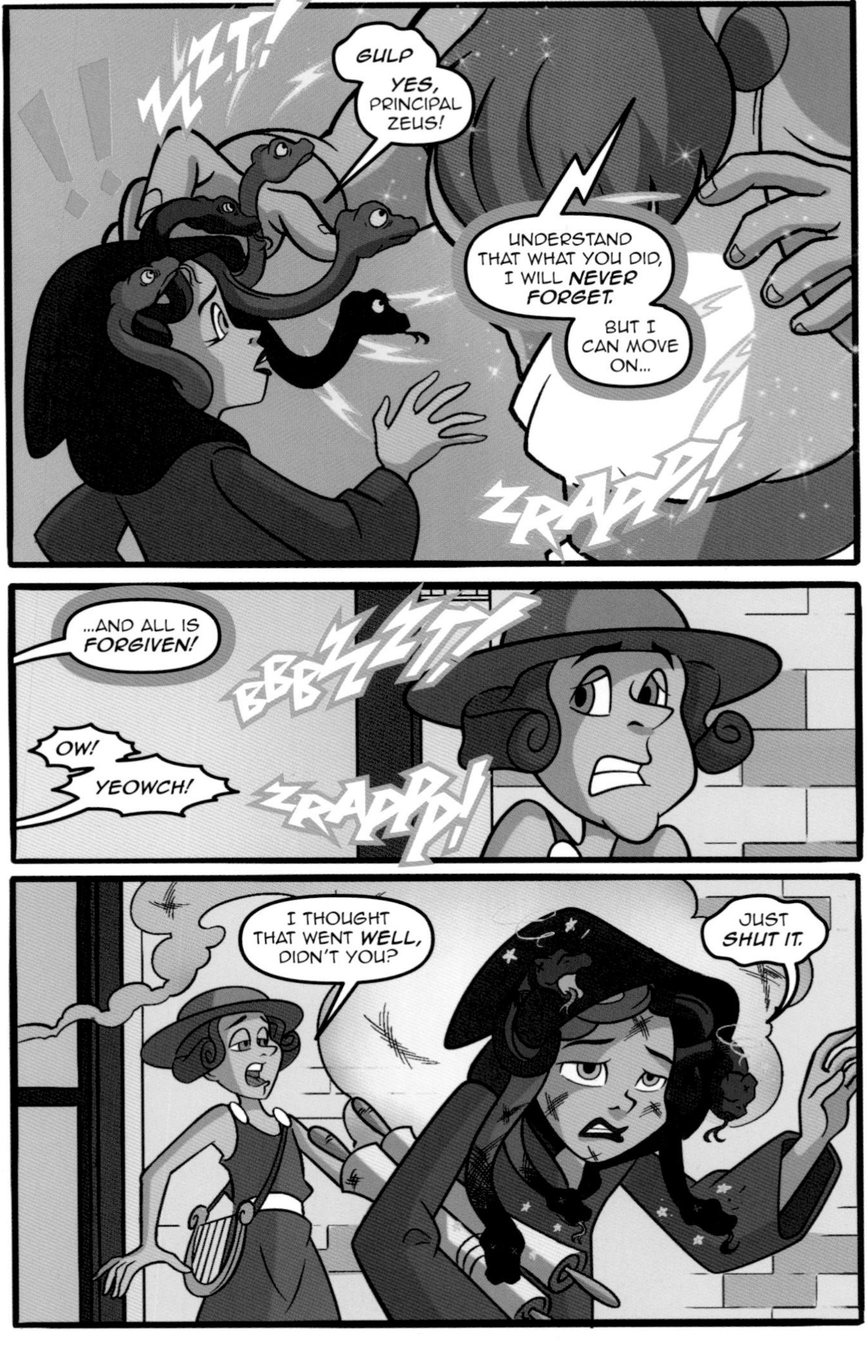

VVZZT!
GULP
YES, PRINCIPAL ZEUS!
UNDERSTAND THAT WHAT YOU DID, I WILL NEVER FORGET.
BUT I CAN MOVE ON...
ZRAPP!
...AND ALL IS FORGIVEN!
BBBZZZT!
OW!
YEOWCH!
ZRAPPP!
I THOUGHT THAT WENT WELL, DIDN'T YOU?
JUST SHUT IT.

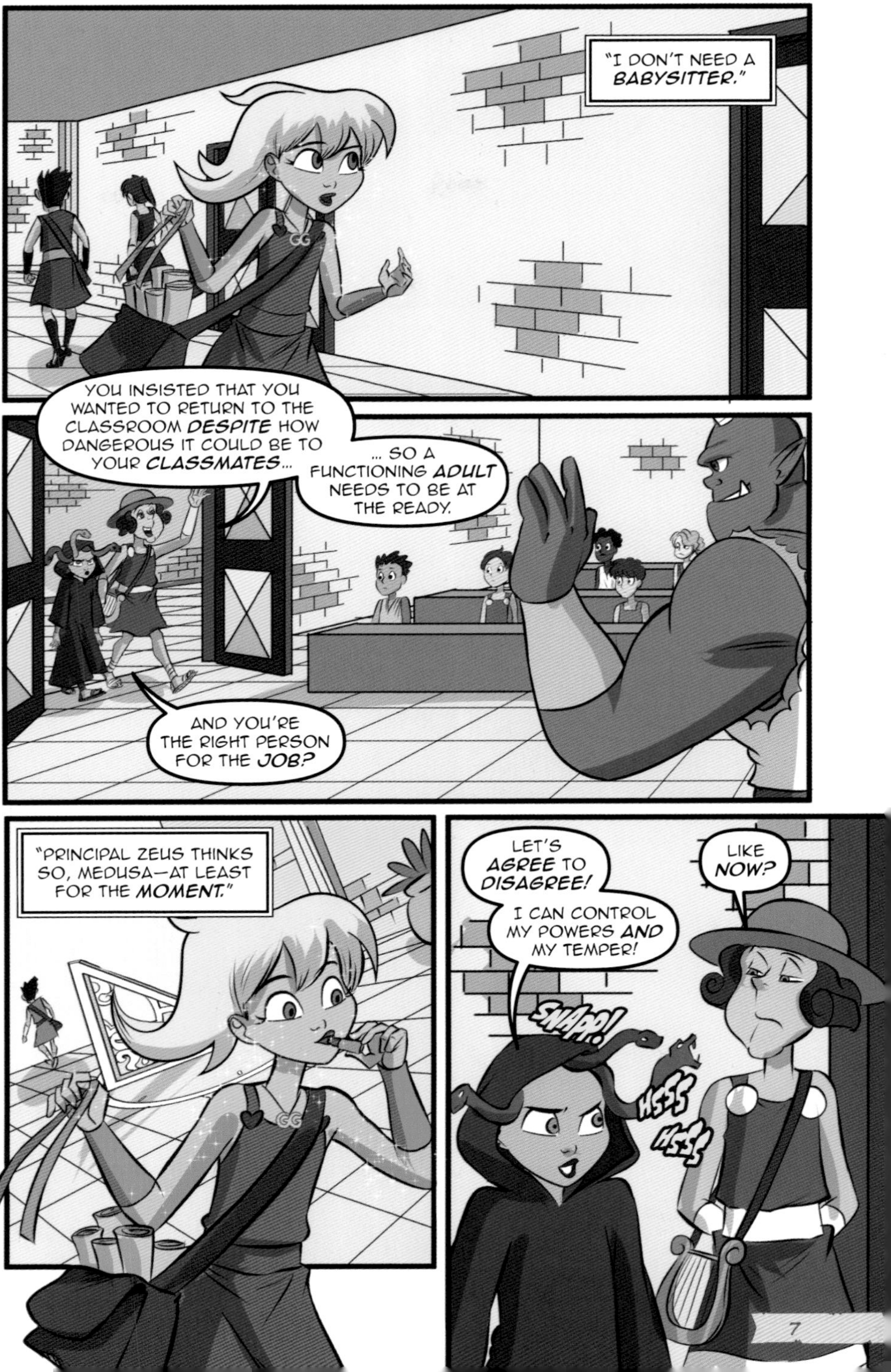
"I DON'T NEED A BABYSITTER."
YOU INSISTED THAT YOU WANTED TO RETURN TO THE CLASSROOM DESPITE HOW DANGEROUS IT COULD BE TO YOUR CLASSMATES...
... SO A FUNCTIONING ADULT NEEDS TO BE AT THE READY.
AND YOU'RE THE RIGHT PERSON FOR THE JOB?
"PRINCIPAL ZEUS THINKS SO, MEDUSA—AT LEAST FOR THE MOMENT."
LET'S AGREE TO DISAGREE!
I CAN CONTROL MY POWERS AND MY TEMPER!
LIKE NOW?
SNAPP!
HSSS
HSSS

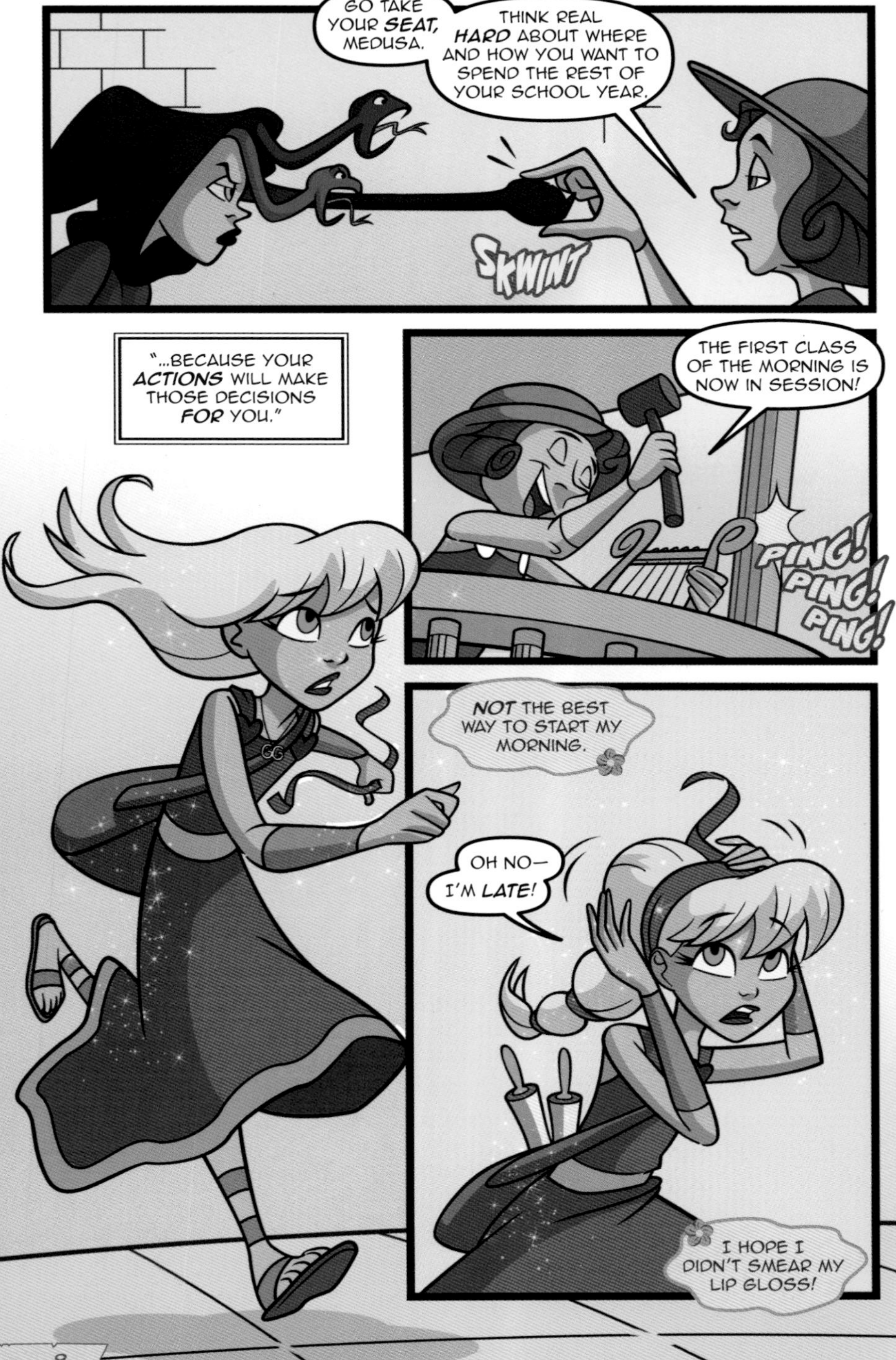
GO TAKE YOUR SEAT, MEDUSA.
THINK REAL HARD ABOUT WHERE AND HOW YOU WANT TO SPEND THE REST OF YOUR SCHOOL YEAR.
SKWINT
"...BECAUSE YOUR ACTIONS WILL MAKE THOSE DECISIONS FOR YOU."
THE FIRST CLASS OF THE MORNING IS NOW IN SESSION!
PING! PING! PING!
NOT THE BEST WAY TO START MY MORNING.
OH NO— I'M LATE!
I HOPE I DIDN'T SMEAR MY LIP GLOSS!

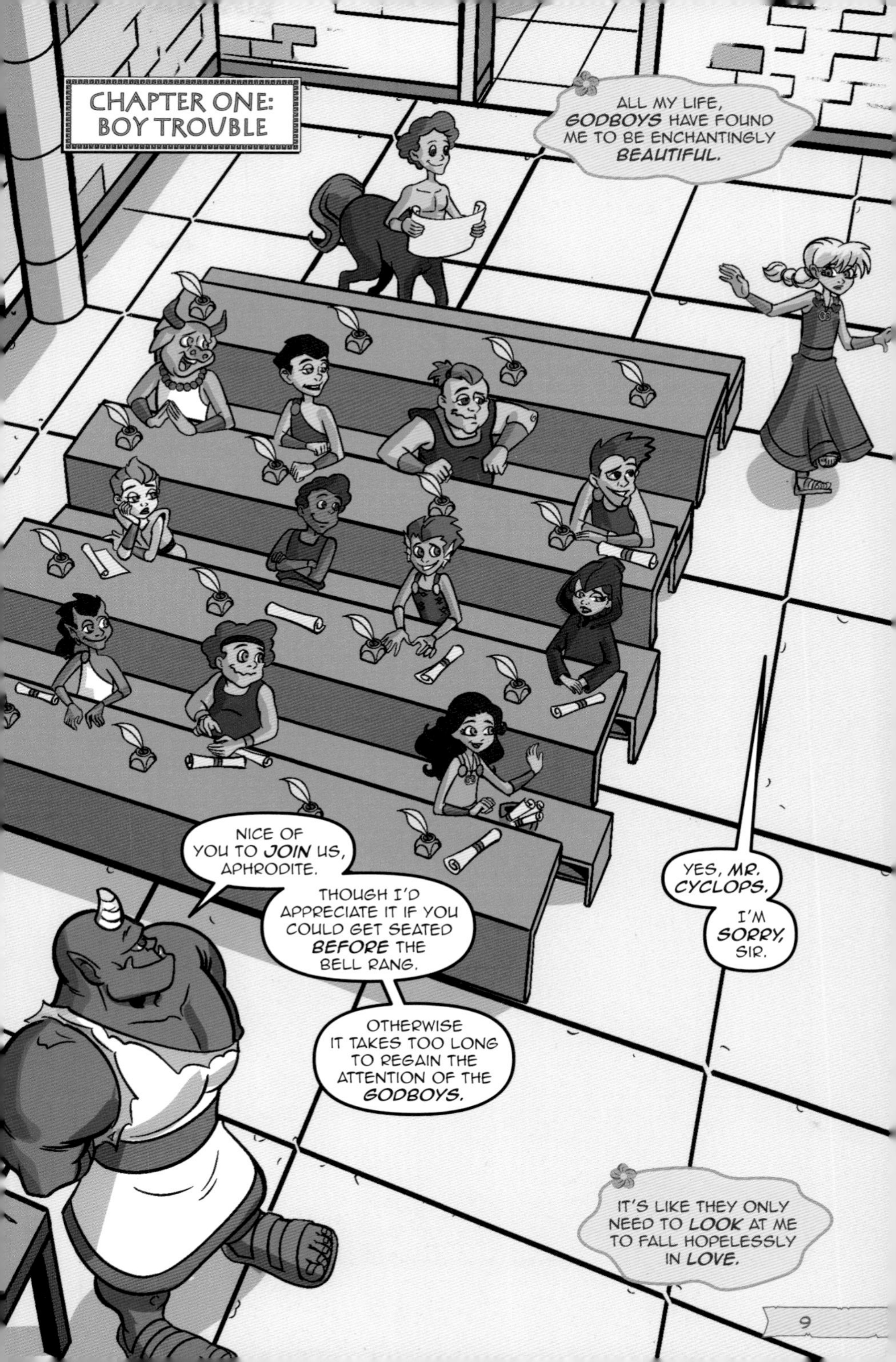
CHAPTER ONE: BOY TROUBLE
ALL MY LIFE, GODBOYS HAVE FOUND ME TO BE ENCHANTINGLY BEAUTIFUL.
NICE OF YOU TO JOIN US, APHRODITE.
THOUGH I'D APPRECIATE IT IF YOU COULD GET SEATED BEFORE THE BELL RANG.
OTHERWISE IT TAKES TOO LONG TO REGAIN THE ATTENTION OF THE GODBOYS.
YES, MR. CYCLOPS.
I'M SORRY, SIR.
IT'S LIKE THEY ONLY NEED TO LOOK AT ME TO FALL HOPELESSLY IN LOVE.

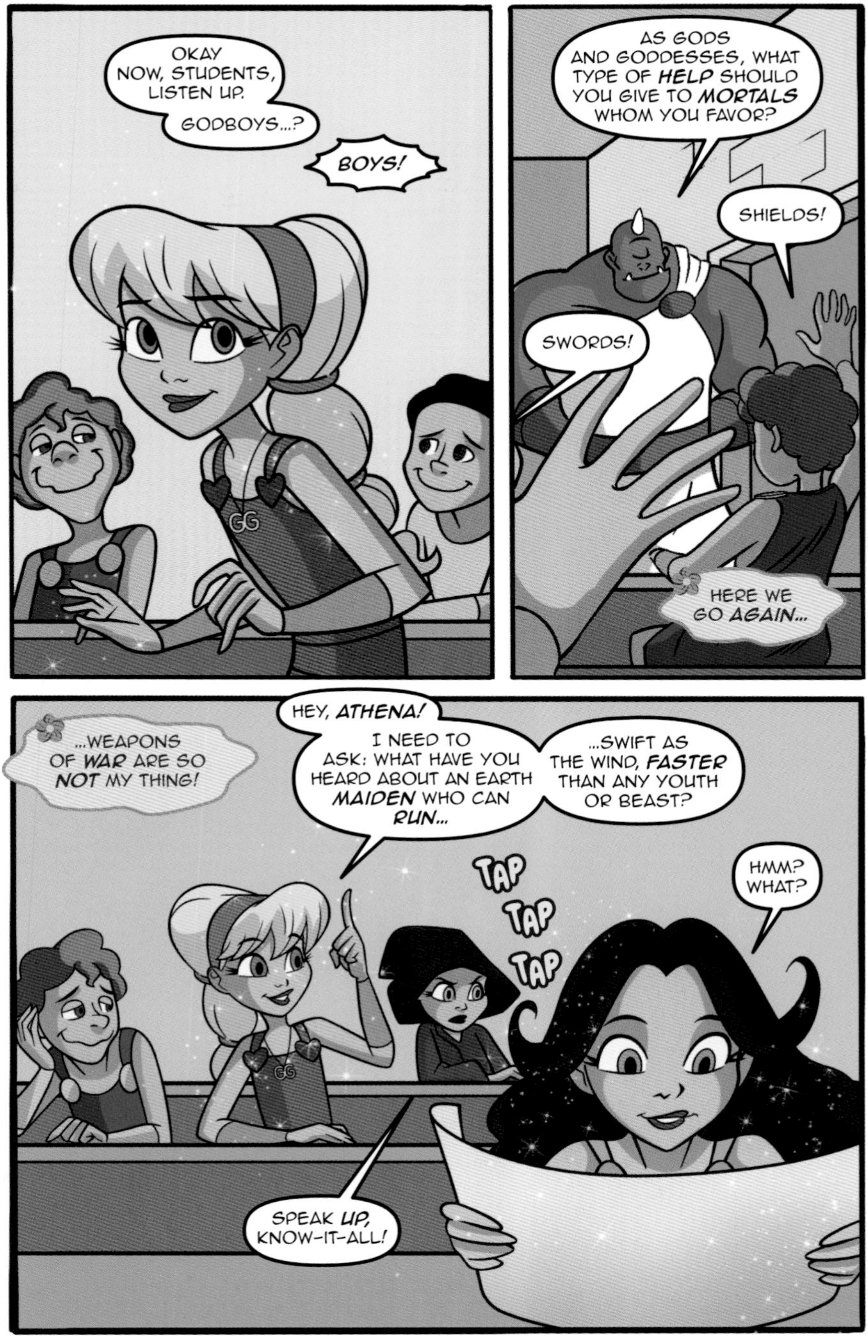
OKAY NOW, STUDENTS, LISTEN UP.
GODBOYS...?
BOYS!
AS GODS AND GODDESSES, WHAT TYPE OF HELP SHOULD YOU GIVE TO MORTALS WHOM YOU FAVOR?
SHIELDS!
SWORDS!
HERE WE GO AGAIN...
...WEAPONS OF WAR ARE SO NOT MY THING!
HEY, ATHENA!
I NEED TO ASK: WHAT HAVE YOU HEARD ABOUT AN EARTH MAIDEN WHO CAN RUN...
...SWIFT AS THE WIND, FASTER THAN ANY YOUTH OR BEAST?
TAP
TAP
TAP
HMM? WHAT?
SPEAK UP, KNOW-IT-ALL!

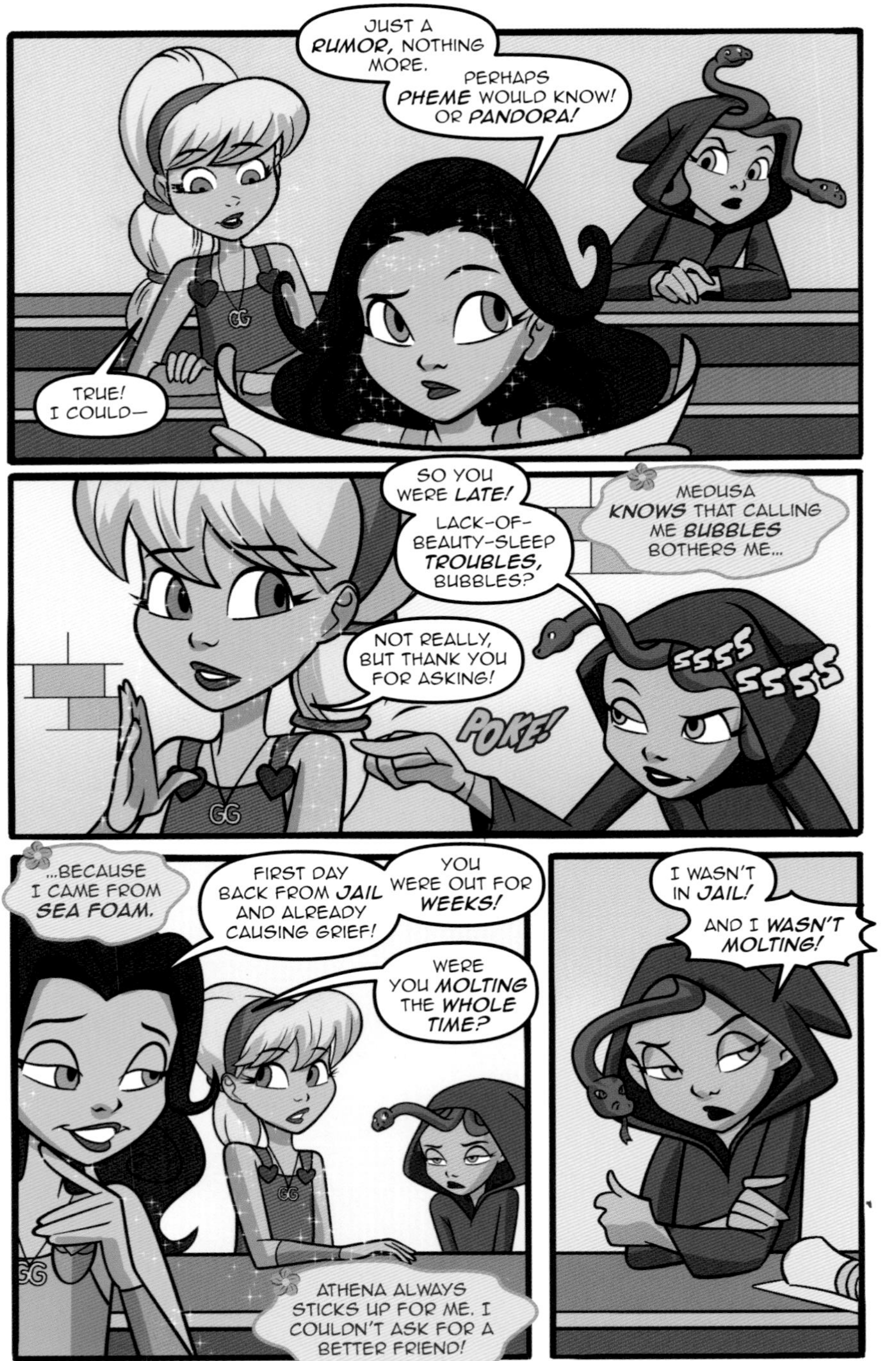

JUST A RUMOR, NOTHING MORE.
PERHAPS PHEME WOULD KNOW! OR PANDORA!
TRUE! I COULD—
SO YOU WERE LATE!
LACK-OF-BEAUTY-SLEEP TROUBLES, BUBBLES?
MEDUSA KNOWS THAT CALLING ME BUBBLES BOTHERS ME...
NOT REALLY, BUT THANK YOU FOR ASKING!
SSSS SSSS
POKE!
...BECAUSE I CAME FROM SEA FOAM.
FIRST DAY BACK FROM JAIL AND ALREADY CAUSING GRIEF!
YOU WERE OUT FOR WEEKS!
WERE YOU MOLTING THE WHOLE TIME?
ATHENA ALWAYS STICKS UP FOR ME. I COULDN'T ASK FOR A BETTER FRIEND!
I WASN'T IN JAIL!
AND I WASN'T MOLTING!

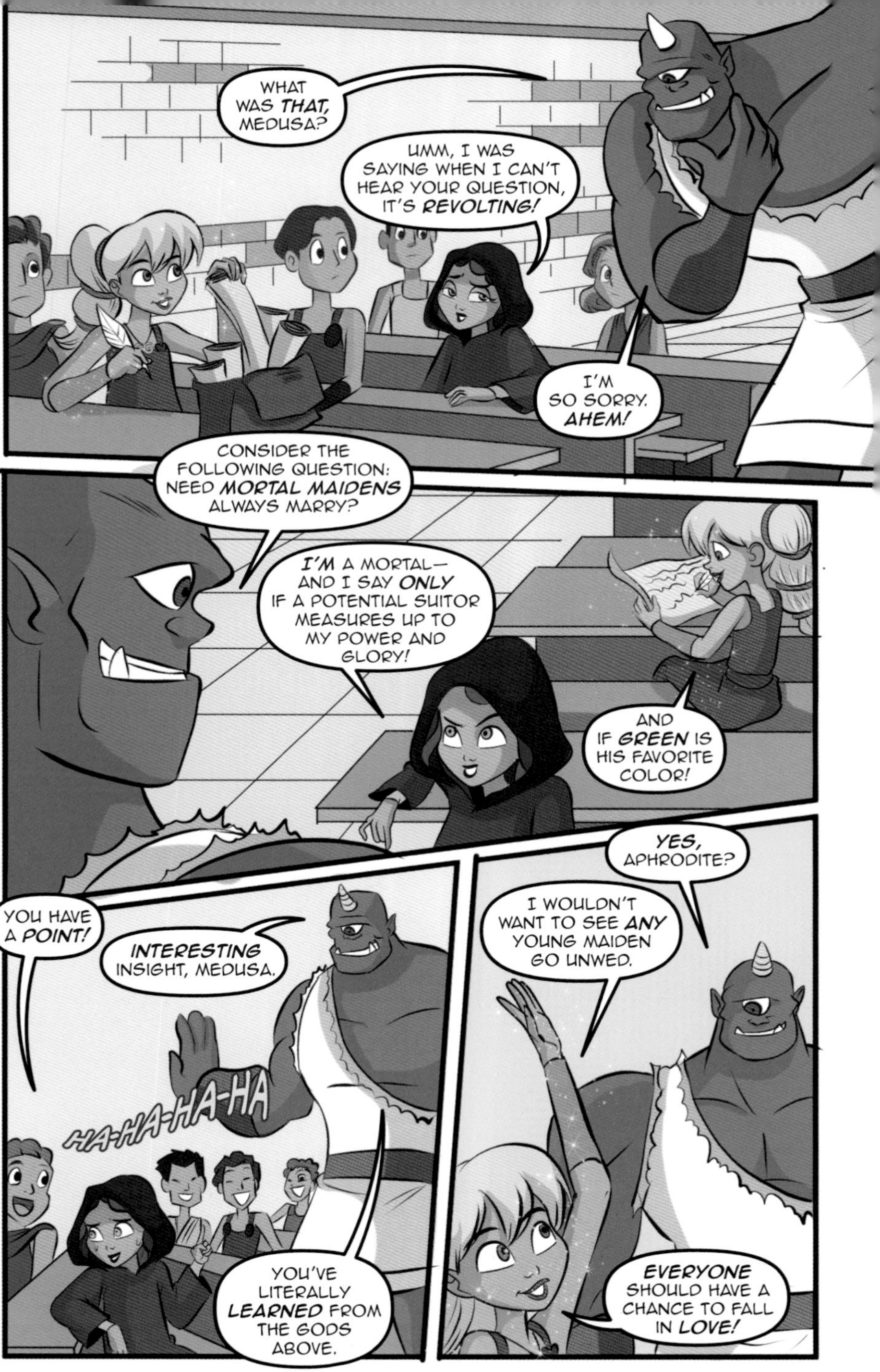
WHAT WAS THAT, MEDUSA?
UMM, I WAS SAYING WHEN I CAN'T HEAR YOUR QUESTION, IT'S REVOLTING!
I'M SO SORRY. AHEM!
CONSIDER THE FOLLOWING QUESTION: NEED MORTAL MAIDENS ALWAYS MARRY?
I'M A MORTAL— AND I SAY ONLY IF A POTENTIAL SUITOR MEASURES UP TO MY POWER AND GLORY!
AND IF GREEN IS HIS FAVORITE COLOR!
YOU HAVE A POINT!
INTERESTING INSIGHT, MEDUSA.
HA-HA-HA-HA-HA
YOU'VE LITERALLY LEARNED FROM THE GODS ABOVE.
YES, APHRODITE?
I WOULDN'T WANT TO SEE ANY YOUNG MAIDEN GO UNWED.
EVERYONE SHOULD HAVE A CHANCE TO FALL IN LOVE!

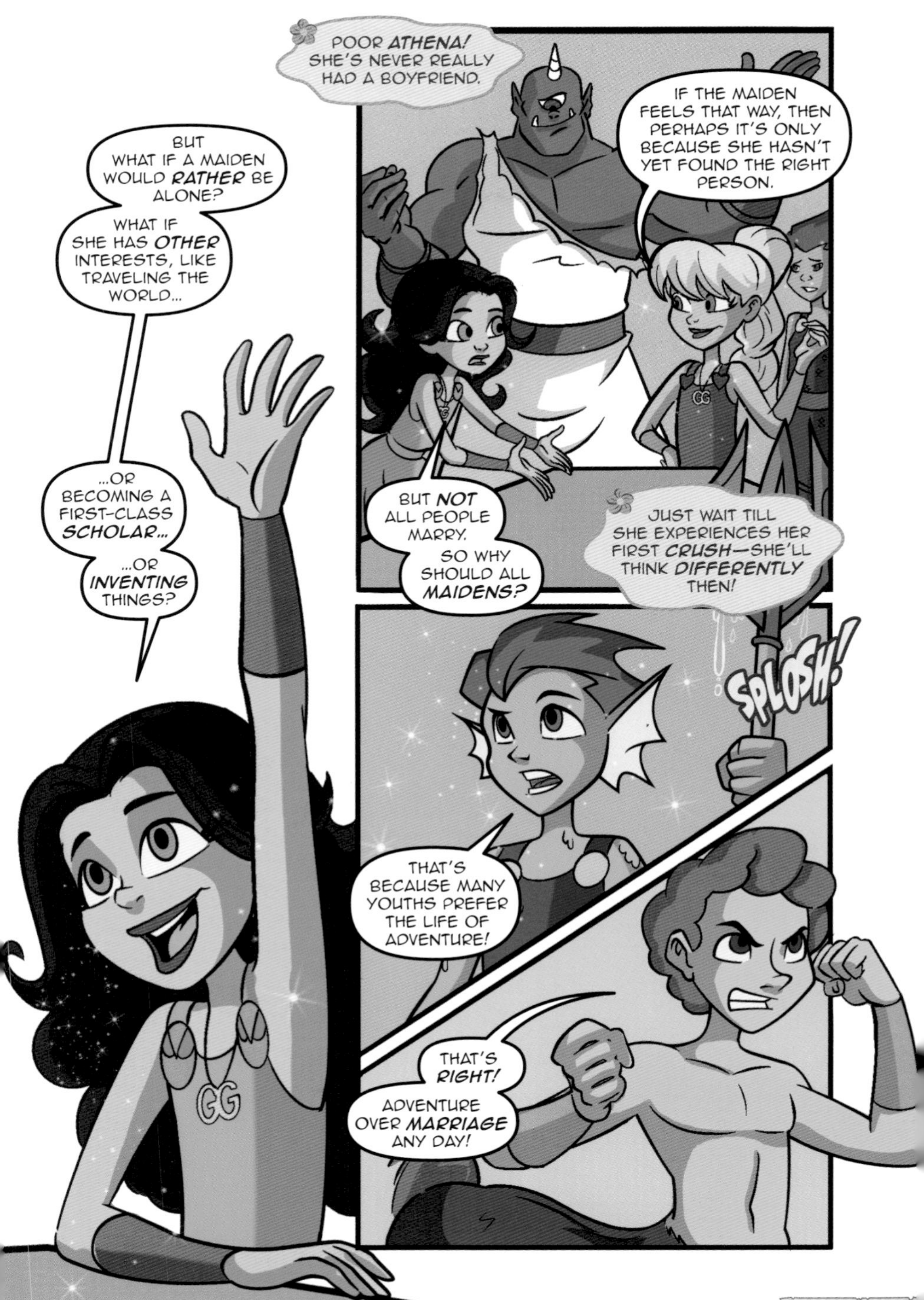
BUT WHAT IF A MAIDEN WOULD RATHER BE ALONE?
WHAT IF SHE HAS OTHER INTERESTS, LIKE TRAVELING THE WORLD...
...OR BECOMING A FIRST-CLASS SCHOLAR...
...OR INVENTING THINGS?
POOR ATHENA! SHE'S NEVER REALLY HAD A BOYFRIEND.
IF THE MAIDEN FEELS THAT WAY, THEN PERHAPS IT'S ONLY BECAUSE SHE HASN'T YET FOUND THE RIGHT PERSON.
BUT NOT ALL PEOPLE MARRY.
SO WHY SHOULD ALL MAIDENS?
JUST WAIT TILL SHE EXPERIENCES HER FIRST CRUSH—SHE'LL THINK DIFFERENTLY THEN!
SPLOSH!
THAT'S BECAUSE MANY YOUTHS PREFER THE LIFE OF ADVENTURE!
THAT'S RIGHT!
ADVENTURE OVER MARRIAGE ANY DAY!

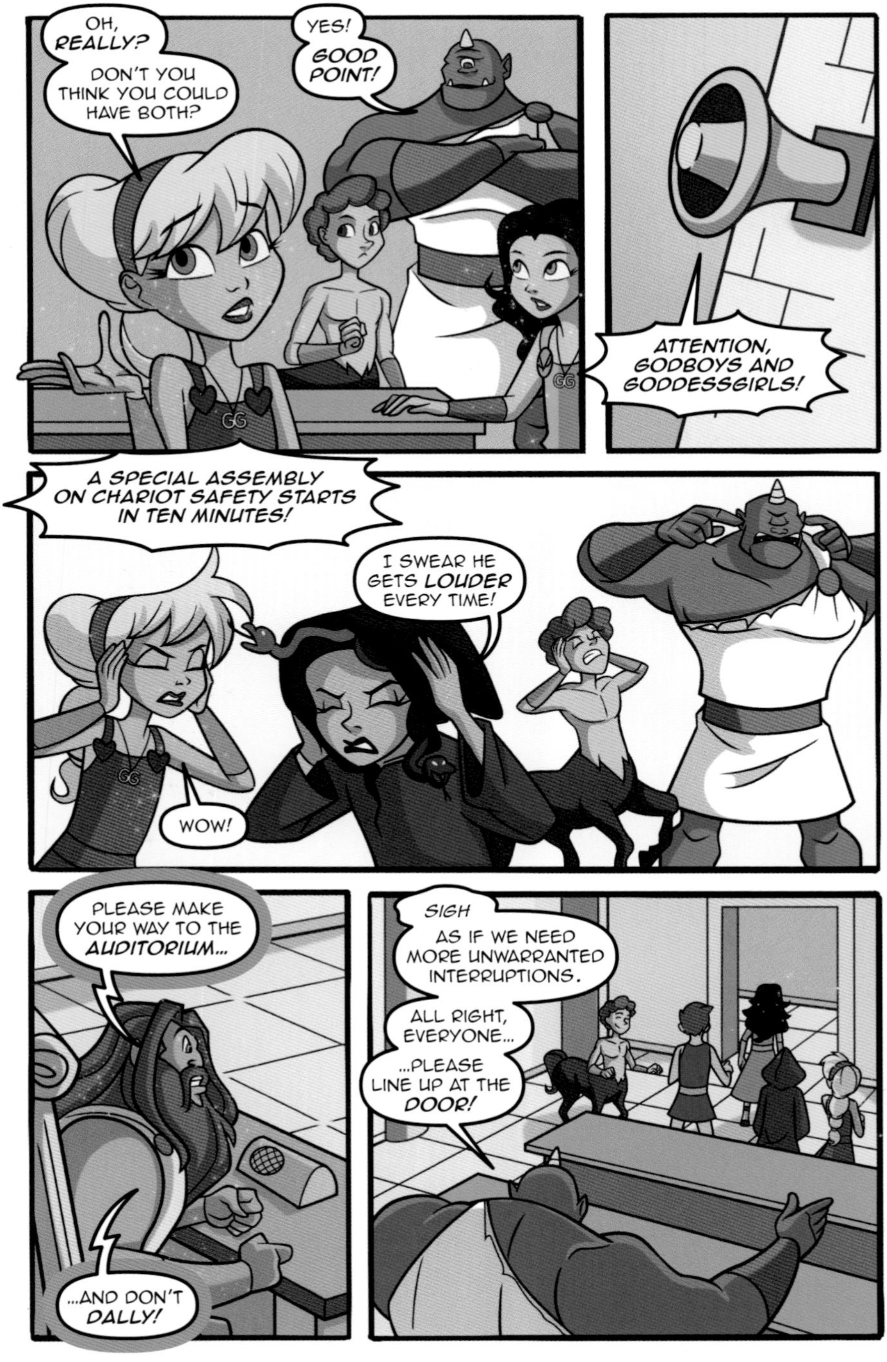
OH, REALLY?
DON'T YOU THINK YOU COULD HAVE BOTH?
YES! GOOD POINT!
ATTENTION, GODBOYS AND GODDESSGIRLS!
A SPECIAL ASSEMBLY ON CHARIOT SAFETY STARTS IN TEN MINUTES!
I SWEAR HE GETS LOUDER EVERY TIME!
WOW!
PLEASE MAKE YOUR WAY TO THE AUDITORIUM...
...AND DON'T DALLY!
SIGH
AS IF WE NEED MORE UNWARRANTED INTERRUPTIONS.
ALL RIGHT, EVERYONE...
...PLEASE LINE UP AT THE DOOR!

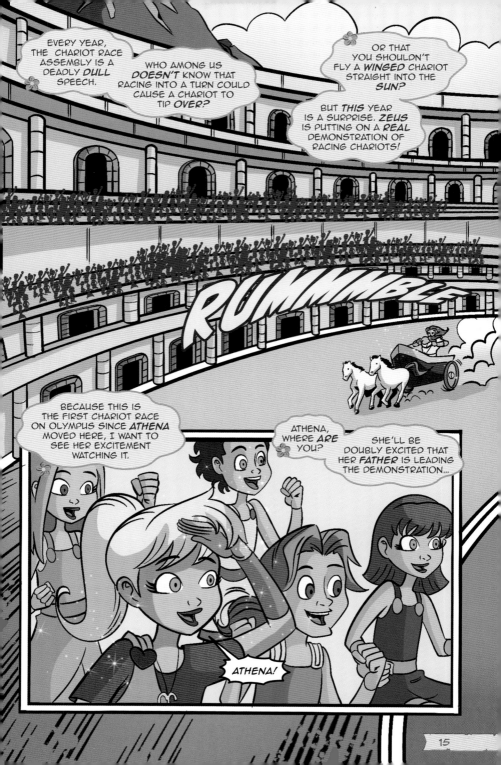

EVERY YEAR, THE CHARIOT RACE ASSEMBLY IS A DEADLY *DULL* SPEECH.

WHO AMONG US *DOESN'T* KNOW THAT RACING INTO A TURN COULD CAUSE A CHARIOT TO TIP *OVER?*

OR THAT YOU SHOULDN'T FLY A *WINGED* CHARIOT STRAIGHT INTO THE *SUN?*

BUT *THIS* YEAR IS A SURPRISE. *ZEUS* IS PUTTING ON A *REAL* DEMONSTRATION OF RACING CHARIOTS!

RUMMMMBLE

BECAUSE THIS IS THE FIRST CHARIOT RACE ON OLYMPUS SINCE *ATHENA* MOVED HERE, I WANT TO SEE HER EXCITEMENT WATCHING IT.

ATHENA, WHERE *ARE* YOU?

SHE'LL BE DOUBLY EXCITED THAT HER *FATHER* IS LEADING THE DEMONSTRATION...

ATHENA!

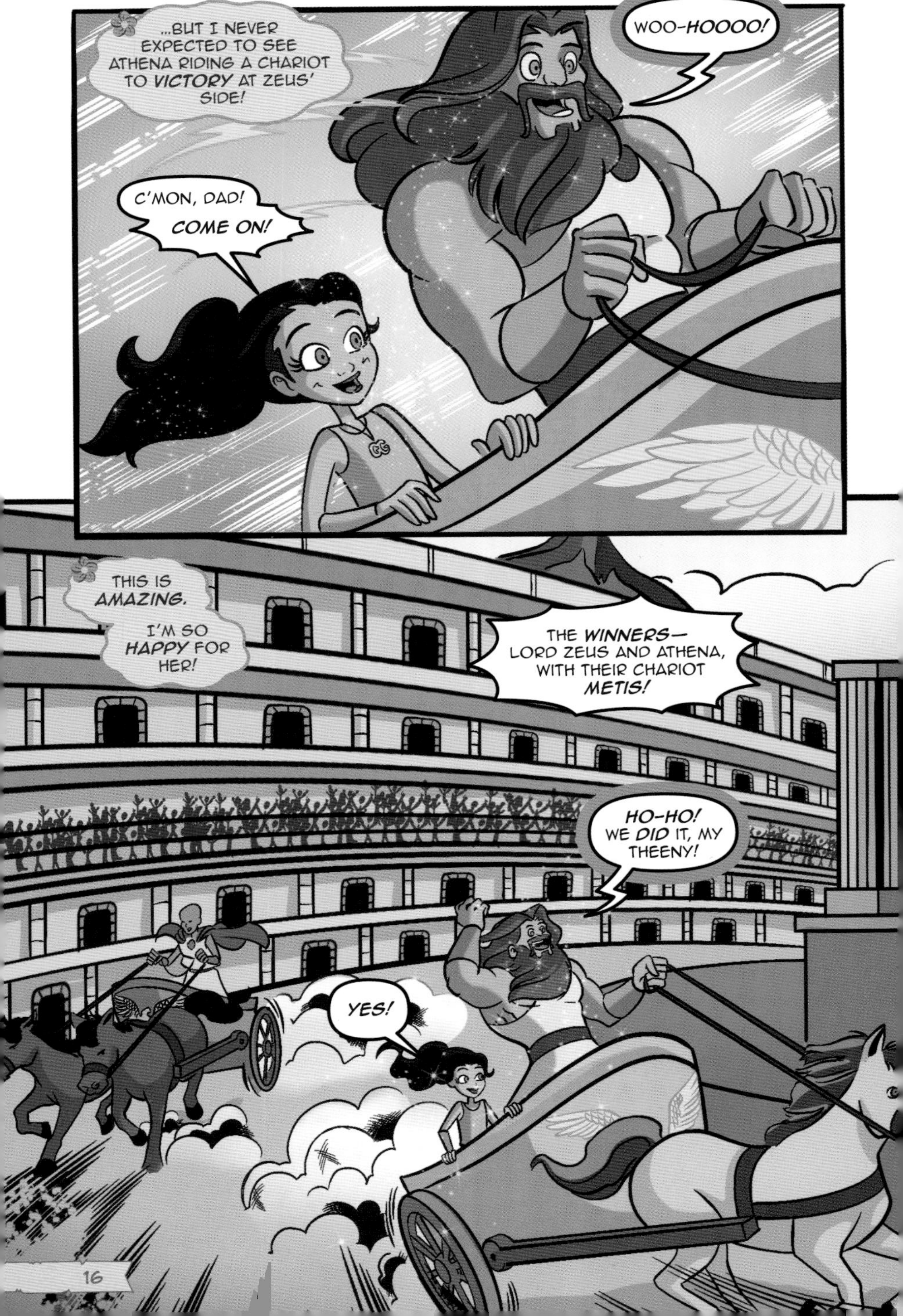
...BUT I NEVER EXPECTED TO SEE ATHENA RIDING A CHARIOT TO VICTORY AT ZEUS' SIDE!
WOO-HOOOO!
C'MON, DAD! COME ON!
THIS IS AMAZING.
I'M SO HAPPY FOR HER!
THE WINNERS— LORD ZEUS AND ATHENA, WITH THEIR CHARIOT METIS!
HO-HO! WE DID IT, MY THEENY!
YES!

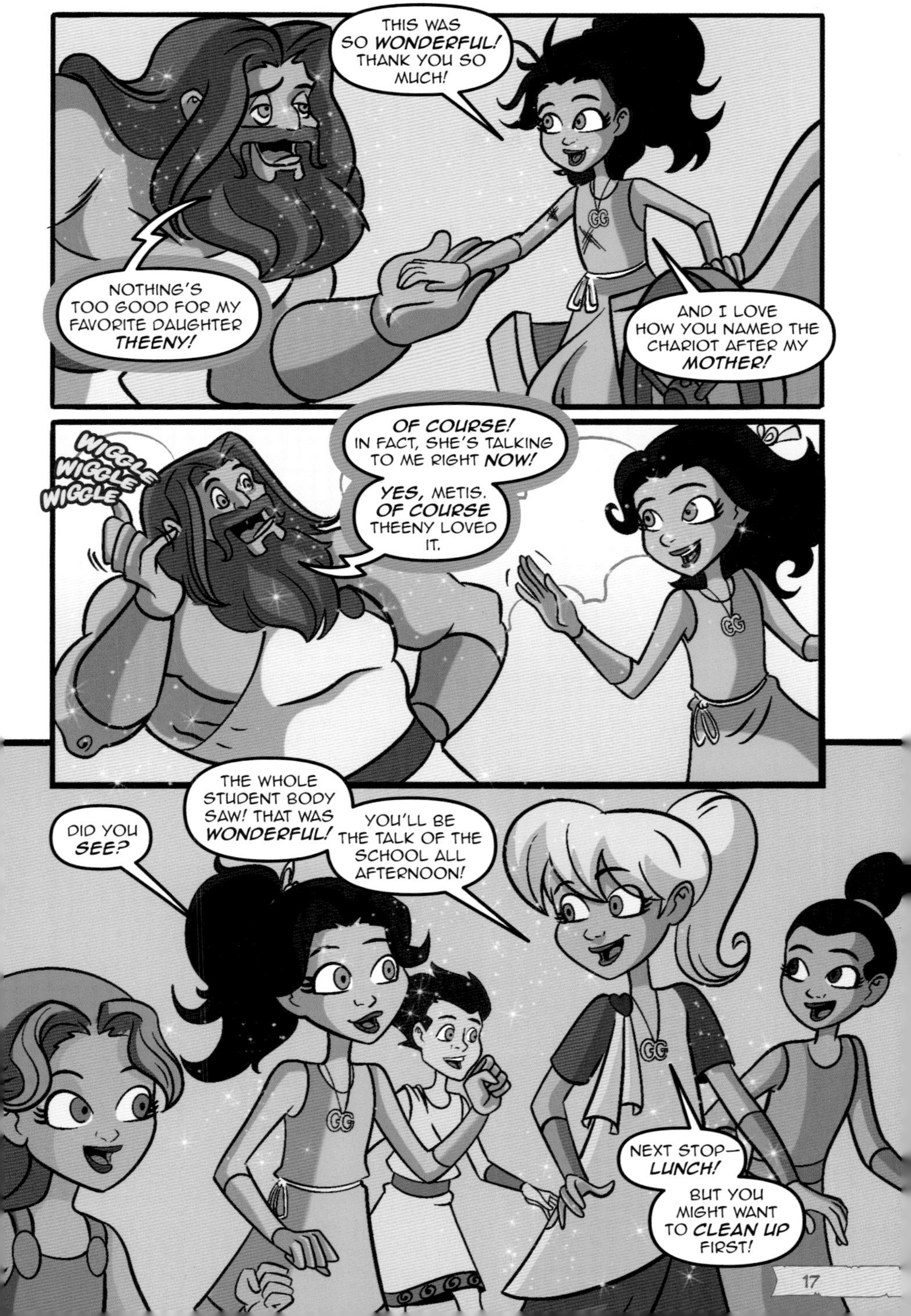

THIS WAS SO WONDERFUL! THANK YOU SO MUCH!
NOTHING'S TOO GOOD FOR MY FAVORITE DAUGHTER THEENY!
AND I LOVE HOW YOU NAMED THE CHARIOT AFTER MY MOTHER!
WIGGLE WIGGLE WIGGLE
OF COURSE! IN FACT, SHE'S TALKING TO ME RIGHT NOW!
YES, METIS. OF COURSE THEENY LOVED IT.
DID YOU SEE?
THE WHOLE STUDENT BODY SAW! THAT WAS WONDERFUL!
YOU'LL BE THE TALK OF THE SCHOOL ALL AFTERNOON!
NEXT STOP— LUNCH!
BUT YOU MIGHT WANT TO CLEAN UP FIRST!

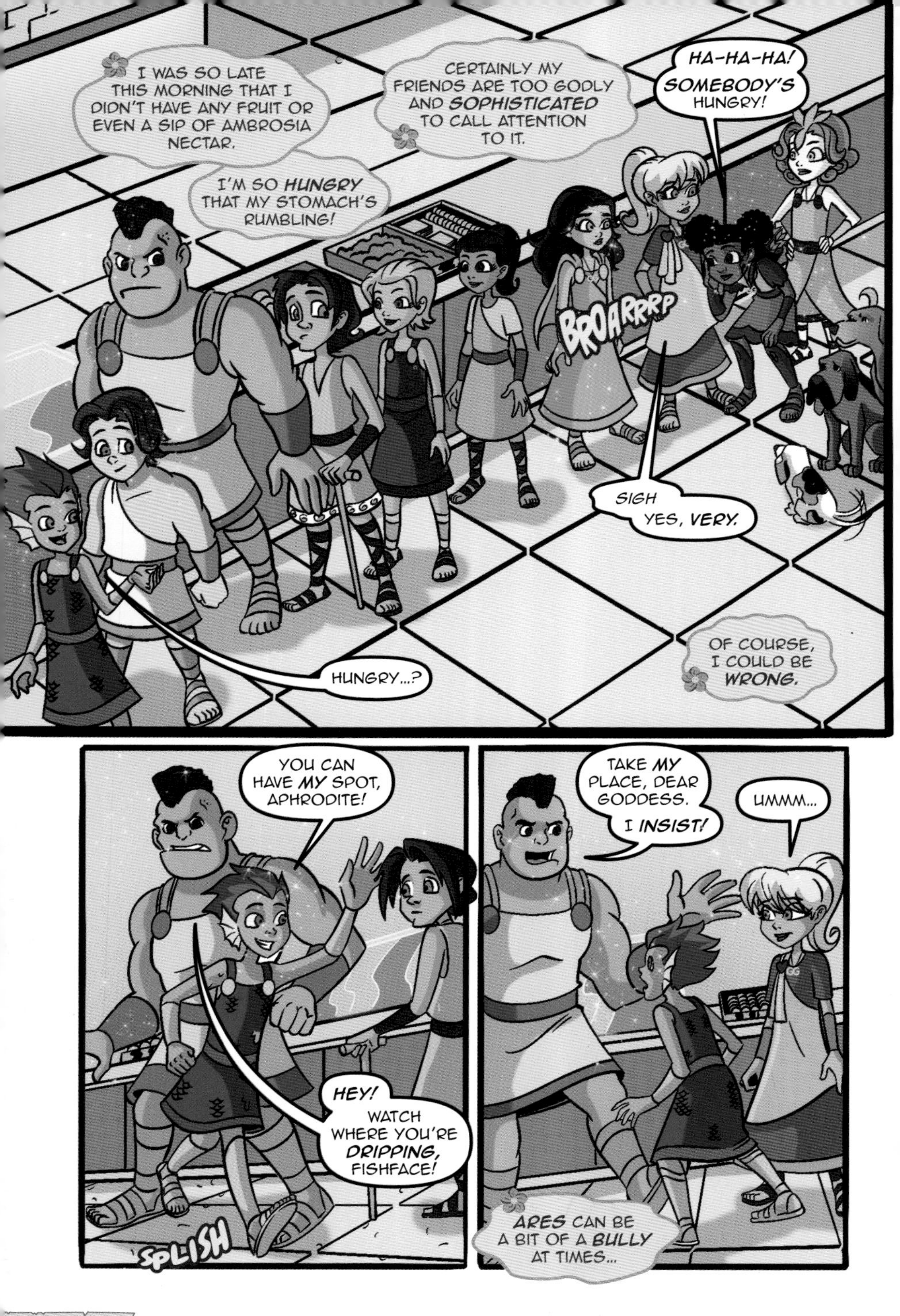
I WAS SO LATE THIS MORNING THAT I DIDN'T HAVE ANY FRUIT OR EVEN A SIP OF AMBROSIA NECTAR.
I'M SO HUNGRY THAT MY STOMACH'S RUMBLING!
CERTAINLY MY FRIENDS ARE TOO GODLY AND SOPHISTICATED TO CALL ATTENTION TO IT.
HA-HA-HA! SOMEBODY'S HUNGRY!
BROARRRP
SIGH
YES, VERY.
HUNGRY...?
OF COURSE, I COULD BE WRONG.
YOU CAN HAVE MY SPOT, APHRODITE!
HEY! WATCH WHERE YOU'RE DRIPPING, FISHFACE!
SPLISH
TAKE MY PLACE, DEAR GODDESS.
I INSIST!
UMMM...
ARES CAN BE A BIT OF A BULLY AT TIMES...

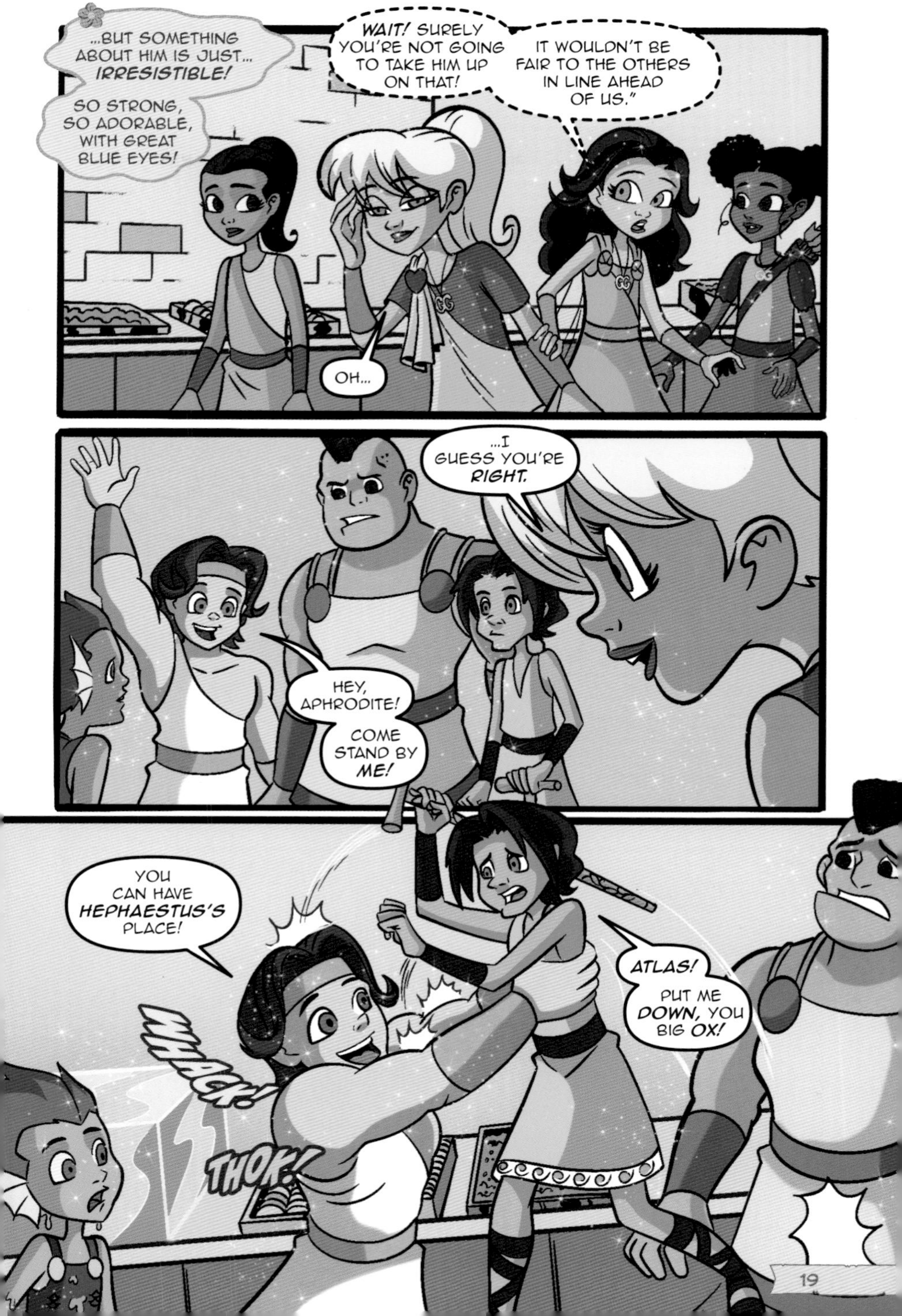
...BUT SOMETHING ABOUT HIM IS JUST... IRRESISTIBLE!
SO STRONG, SO ADORABLE, WITH GREAT BLUE EYES!
WAIT! SURELY YOU'RE NOT GOING TO TAKE HIM UP ON THAT!
IT WOULDN'T BE FAIR TO THE OTHERS IN LINE AHEAD OF US."
OH...
...I GUESS YOU'RE RIGHT.
HEY, APHRODITE!
COME STAND BY ME!
YOU CAN HAVE HEPHAESTUS'S PLACE!
ATLAS!
PUT ME DOWN, YOU BIG OX!
WHACK!
THOK!

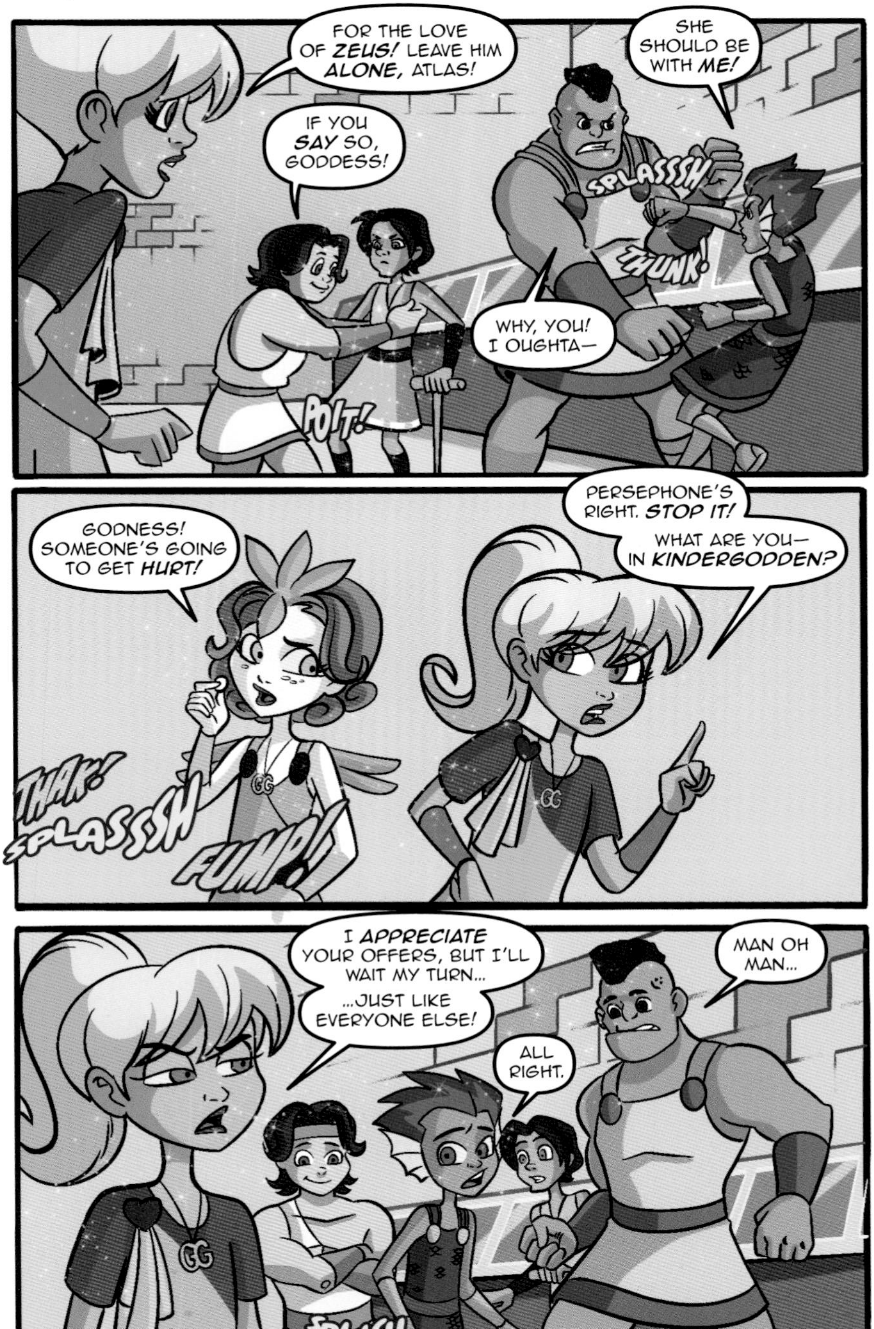

FOR THE LOVE OF ZEUS! LEAVE HIM ALONE, ATLAS!
IF YOU SAY SO, GODDESS!
SHE SHOULD BE WITH ME!
SPLASSSH
THUNK!
WHY, YOU! I OUGHTA—
POIT!
GODNESS! SOMEONE'S GOING TO GET HURT!
PERSEPHONE'S RIGHT. STOP IT!
WHAT ARE YOU— IN KINDERGODDEN?
THAK!
SPLASSSH
FUMP!
I APPRECIATE YOUR OFFERS, BUT I'LL WAIT MY TURN...
...JUST LIKE EVERYONE ELSE!
ALL RIGHT.
MAN OH MAN...
SPLISH

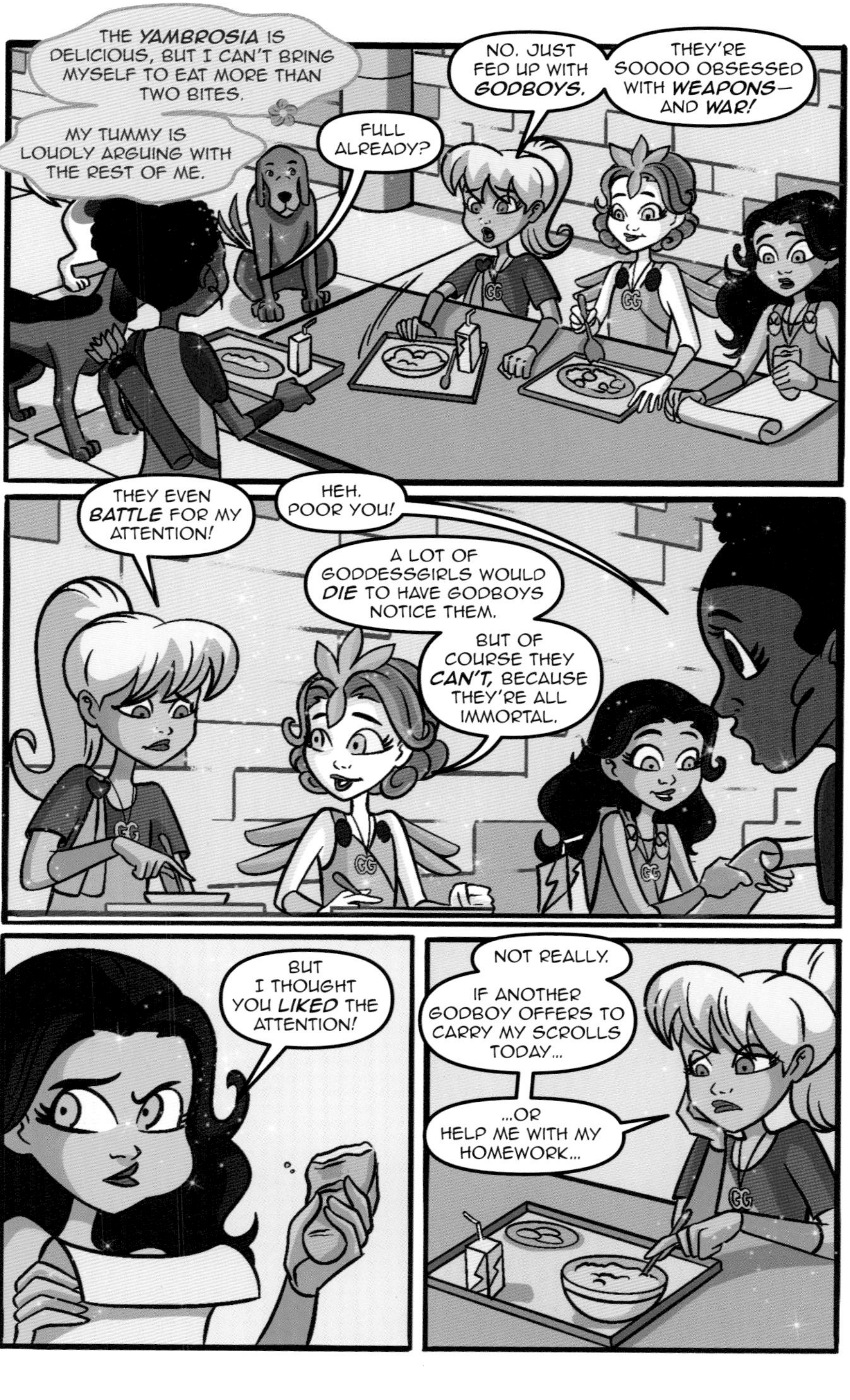
THE *YAMBROSIA* IS DELICIOUS, BUT I CAN'T BRING MYSELF TO EAT MORE THAN TWO BITES.
MY TUMMY IS LOUDLY ARGUING WITH THE REST OF ME.
FULL ALREADY?
NO. JUST FED UP WITH *GODBOYS.*
THEY'RE SOOOO OBSESSED WITH *WEAPONS*— AND *WAR!*
THEY EVEN *BATTLE* FOR MY ATTENTION!
HEH. POOR YOU!
A LOT OF GODDESSGIRLS WOULD *DIE* TO HAVE GODBOYS NOTICE THEM.
BUT OF COURSE THEY *CAN'T,* BECAUSE THEY'RE ALL IMMORTAL.
BUT I THOUGHT YOU *LIKED* THE ATTENTION!
NOT REALLY.
IF ANOTHER GODBOY OFFERS TO CARRY MY SCROLLS TODAY...
...OR HELP ME WITH MY HOMEWORK...

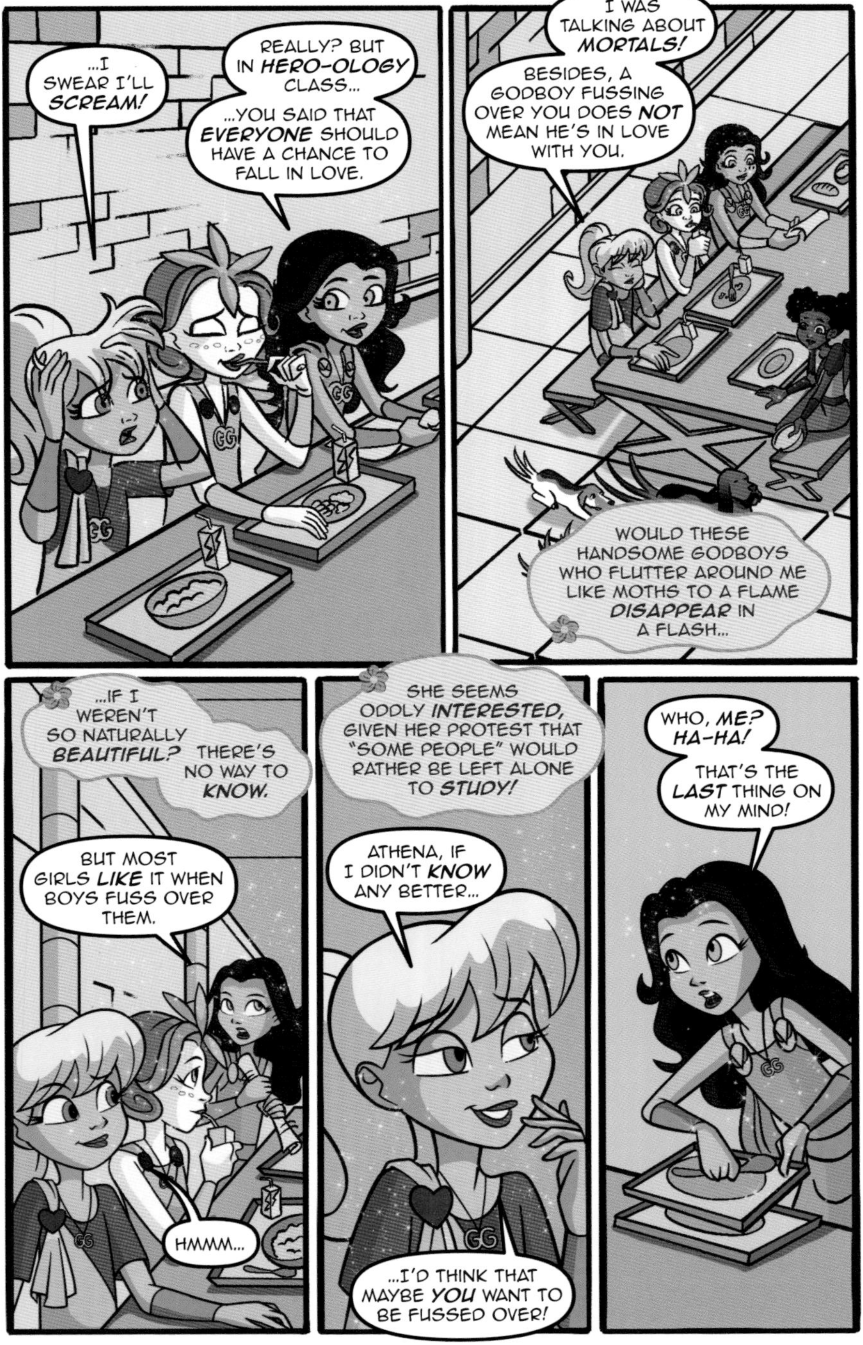

...I SWEAR I'LL SCREAM!
REALLY? BUT IN HERO-OLOGY CLASS...
...YOU SAID THAT EVERYONE SHOULD HAVE A CHANCE TO FALL IN LOVE.
I WAS TALKING ABOUT MORTALS!
BESIDES, A GODBOY FUSSING OVER YOU DOES NOT MEAN HE'S IN LOVE WITH YOU.
WOULD THESE HANDSOME GODBOYS WHO FLUTTER AROUND ME LIKE MOTHS TO A FLAME DISAPPEAR IN A FLASH...
...IF I WEREN'T SO NATURALLY BEAUTIFUL? THERE'S NO WAY TO KNOW.
BUT MOST GIRLS LIKE IT WHEN BOYS FUSS OVER THEM.
HMMM...
SHE SEEMS ODDLY INTERESTED, GIVEN HER PROTEST THAT "SOME PEOPLE" WOULD RATHER BE LEFT ALONE TO STUDY!
ATHENA, IF I DIDN'T KNOW ANY BETTER...
...I'D THINK THAT MAYBE YOU WANT TO BE FUSSED OVER!
WHO, ME? HA-HA!
THAT'S THE LAST THING ON MY MIND!

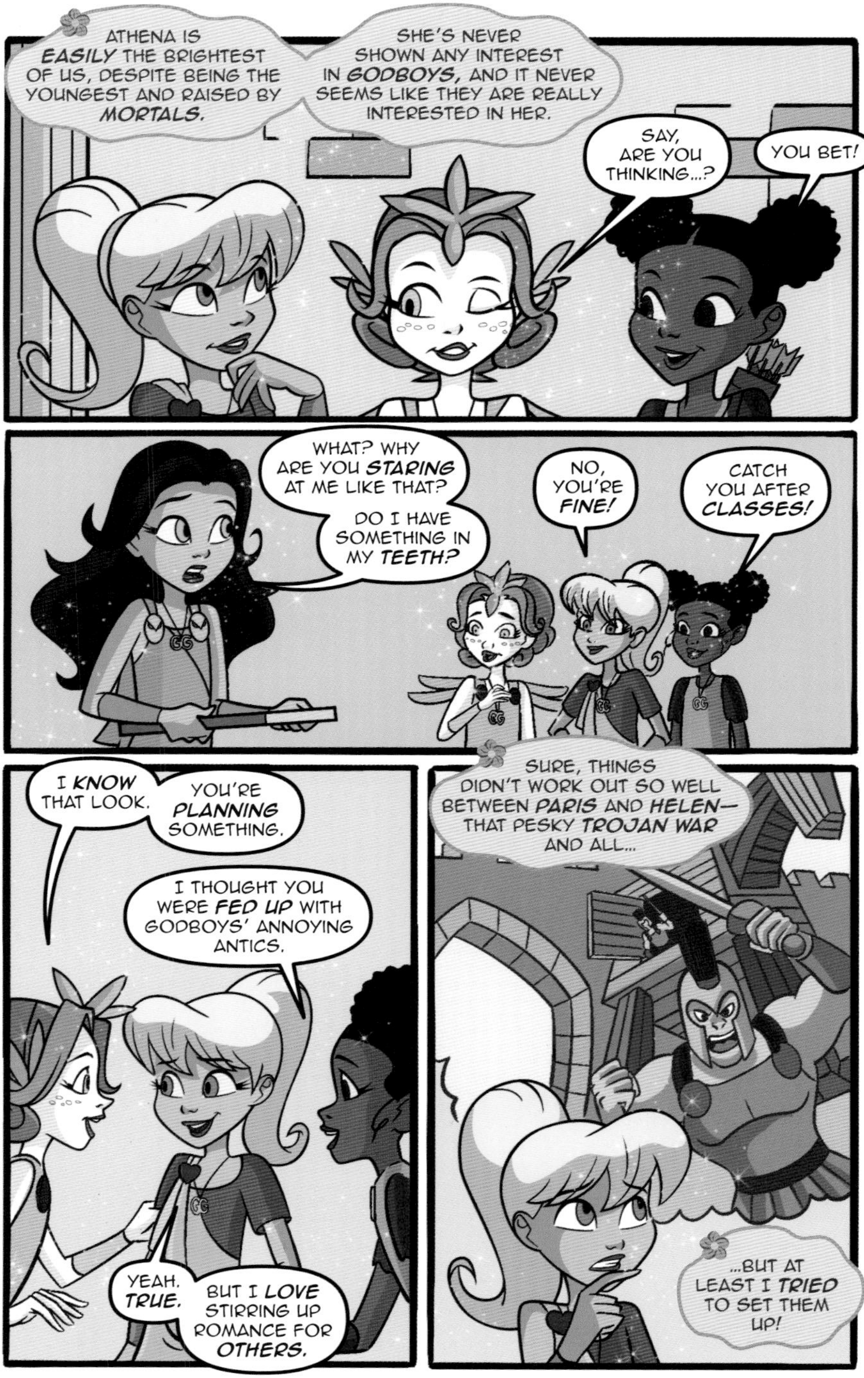
ATHENA IS EASILY THE BRIGHTEST OF US, DESPITE BEING THE YOUNGEST AND RAISED BY MORTALS.
SHE'S NEVER SHOWN ANY INTEREST IN GODBOYS, AND IT NEVER SEEMS LIKE THEY ARE REALLY INTERESTED IN HER.
SAY, ARE YOU THINKING...?
YOU BET!
WHAT? WHY ARE YOU STARING AT ME LIKE THAT?
DO I HAVE SOMETHING IN MY TEETH?
NO, YOU'RE FINE!
CATCH YOU AFTER CLASSES!
I KNOW THAT LOOK.
YOU'RE PLANNING SOMETHING.
I THOUGHT YOU WERE FED UP WITH GODBOYS' ANNOYING ANTICS.
YEAH. TRUE.
BUT I LOVE STIRRING UP ROMANCE FOR OTHERS.
SURE, THINGS DIDN'T WORK OUT SO WELL BETWEEN PARIS AND HELEN—THAT PESKY TROJAN WAR AND ALL...
...BUT AT LEAST I TRIED TO SET THEM UP!

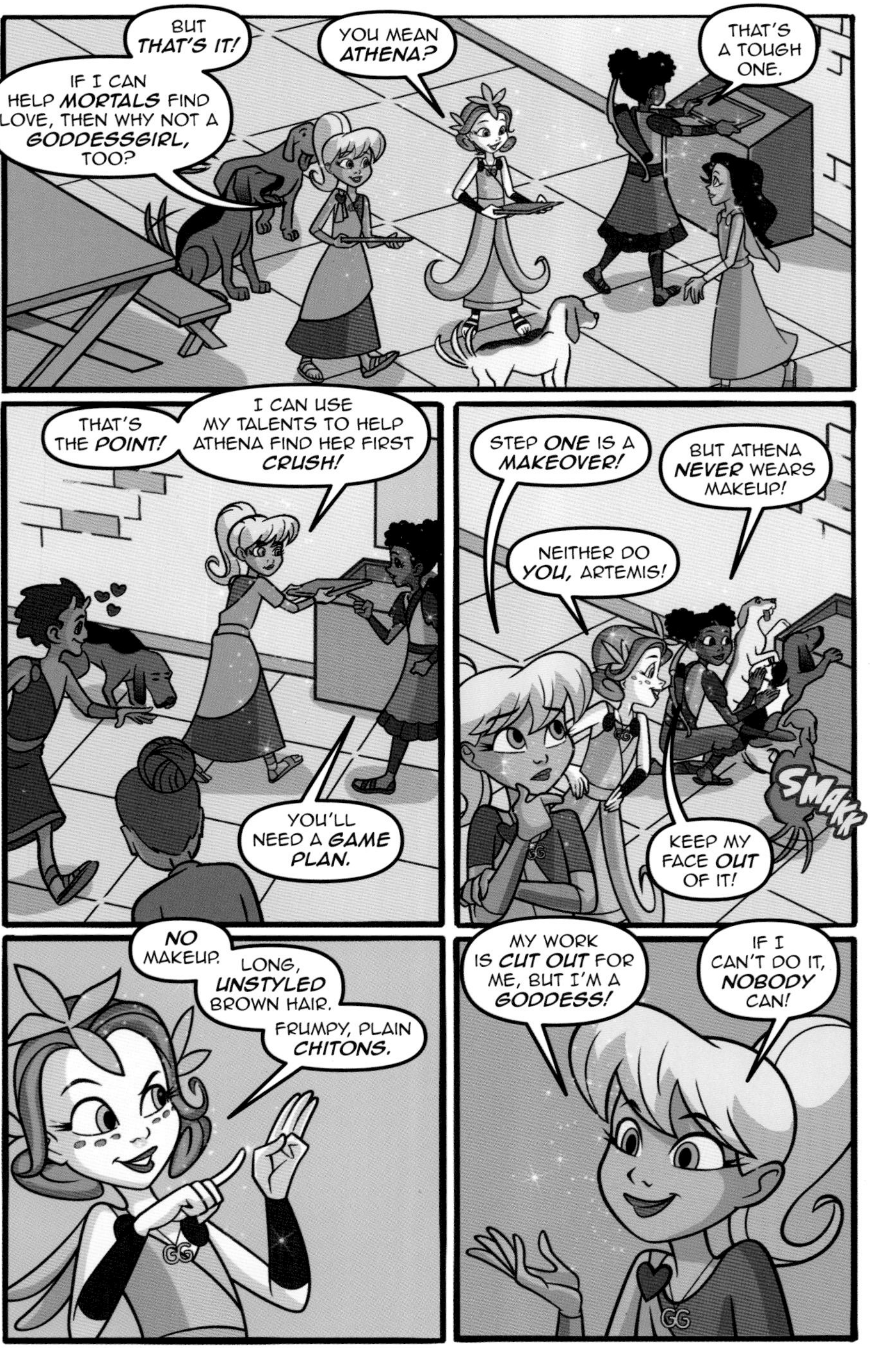
BUT THAT'S IT!
IF I CAN HELP MORTALS FIND LOVE, THEN WHY NOT A GODDESSGIRL, TOO?
YOU MEAN ATHENA?
THAT'S A TOUGH ONE.
THAT'S THE POINT!
I CAN USE MY TALENTS TO HELP ATHENA FIND HER FIRST CRUSH!
YOU'LL NEED A GAME PLAN.
STEP ONE IS A MAKEOVER!
BUT ATHENA NEVER WEARS MAKEUP!
NEITHER DO YOU, ARTEMIS!
KEEP MY FACE OUT OF IT!
SMAKK
NO MAKEUP.
LONG, UNSTYLED BROWN HAIR.
FRUMPY, PLAIN CHITONS.
MY WORK IS CUT OUT FOR ME, BUT I'M A GODDESS!
IF I CAN'T DO IT, NOBODY CAN!

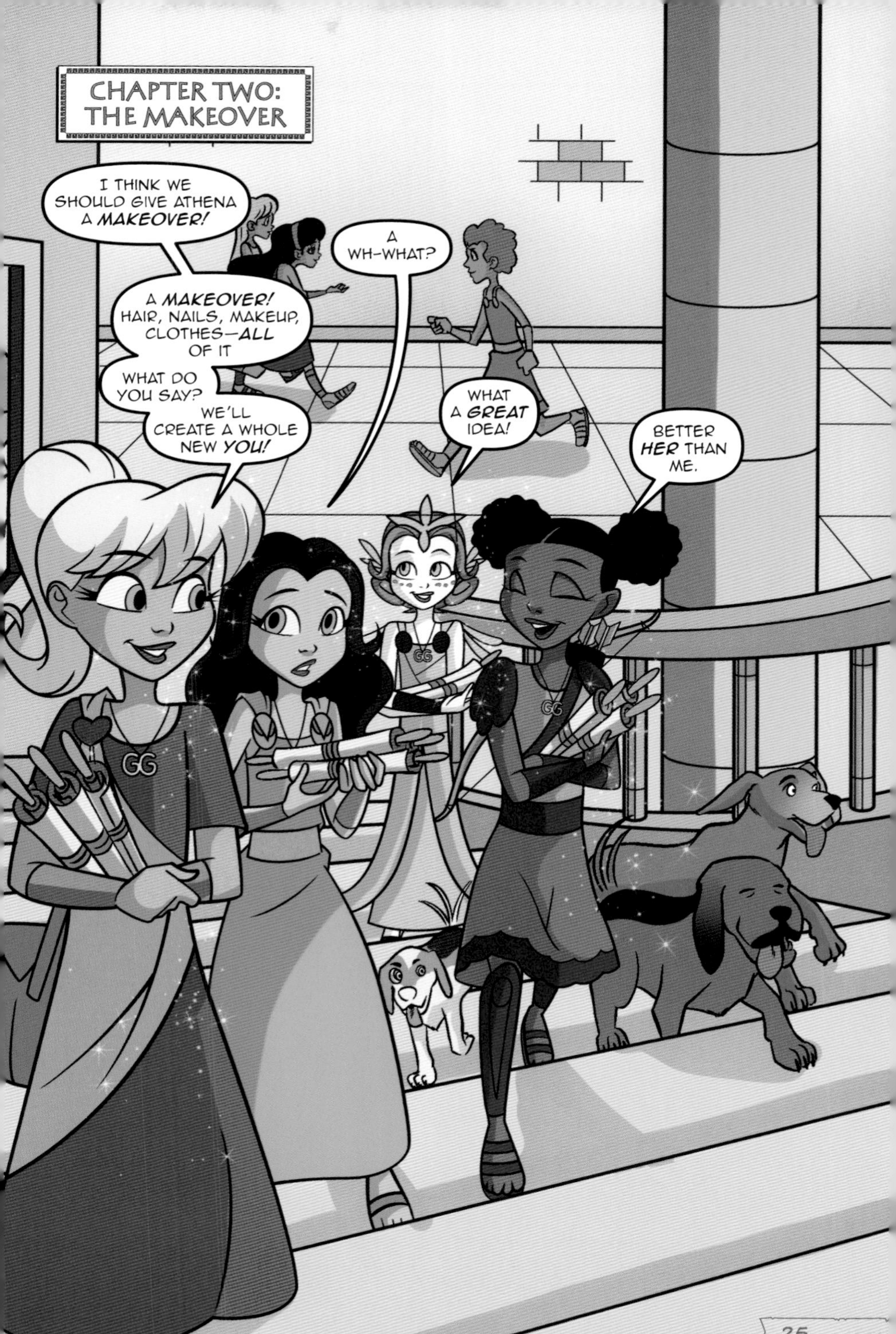
CHAPTER TWO: THE MAKEOVER
I THINK WE SHOULD GIVE ATHENA A *MAKEOVER!*
A WH-WHAT?
A *MAKEOVER!* HAIR, NAILS, MAKEUP, CLOTHES—*ALL* OF IT
WHAT DO YOU SAY?
WE'LL CREATE A WHOLE NEW *YOU!*
WHAT A *GREAT* IDEA!
BETTER *HER* THAN ME.

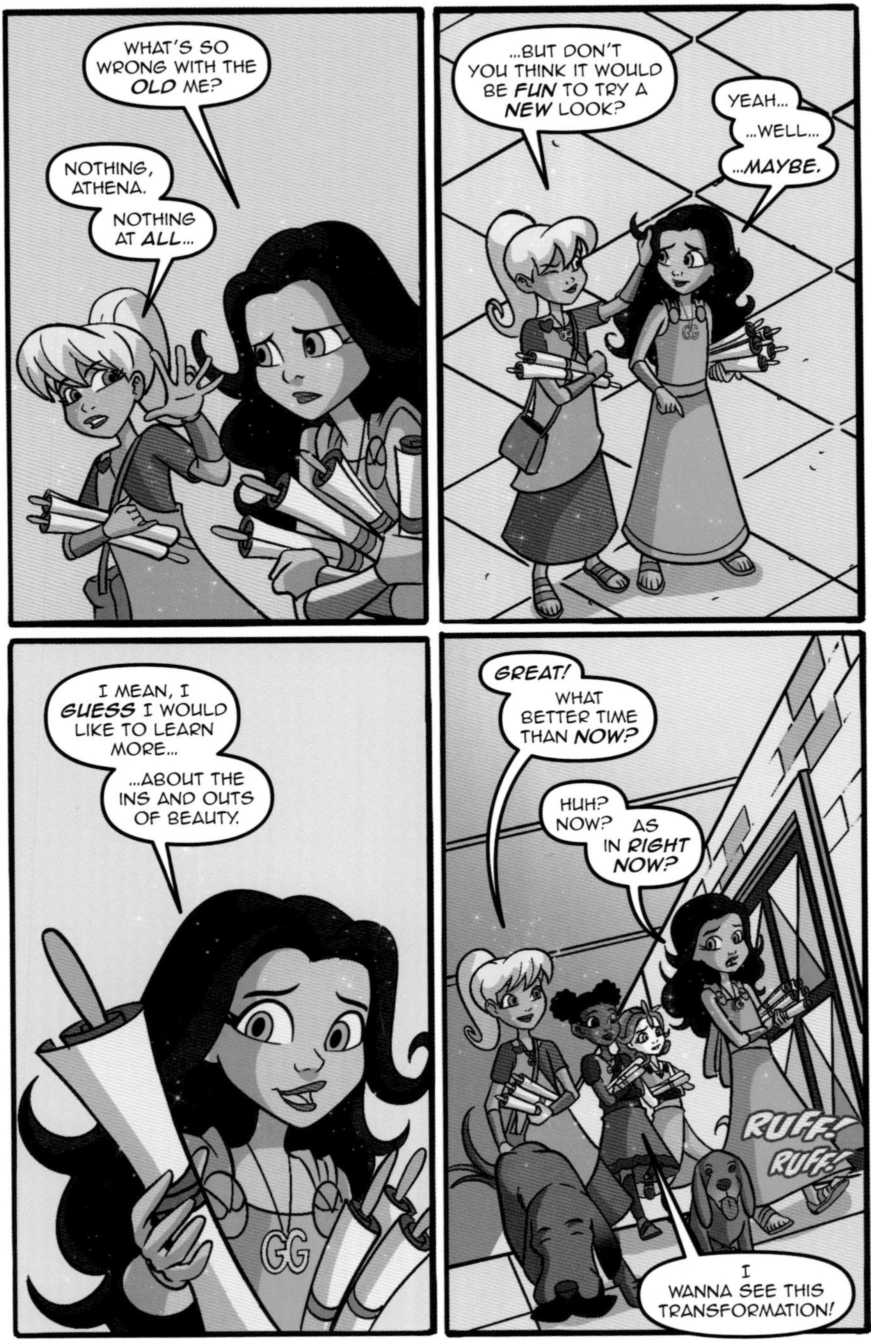
WHAT'S SO WRONG WITH THE OLD ME?
NOTHING, ATHENA.
NOTHING AT ALL...
...BUT DON'T YOU THINK IT WOULD BE FUN TO TRY A NEW LOOK?
YEAH...
...WELL...
...MAYBE.
I MEAN, I GUESS I WOULD LIKE TO LEARN MORE...
...ABOUT THE INS AND OUTS OF BEAUTY.
GREAT!
WHAT BETTER TIME THAN NOW?
HUH? NOW?
AS IN RIGHT NOW?
RUFF!
RUFF!
I WANNA SEE THIS TRANSFORMATION!

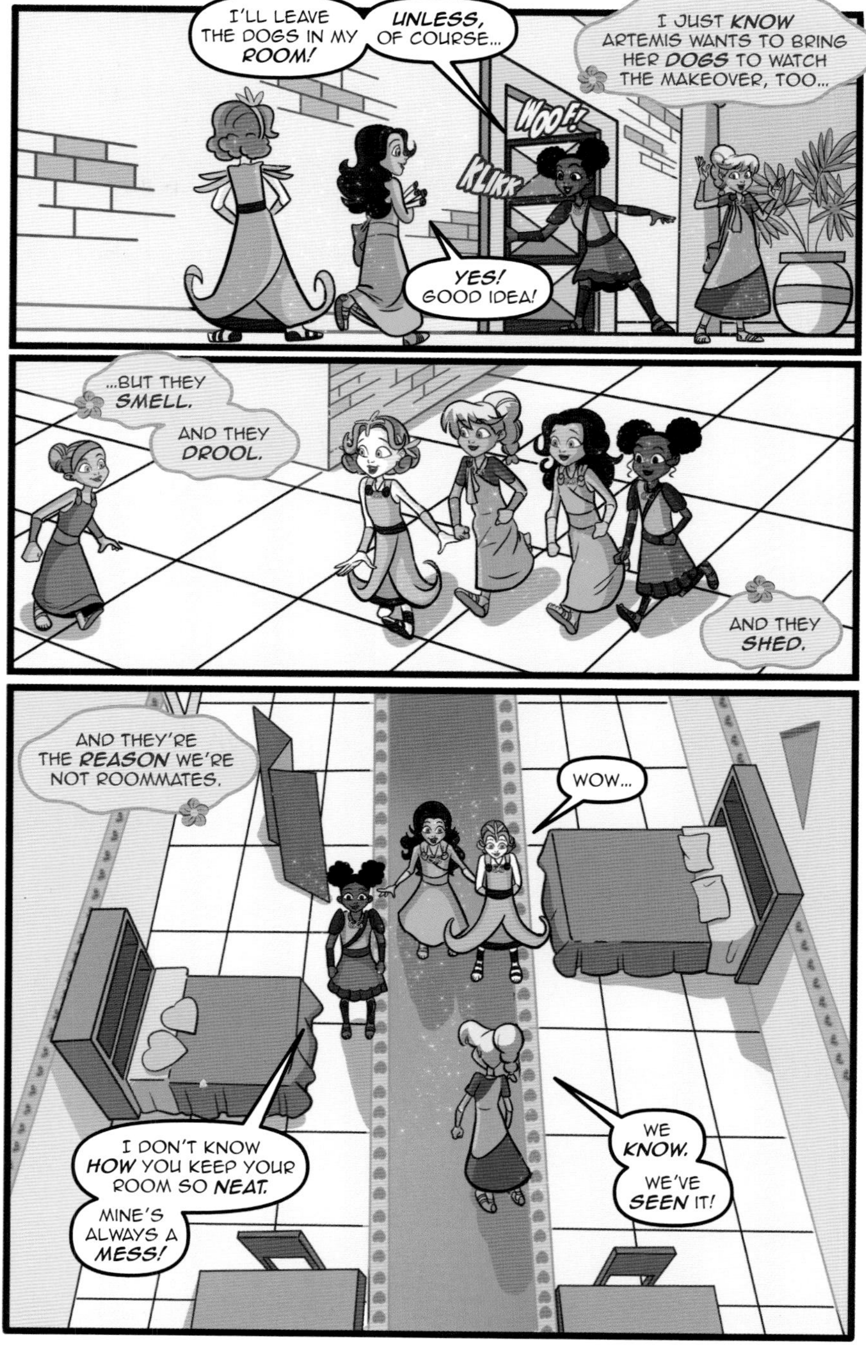
I'LL LEAVE THE DOGS IN MY ROOM!
UNLESS, OF COURSE...
I JUST KNOW ARTEMIS WANTS TO BRING HER DOGS TO WATCH THE MAKEOVER, TOO...
WOOF!
KLIKK
YES! GOOD IDEA!
...BUT THEY SMELL.
AND THEY DROOL.
AND THEY SHED.
AND THEY'RE THE REASON WE'RE NOT ROOMMATES.
WOW...
I DON'T KNOW HOW YOU KEEP YOUR ROOM SO NEAT.
MINE'S ALWAYS A MESS!
WE KNOW.
WE'VE SEEN IT!

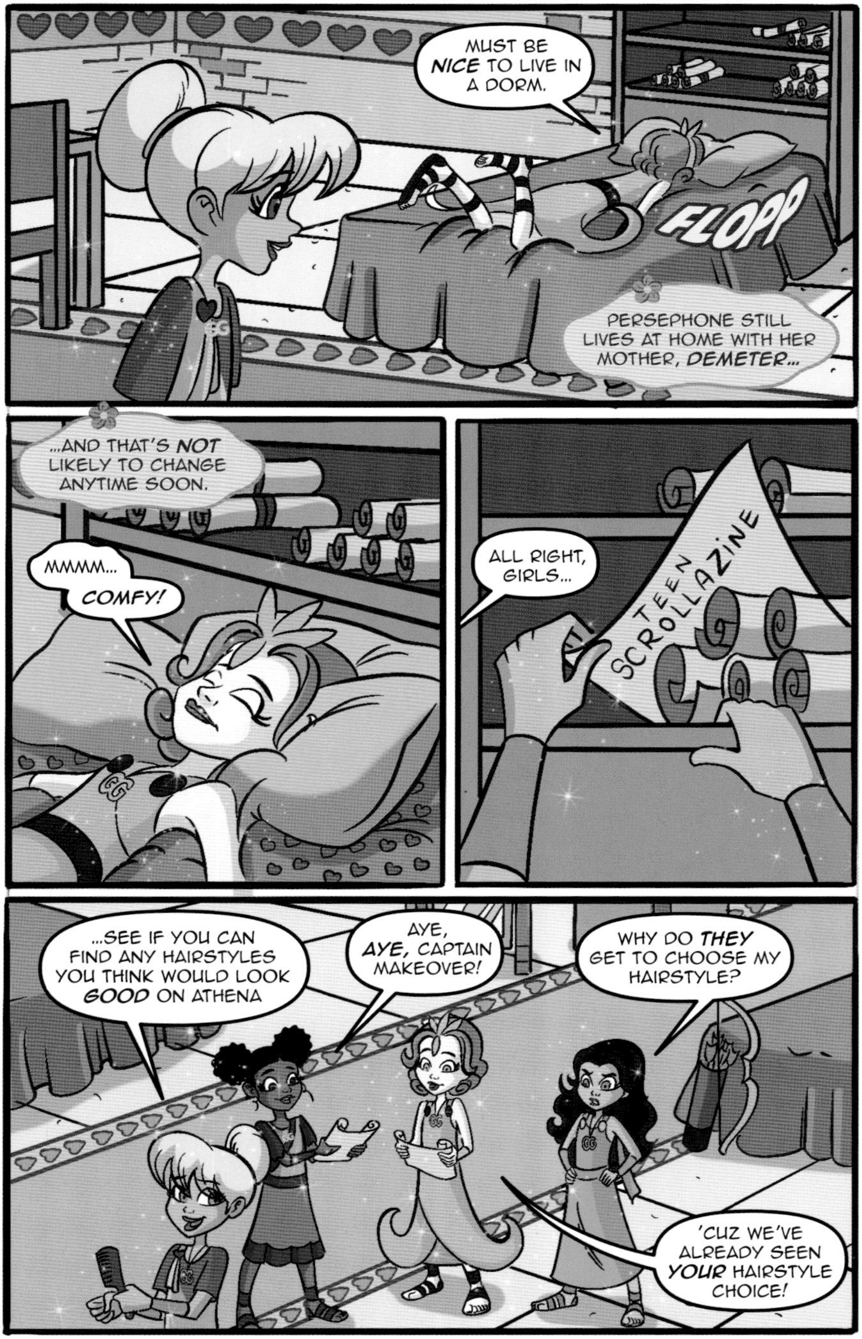
MUST BE NICE TO LIVE IN A DORM.
FLOPP
PERSEPHONE STILL LIVES AT HOME WITH HER MOTHER, DEMETER...
...AND THAT'S NOT LIKELY TO CHANGE ANYTIME SOON.
MMMM... COMFY!
ALL RIGHT, GIRLS...
TEEN SCROLLAZINE
...SEE IF YOU CAN FIND ANY HAIRSTYLES YOU THINK WOULD LOOK GOOD ON ATHENA
AYE, AYE, CAPTAIN MAKEOVER!
WHY DO THEY GET TO CHOOSE MY HAIRSTYLE?
'CUZ WE'VE ALREADY SEEN YOUR HAIRSTYLE CHOICE!

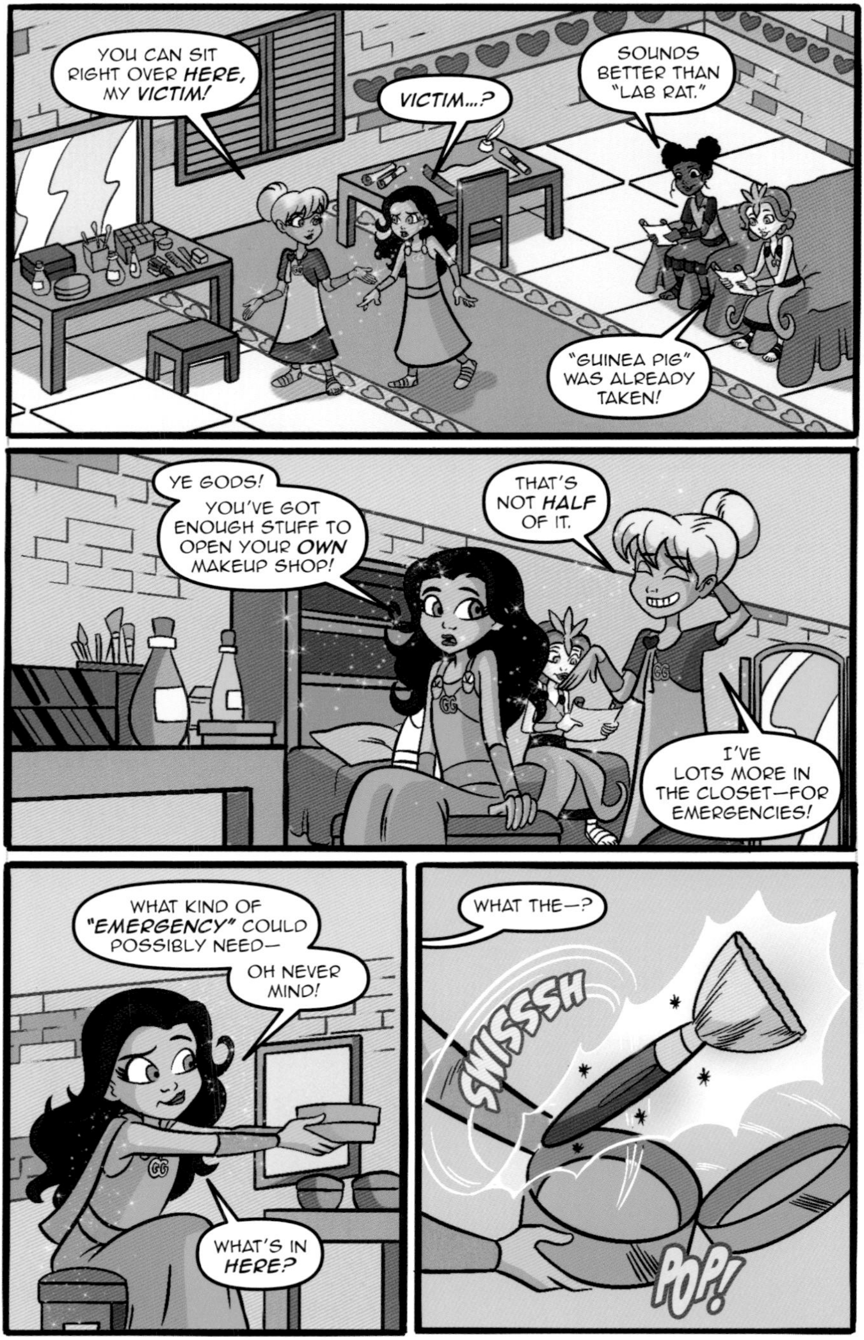
YOU CAN SIT RIGHT OVER HERE, MY VICTIM!
VICTIM...?
SOUNDS BETTER THAN "LAB RAT."
"GUINEA PIG" WAS ALREADY TAKEN!
YE GODS!
YOU'VE GOT ENOUGH STUFF TO OPEN YOUR OWN MAKEUP SHOP!
THAT'S NOT HALF OF IT.
I'VE LOTS MORE IN THE CLOSET—FOR EMERGENCIES!
WHAT KIND OF "EMERGENCY" COULD POSSIBLY NEED—
OH NEVER MIND!
WHAT'S IN HERE?
WHAT THE—?
SWISSSH
POP!

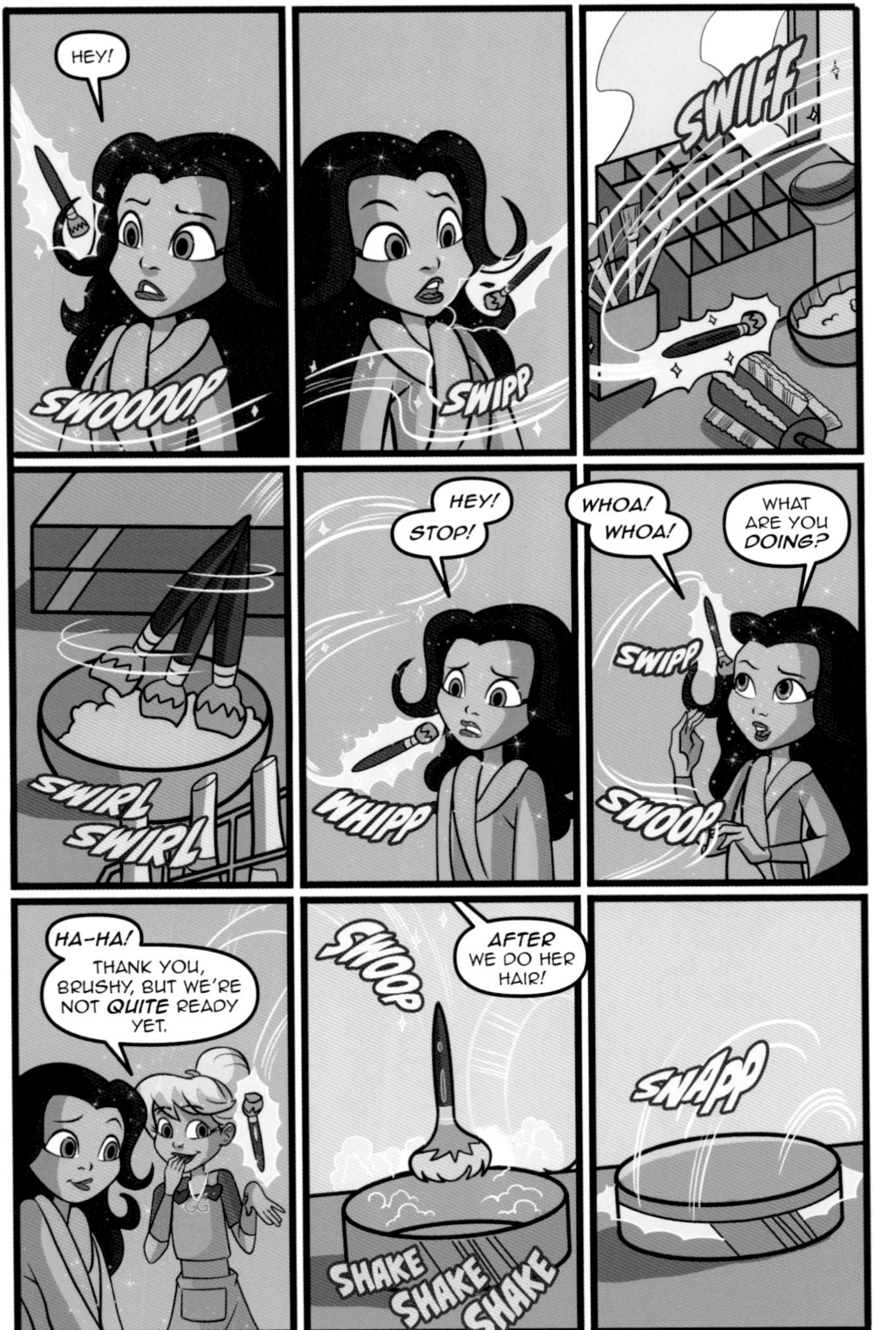
HEY!
SWOOOOP
SWIPP
SWIFF
SWIRL
SWIRL
HEY! STOP!
WHIPP
WHOA! WHOA!
WHAT ARE YOU DOING?
SWIPP
SWOOP
HA-HA!
THANK YOU, BRUSHY, BUT WE'RE NOT QUITE READY YET.
SWOOP
AFTER WE DO HER HAIR!
SHAKE
SHAKE
SHAKE
SNAPP

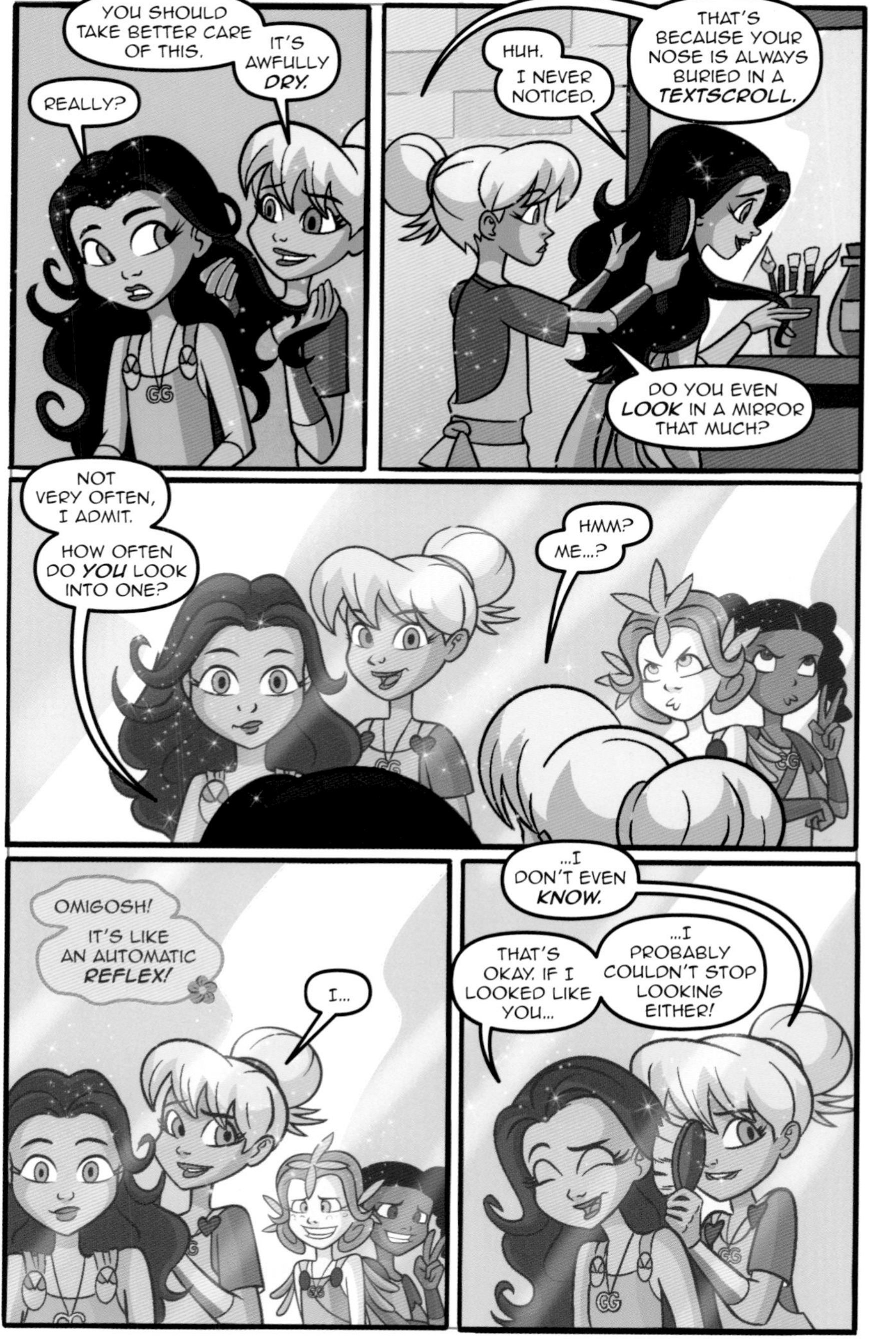
YOU SHOULD TAKE BETTER CARE OF THIS.
IT'S AWFULLY DRY.
REALLY?
HUH. I NEVER NOTICED.
THAT'S BECAUSE YOUR NOSE IS ALWAYS BURIED IN A TEXTSCROLL.
DO YOU EVEN LOOK IN A MIRROR THAT MUCH?
NOT VERY OFTEN, I ADMIT.
HOW OFTEN DO YOU LOOK INTO ONE?
HMM? ME...?
OMIGOSH! IT'S LIKE AN AUTOMATIC REFLEX!
I...
...I DON'T EVEN KNOW.
THAT'S OKAY. IF I LOOKED LIKE YOU...
...I PROBABLY COULDN'T STOP LOOKING EITHER!

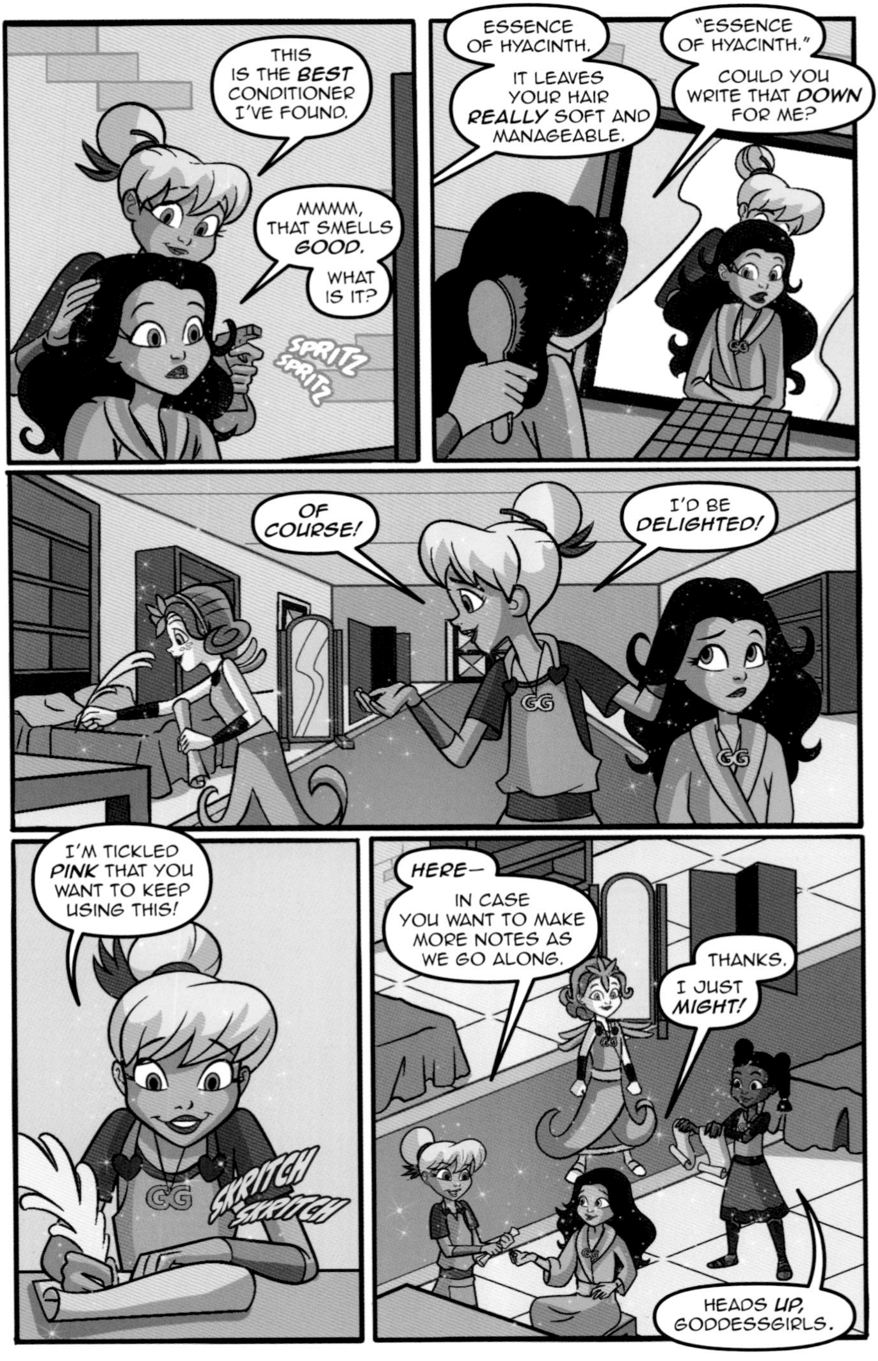

THIS IS THE BEST CONDITIONER I'VE FOUND.
MMMM, THAT SMELLS GOOD.
WHAT IS IT?
SPRITZ SPRITZ
ESSENCE OF HYACINTH.
IT LEAVES YOUR HAIR REALLY SOFT AND MANAGEABLE.
"ESSENCE OF HYACINTH."
COULD YOU WRITE THAT DOWN FOR ME?
OF COURSE!
I'D BE DELIGHTED!
I'M TICKLED PINK THAT YOU WANT TO KEEP USING THIS!
SKRITCH SKRITCH
HERE—
IN CASE YOU WANT TO MAKE MORE NOTES AS WE GO ALONG.
THANKS. I JUST MIGHT!
HEADS UP, GODDESSGIRLS.

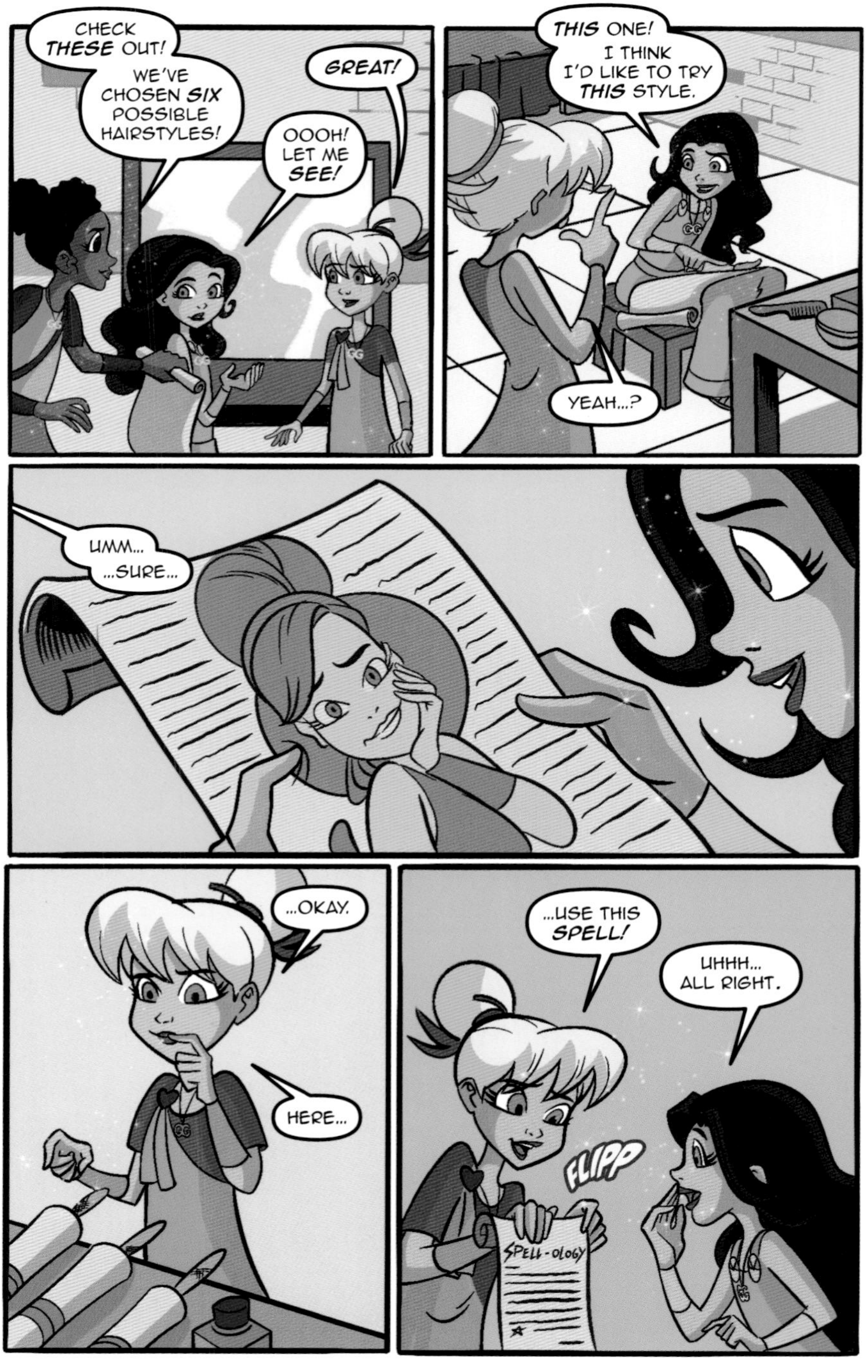
CHECK THESE OUT!
WE'VE CHOSEN SIX POSSIBLE HAIRSTYLES!
OOOH! LET ME SEE!
GREAT!
THIS ONE!
I THINK I'D LIKE TO TRY THIS STYLE.
YEAH...?
UMM... ...SURE...
...OKAY.
HERE...
...USE THIS SPELL!
UHHH... ALL RIGHT.
FLIPP
SPELL-OLOGY

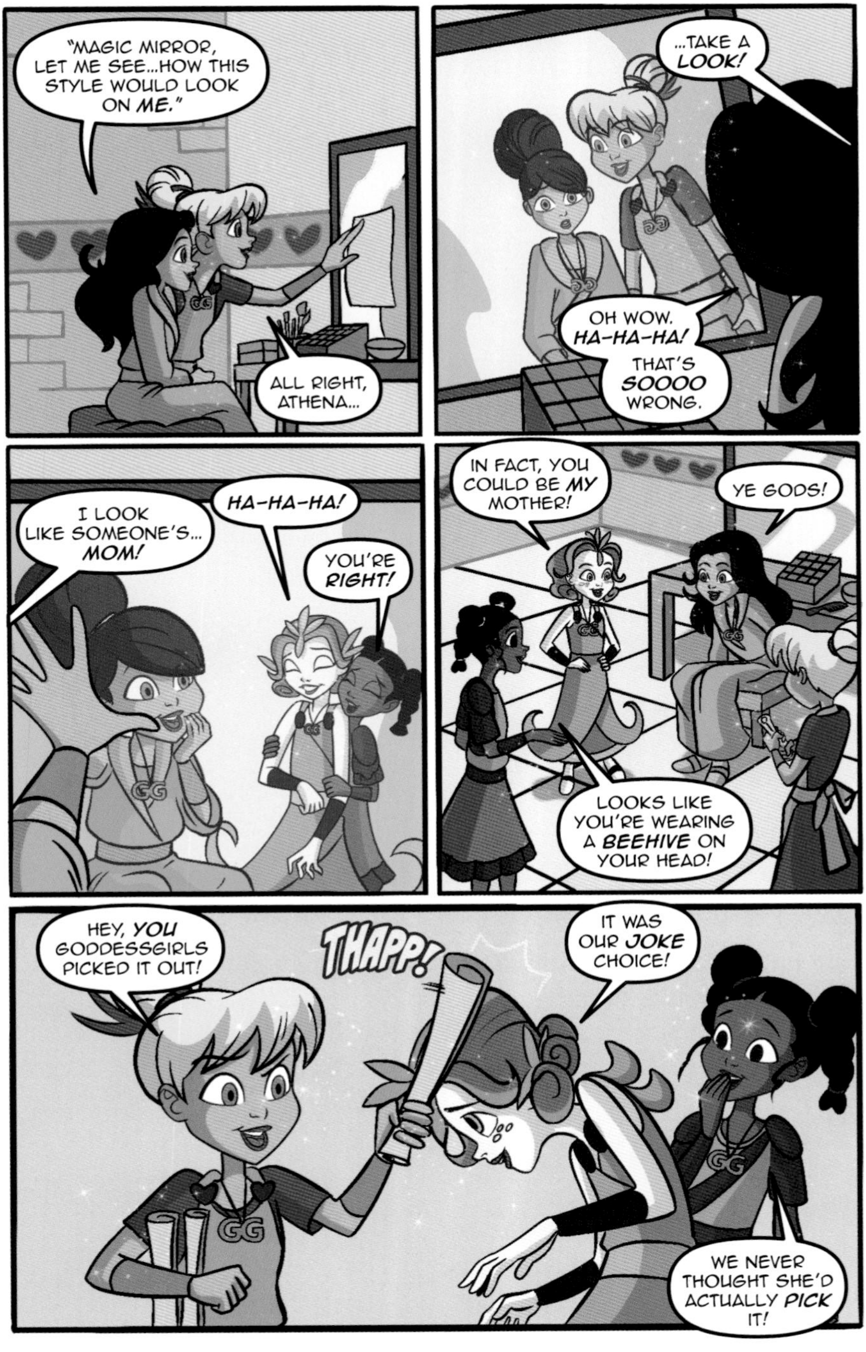
"MAGIC MIRROR, LET ME SEE...HOW THIS STYLE WOULD LOOK ON ME."
ALL RIGHT, ATHENA...
...TAKE A LOOK!
OH WOW. HA-HA-HA!
THAT'S SOOOO WRONG.
I LOOK LIKE SOMEONE'S... MOM!
HA-HA-HA!
YOU'RE RIGHT!
IN FACT, YOU COULD BE MY MOTHER!
YE GODS!
LOOKS LIKE YOU'RE WEARING A BEEHIVE ON YOUR HEAD!
HEY, YOU GODDESSGIRLS PICKED IT OUT!
THAPP!
IT WAS OUR JOKE CHOICE!
WE NEVER THOUGHT SHE'D ACTUALLY PICK IT!

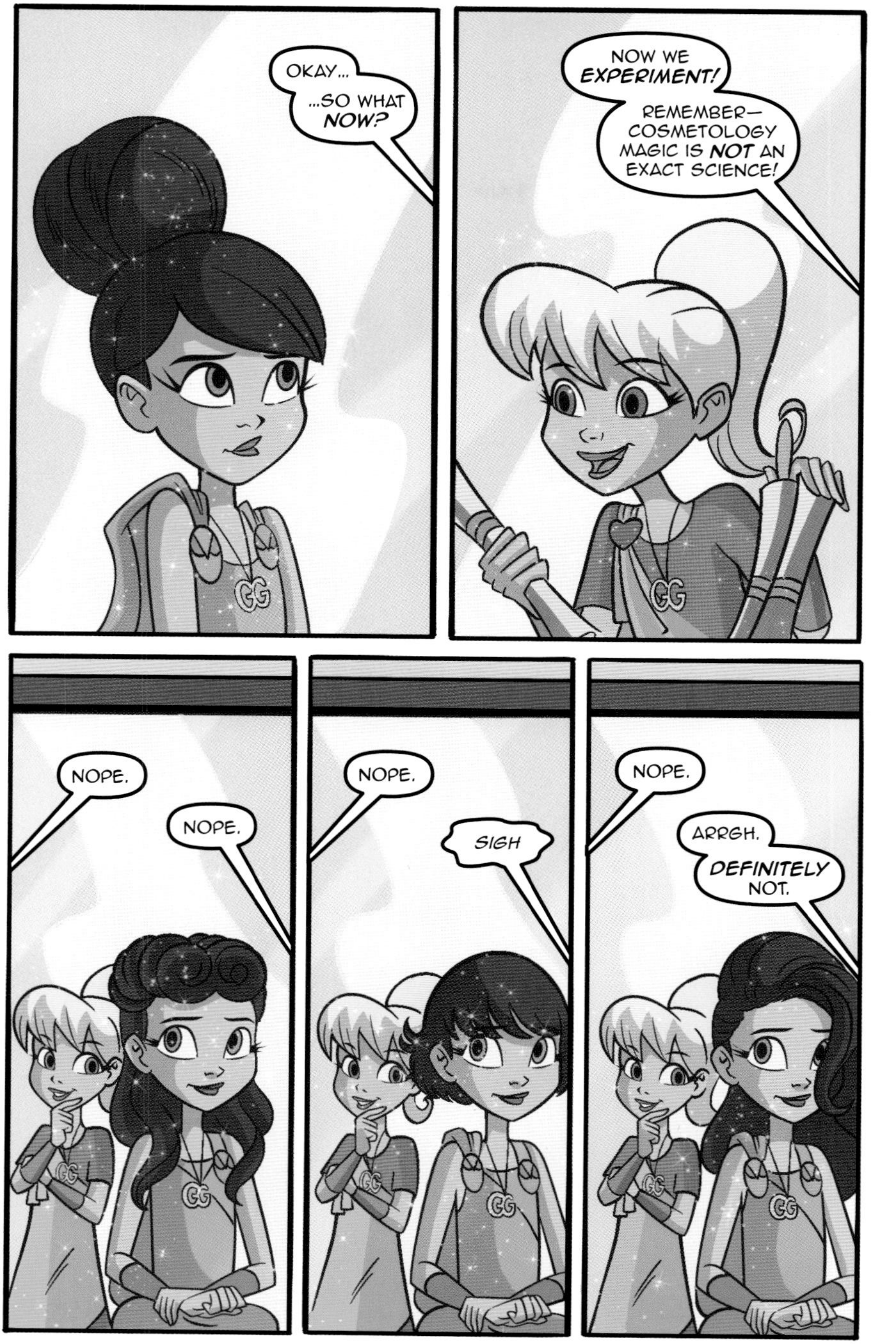
OKAY...
...SO WHAT NOW?
NOW WE EXPERIMENT!
REMEMBER—COSMETOLOGY MAGIC IS NOT AN EXACT SCIENCE!
NOPE.
NOPE.
NOPE.
SIGH
NOPE.
ARRGH.
DEFINITELY NOT.

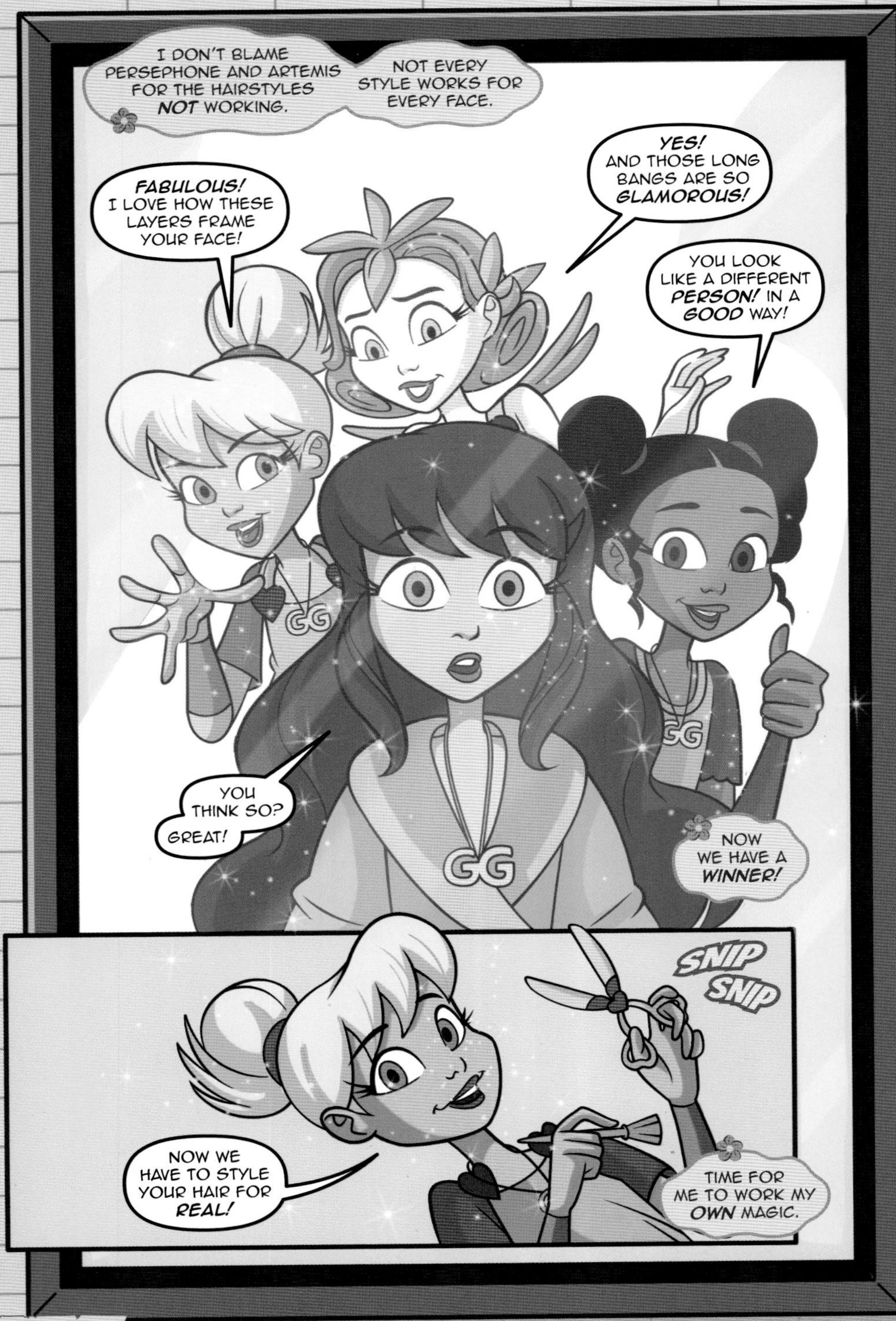
I DON'T BLAME PERSEPHONE AND ARTEMIS FOR THE HAIRSTYLES NOT WORKING.
NOT EVERY STYLE WORKS FOR EVERY FACE.
FABULOUS! I LOVE HOW THESE LAYERS FRAME YOUR FACE!
YES! AND THOSE LONG BANGS ARE SO GLAMOROUS!
YOU LOOK LIKE A DIFFERENT PERSON! IN A GOOD WAY!
YOU THINK SO?
GREAT!
NOW WE HAVE A WINNER!
SNIP SNIP
NOW WE HAVE TO STYLE YOUR HAIR FOR REAL!
TIME FOR ME TO WORK MY OWN MAGIC.

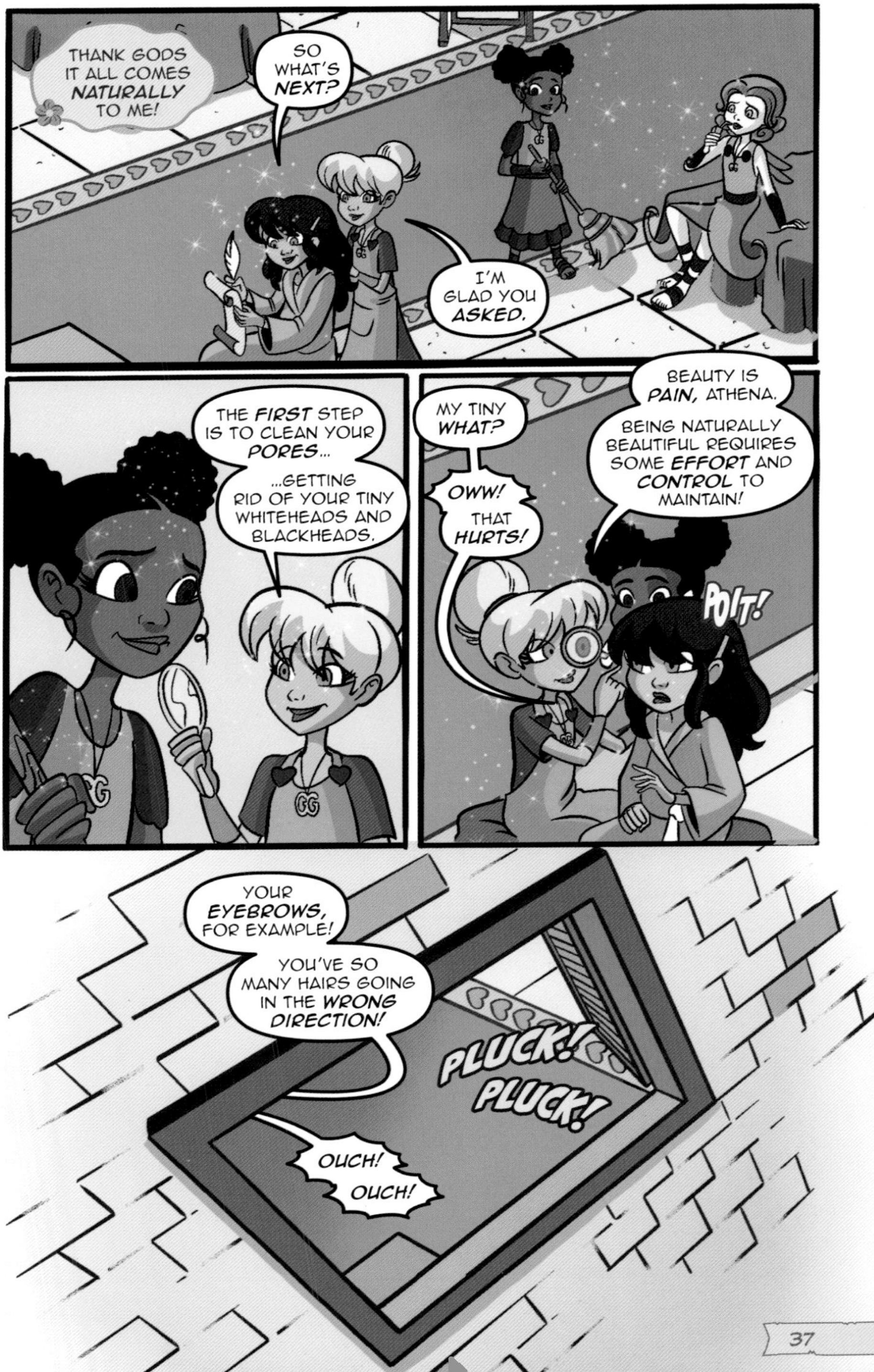
THANK GODS IT ALL COMES NATURALLY TO ME!
SO WHAT'S NEXT?
I'M GLAD YOU ASKED.
THE FIRST STEP IS TO CLEAN YOUR PORES...
...GETTING RID OF YOUR TINY WHITEHEADS AND BLACKHEADS.
MY TINY WHAT?
OWW!
THAT HURTS!
BEAUTY IS PAIN, ATHENA.
BEING NATURALLY BEAUTIFUL REQUIRES SOME EFFORT AND CONTROL TO MAINTAIN!
POIT!
YOUR EYEBROWS, FOR EXAMPLE!
YOU'VE SO MANY HAIRS GOING IN THE WRONG DIRECTION!
PLUCK! PLUCK!
OUCH!
OUCH!

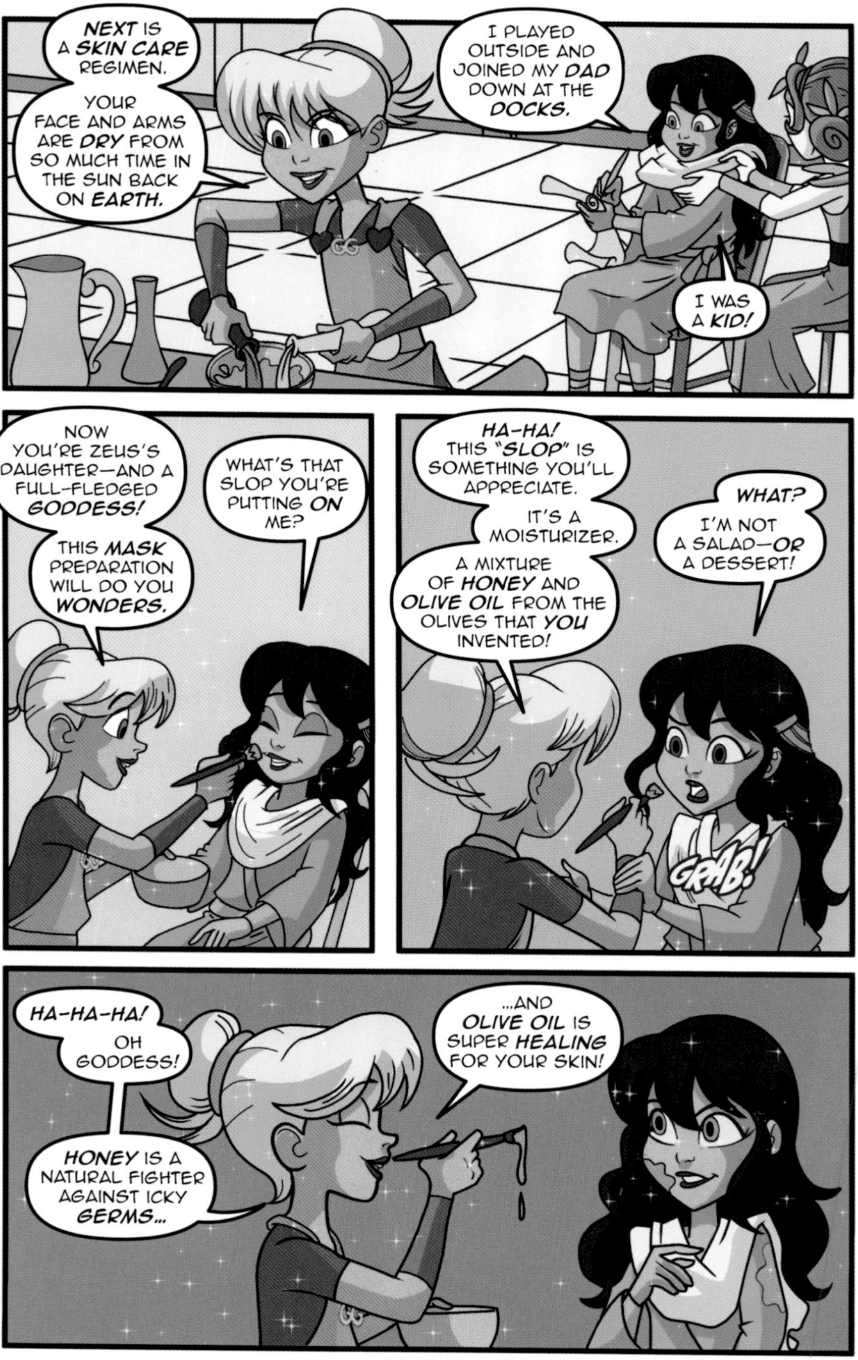
NEXT IS A SKIN CARE REGIMEN.
YOUR FACE AND ARMS ARE DRY FROM SO MUCH TIME IN THE SUN BACK ON EARTH.
I PLAYED OUTSIDE AND JOINED MY DAD DOWN AT THE DOCKS.
I WAS A KID!
NOW YOU'RE ZEUS'S DAUGHTER—AND A FULL-FLEDGED GODDESS!
THIS MASK PREPARATION WILL DO YOU WONDERS.
WHAT'S THAT SLOP YOU'RE PUTTING ON ME?
HA-HA! THIS "SLOP" IS SOMETHING YOU'LL APPRECIATE.
IT'S A MOISTURIZER.
A MIXTURE OF HONEY AND OLIVE OIL FROM THE OLIVES THAT YOU INVENTED!
WHAT? I'M NOT A SALAD—OR A DESSERT!
GRAB!
HA-HA-HA! OH GODDESS!
HONEY IS A NATURAL FIGHTER AGAINST ICKY GERMS...
...AND OLIVE OIL IS SUPER HEALING FOR YOUR SKIN!

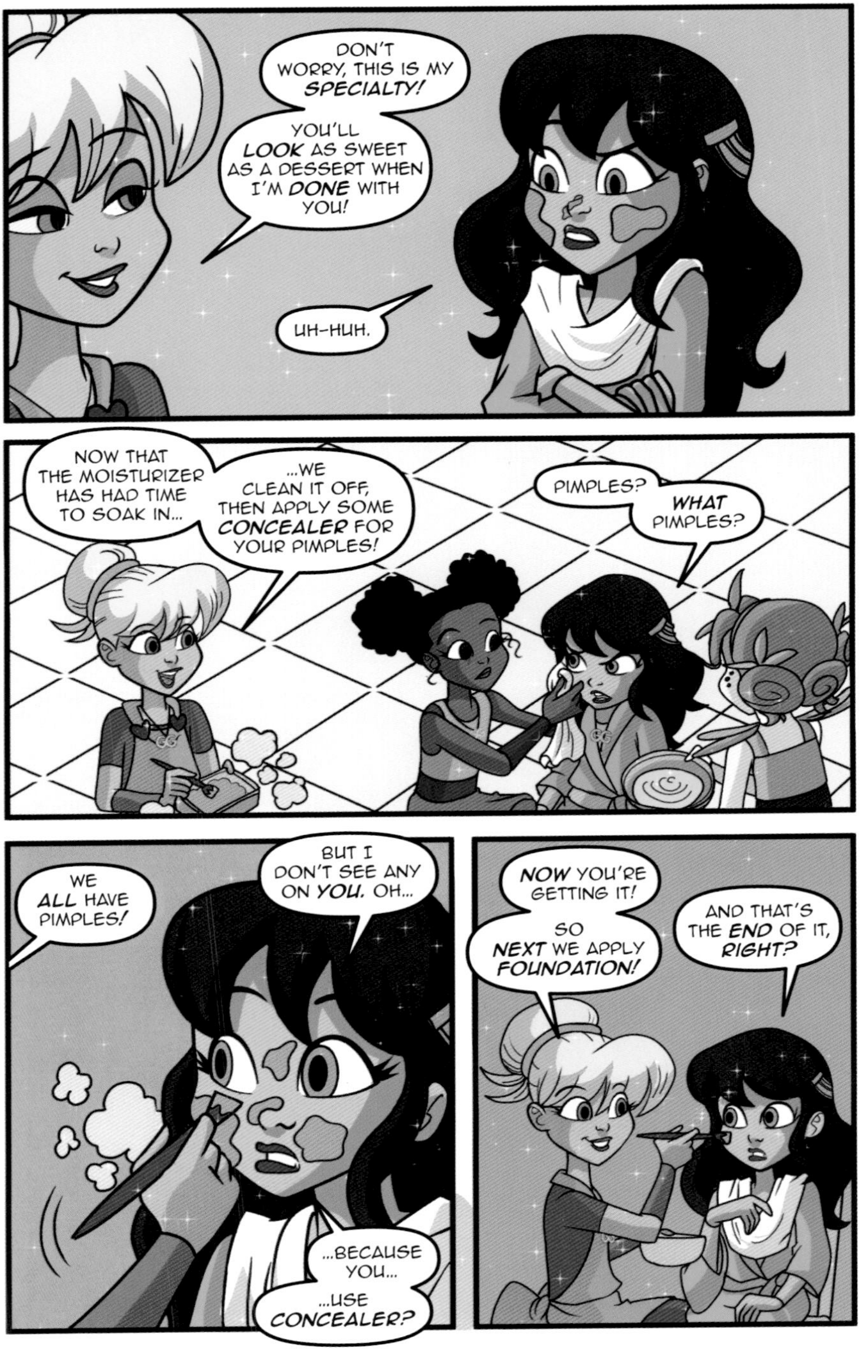
DON'T WORRY, THIS IS MY SPECIALTY!
YOU'LL LOOK AS SWEET AS A DESSERT WHEN I'M DONE WITH YOU!
UH-HUH.
NOW THAT THE MOISTURIZER HAS HAD TIME TO SOAK IN...
...WE CLEAN IT OFF, THEN APPLY SOME CONCEALER FOR YOUR PIMPLES!
PIMPLES?
WHAT PIMPLES?
WE ALL HAVE PIMPLES!
BUT I DON'T SEE ANY ON YOU. OH...
...BECAUSE YOU...
...USE CONCEALER?
NOW YOU'RE GETTING IT!
SO NEXT WE APPLY FOUNDATION!
AND THAT'S THE END OF IT, RIGHT?

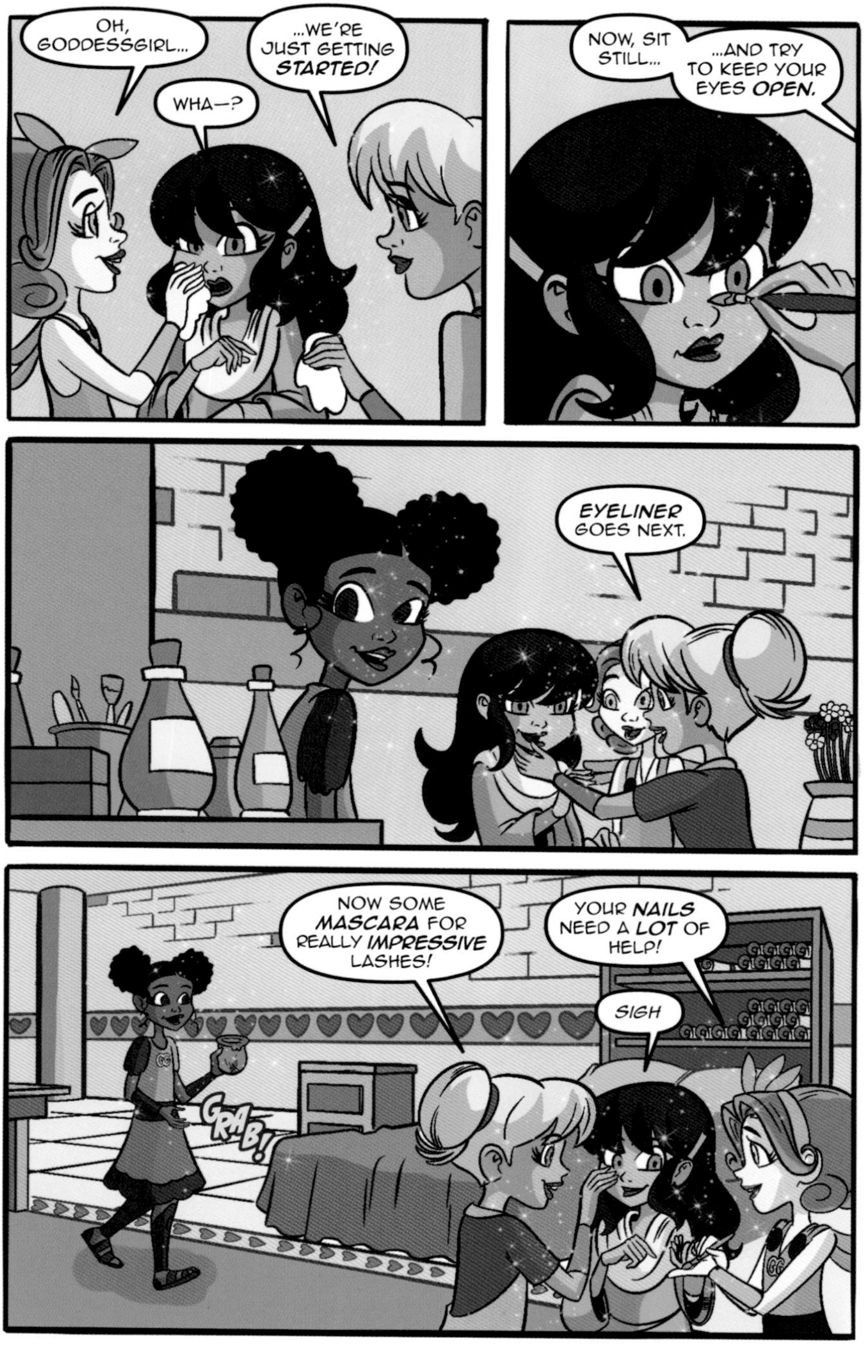
OH, GODDESSGIRL...
WHA—?
...WE'RE JUST GETTING STARTED!
NOW, SIT STILL...
...AND TRY TO KEEP YOUR EYES OPEN.
EYELINER GOES NEXT.
NOW SOME MASCARA FOR REALLY IMPRESSIVE LASHES!
YOUR NAILS NEED A LOT OF HELP!
SIGH
GRAB!

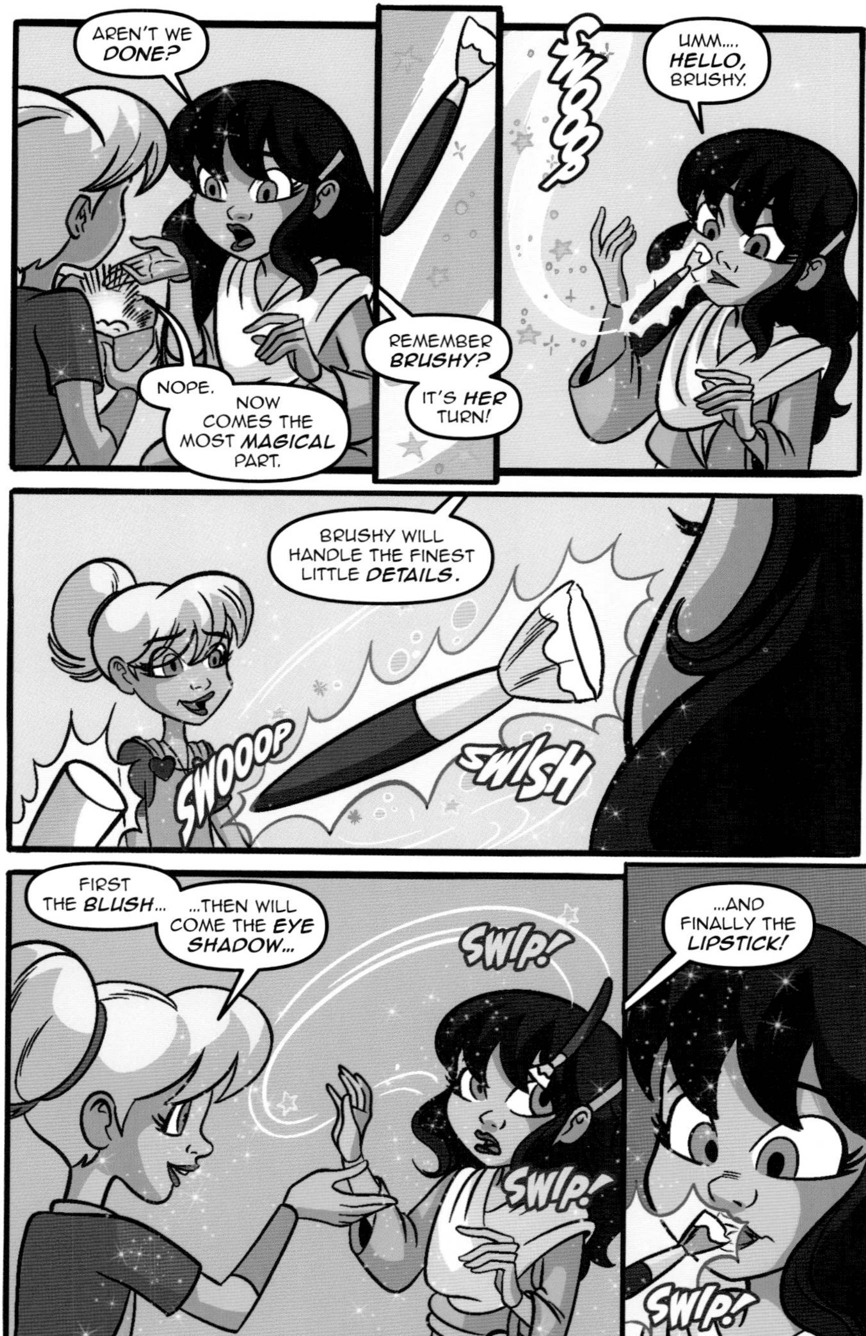

AREN'T WE DONE?
NOPE. NOW COMES THE MOST MAGICAL PART.
REMEMBER BRUSHY?
IT'S HER TURN!
SWOOOP
UMM.... HELLO, BRUSHY.
BRUSHY WILL HANDLE THE FINEST LITTLE DETAILS.
SWOOOP
SWISH
FIRST THE BLUSH...
...THEN WILL COME THE EYE SHADOW...
SWIP!
SWIP!
...AND FINALLY THE LIPSTICK!
SWIP!

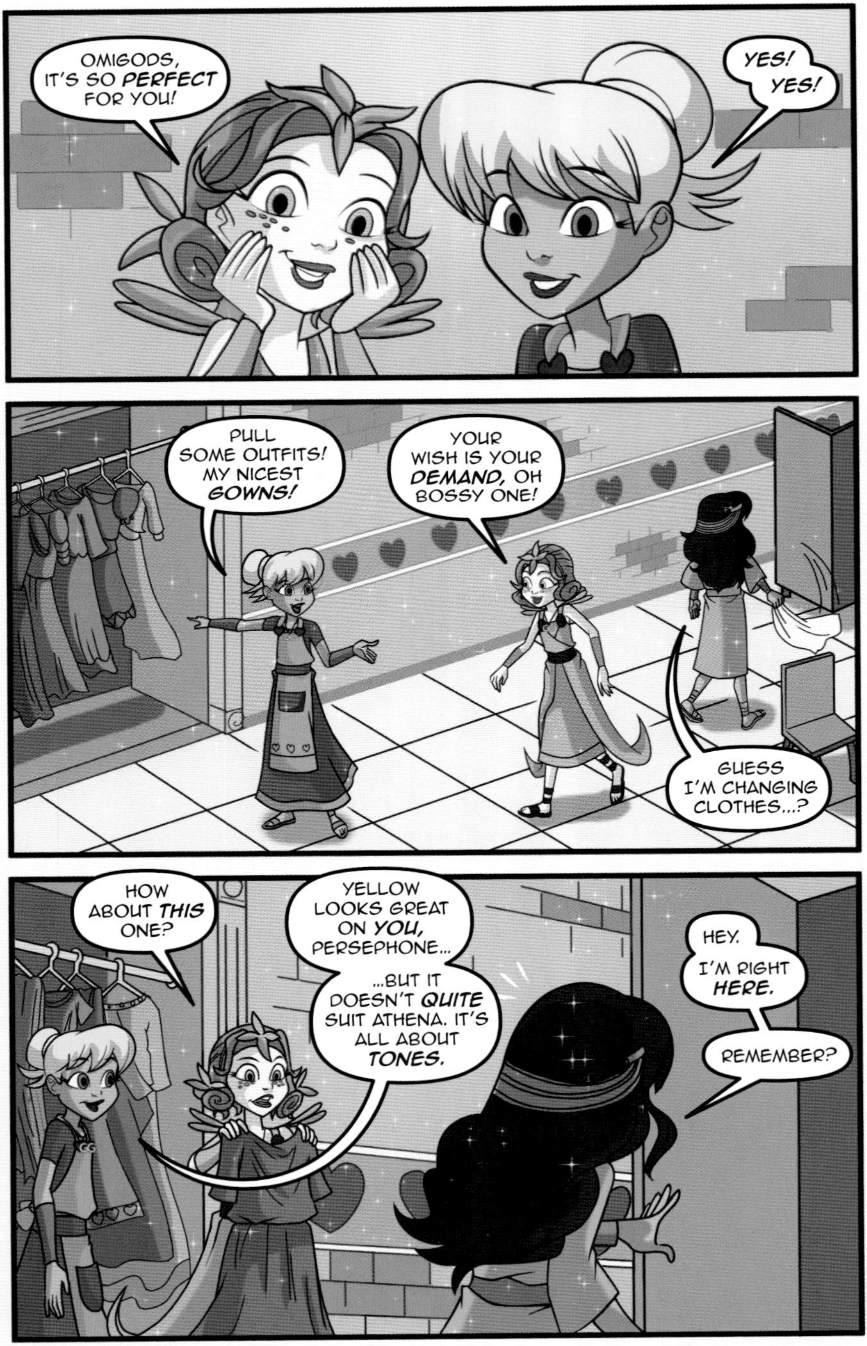
OMIGODS, IT'S SO **PERFECT** FOR YOU!
YES! YES!
PULL SOME OUTFITS! MY NICEST **GOWNS!**
YOUR WISH IS YOUR **DEMAND,** OH BOSSY ONE!
GUESS I'M CHANGING CLOTHES...?
HOW ABOUT **THIS** ONE?
YELLOW LOOKS GREAT ON **YOU,** PERSEPHONE...
...BUT IT DOESN'T **QUITE** SUIT ATHENA. IT'S ALL ABOUT **TONES.**
HEY. I'M RIGHT **HERE.**
REMEMBER?

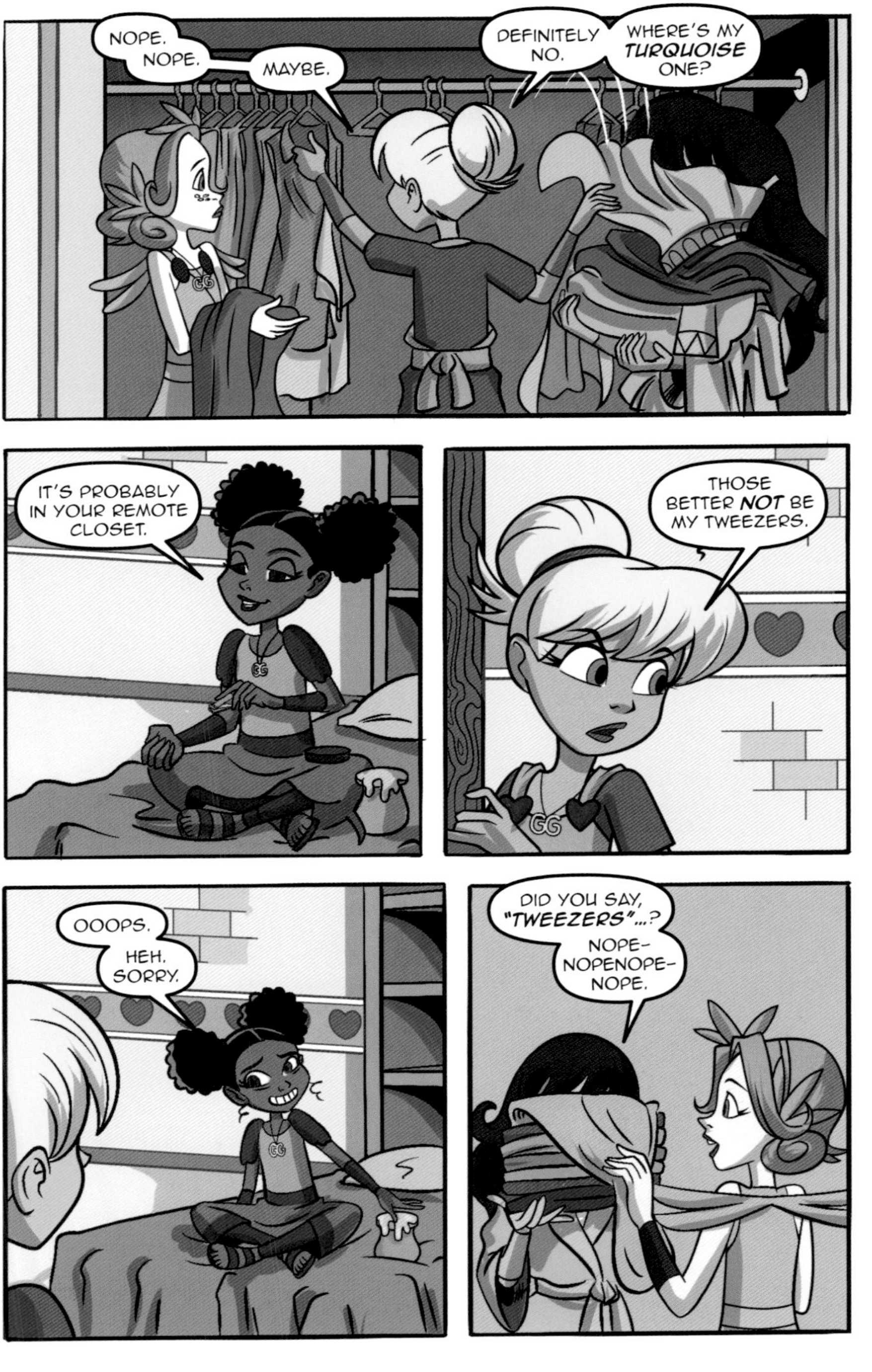
NOPE. NOPE.
MAYBE.
DEFINITELY NO.
WHERE'S MY *TURQUOISE* ONE?
IT'S PROBABLY IN YOUR REMOTE CLOSET.
THOSE BETTER *NOT* BE MY TWEEZERS.
OOOPS.
HEH. SORRY.
DID YOU SAY, *"TWEEZERS"*...?
NOPE-NOPENOPE-NOPE.

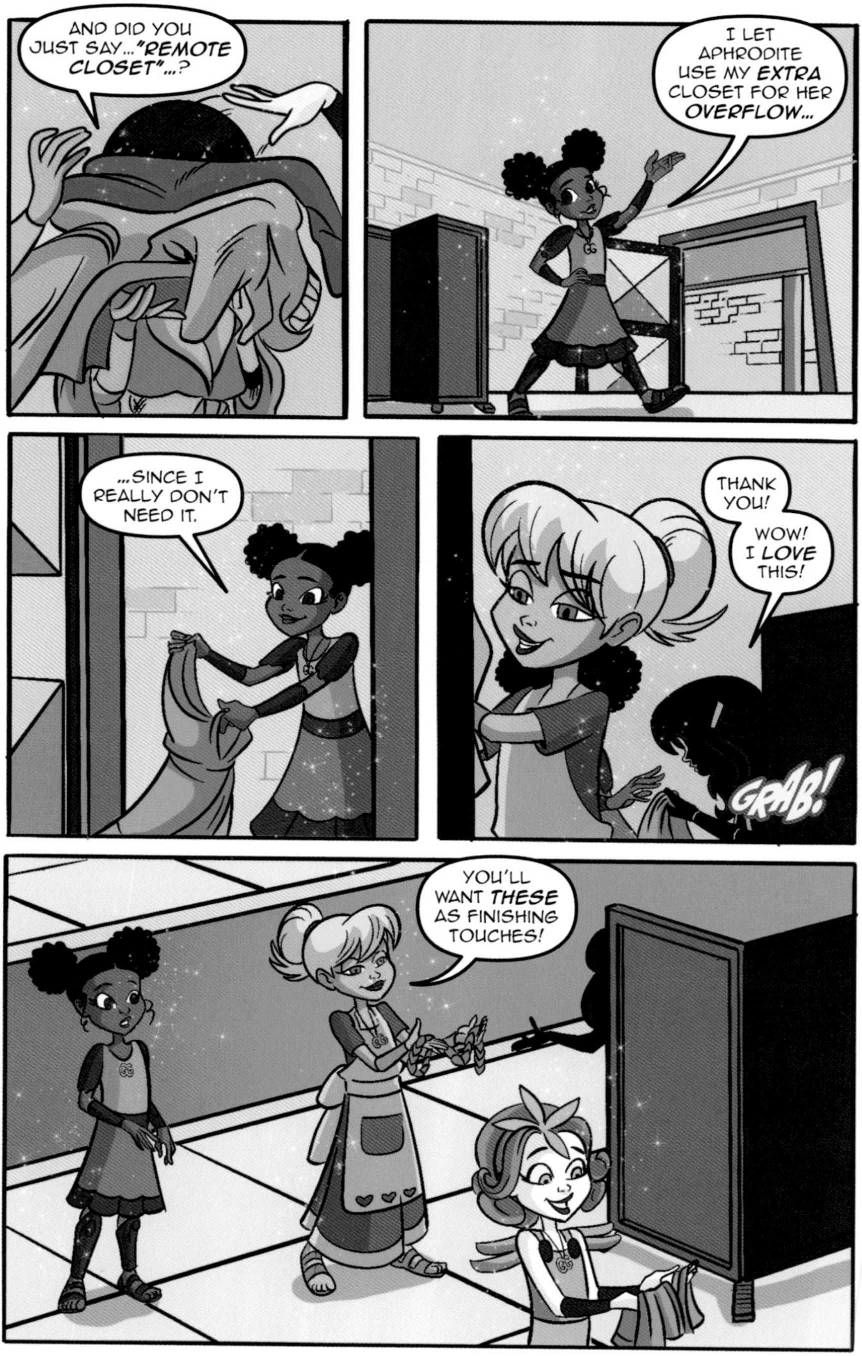
AND DID YOU JUST SAY..."REMOTE CLOSET"...?
I LET APHRODITE USE MY EXTRA CLOSET FOR HER OVERFLOW...
...SINCE I REALLY DON'T NEED IT.
THANK YOU!
WOW! I LOVE THIS!
GRAB!
YOU'LL WANT THESE AS FINISHING TOUCHES!

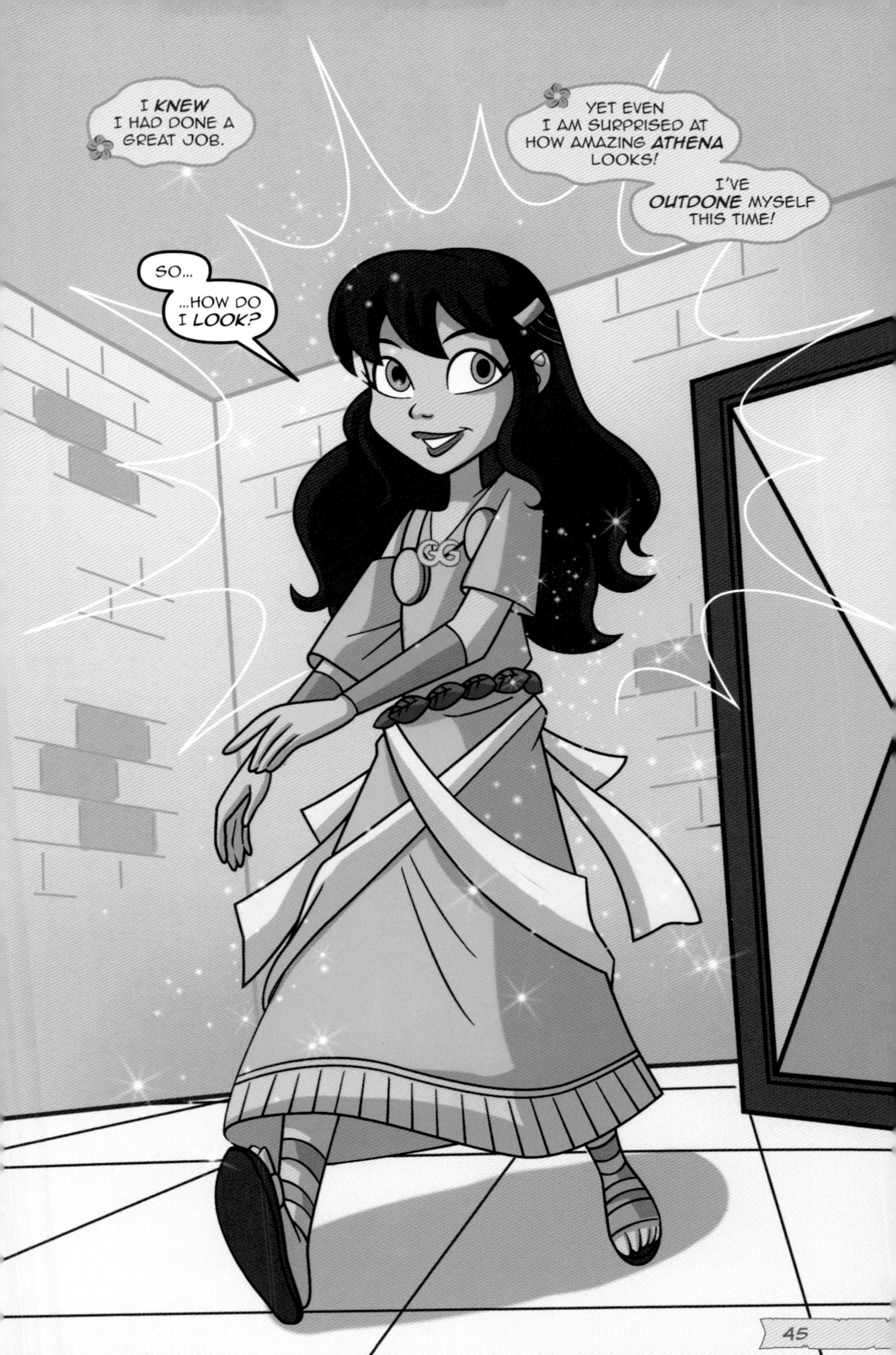
I KNEW I HAD DONE A GREAT JOB.
YET EVEN I AM SURPRISED AT HOW AMAZING ATHENA LOOKS!
I'VE OUTDONE MYSELF THIS TIME!
SO...
...HOW DO I LOOK?

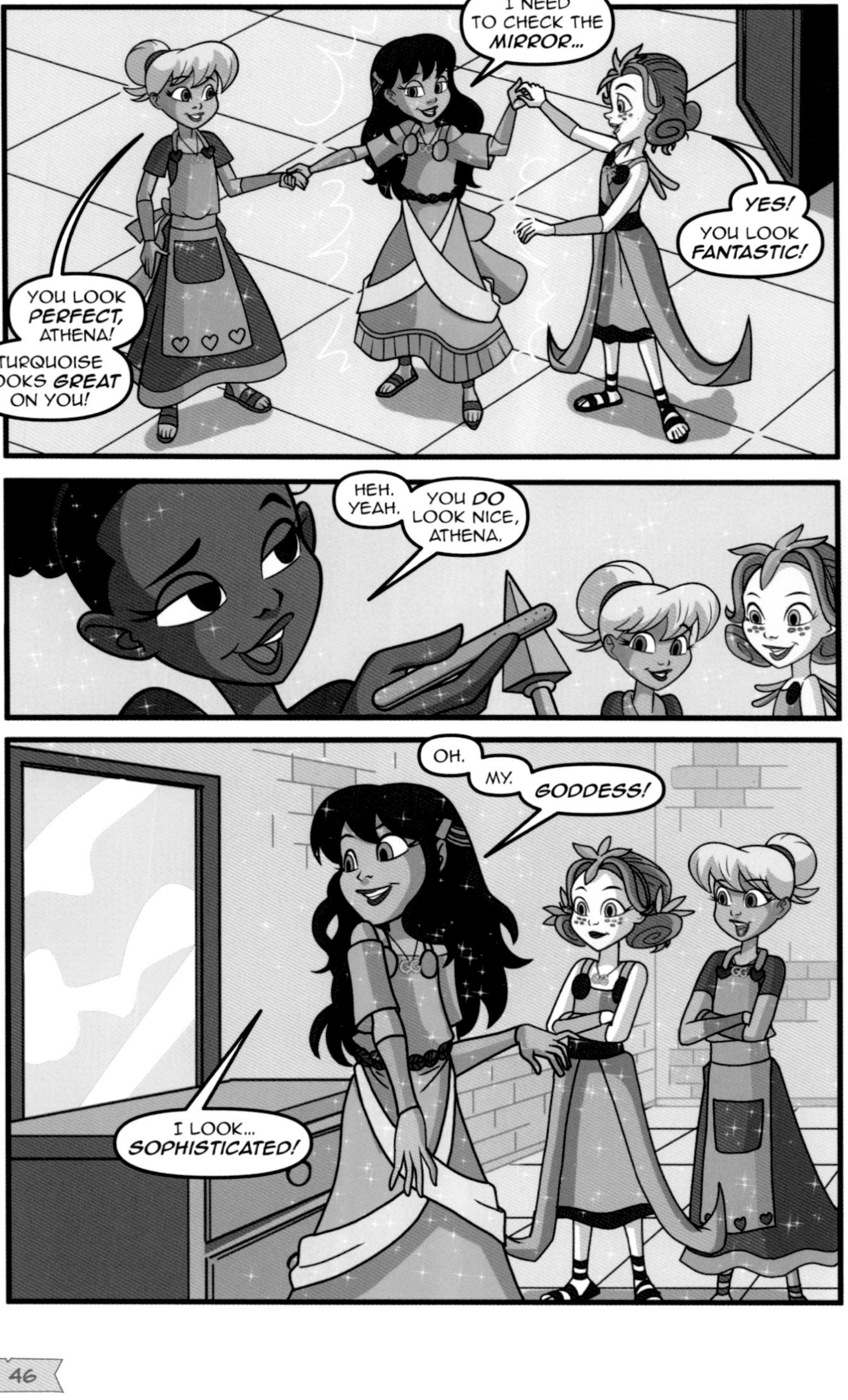
I NEED TO CHECK THE MIRROR...
YOU LOOK PERFECT, ATHENA!
TURQUOISE LOOKS GREAT ON YOU!
YES! YOU LOOK FANTASTIC!
HEH. YEAH.
YOU DO LOOK NICE, ATHENA.
OH.
MY.
GODDESS!
I LOOK... SOPHISTICATED!

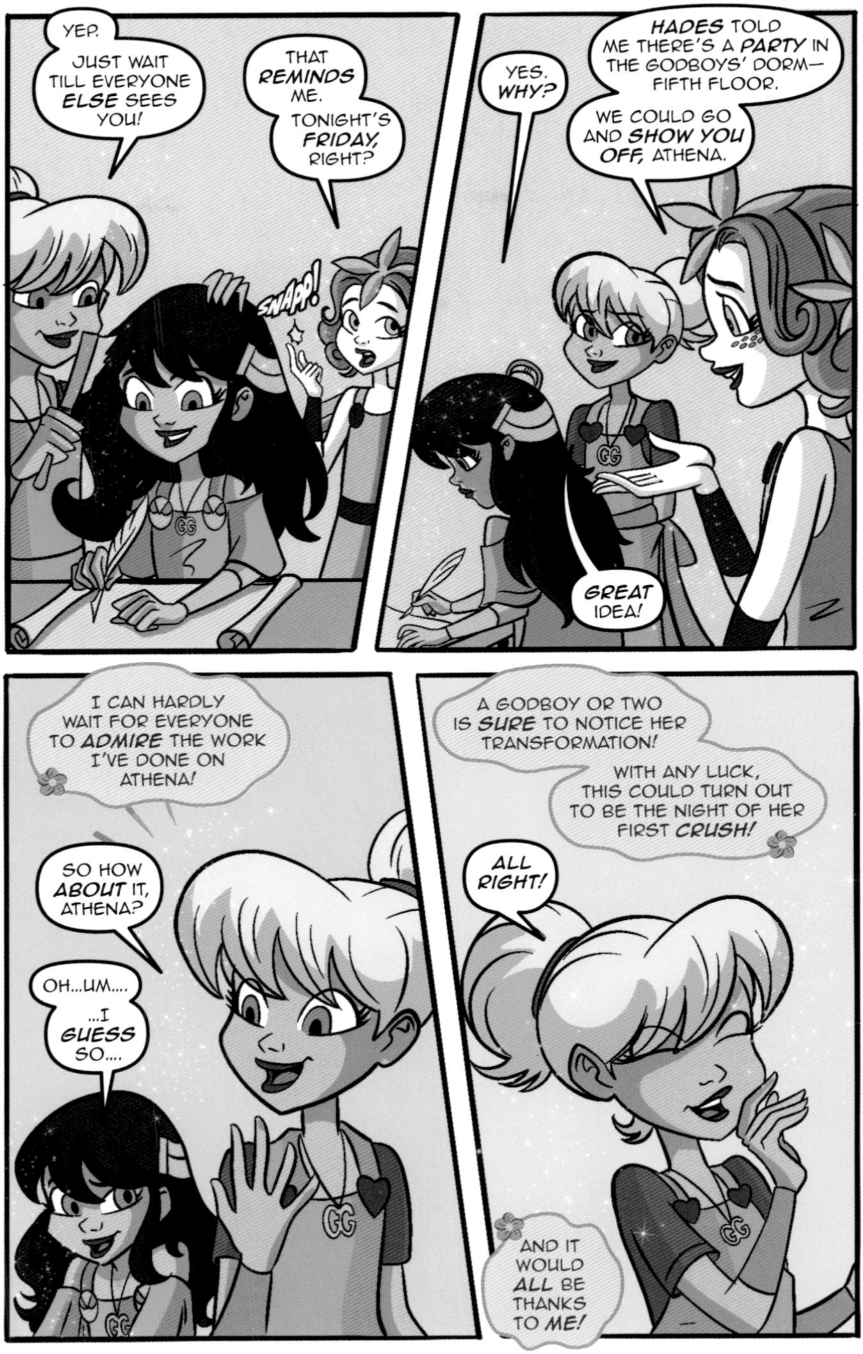
YEP.
JUST WAIT TILL EVERYONE ELSE SEES YOU!
THAT REMINDS ME.
TONIGHT'S FRIDAY, RIGHT?
SNAPP!
YES. WHY?
HADES TOLD ME THERE'S A PARTY IN THE GODBOYS' DORM—FIFTH FLOOR.
WE COULD GO AND SHOW YOU OFF, ATHENA.
GREAT IDEA!
I CAN HARDLY WAIT FOR EVERYONE TO ADMIRE THE WORK I'VE DONE ON ATHENA!
SO HOW ABOUT IT, ATHENA?
OH...UM....
...I GUESS SO....
A GODBOY OR TWO IS SURE TO NOTICE HER TRANSFORMATION!
WITH ANY LUCK, THIS COULD TURN OUT TO BE THE NIGHT OF HER FIRST CRUSH!
ALL RIGHT!
AND IT WOULD ALL BE THANKS TO ME!

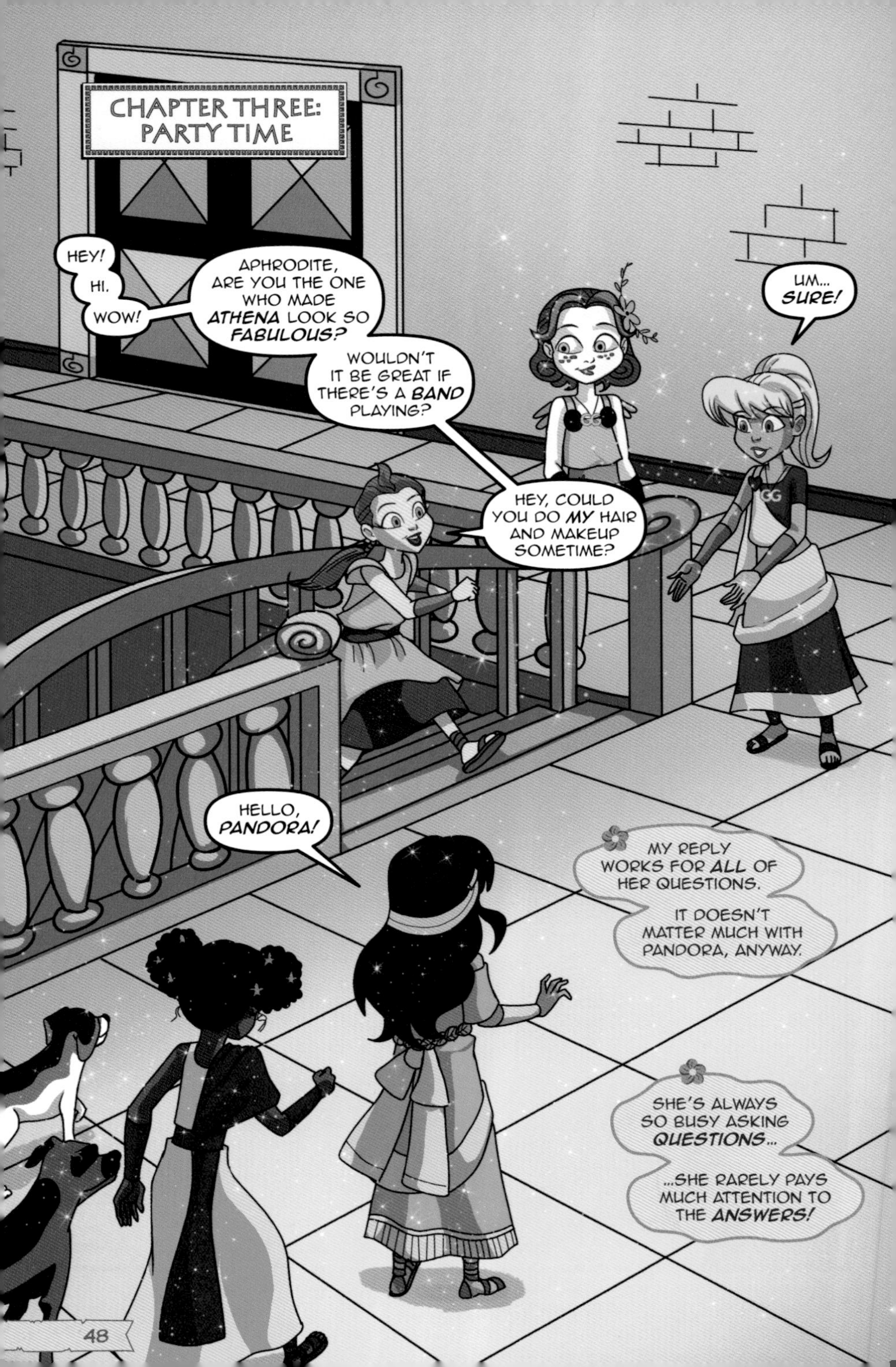
CHAPTER THREE: PARTY TIME
HEY!
HI.
WOW!
APHRODITE, ARE YOU THE ONE WHO MADE ATHENA LOOK SO FABULOUS?
WOULDN'T IT BE GREAT IF THERE'S A BAND PLAYING?
HEY, COULD YOU DO MY HAIR AND MAKEUP SOMETIME?
UM... SURE!
HELLO, PANDORA!
MY REPLY WORKS FOR ALL OF HER QUESTIONS.
IT DOESN'T MATTER MUCH WITH PANDORA, ANYWAY.
SHE'S ALWAYS SO BUSY ASKING QUESTIONS...
...SHE RARELY PAYS MUCH ATTENTION TO THE ANSWERS!

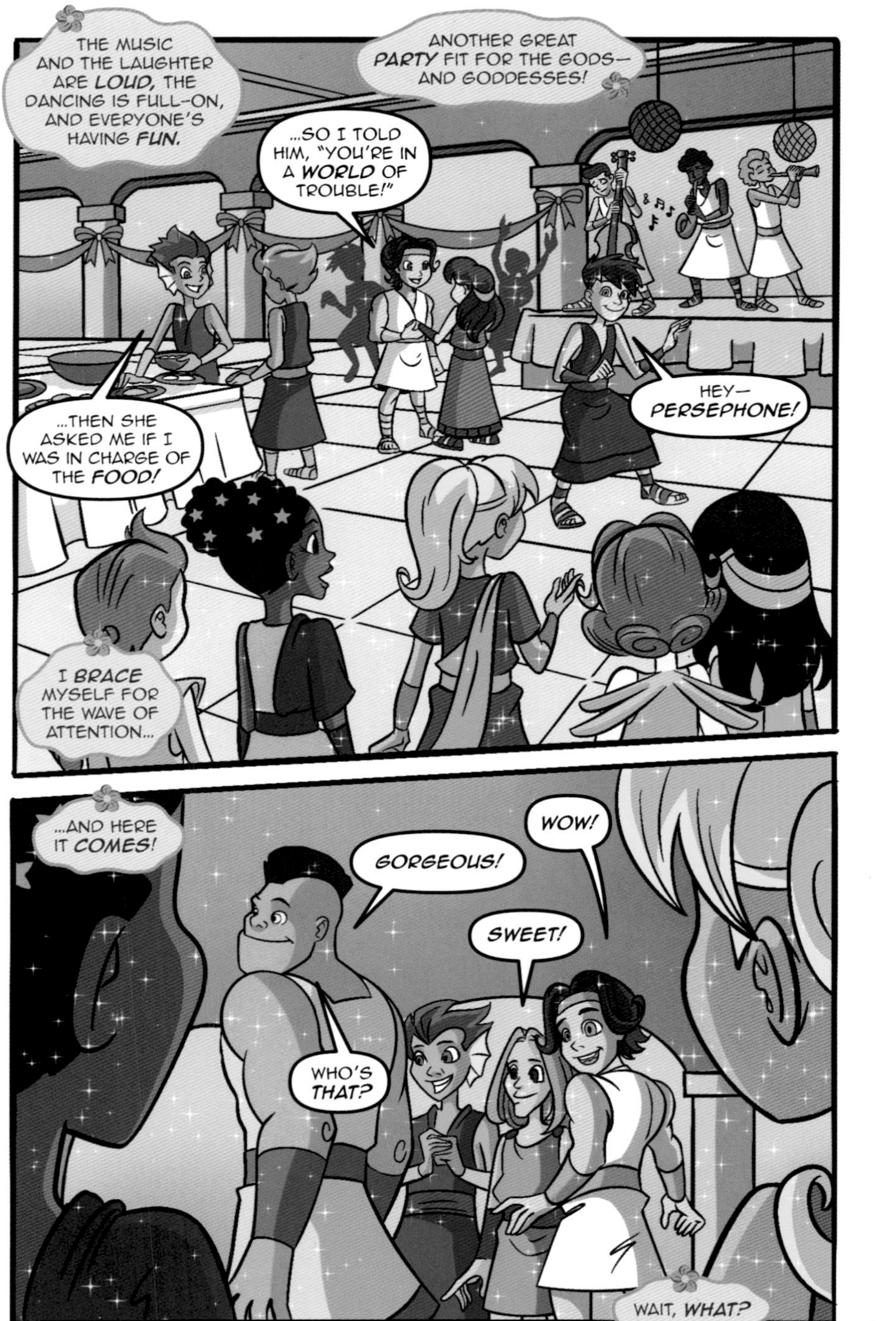
THE MUSIC AND THE LAUGHTER ARE LOUD, THE DANCING IS FULL-ON, AND EVERYONE'S HAVING FUN.
ANOTHER GREAT PARTY FIT FOR THE GODS— AND GODDESSES!
...SO I TOLD HIM, "YOU'RE IN A WORLD OF TROUBLE!"
...THEN SHE ASKED ME IF I WAS IN CHARGE OF THE FOOD!
HEY— PERSEPHONE!
I BRACE MYSELF FOR THE WAVE OF ATTENTION...
...AND HERE IT COMES!
GORGEOUS!
WOW!
SWEET!
WHO'S THAT?
WAIT, WHAT?

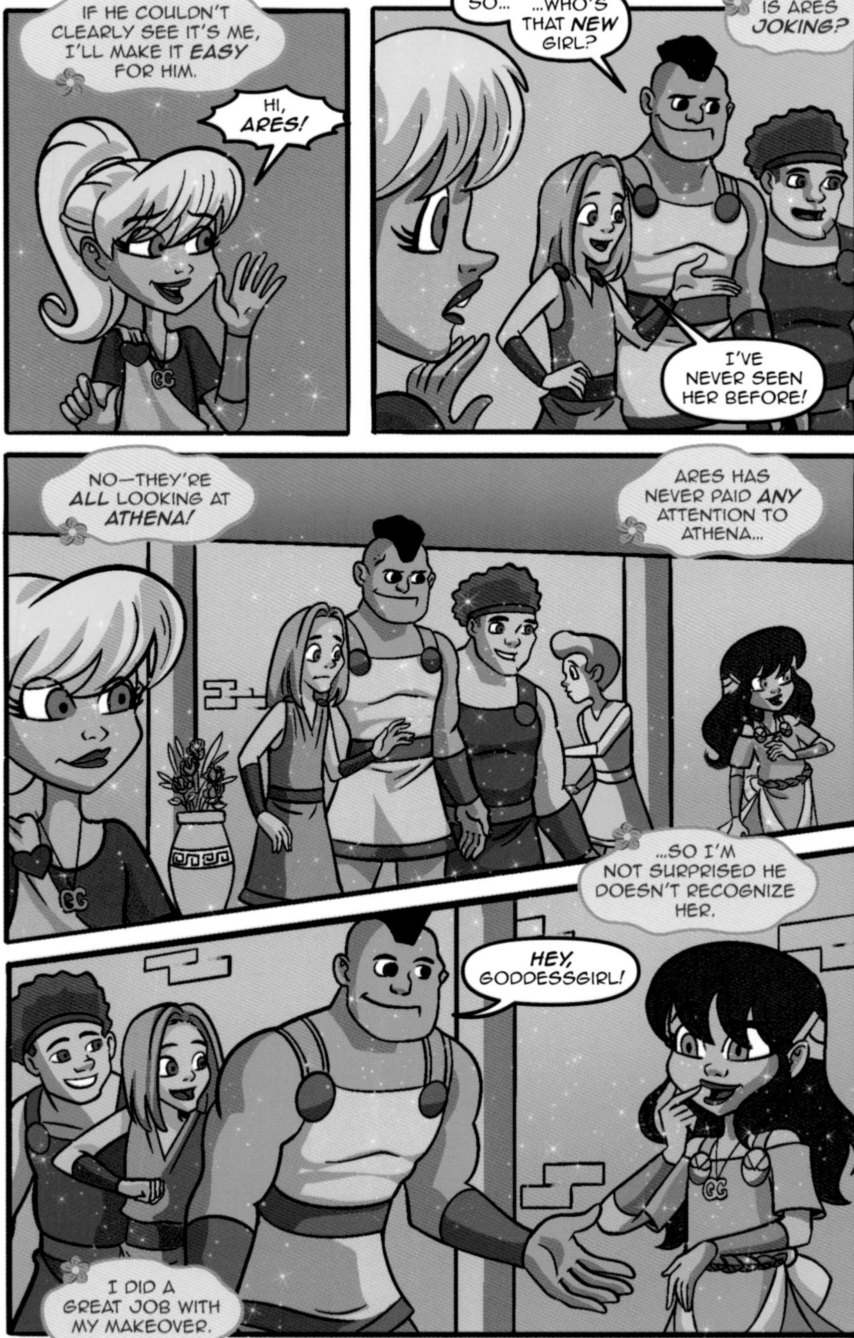
IF HE COULDN'T CLEARLY SEE IT'S ME, I'LL MAKE IT EASY FOR HIM.
HI, ARES!
SO...
...WHO'S THAT NEW GIRL?
IS ARES JOKING?
I'VE NEVER SEEN HER BEFORE!
NO—THEY'RE ALL LOOKING AT ATHENA!
ARES HAS NEVER PAID ANY ATTENTION TO ATHENA...
...SO I'M NOT SURPRISED HE DOESN'T RECOGNIZE HER.
HEY, GODDESSGIRL!
I DID A GREAT JOB WITH MY MAKEOVER.

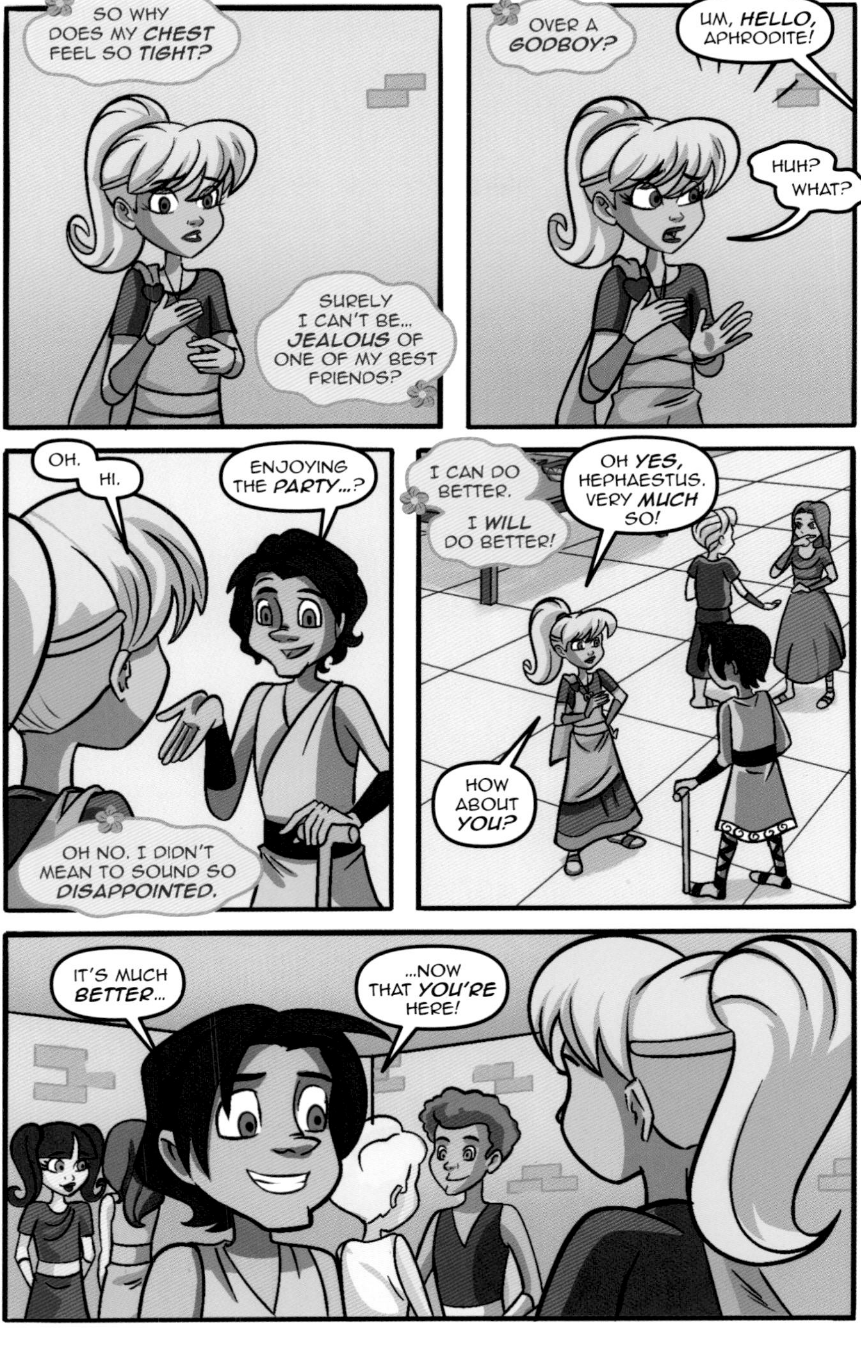
SO WHY DOES MY CHEST FEEL SO TIGHT?
SURELY I CAN'T BE... JEALOUS OF ONE OF MY BEST FRIENDS?
OVER A GODBOY?
UM, HELLO, APHRODITE!
HUH? WHAT?
OH. HI.
ENJOYING THE PARTY...?
OH NO. I DIDN'T MEAN TO SOUND SO DISAPPOINTED.
I CAN DO BETTER.
I WILL DO BETTER!
OH YES, HEPHAESTUS. VERY MUCH SO!
HOW ABOUT YOU?
IT'S MUCH BETTER...
...NOW THAT YOU'RE HERE!

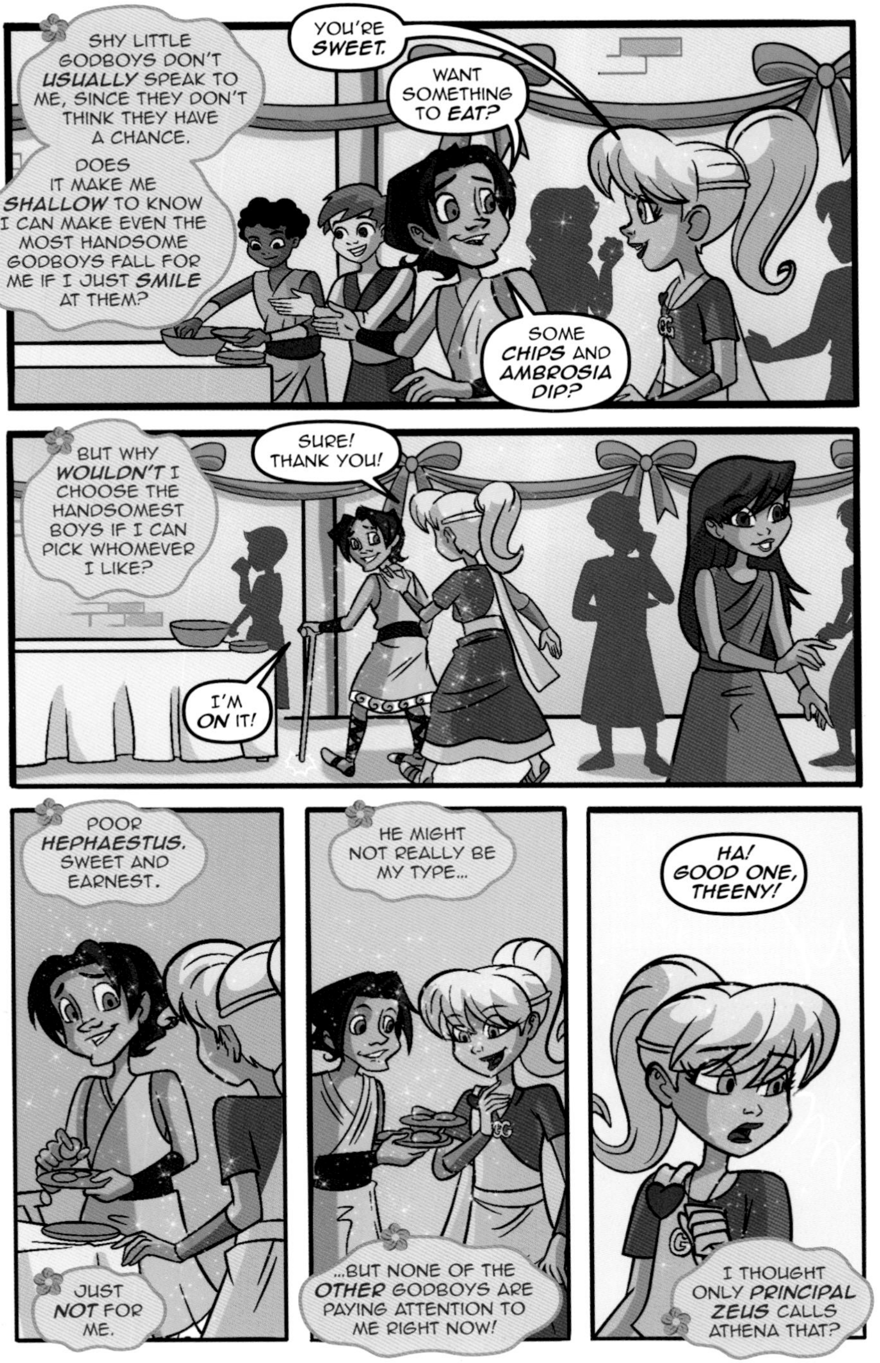
SHY LITTLE GODBOYS DON'T USUALLY SPEAK TO ME, SINCE THEY DON'T THINK THEY HAVE A CHANCE.
YOU'RE SWEET.
WANT SOMETHING TO EAT?
DOES IT MAKE ME SHALLOW TO KNOW I CAN MAKE EVEN THE MOST HANDSOME GODBOYS FALL FOR ME IF I JUST SMILE AT THEM?
SOME CHIPS AND AMBROSIA DIP?
BUT WHY WOULDN'T I CHOOSE THE HANDSOMEST BOYS IF I CAN PICK WHOMEVER I LIKE?
SURE! THANK YOU!
I'M ON IT!
POOR HEPHAESTUS. SWEET AND EARNEST.
JUST NOT FOR ME.
HE MIGHT NOT REALLY BE MY TYPE...
...BUT NONE OF THE OTHER GODBOYS ARE PAYING ATTENTION TO ME RIGHT NOW!
HA! GOOD ONE, THEENY!
I THOUGHT ONLY PRINCIPAL ZEUS CALLS ATHENA THAT?

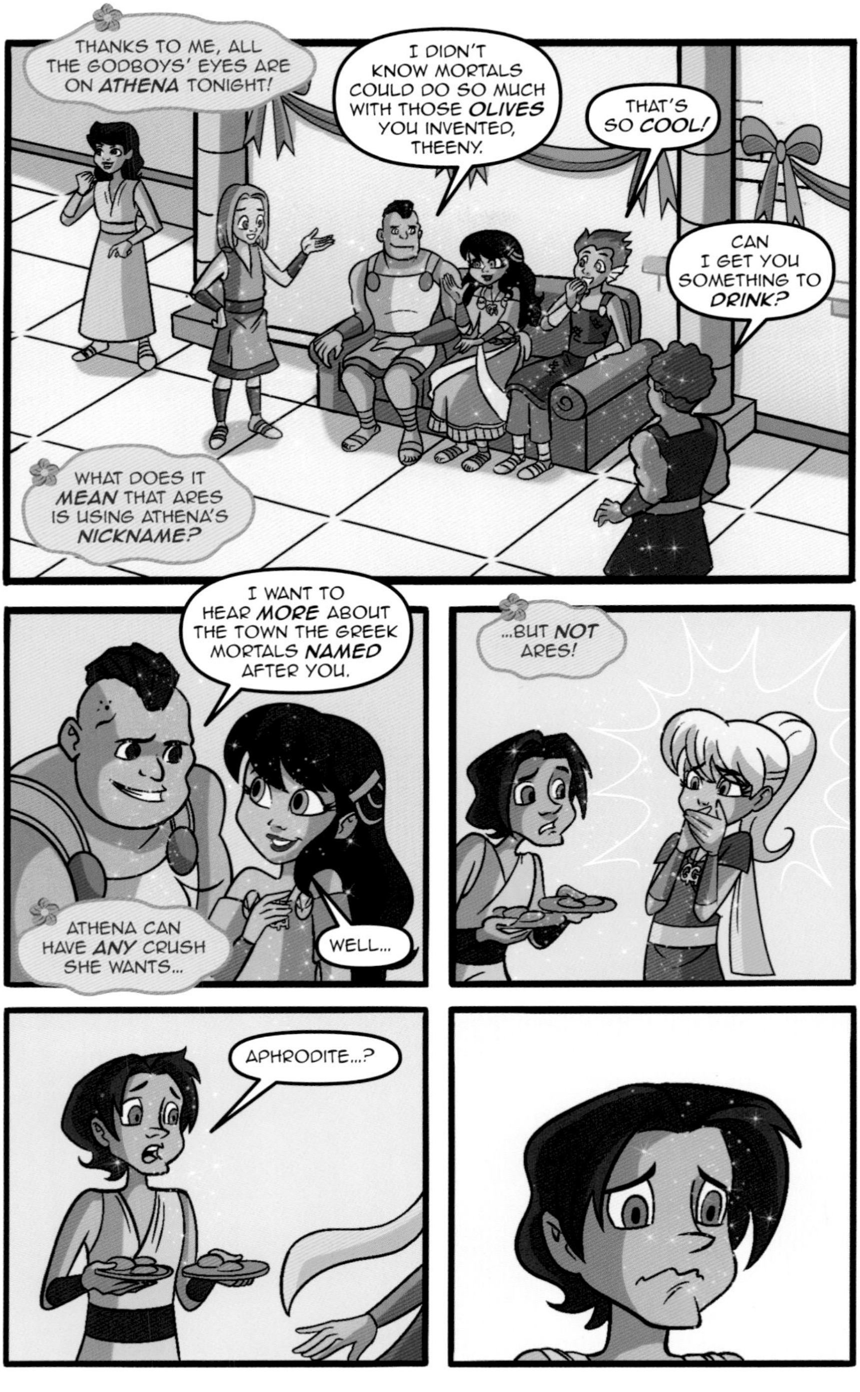
THANKS TO ME, ALL THE GODBOYS' EYES ARE ON ATHENA TONIGHT!
I DIDN'T KNOW MORTALS COULD DO SO MUCH WITH THOSE OLIVES YOU INVENTED, THEENY.
THAT'S SO COOL!
CAN I GET YOU SOMETHING TO DRINK?
WHAT DOES IT MEAN THAT ARES IS USING ATHENA'S NICKNAME?
I WANT TO HEAR MORE ABOUT THE TOWN THE GREEK MORTALS NAMED AFTER YOU.
ATHENA CAN HAVE ANY CRUSH SHE WANTS...
WELL...
...BUT NOT ARES!
APHRODITE...?

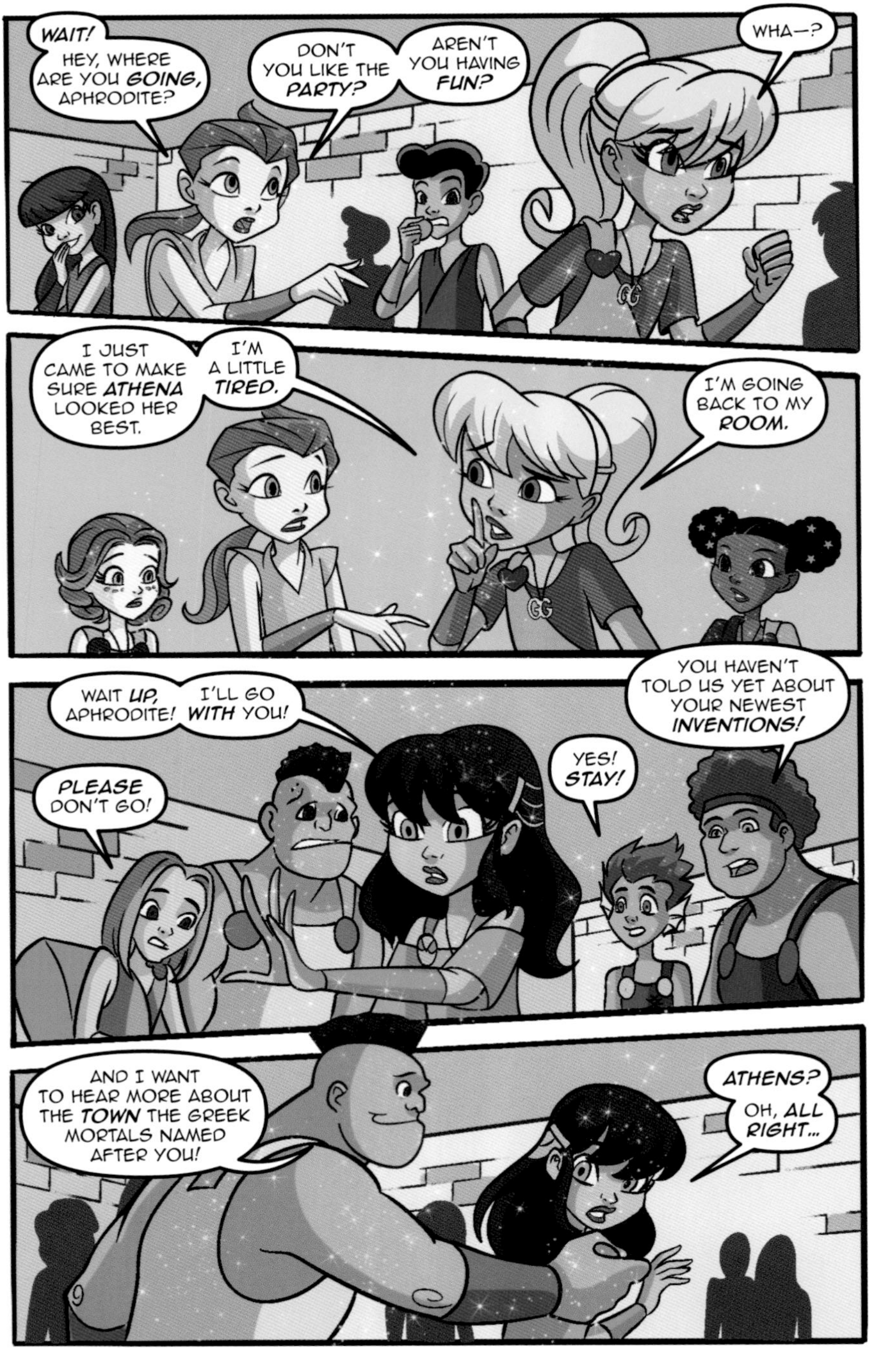
WAIT! HEY, WHERE ARE YOU GOING, APHRODITE?
DON'T YOU LIKE THE PARTY?
AREN'T YOU HAVING FUN?
WHA—?
I JUST CAME TO MAKE SURE ATHENA LOOKED HER BEST.
I'M A LITTLE TIRED.
I'M GOING BACK TO MY ROOM.
WAIT UP, APHRODITE!
I'LL GO WITH YOU!
YOU HAVEN'T TOLD US YET ABOUT YOUR NEWEST INVENTIONS!
PLEASE DON'T GO!
YES! STAY!
AND I WANT TO HEAR MORE ABOUT THE TOWN THE GREEK MORTALS NAMED AFTER YOU!
ATHENS?
OH, ALL RIGHT...

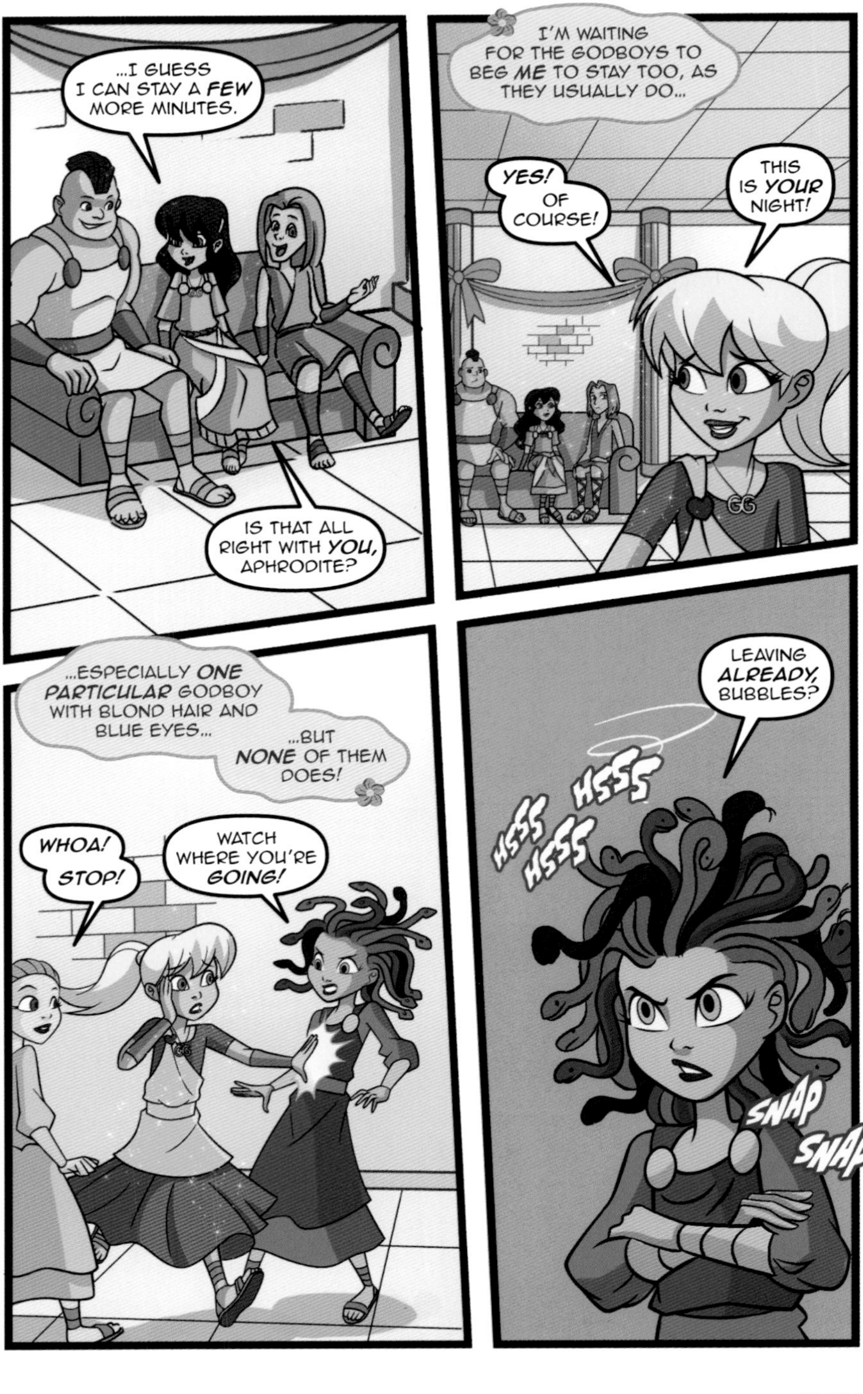
...I GUESS I CAN STAY A FEW MORE MINUTES.
IS THAT ALL RIGHT WITH YOU, APHRODITE?
I'M WAITING FOR THE GODBOYS TO BEG ME TO STAY TOO, AS THEY USUALLY DO...
YES! OF COURSE!
THIS IS YOUR NIGHT!
...ESPECIALLY ONE PARTICULAR GODBOY WITH BLOND HAIR AND BLUE EYES...
...BUT NONE OF THEM DOES!
WHOA! STOP!
WATCH WHERE YOU'RE GOING!
LEAVING ALREADY, BUBBLES?
HSSS HSSS HSSS
SNAP SNAP

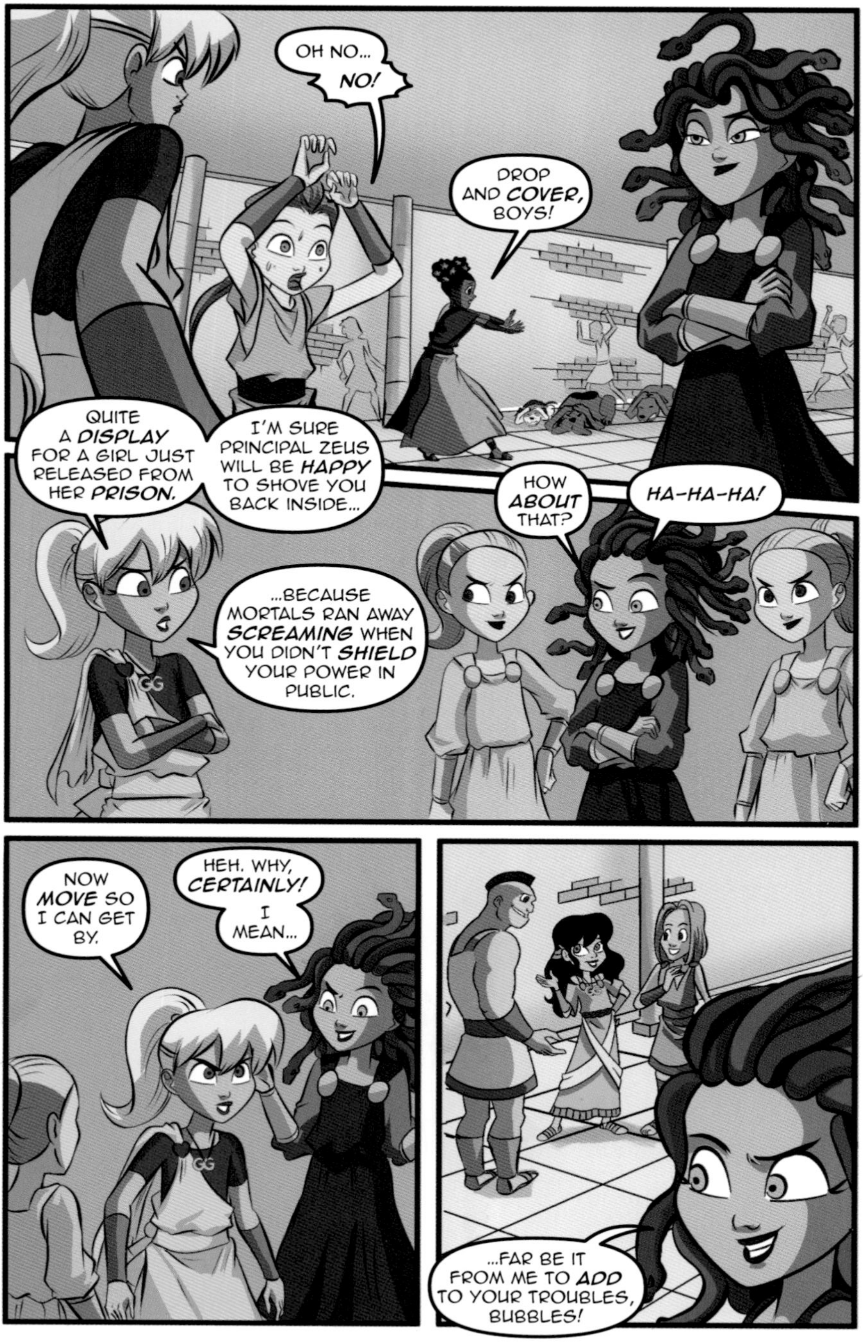
OH NO... NO!
DROP AND COVER, BOYS!
QUITE A DISPLAY FOR A GIRL JUST RELEASED FROM HER PRISON.
I'M SURE PRINCIPAL ZEUS WILL BE HAPPY TO SHOVE YOU BACK INSIDE...
HOW ABOUT THAT?
HA-HA-HA!
...BECAUSE MORTALS RAN AWAY SCREAMING WHEN YOU DIDN'T SHIELD YOUR POWER IN PUBLIC.
NOW MOVE SO I CAN GET BY.
HEH. WHY, CERTAINLY!
I MEAN...
...FAR BE IT FROM ME TO ADD TO YOUR TROUBLES, BUBBLES!

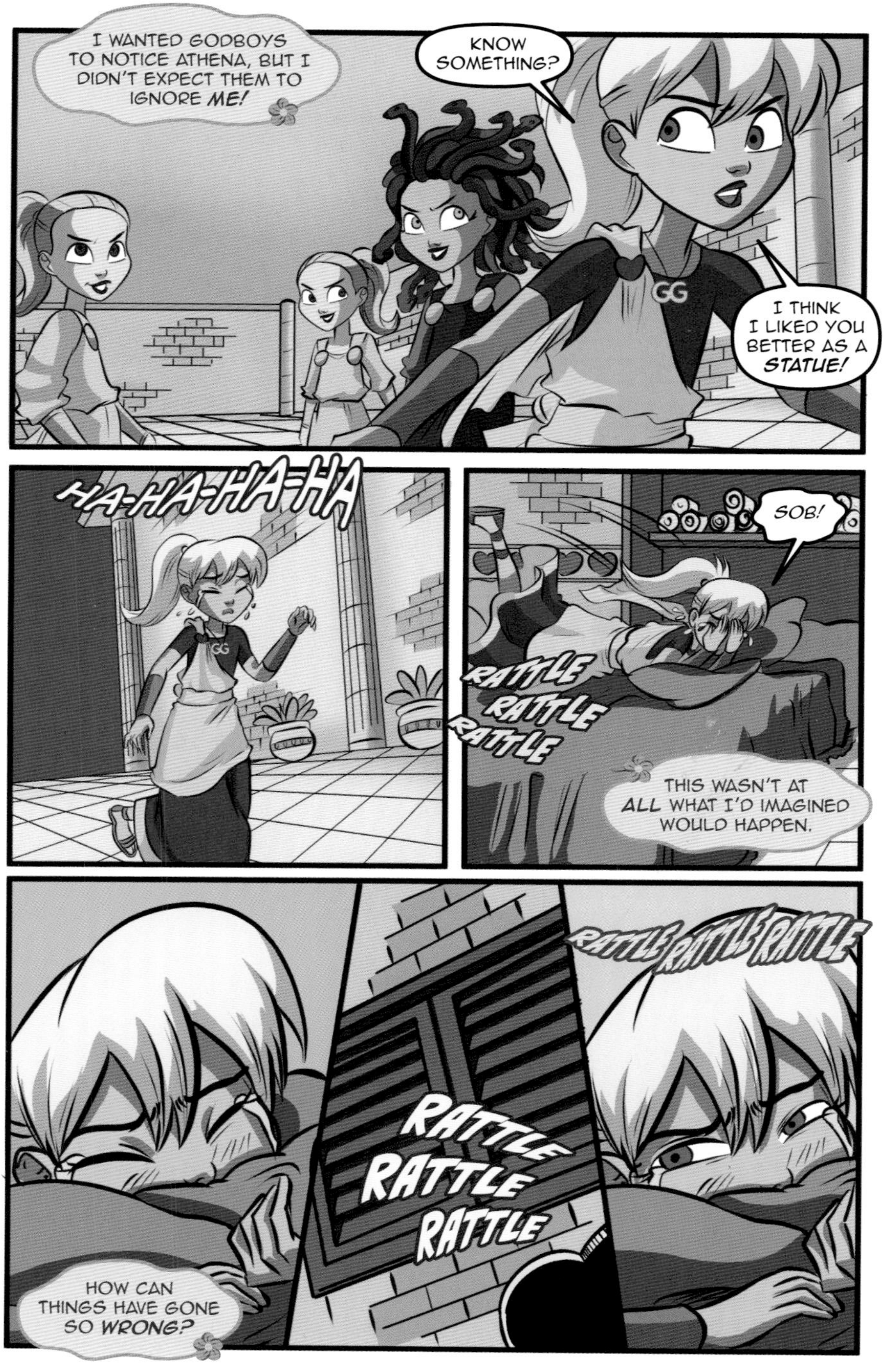
I WANTED GODBOYS TO NOTICE ATHENA, BUT I DIDN'T EXPECT THEM TO IGNORE ME!
KNOW SOMETHING?
GG
I THINK I LIKED YOU BETTER AS A STATUE!
HA-HA-HA-HA-HA
GG
SOB!
RATTLE RATTLE RATTLE
THIS WASN'T AT ALL WHAT I'D IMAGINED WOULD HAPPEN.
RATTLE RATTLE RATTLE
RATTLE RATTLE RATTLE
HOW CAN THINGS HAVE GONE SO WRONG?

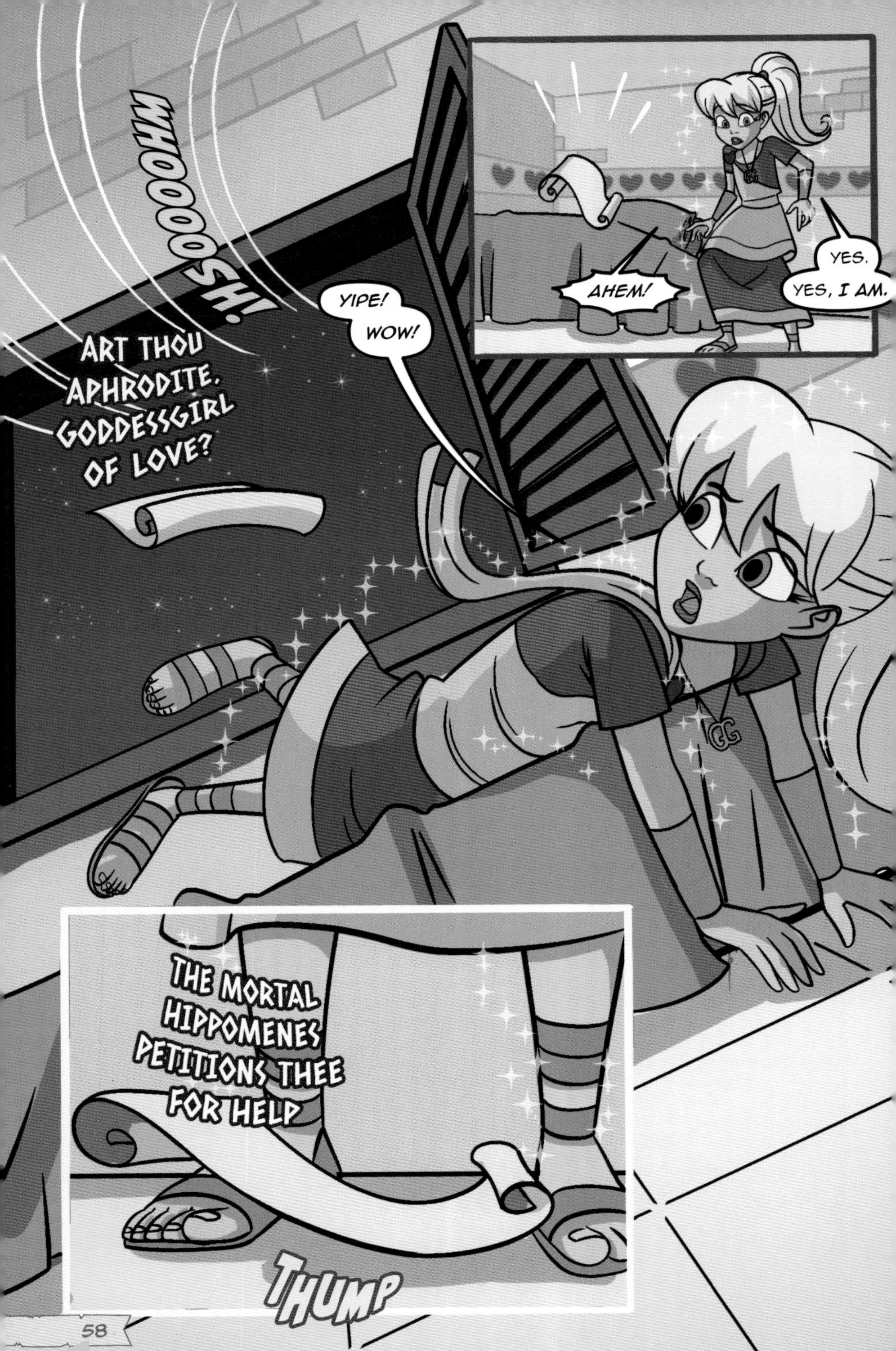
WHOOOOSH!
ART THOU APHRODITE, GODDESSGIRL OF LOVE?
YIPE!
WOW!
AHEM!
YES.
YES, I AM.
THE MORTAL HIPPOMENES PETITIONS THEE FOR HELP
THUMP

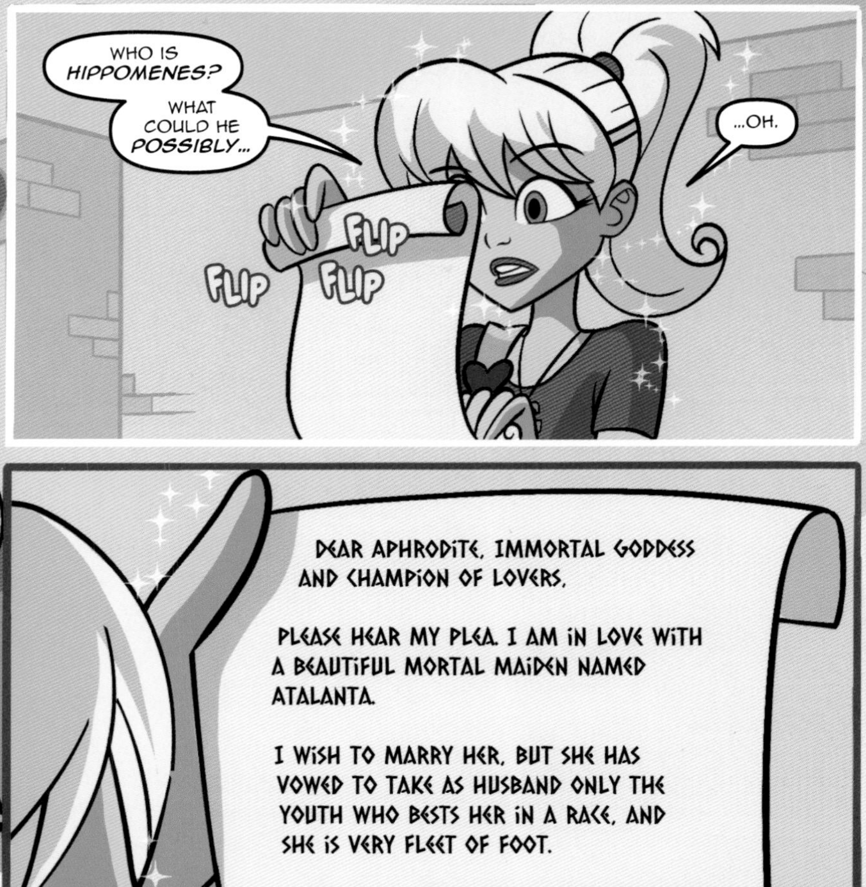
WHO IS HIPPOMENES? WHAT COULD HE POSSIBLY...
...OH.
FLIP FLIP FLIP FLIP
DEAR APHRODITE, IMMORTAL GODDESS AND CHAMPION OF LOVERS,
PLEASE HEAR MY PLEA. I AM IN LOVE WITH A BEAUTIFUL MORTAL MAIDEN NAMED ATALANTA.
I WISH TO MARRY HER, BUT SHE HAS VOWED TO TAKE AS HUSBAND ONLY THE YOUTH WHO BESTS HER IN A RACE, AND SHE IS VERY FLEET OF FOOT.
HER FATHER, KING SCHOENEUS, HAS MADE A LAW THAT THOSE SEEKING HER HAND WHO LOSE AGAINST HER SHALL ALSO LOSE THEIR LIVES.
I AM PREPARED TO FORFEIT MY LIFE FOR LOVE BUT WOULD REALLY RATHER NOT.
SO, I'M HOPING FOR YOUR DIVINE ASSISTANCE IN THIS MATTER.
YOUR DEVOTED FOLLOWER,
HIPPOMENES

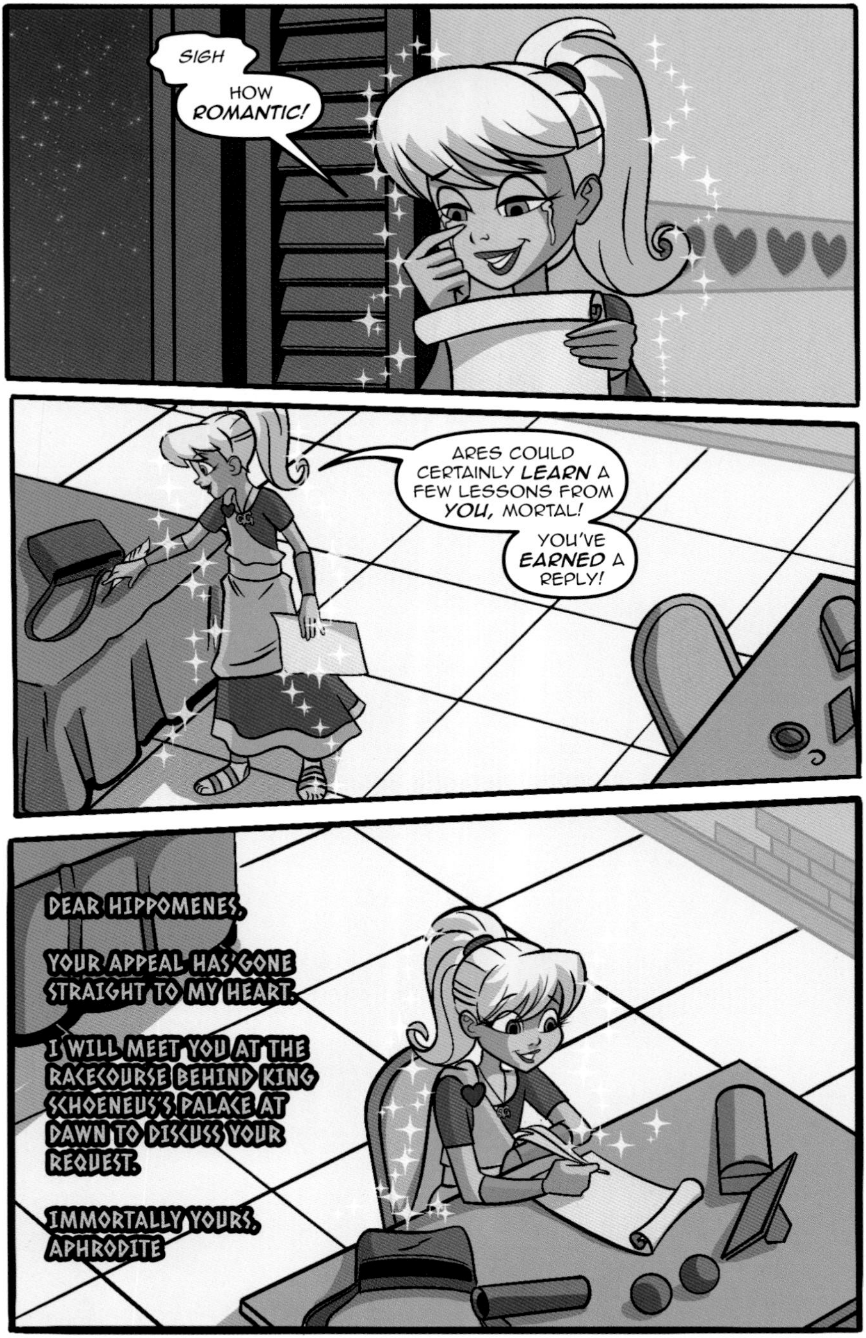
SIGH
HOW ROMANTIC!
ARES COULD CERTAINLY LEARN A FEW LESSONS FROM YOU, MORTAL!
YOU'VE EARNED A REPLY!
DEAR HIPPOMENES,
YOUR APPEAL HAS GONE STRAIGHT TO MY HEART.
I WILL MEET YOU AT THE RACECOURSE BEHIND KING SCHOENEUS'S PALACE AT DAWN TO DISCUSS YOUR REQUEST.
IMMORTALLY YOURS,
APHRODITE

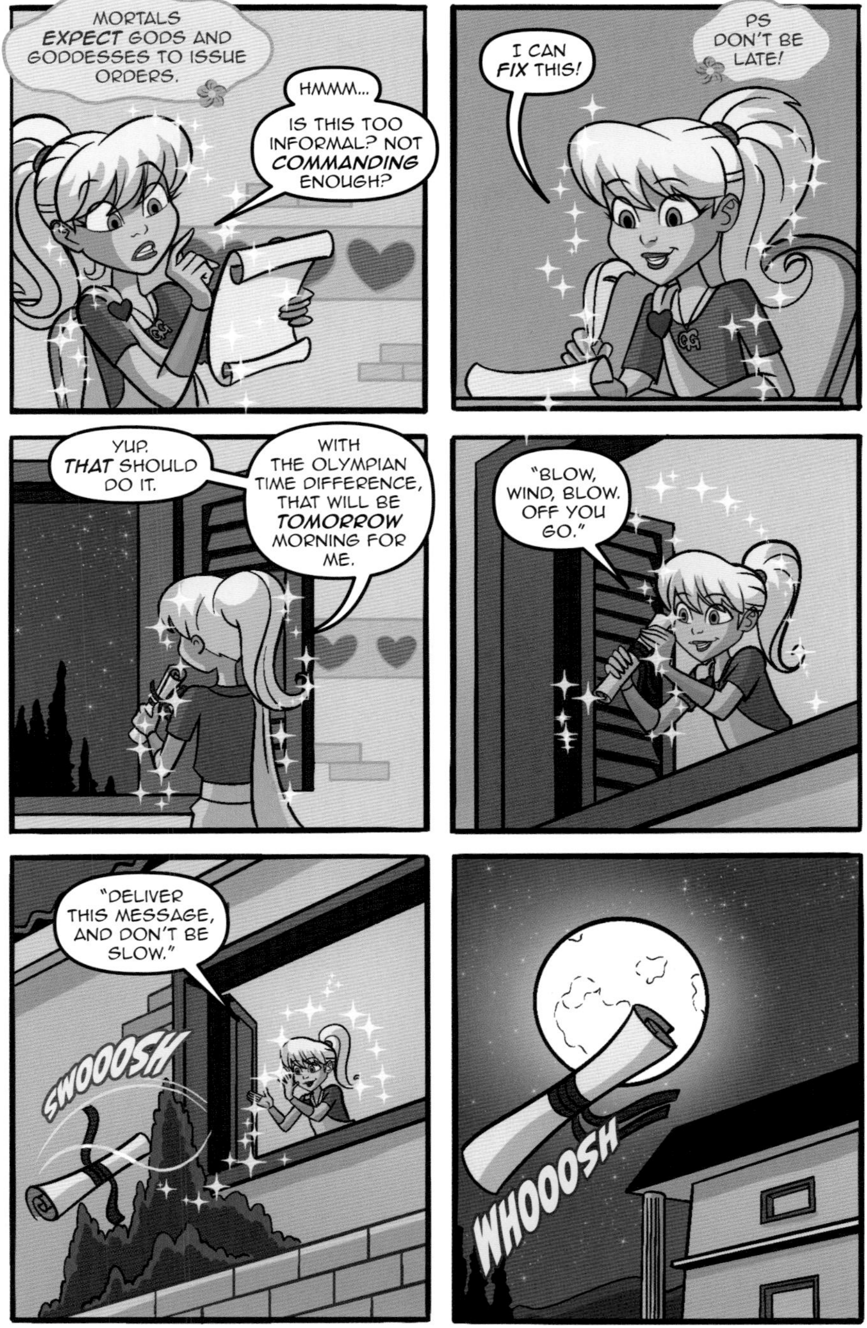

MORTALS *EXPECT* GODS AND GODDESSES TO ISSUE ORDERS.
HMMM...
IS THIS TOO INFORMAL? NOT *COMMANDING* ENOUGH?
I CAN *FIX* THIS!
PS DON'T BE LATE!
YUP. *THAT* SHOULD DO IT.
WITH THE OLYMPIAN TIME DIFFERENCE, THAT WILL BE *TOMORROW* MORNING FOR ME.
"BLOW, WIND, BLOW. OFF YOU GO."
"DELIVER THIS MESSAGE, AND DON'T BE SLOW."
SWOOOSH
WHOOOSH

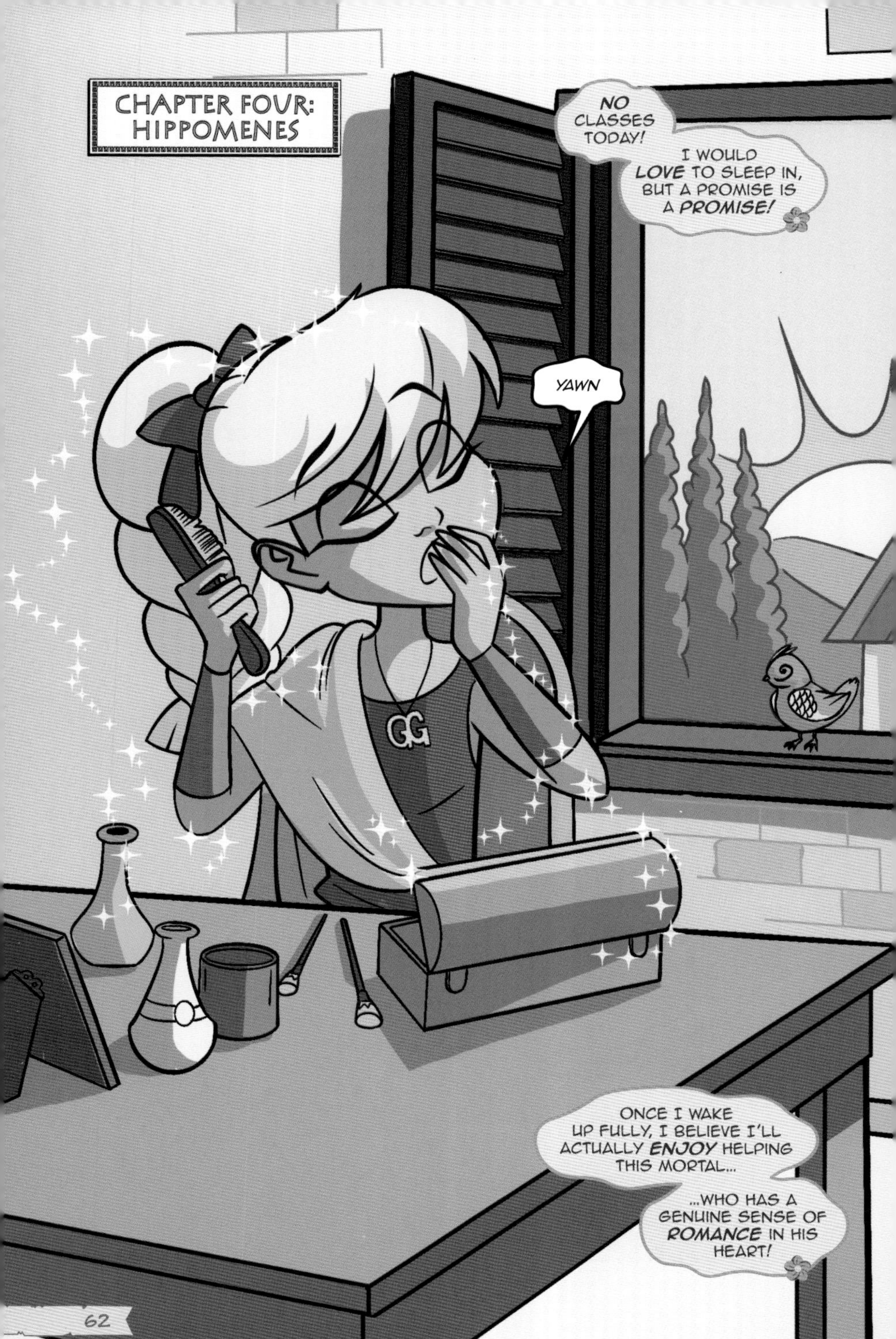

CHAPTER FOUR: HIPPOMENES
NO CLASSES TODAY!
I WOULD LOVE TO SLEEP IN, BUT A PROMISE IS A PROMISE!
YAWN
GG
ONCE I WAKE UP FULLY, I BELIEVE I'LL ACTUALLY ENJOY HELPING THIS MORTAL...
...WHO HAS A GENUINE SENSE OF ROMANCE IN HIS HEART!

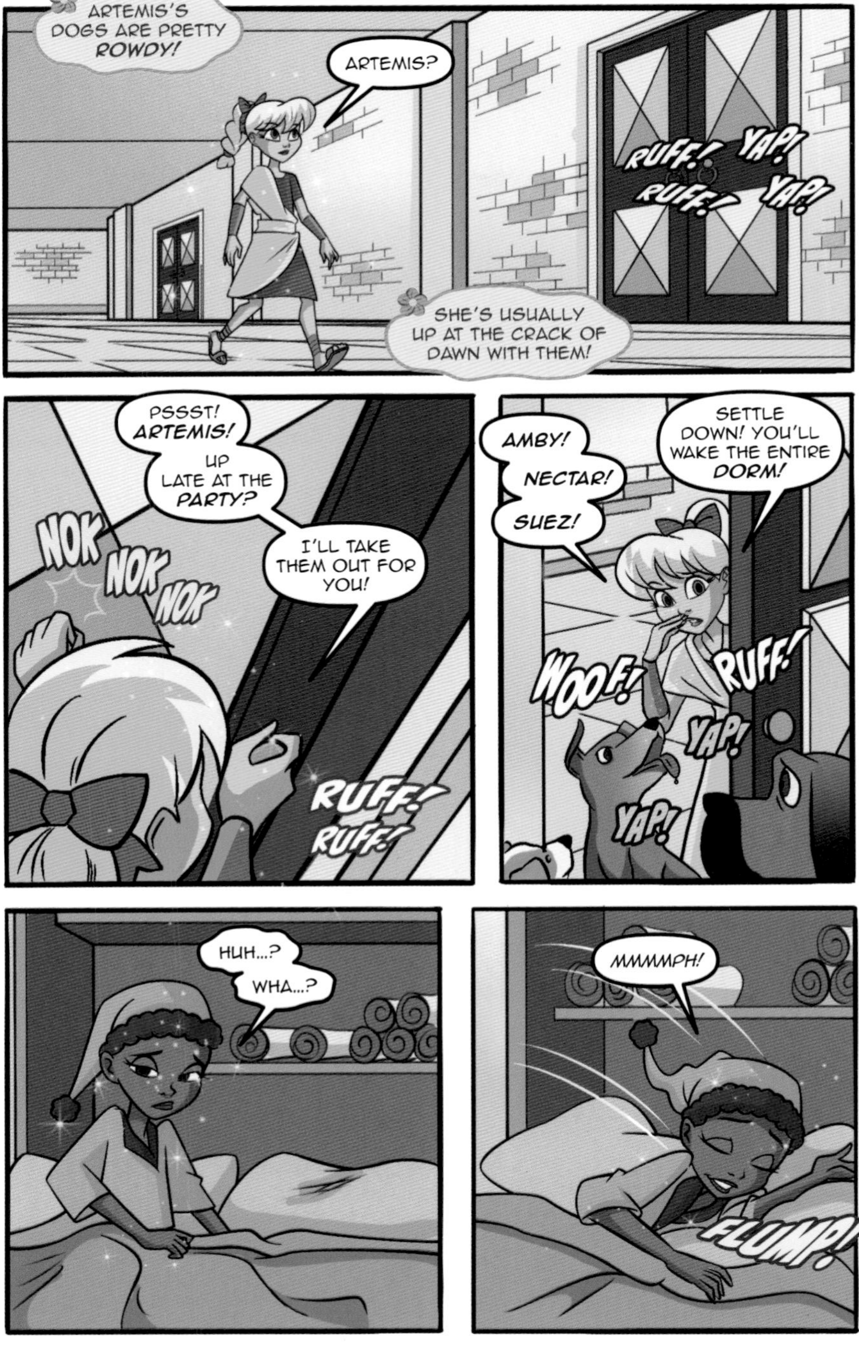
ARTEMIS'S DOGS ARE PRETTY ROWDY!
ARTEMIS?
RUFF! YAP! RUFF! YAP!
SHE'S USUALLY UP AT THE CRACK OF DAWN WITH THEM!
NOK NOK NOK
PSSST! ARTEMIS!
UP LATE AT THE PARTY?
I'LL TAKE THEM OUT FOR YOU!
RUFF! RUFF!
AMBY!
NECTAR!
SUEZ!
SETTLE DOWN! YOU'LL WAKE THE ENTIRE DORM!
WOOF! RUFF! YAP! YAP!
HUH...?
WHA...?
MMMMPH!
FLUMP!

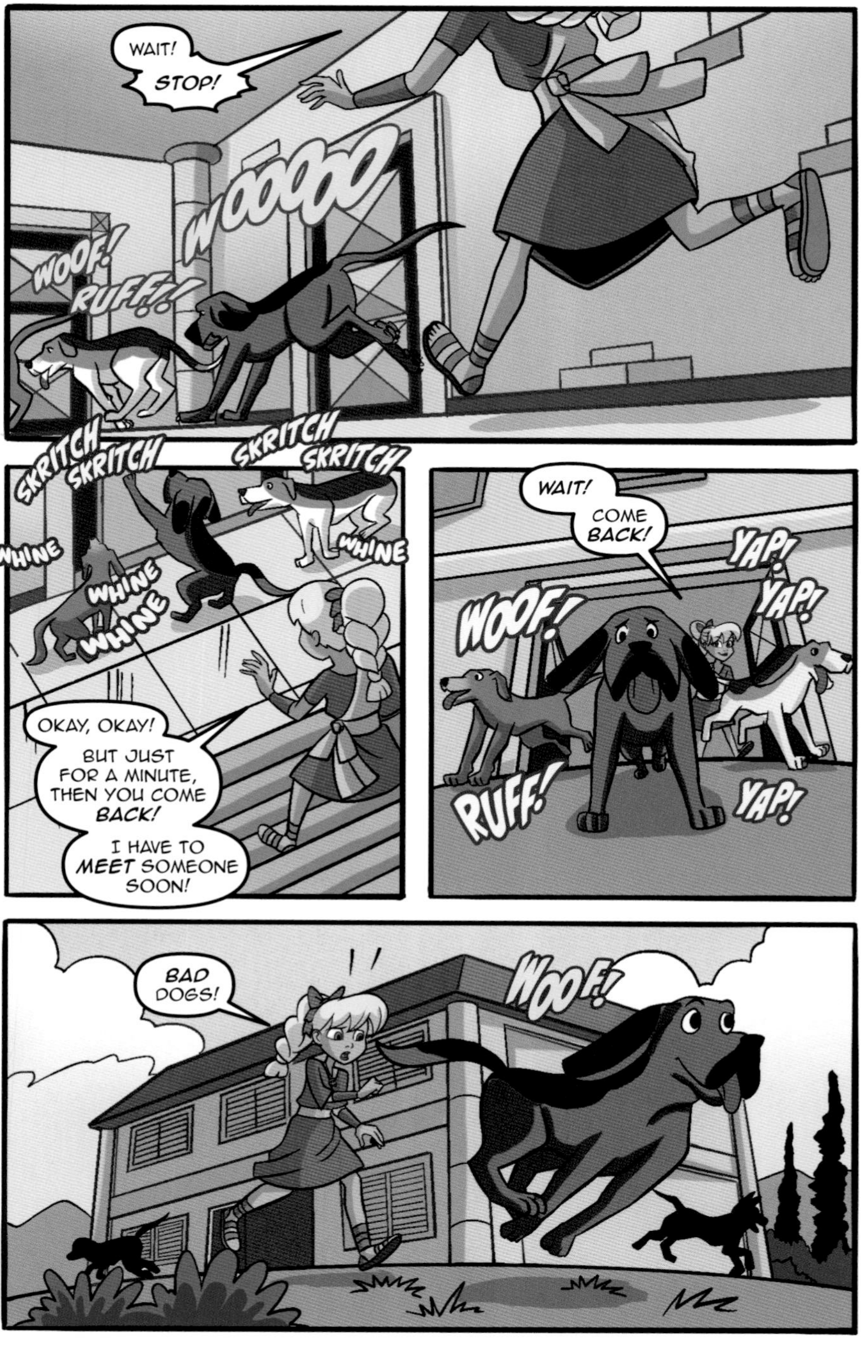

WAIT!
STOP!
WOOOOO
WOOF!
RUFF!!
SKRITCH
SKRITCH
SKRITCH
SKRITCH
WHINE
WHINE
WHINE
WHINE
OKAY, OKAY!
BUT JUST FOR A MINUTE, THEN YOU COME BACK!
I HAVE TO MEET SOMEONE SOON!
WAIT!
COME BACK!
YAP!
YAP!
WOOF!
RUFF!
YAP!
BAD DOGS!
WOOF!

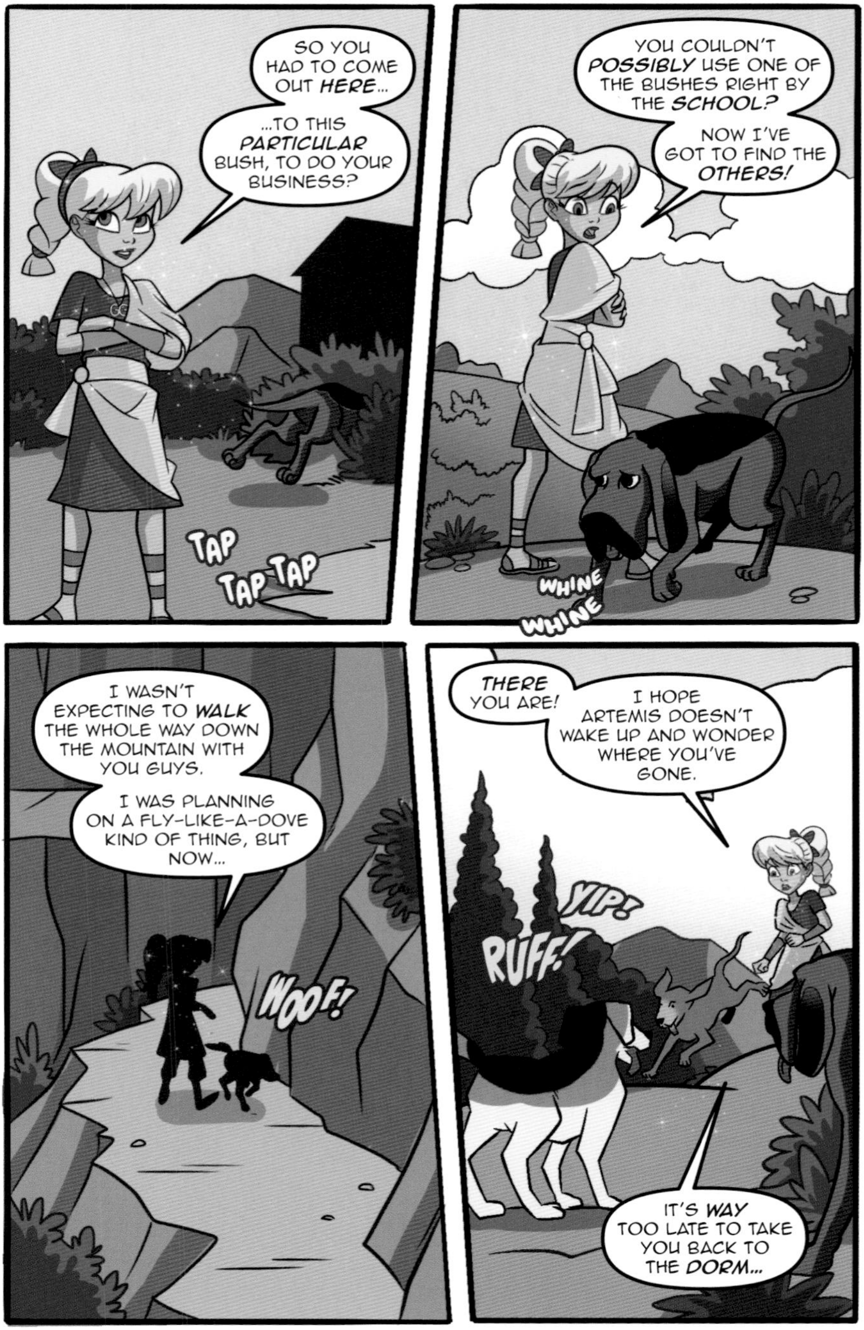
SO YOU HAD TO COME OUT HERE...
...TO THIS PARTICULAR BUSH, TO DO YOUR BUSINESS?
TAP
TAP TAP
YOU COULDN'T POSSIBLY USE ONE OF THE BUSHES RIGHT BY THE SCHOOL?
NOW I'VE GOT TO FIND THE OTHERS!
WHINE
WHINE
I WASN'T EXPECTING TO WALK THE WHOLE WAY DOWN THE MOUNTAIN WITH YOU GUYS.
I WAS PLANNING ON A FLY-LIKE-A-DOVE KIND OF THING, BUT NOW...
WOOF!
THERE YOU ARE!
I HOPE ARTEMIS DOESN'T WAKE UP AND WONDER WHERE YOU'VE GONE.
YIP!
RUFF!
IT'S WAY TOO LATE TO TAKE YOU BACK TO THE DORM...

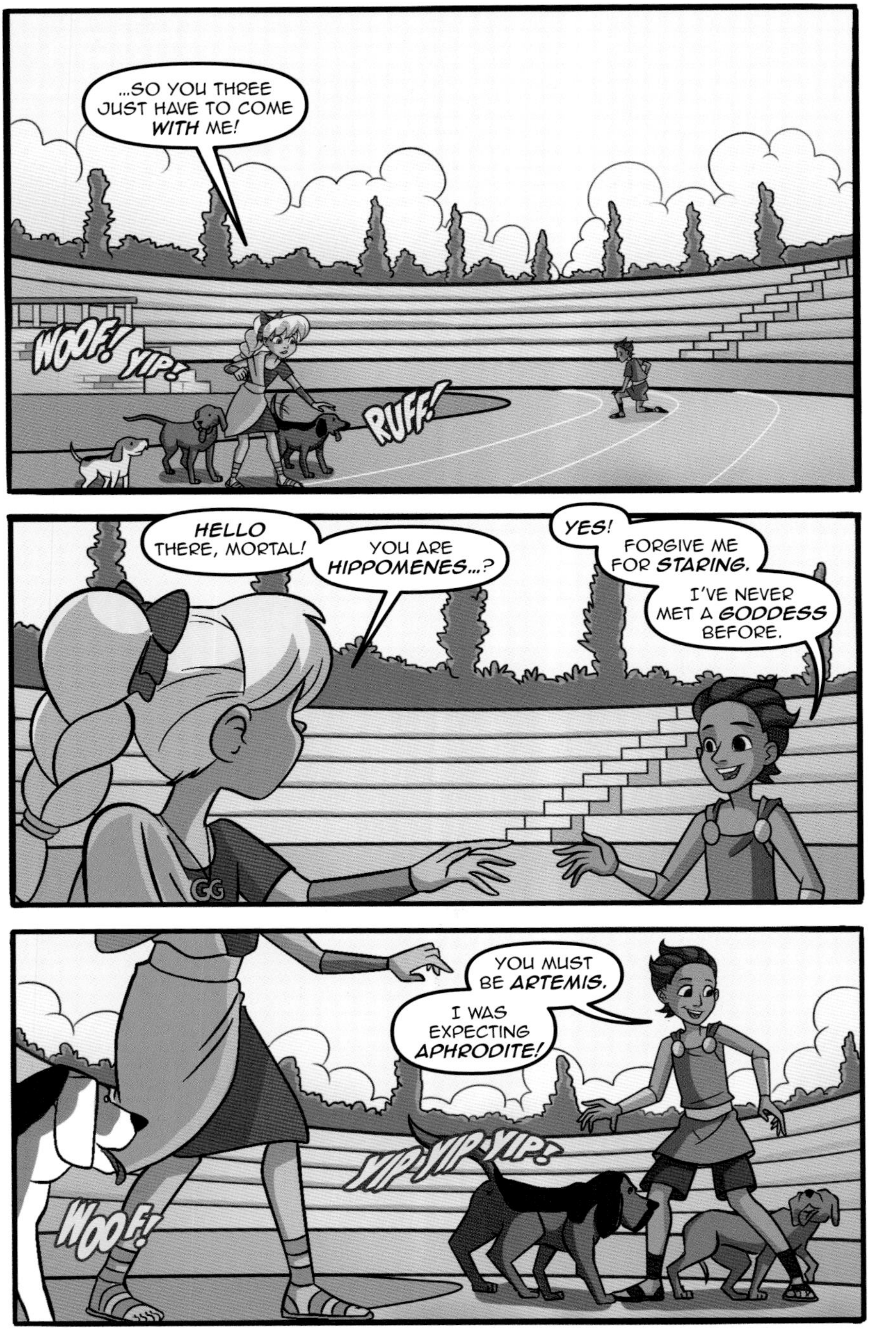

...SO YOU THREE JUST HAVE TO COME WITH ME!
WOOF! YIP!
RUFF!
HELLO THERE, MORTAL!
YOU ARE HIPPOMENES...?
YES!
FORGIVE ME FOR STARING.
I'VE NEVER MET A GODDESS BEFORE.
GG
YOU MUST BE ARTEMIS.
I WAS EXPECTING APHRODITE!
YIP-YIP-YIP!
WOOF!

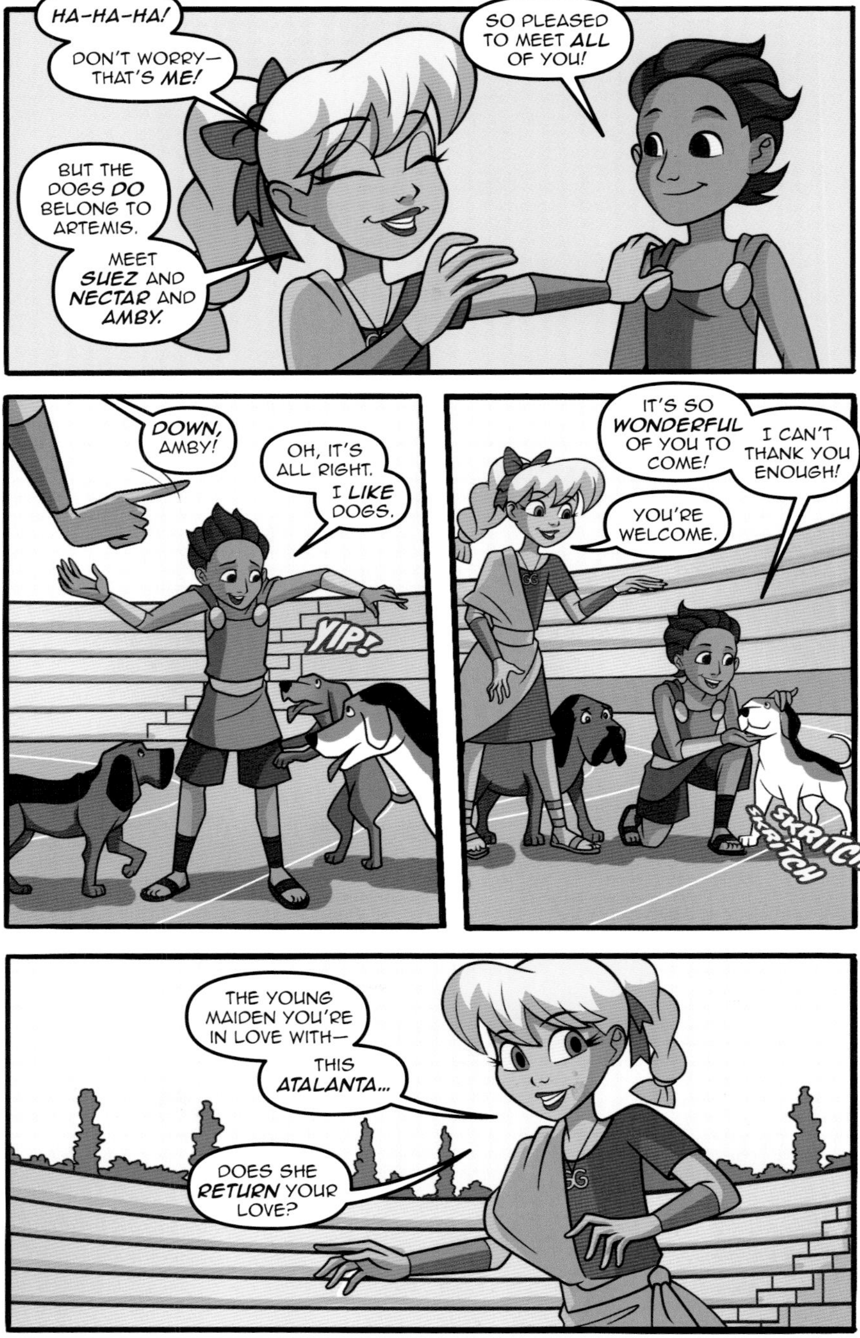
HA-HA-HA!
DON'T WORRY— THAT'S ME!
SO PLEASED TO MEET ALL OF YOU!
BUT THE DOGS DO BELONG TO ARTEMIS.
MEET SUEZ AND NECTAR AND AMBY.
DOWN, AMBY!
OH, IT'S ALL RIGHT.
I LIKE DOGS.
YIP!
IT'S SO WONDERFUL OF YOU TO COME!
I CAN'T THANK YOU ENOUGH!
YOU'RE WELCOME.
SKRITCH
SKRITCH
THE YOUNG MAIDEN YOU'RE IN LOVE WITH—
THIS ATALANTA...
DOES SHE RETURN YOUR LOVE?

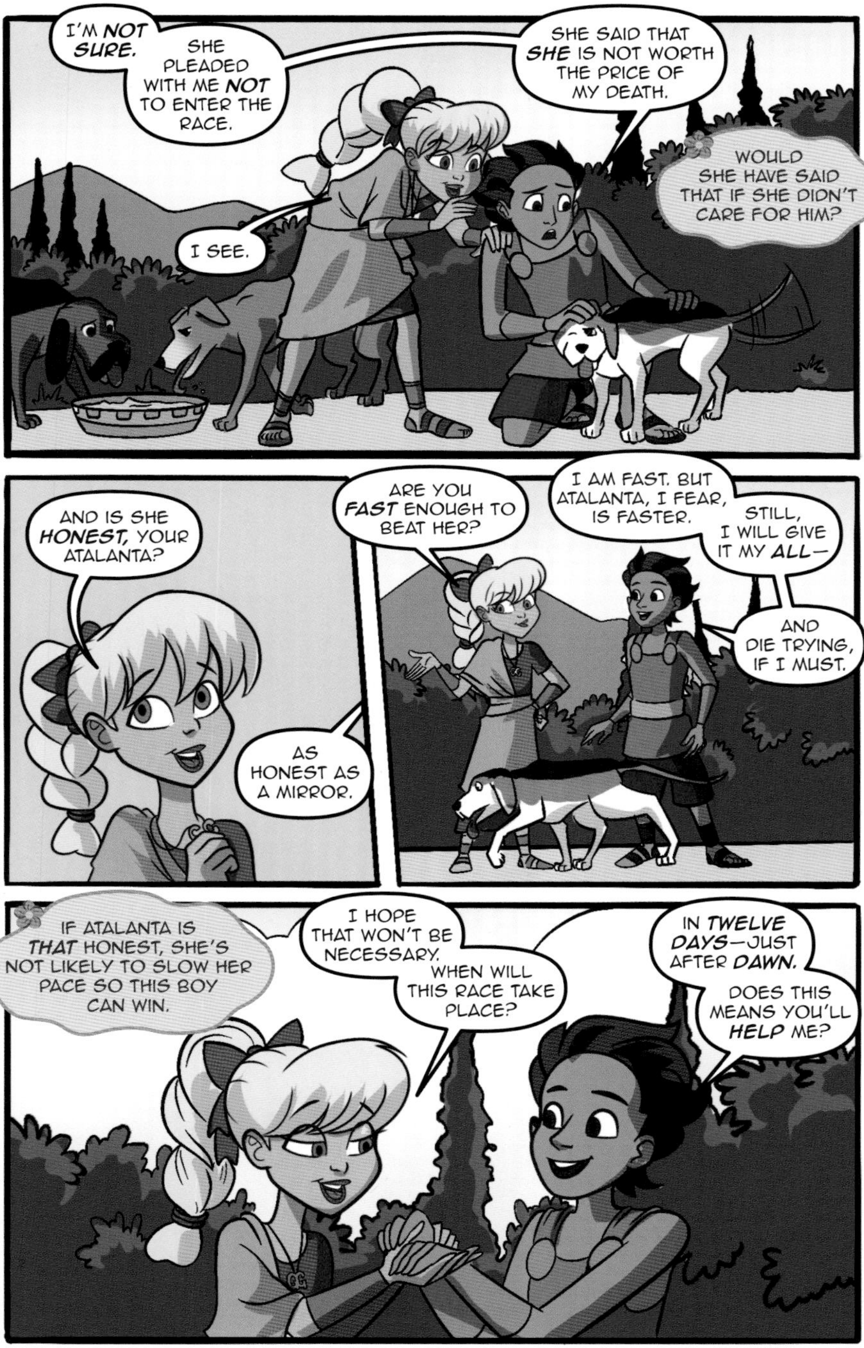
I'M **NOT** **SURE.**
SHE PLEADED WITH ME **NOT** TO ENTER THE RACE.
SHE SAID THAT **SHE** IS NOT WORTH THE PRICE OF MY DEATH.
I SEE.
WOULD SHE HAVE SAID THAT IF SHE DIDN'T CARE FOR HIM?
AND IS SHE **HONEST,** YOUR ATALANTA?
AS HONEST AS A MIRROR.
ARE YOU **FAST** ENOUGH TO BEAT HER?
I AM FAST. BUT ATALANTA, I FEAR, IS FASTER.
STILL, I WILL GIVE IT MY **ALL**—
AND DIE TRYING, IF I MUST.
IF ATALANTA IS **THAT** HONEST, SHE'S NOT LIKELY TO SLOW HER PACE SO THIS BOY CAN WIN.
I HOPE THAT WON'T BE NECESSARY.
WHEN WILL THIS RACE TAKE PLACE?
IN **TWELVE** **DAYS**—JUST AFTER **DAWN.**
DOES THIS MEANS YOU'LL **HELP** ME?

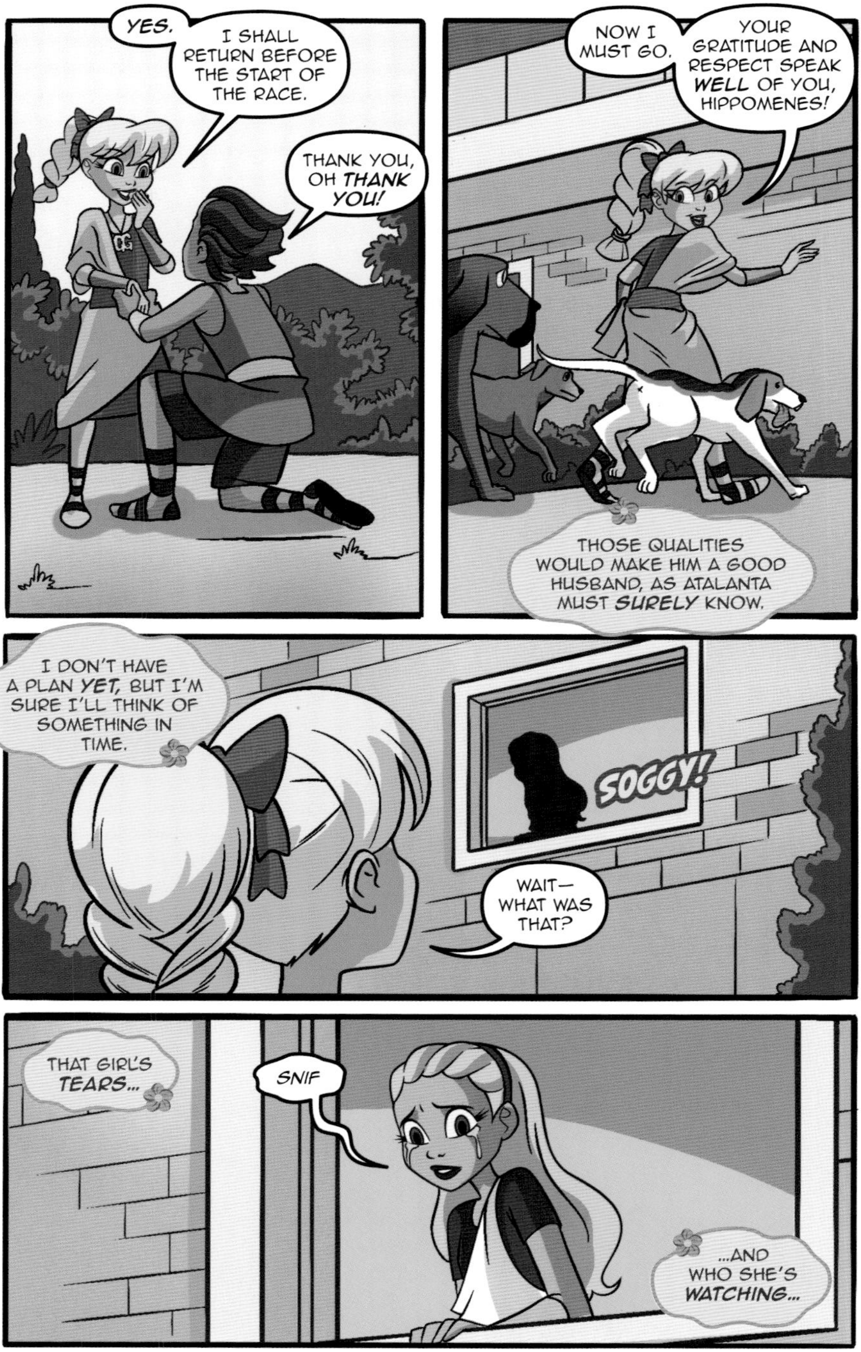
YES.
I SHALL RETURN BEFORE THE START OF THE RACE.
THANK YOU, OH *THANK YOU!*
NOW I MUST GO.
YOUR GRATITUDE AND RESPECT SPEAK *WELL* OF YOU, HIPPOMENES!
THOSE QUALITIES WOULD MAKE HIM A GOOD HUSBAND, AS ATALANTA MUST *SURELY* KNOW.
I DON'T HAVE A PLAN *YET,* BUT I'M SURE I'LL THINK OF SOMETHING IN TIME.
SOGGY!
WAIT— WHAT WAS THAT?
THAT GIRL'S *TEARS...*
SNIF
...AND WHO SHE'S *WATCHING...*

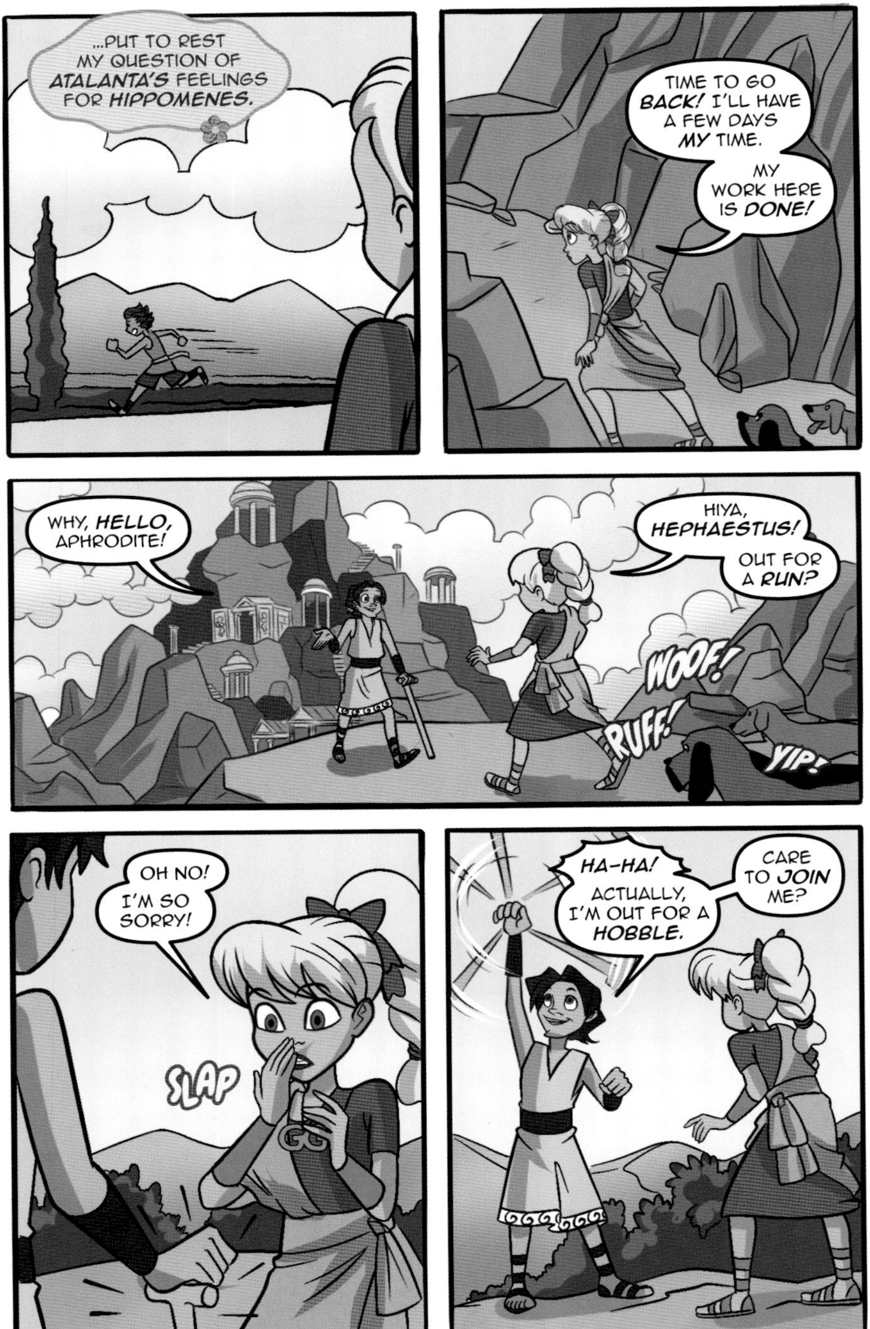
...PUT TO REST MY QUESTION OF ATALANTA'S FEELINGS FOR HIPPOMENES.
TIME TO GO BACK! I'LL HAVE A FEW DAYS MY TIME.
MY WORK HERE IS DONE!
WHY, HELLO, APHRODITE!
HIYA, HEPHAESTUS!
OUT FOR A RUN?
WOOF!
RUFF!
YIP!
OH NO! I'M SO SORRY!
SLAP
HA-HA! ACTUALLY, I'M OUT FOR A HOBBLE.
CARE TO JOIN ME?

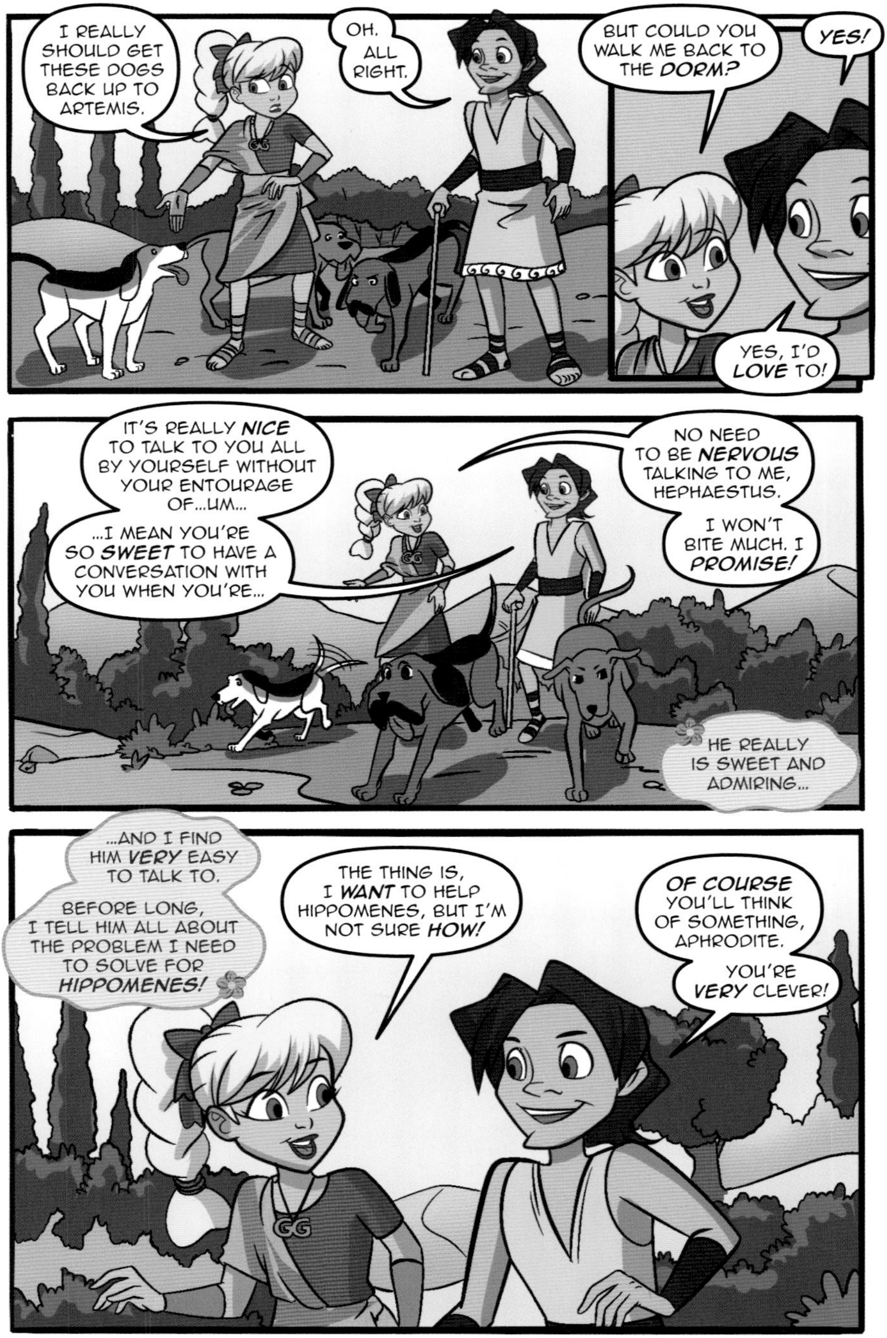
I REALLY SHOULD GET THESE DOGS BACK UP TO ARTEMIS.
OH. ALL RIGHT.
BUT COULD YOU WALK ME BACK TO THE *DORM?*
YES!
YES, I'D *LOVE* TO!
IT'S REALLY *NICE* TO TALK TO YOU ALL BY YOURSELF WITHOUT YOUR ENTOURAGE OF...UM...
...I MEAN YOU'RE SO *SWEET* TO HAVE A CONVERSATION WITH YOU WHEN YOU'RE...
NO NEED TO BE *NERVOUS* TALKING TO ME, HEPHAESTUS.
I WON'T BITE MUCH. I *PROMISE!*
HE REALLY IS SWEET AND ADMIRING...
...AND I FIND HIM *VERY* EASY TO TALK TO.
BEFORE LONG, I TELL HIM ALL ABOUT THE PROBLEM I NEED TO SOLVE FOR *HIPPOMENES!*
THE THING IS, I *WANT* TO HELP HIPPOMENES, BUT I'M NOT SURE *HOW!*
OF COURSE YOU'LL THINK OF SOMETHING, APHRODITE.
YOU'RE *VERY* CLEVER!

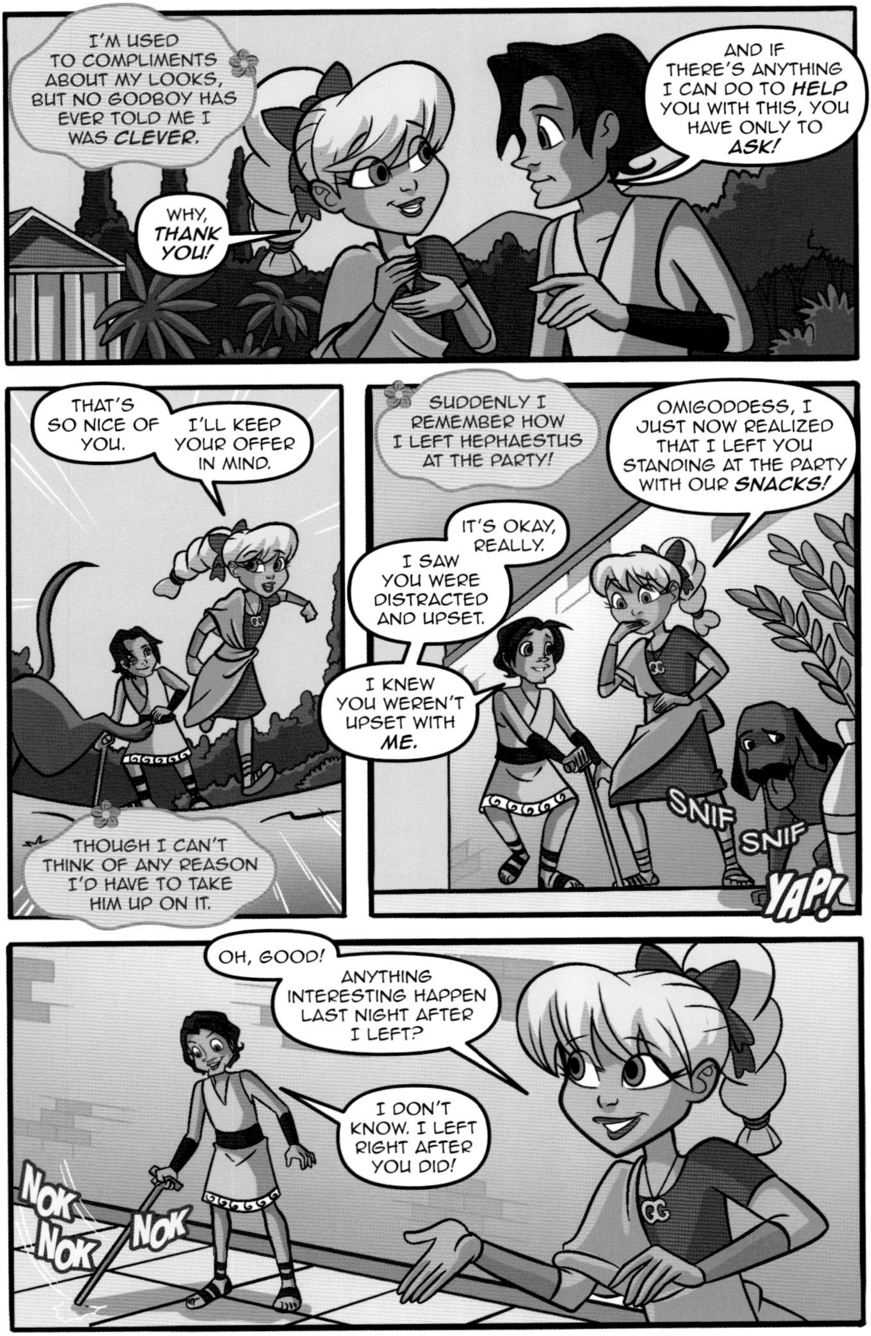
I'M USED TO COMPLIMENTS ABOUT MY LOOKS, BUT NO GODBOY HAS EVER TOLD ME I WAS *CLEVER.*
WHY, *THANK YOU!*
AND IF THERE'S ANYTHING I CAN DO TO *HELP* YOU WITH THIS, YOU HAVE ONLY TO *ASK!*
THAT'S SO NICE OF YOU.
I'LL KEEP YOUR OFFER IN MIND.
THOUGH I CAN'T THINK OF ANY REASON I'D HAVE TO TAKE HIM UP ON IT.
SUDDENLY I REMEMBER HOW I LEFT HEPHAESTUS AT THE PARTY!
OMIGODDESS, I JUST NOW REALIZED THAT I LEFT YOU STANDING AT THE PARTY WITH OUR *SNACKS!*
IT'S OKAY, REALLY.
I SAW YOU WERE DISTRACTED AND UPSET.
I KNEW YOU WEREN'T UPSET WITH *ME.*
SNIF
SNIF
YAP!
OH, GOOD!
ANYTHING INTERESTING HAPPEN LAST NIGHT AFTER I LEFT?
I DON'T KNOW. I LEFT RIGHT AFTER YOU DID!
NOK
NOK
NOK

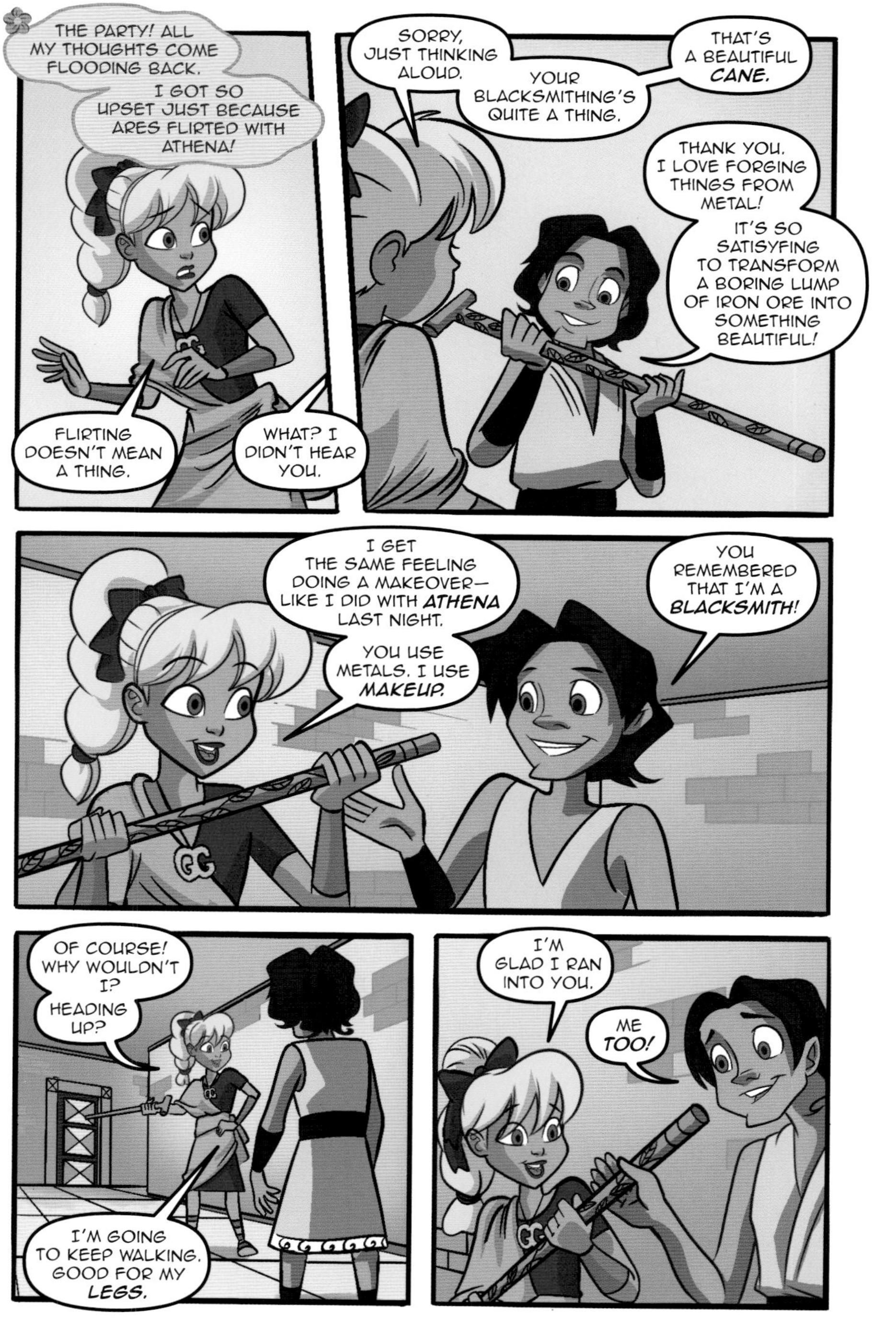
THE PARTY! ALL MY THOUGHTS COME FLOODING BACK.
I GOT SO UPSET JUST BECAUSE ARES FLIRTED WITH ATHENA!
FLIRTING DOESN'T MEAN A THING.
WHAT? I DIDN'T HEAR YOU.
SORRY, JUST THINKING ALOUD.
YOUR BLACKSMITHING'S QUITE A THING.
THAT'S A BEAUTIFUL *CANE.*
THANK YOU. I LOVE FORGING THINGS FROM METAL!
IT'S SO SATISYFING TO TRANSFORM A BORING LUMP OF IRON ORE INTO SOMETHING BEAUTIFUL!
I GET THE SAME FEELING DOING A MAKEOVER—LIKE I DID WITH *ATHENA* LAST NIGHT.
YOU USE METALS. I USE *MAKEUP.*
YOU REMEMBERED THAT I'M A *BLACKSMITH!*
OF COURSE! WHY WOULDN'T I?
HEADING UP?
I'M GOING TO KEEP WALKING. GOOD FOR MY *LEGS.*
I'M GLAD I RAN INTO YOU.
ME *TOO!*

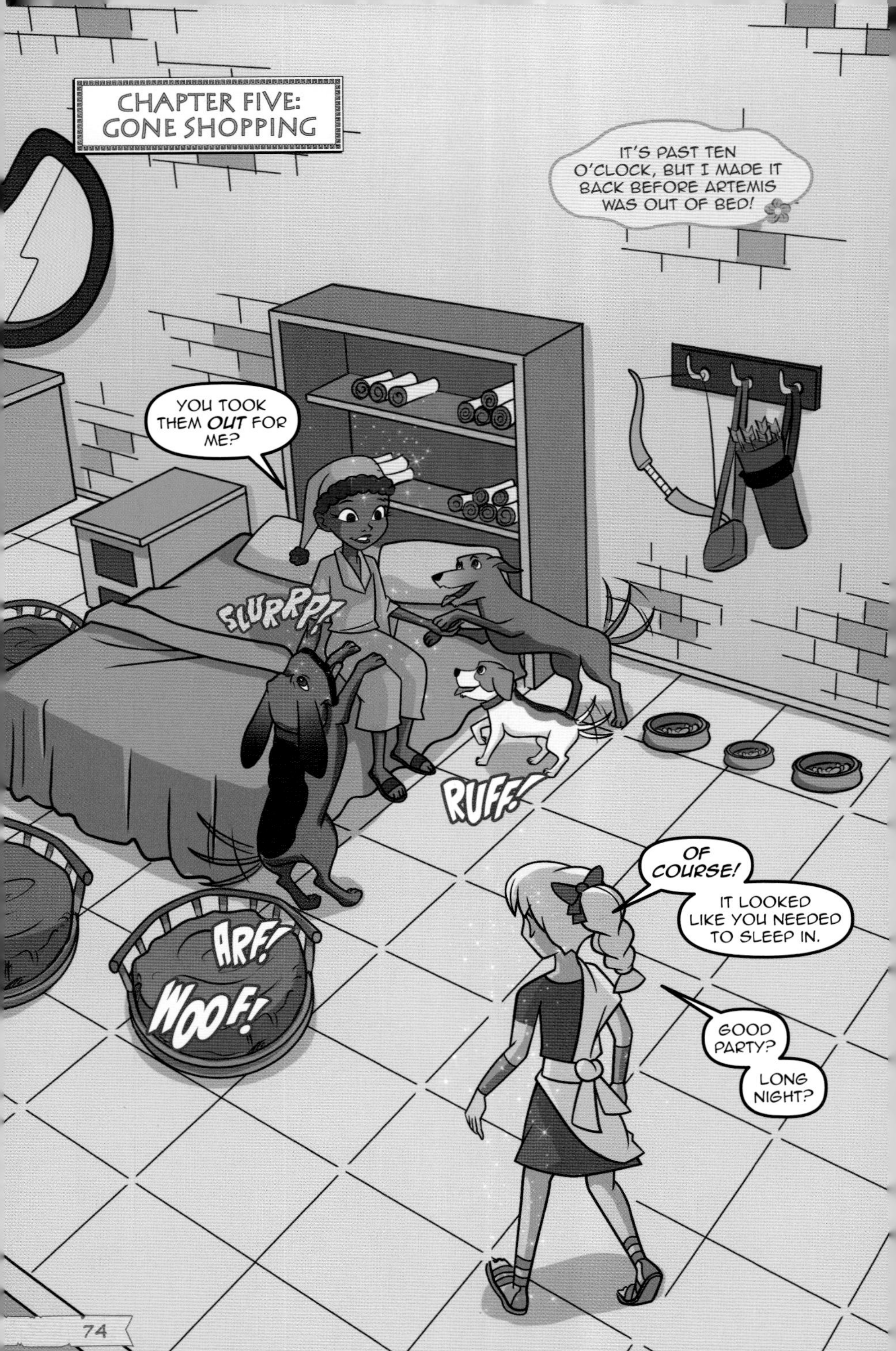
CHAPTER FIVE:
GONE SHOPPING
IT'S PAST TEN O'CLOCK, BUT I MADE IT BACK BEFORE ARTEMIS WAS OUT OF BED!
YOU TOOK THEM OUT FOR ME?
SLURRP!
RUFF!
OF COURSE!
IT LOOKED LIKE YOU NEEDED TO SLEEP IN.
ARF!
WOOF!
GOOD PARTY?
LONG NIGHT?

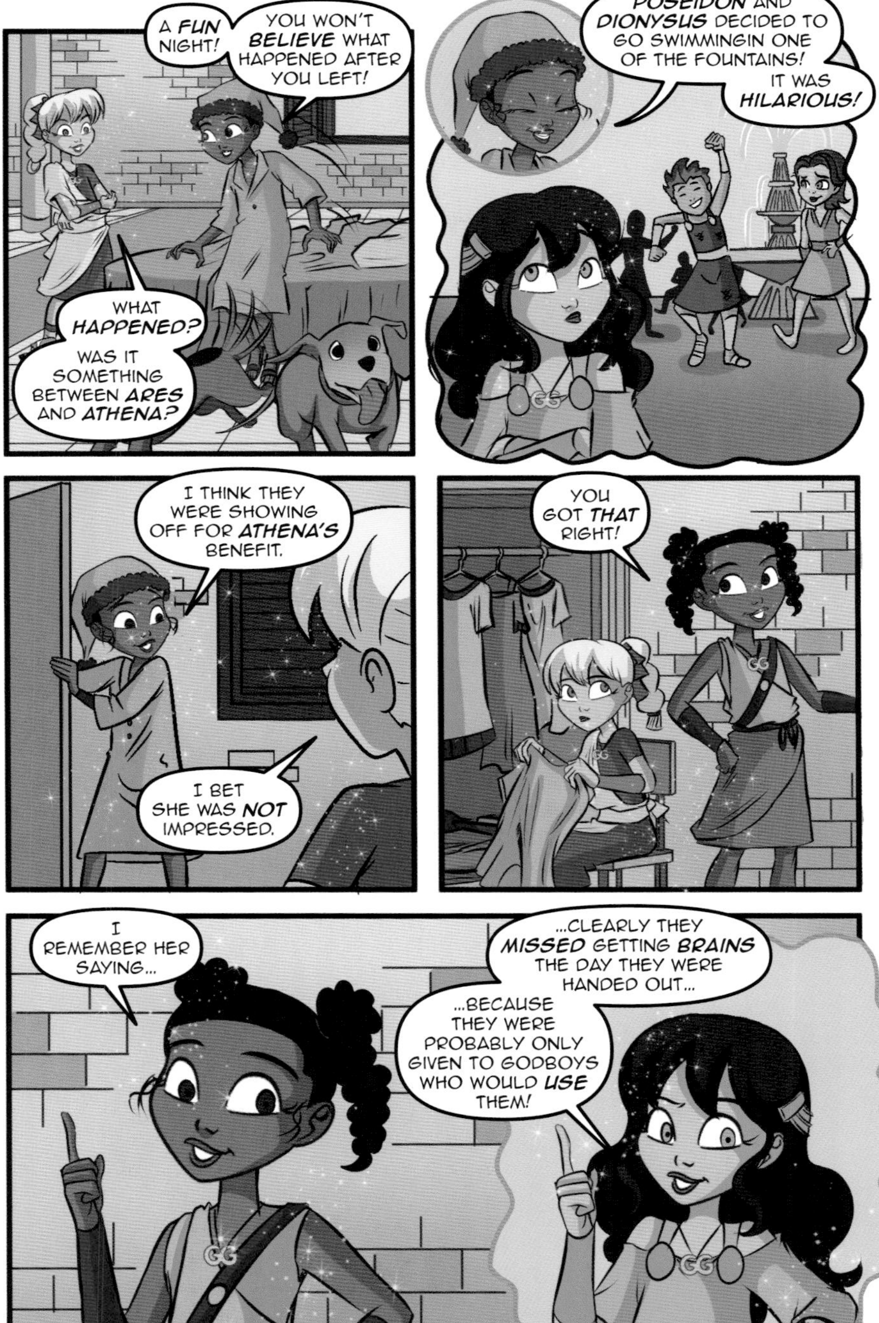
A FUN NIGHT!
YOU WON'T BELIEVE WHAT HAPPENED AFTER YOU LEFT!
WHAT HAPPENED?
WAS IT SOMETHING BETWEEN ARES AND ATHENA?
POSEIDON AND DIONYSUS DECIDED TO GO SWIMMINGIN ONE OF THE FOUNTAINS!
IT WAS HILARIOUS!
I THINK THEY WERE SHOWING OFF FOR ATHENA'S BENEFIT.
I BET SHE WAS NOT IMPRESSED.
YOU GOT THAT RIGHT!
I REMEMBER HER SAYING...
...CLEARLY THEY MISSED GETTING BRAINS THE DAY THEY WERE HANDED OUT...
...BECAUSE THEY WERE PROBABLY ONLY GIVEN TO GODBOYS WHO WOULD USE THEM!

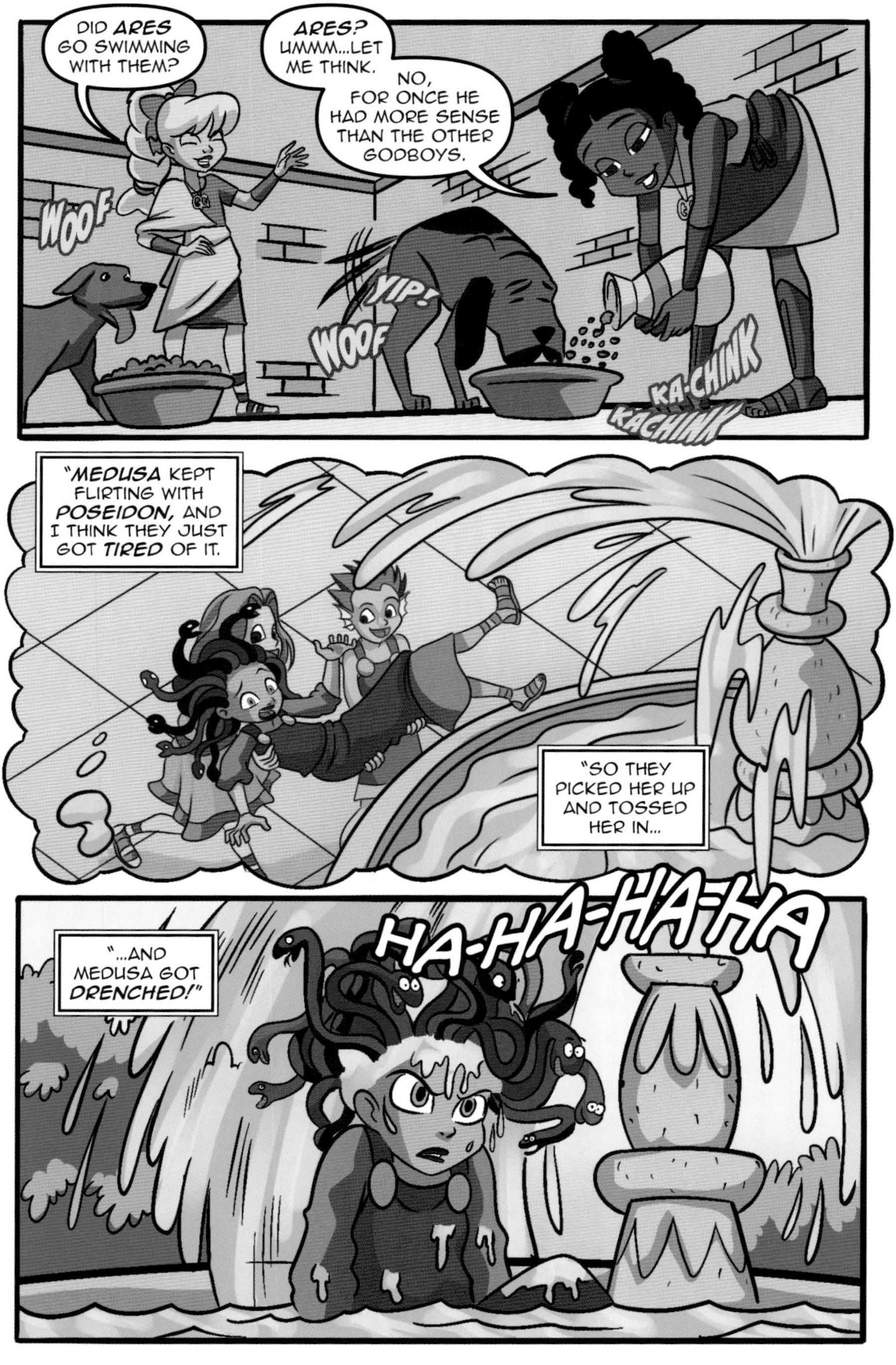
DID ARES GO SWIMMING WITH THEM?
ARES? UMMM...LET ME THINK.
NO, FOR ONCE HE HAD MORE SENSE THAN THE OTHER GODBOYS.
WOOF
YIP!
WOOF
KA-CHINK
KACHINK
"MEDUSA KEPT FLIRTING WITH POSEIDON, AND I THINK THEY JUST GOT TIRED OF IT.
"SO THEY PICKED HER UP AND TOSSED HER IN...
HA-HA-HA-HA
"...AND MEDUSA GOT DRENCHED!"

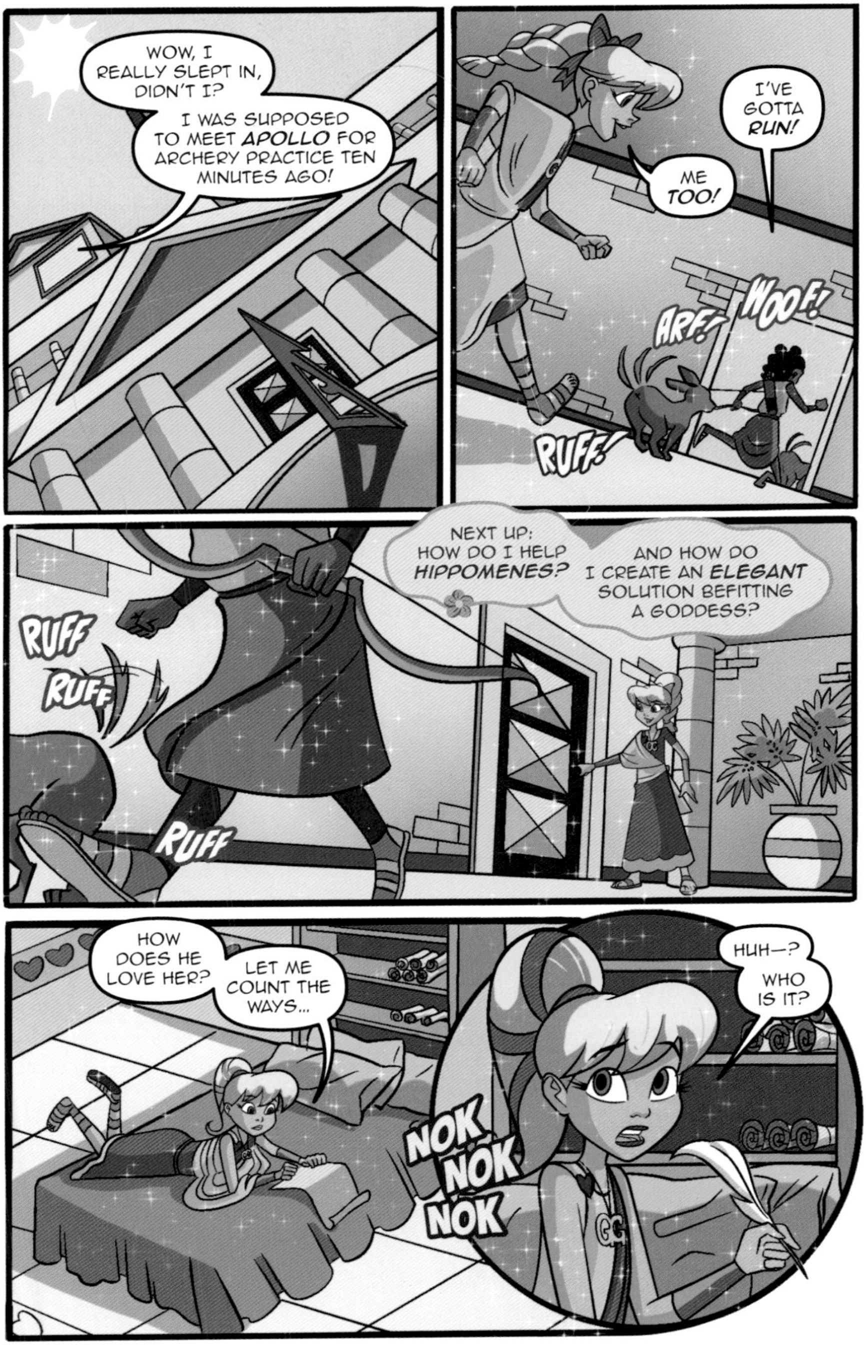
WOW, I REALLY SLEPT IN, DIDN'T I?
I WAS SUPPOSED TO MEET APOLLO FOR ARCHERY PRACTICE TEN MINUTES AGO!
I'VE GOTTA RUN!
ME TOO!
ARF!
WOOF!
RUFF!
RUFF
RUFF
RUFF
NEXT UP: HOW DO I HELP HIPPOMENES?
AND HOW DO I CREATE AN ELEGANT SOLUTION BEFITTING A GODDESS?
HOW DOES HE LOVE HER?
LET ME COUNT THE WAYS...
NOK NOK NOK
HUH—?
WHO IS IT?

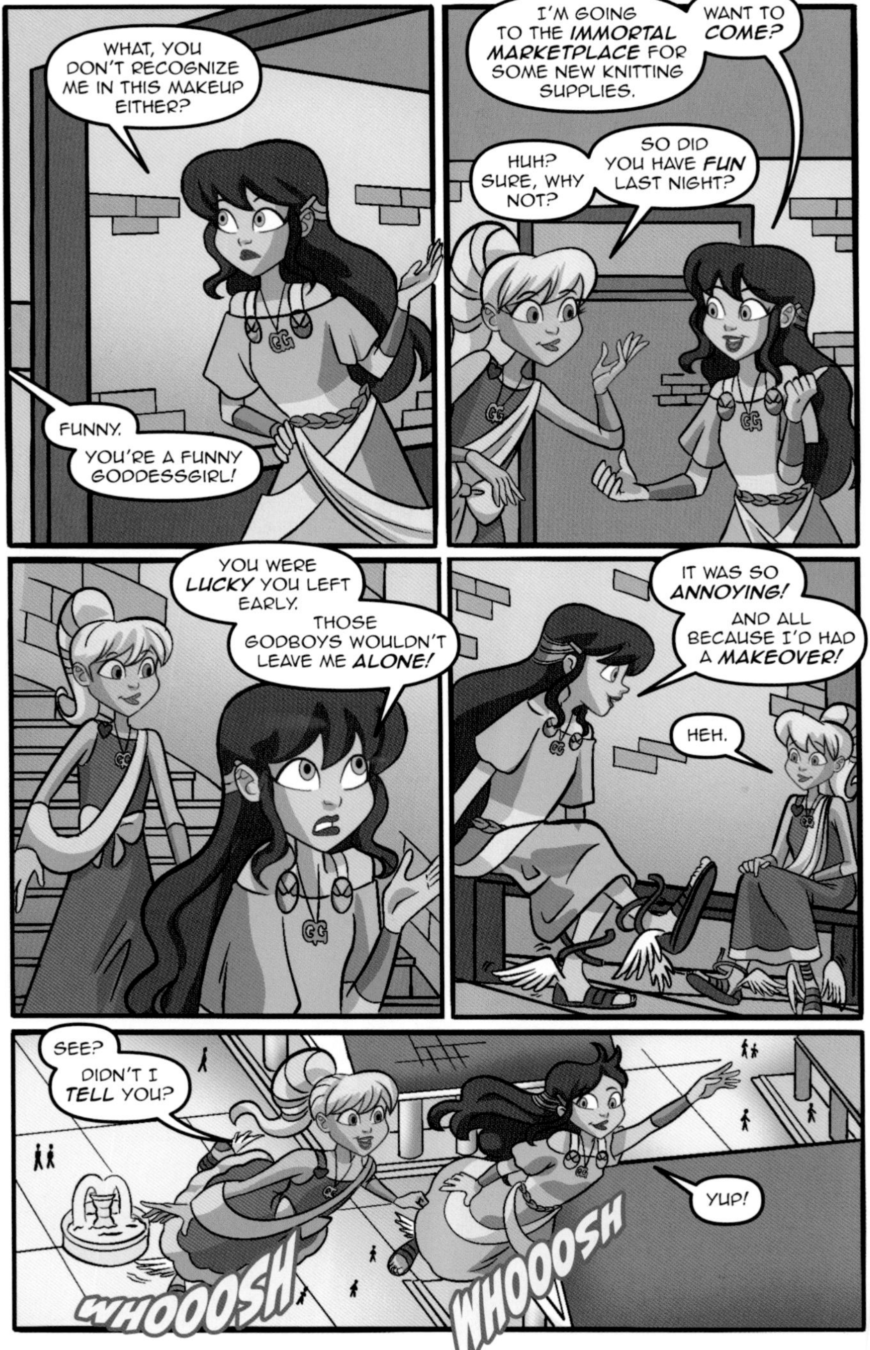
WHAT, YOU DON'T RECOGNIZE ME IN THIS MAKEUP EITHER?
FUNNY. YOU'RE A FUNNY GODDESSGIRL!
I'M GOING TO THE IMMORTAL MARKETPLACE FOR SOME NEW KNITTING SUPPLIES.
WANT TO COME?
HUH? SURE, WHY NOT?
SO DID YOU HAVE FUN LAST NIGHT?
YOU WERE LUCKY YOU LEFT EARLY.
THOSE GODBOYS WOULDN'T LEAVE ME ALONE!
IT WAS SO ANNOYING!
AND ALL BECAUSE I'D HAD A MAKEOVER!
HEH.
SEE?
DIDN'T I TELL YOU?
YUP!
WHOOOSH
WHOOOSH

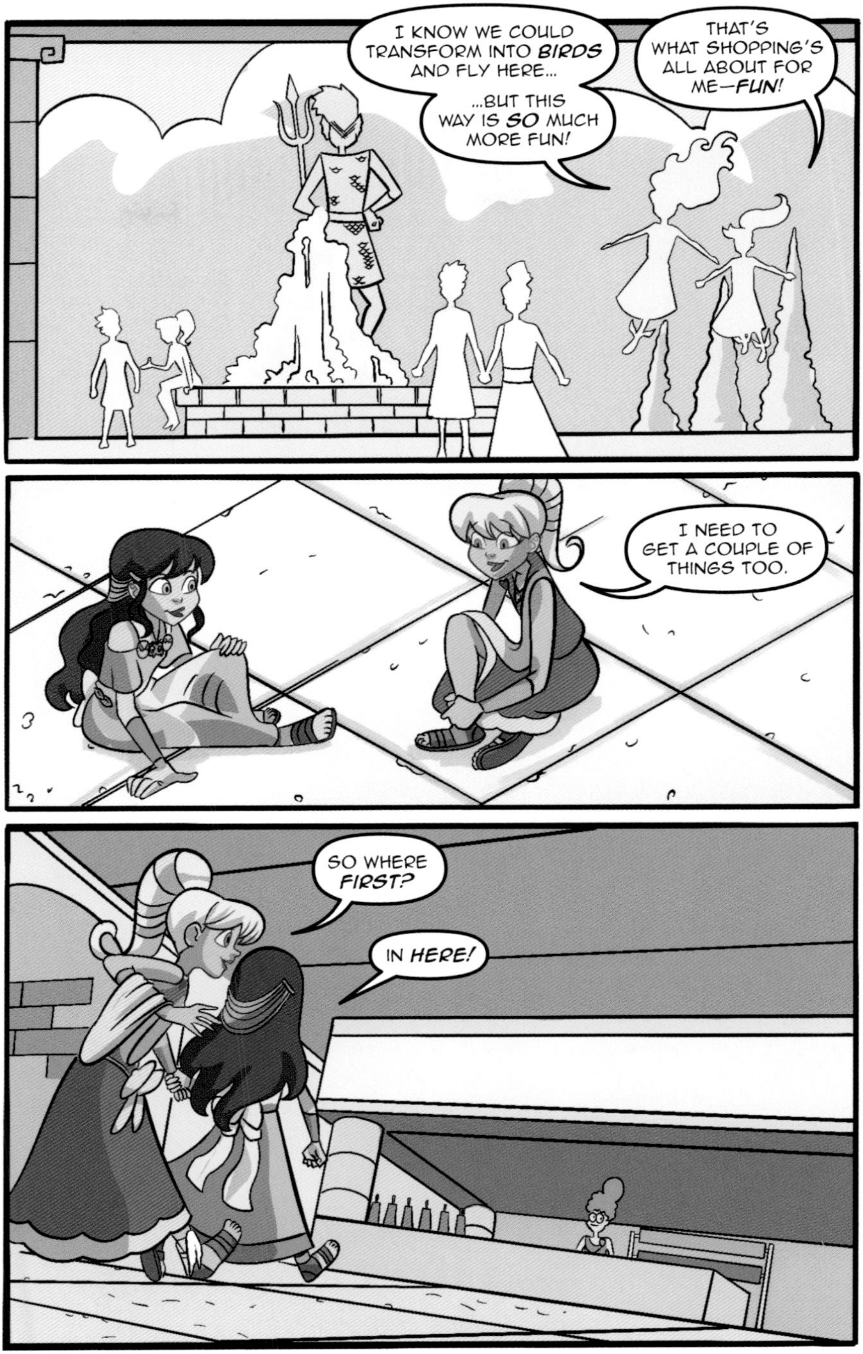
I KNOW WE COULD TRANSFORM INTO *BIRDS* AND FLY HERE...
...BUT THIS WAY IS *SO* MUCH MORE FUN!
THAT'S WHAT SHOPPING'S ALL ABOUT FOR ME—*FUN*!
I NEED TO GET A COUPLE OF THINGS TOO.
SO WHERE *FIRST?*
IN *HERE!*

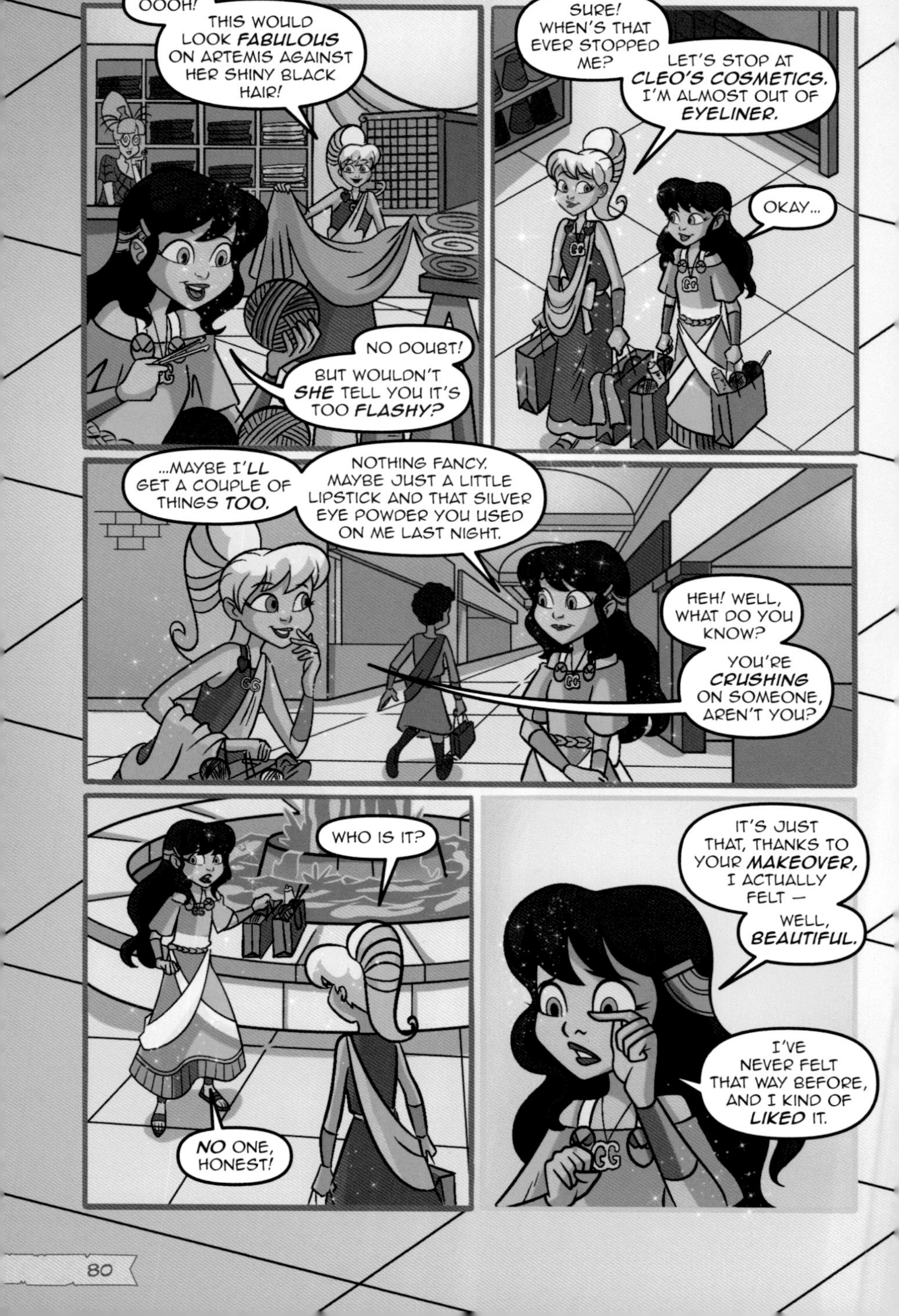
OOOH!
THIS WOULD LOOK FABULOUS ON ARTEMIS AGAINST HER SHINY BLACK HAIR!
NO DOUBT!
BUT WOULDN'T SHE TELL YOU IT'S TOO FLASHY?
SURE! WHEN'S THAT EVER STOPPED ME?
LET'S STOP AT CLEO'S COSMETICS. I'M ALMOST OUT OF EYELINER.
OKAY...
...MAYBE I'LL GET A COUPLE OF THINGS TOO.
NOTHING FANCY. MAYBE JUST A LITTLE LIPSTICK AND THAT SILVER EYE POWDER YOU USED ON ME LAST NIGHT.
HEH! WELL, WHAT DO YOU KNOW?
YOU'RE CRUSHING ON SOMEONE, AREN'T YOU?
WHO IS IT?
NO ONE, HONEST!
IT'S JUST THAT, THANKS TO YOUR MAKEOVER, I ACTUALLY FELT —
WELL, BEAUTIFUL.
I'VE NEVER FELT THAT WAY BEFORE, AND I KIND OF LIKED IT.

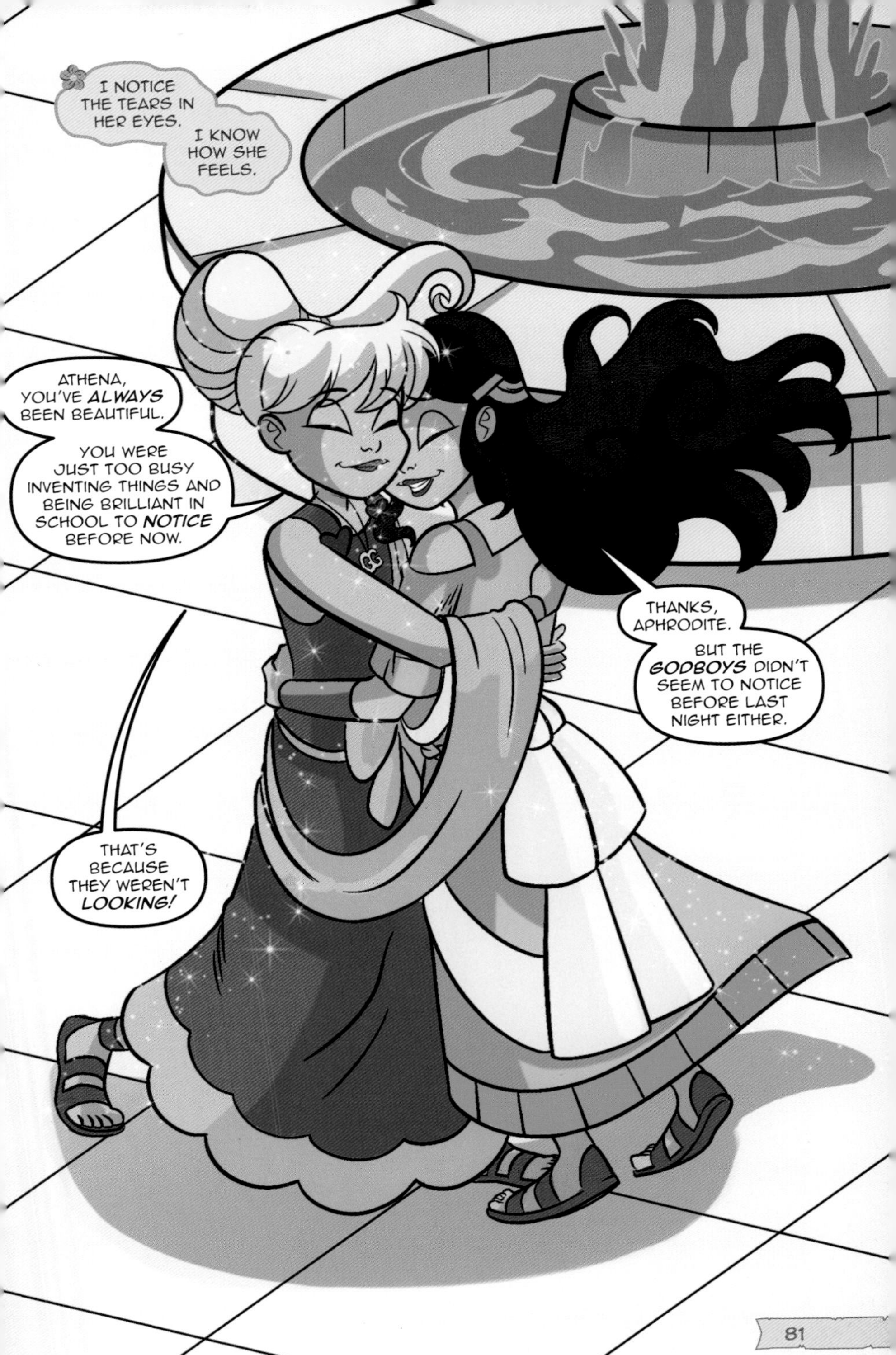
I NOTICE THE TEARS IN HER EYES.
I KNOW HOW SHE FEELS.
ATHENA, YOU'VE ALWAYS BEEN BEAUTIFUL.
YOU WERE JUST TOO BUSY INVENTING THINGS AND BEING BRILLIANT IN SCHOOL TO NOTICE BEFORE NOW.
THANKS, APHRODITE.
BUT THE GODBOYS DIDN'T SEEM TO NOTICE BEFORE LAST NIGHT EITHER.
THAT'S BECAUSE THEY WEREN'T LOOKING!

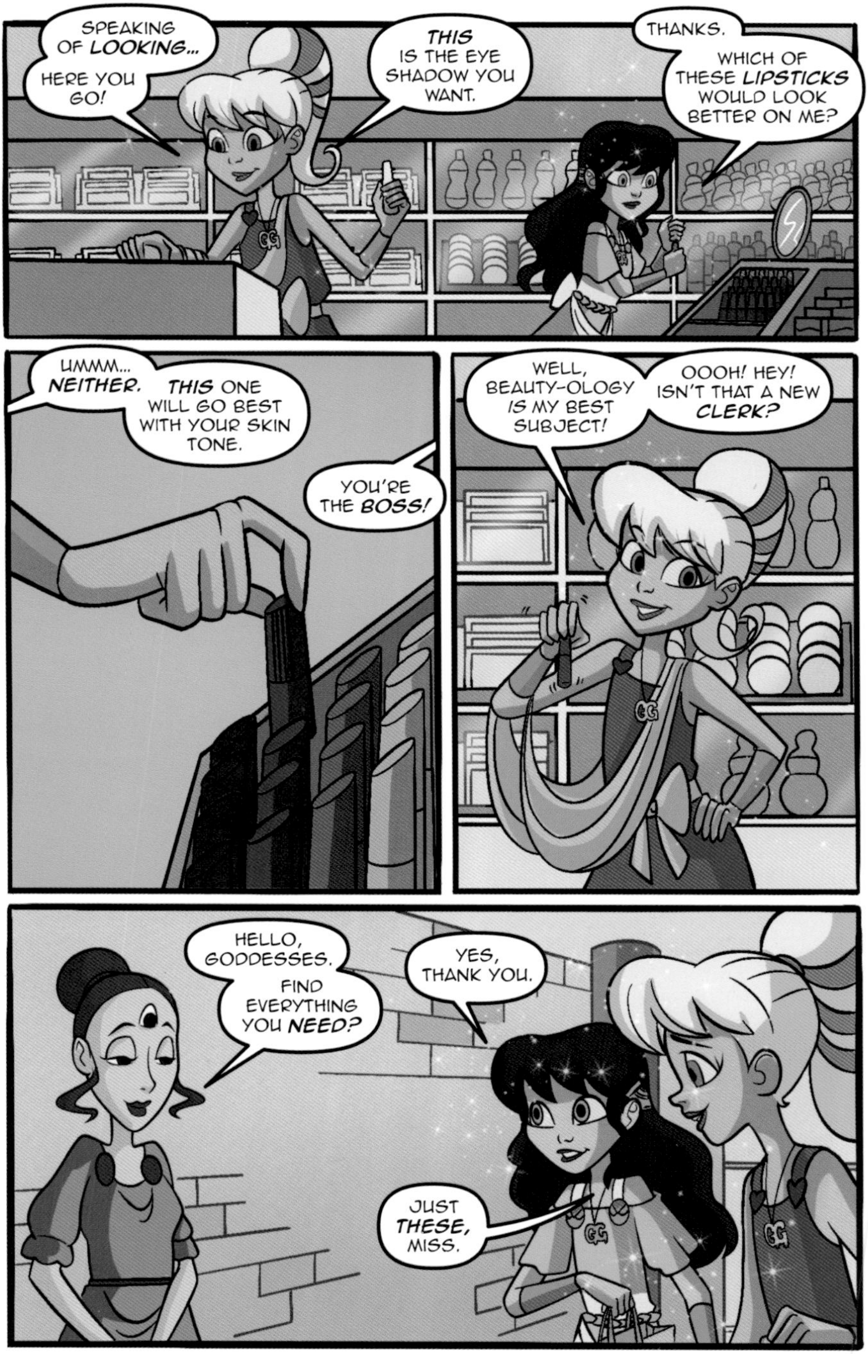
SPEAKING OF LOOKING...
HERE YOU GO!
THIS IS THE EYE SHADOW YOU WANT.
THANKS.
WHICH OF THESE LIPSTICKS WOULD LOOK BETTER ON ME?
UMMM... NEITHER.
THIS ONE WILL GO BEST WITH YOUR SKIN TONE.
YOU'RE THE BOSS!
WELL, BEAUTY-OLOGY IS MY BEST SUBJECT!
OOOH! HEY! ISN'T THAT A NEW CLERK?
HELLO, GODDESSES.
FIND EVERYTHING YOU NEED?
YES, THANK YOU.
JUST THESE, MISS.

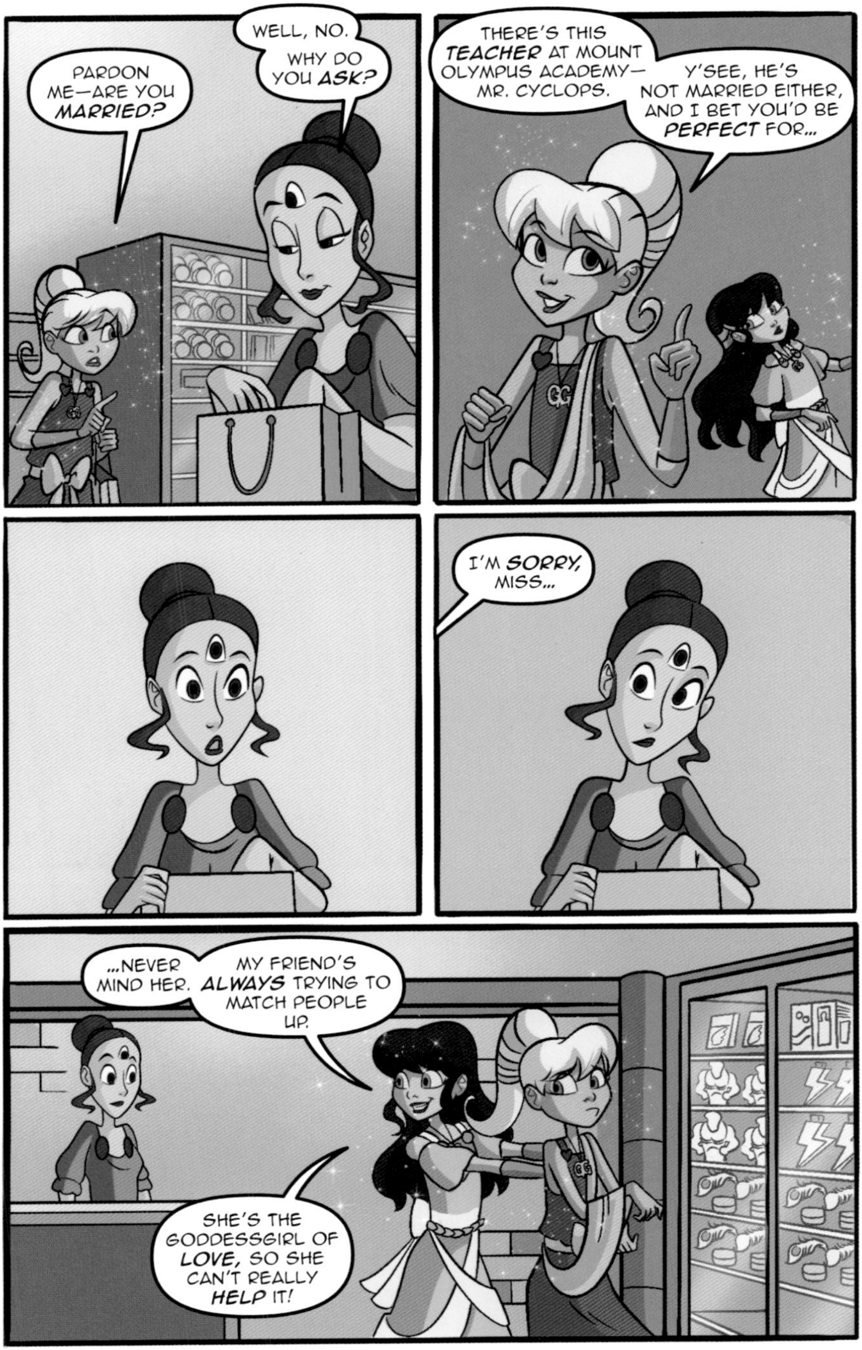
PARDON ME—ARE YOU MARRIED?
WELL, NO. WHY DO YOU ASK?
THERE'S THIS TEACHER AT MOUNT OLYMPUS ACADEMY—MR. CYCLOPS.
Y'SEE, HE'S NOT MARRIED EITHER, AND I BET YOU'D BE PERFECT FOR...
I'M SORRY, MISS...
...NEVER MIND HER.
MY FRIEND'S ALWAYS TRYING TO MATCH PEOPLE UP.
SHE'S THE GODDESSGIRL OF LOVE, SO SHE CAN'T REALLY HELP IT!

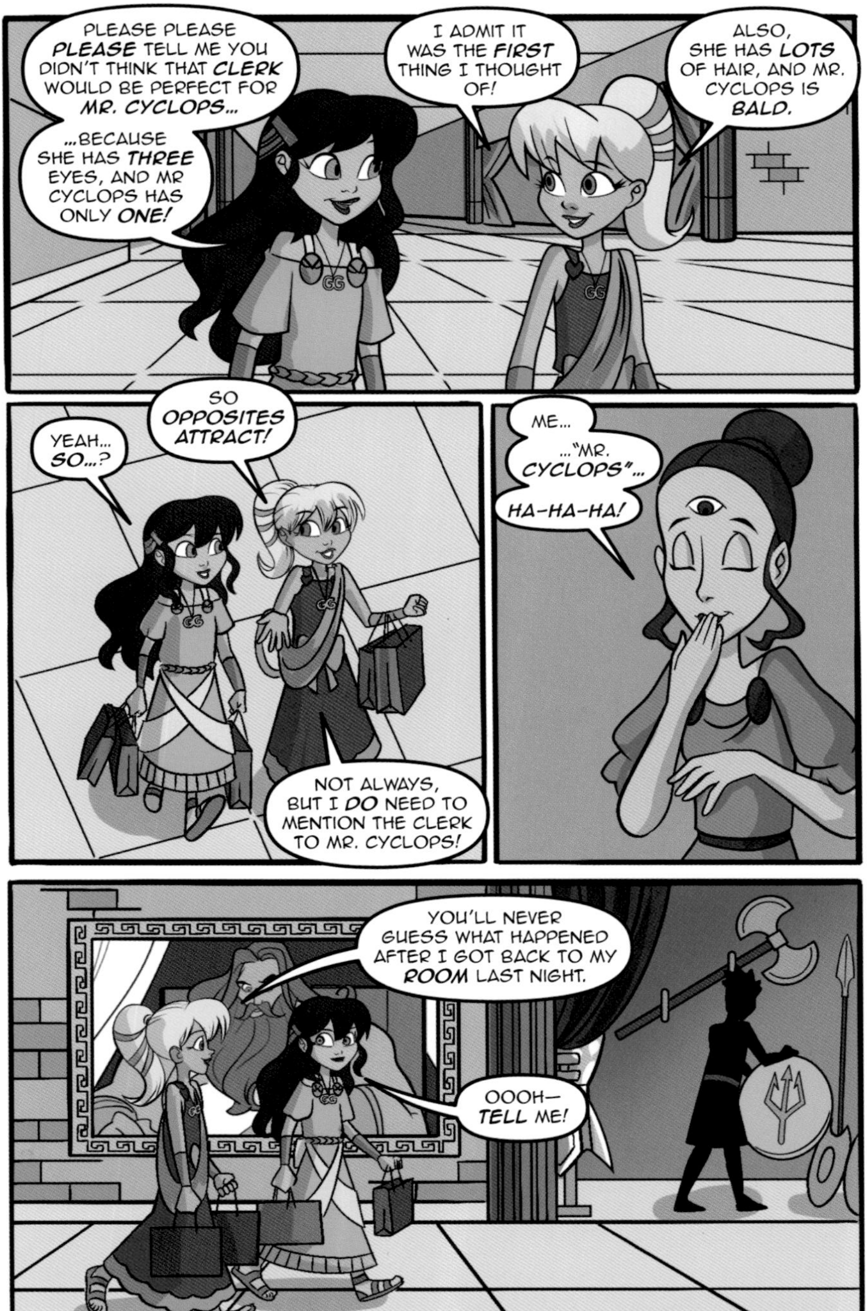
PLEASE PLEASE PLEASE TELL ME YOU DIDN'T THINK THAT CLERK WOULD BE PERFECT FOR MR. CYCLOPS...
...BECAUSE SHE HAS THREE EYES, AND MR CYCLOPS HAS ONLY ONE!
I ADMIT IT WAS THE FIRST THING I THOUGHT OF!
ALSO, SHE HAS LOTS OF HAIR, AND MR. CYCLOPS IS BALD.
YEAH... SO...?
SO OPPOSITES ATTRACT!
NOT ALWAYS, BUT I DO NEED TO MENTION THE CLERK TO MR. CYCLOPS!
ME...
..."MR. CYCLOPS"...
HA-HA-HA!
YOU'LL NEVER GUESS WHAT HAPPENED AFTER I GOT BACK TO MY ROOM LAST NIGHT.
OOOH— TELL ME!

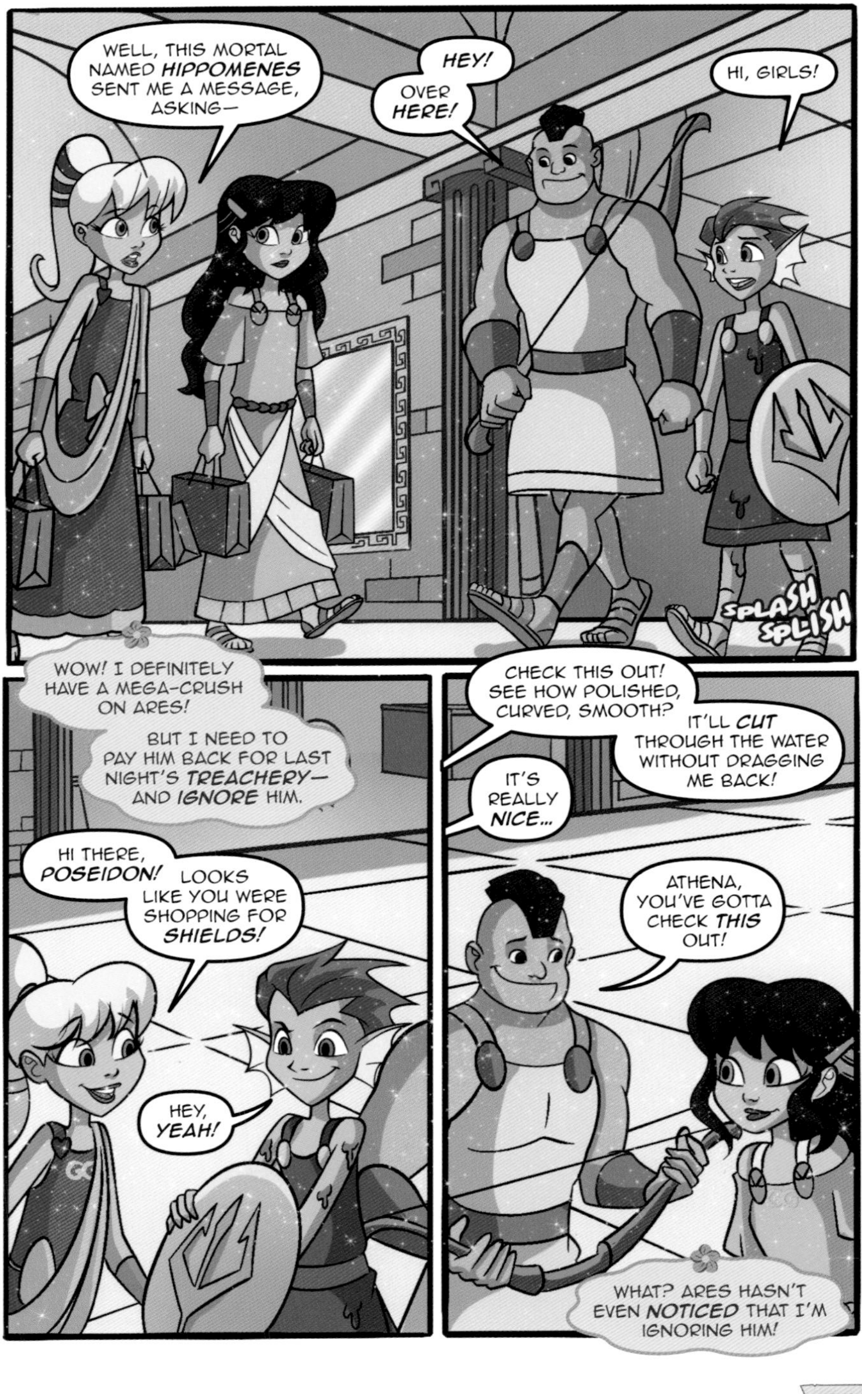
WELL, THIS MORTAL NAMED HIPPOMENES SENT ME A MESSAGE, ASKING—
HEY! OVER HERE!
HI, GIRLS!
SPLASH SPLISH
WOW! I DEFINITELY HAVE A MEGA-CRUSH ON ARES!
BUT I NEED TO PAY HIM BACK FOR LAST NIGHT'S TREACHERY—AND IGNORE HIM.
HI THERE, POSEIDON! LOOKS LIKE YOU WERE SHOPPING FOR SHIELDS!
HEY, YEAH!
CHECK THIS OUT! SEE HOW POLISHED, CURVED, SMOOTH?
IT'LL CUT THROUGH THE WATER WITHOUT DRAGGING ME BACK!
IT'S REALLY NICE...
ATHENA, YOU'VE GOTTA CHECK THIS OUT!
WHAT? ARES HASN'T EVEN NOTICED THAT I'M IGNORING HIM!

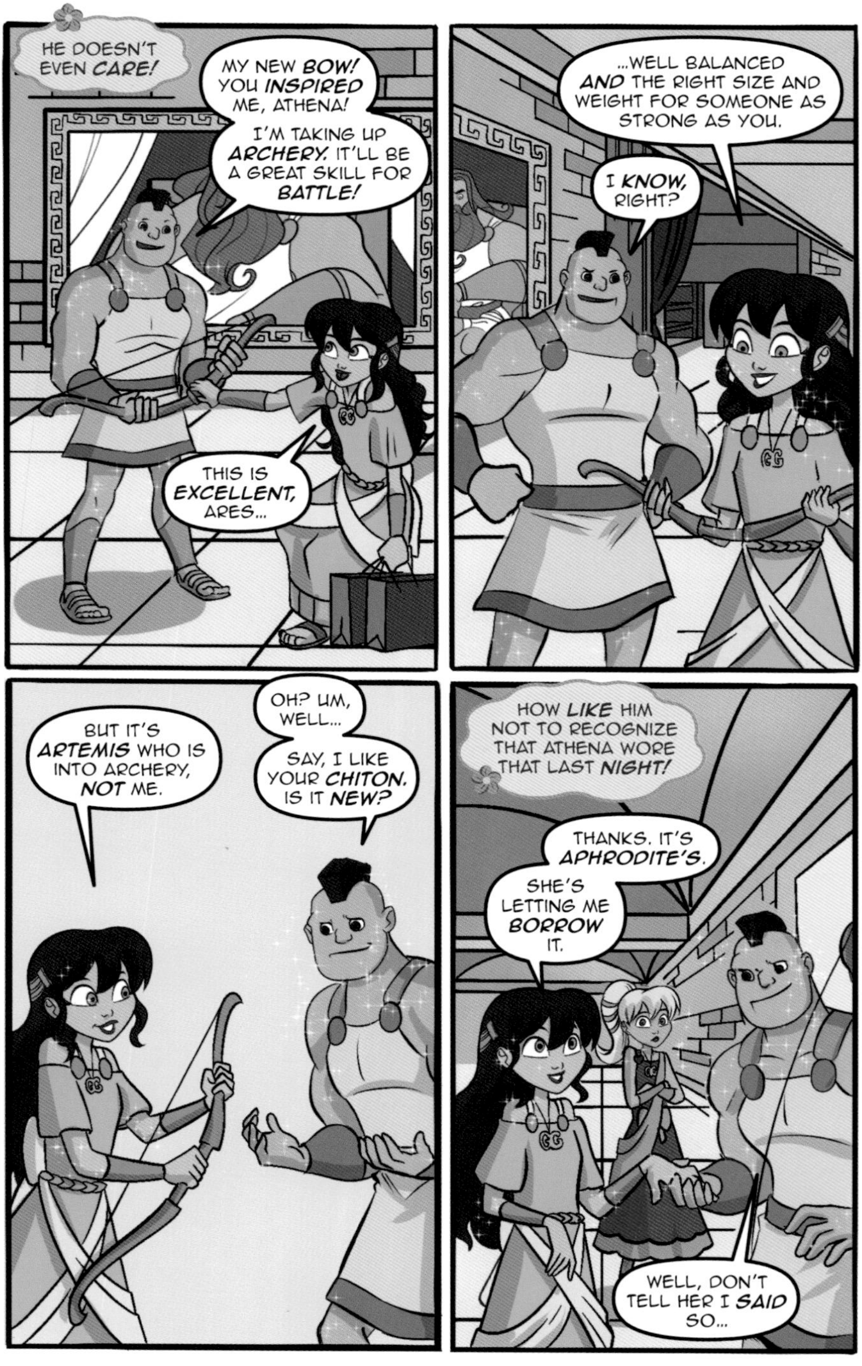
HE DOESN'T EVEN CARE!
MY NEW BOW! YOU INSPIRED ME, ATHENA!
I'M TAKING UP ARCHERY. IT'LL BE A GREAT SKILL FOR BATTLE!
THIS IS EXCELLENT, ARES...
...WELL BALANCED AND THE RIGHT SIZE AND WEIGHT FOR SOMEONE AS STRONG AS YOU.
I KNOW, RIGHT?
BUT IT'S ARTEMIS WHO IS INTO ARCHERY, NOT ME.
OH? UM, WELL...
SAY, I LIKE YOUR CHITON. IS IT NEW?
HOW LIKE HIM NOT TO RECOGNIZE THAT ATHENA WORE THAT LAST NIGHT!
THANKS. IT'S APHRODITE'S.
SHE'S LETTING ME BORROW IT.
WELL, DON'T TELL HER I SAID SO...

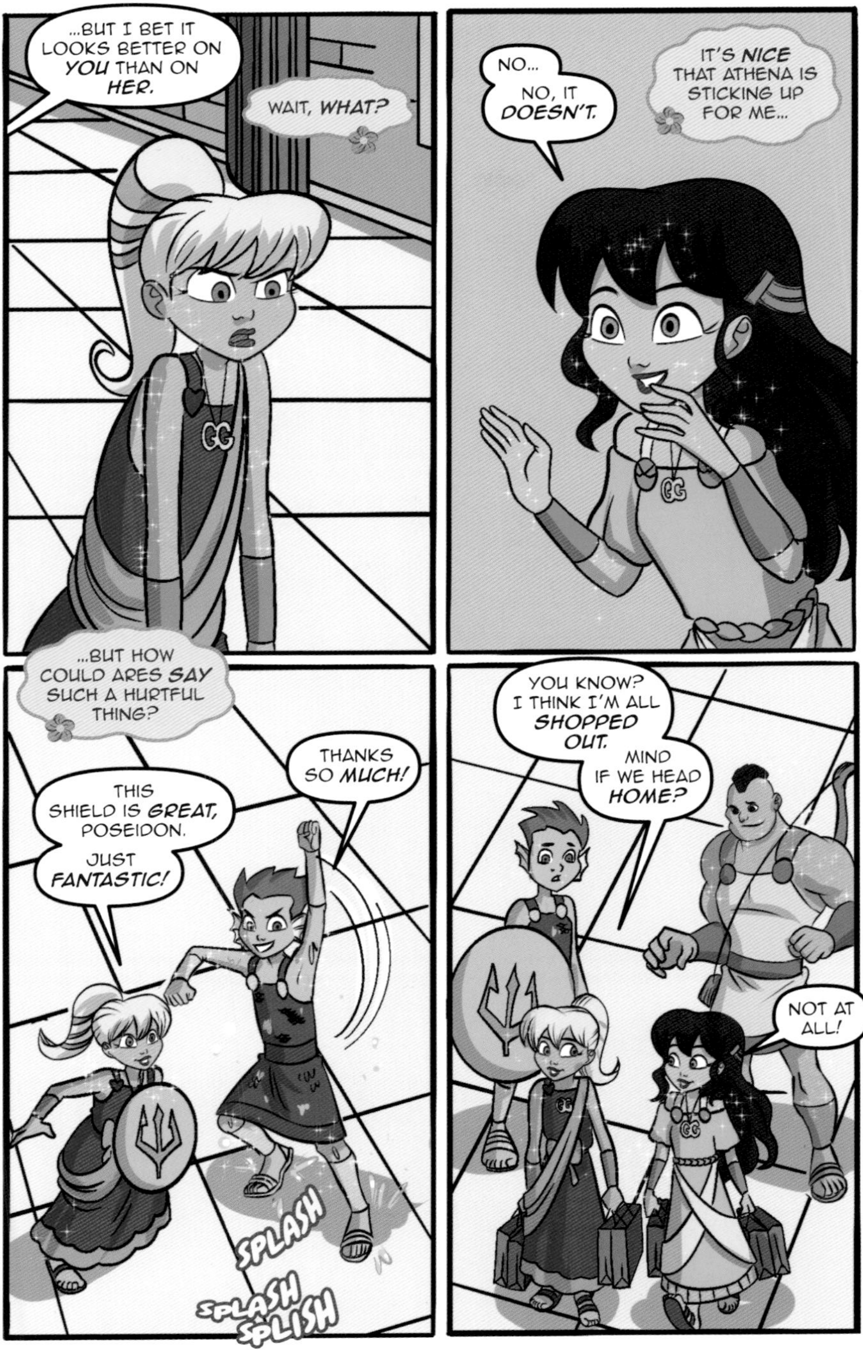
...BUT I BET IT LOOKS BETTER ON YOU THAN ON HER.
WAIT, WHAT?
NO...
NO, IT DOESN'T.
IT'S NICE THAT ATHENA IS STICKING UP FOR ME...
...BUT HOW COULD ARES SAY SUCH A HURTFUL THING?
THIS SHIELD IS GREAT, POSEIDON.
JUST FANTASTIC!
THANKS SO MUCH!
SPLASH
SPLASH
SPLISH
YOU KNOW? I THINK I'M ALL SHOPPED OUT.
MIND IF WE HEAD HOME?
NOT AT ALL!

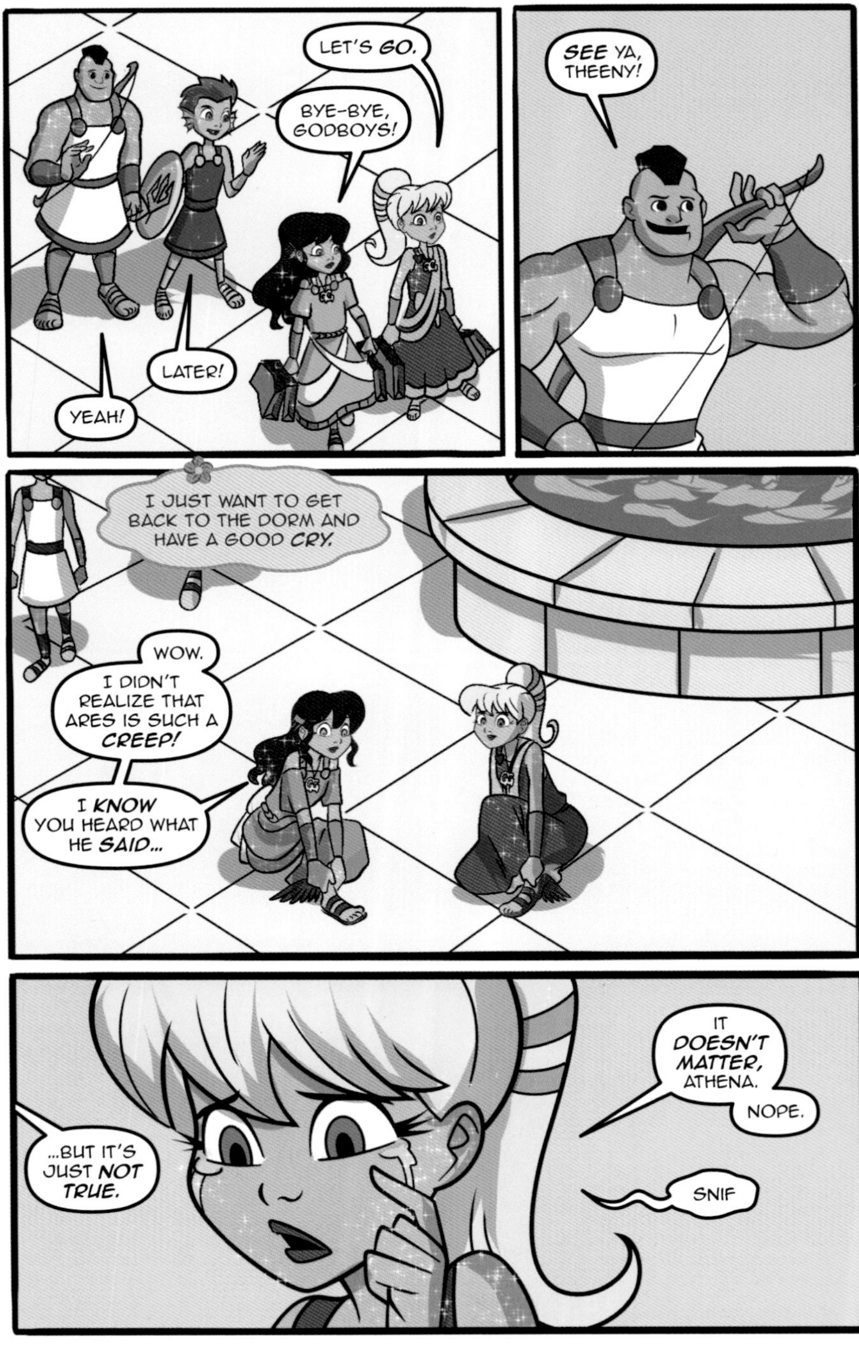
LET'S GO.
BYE-BYE, GODBOYS!
LATER!
YEAH!
SEE YA, THEENY!
I JUST WANT TO GET BACK TO THE DORM AND HAVE A GOOD CRY.
WOW. I DIDN'T REALIZE THAT ARES IS SUCH A CREEP!
I KNOW YOU HEARD WHAT HE SAID...
...BUT IT'S JUST NOT TRUE.
IT DOESN'T MATTER, ATHENA.
NOPE.
SNIF

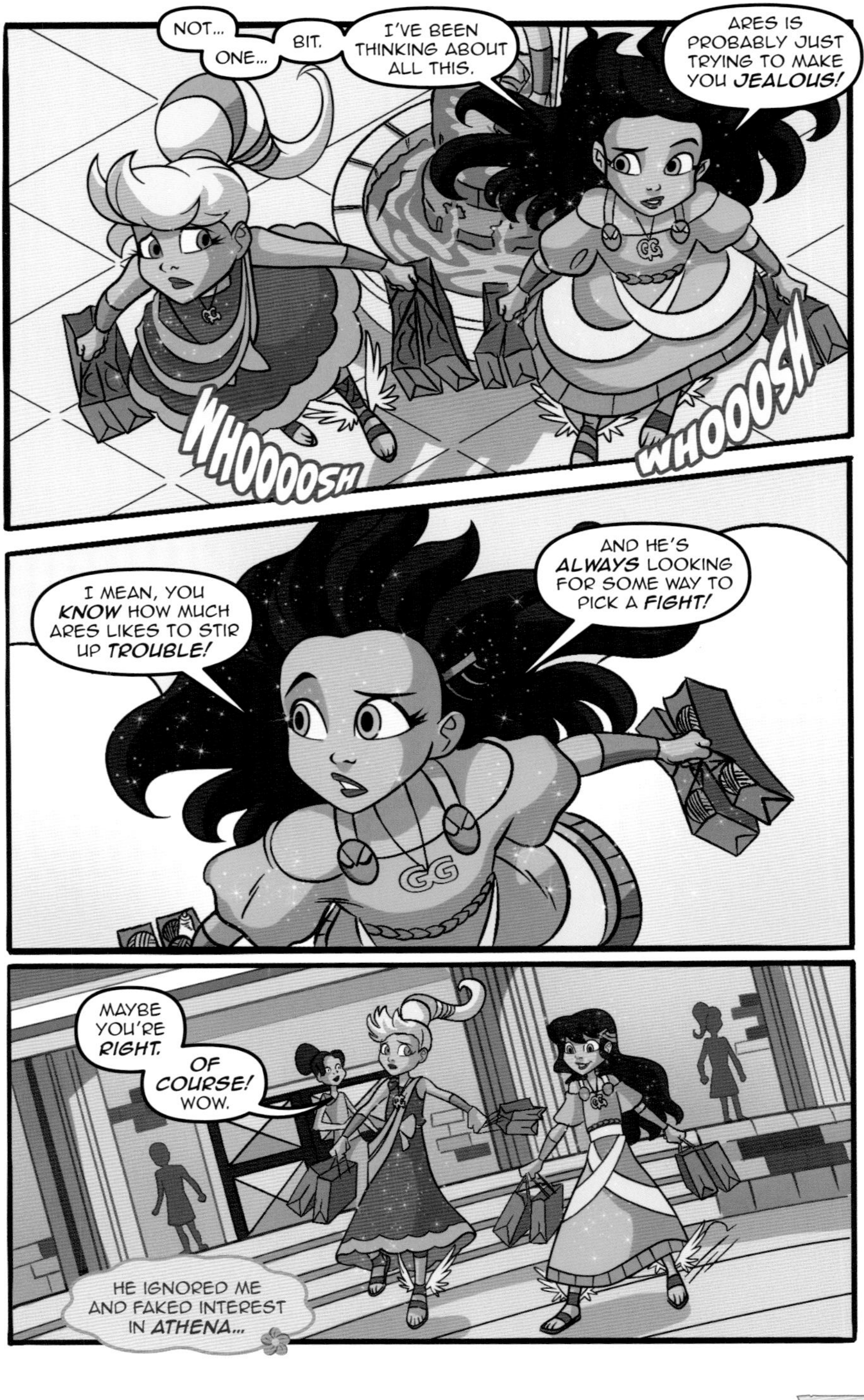
NOT...
ONE...
BIT.
I'VE BEEN THINKING ABOUT ALL THIS.
ARES IS PROBABLY JUST TRYING TO MAKE YOU JEALOUS!
WHOOOOSH
WHOOOSH
I MEAN, YOU KNOW HOW MUCH ARES LIKES TO STIR UP TROUBLE!
AND HE'S ALWAYS LOOKING FOR SOME WAY TO PICK A FIGHT!
MAYBE YOU'RE RIGHT.
OF COURSE! WOW.
HE IGNORED ME AND FAKED INTEREST IN ATHENA...

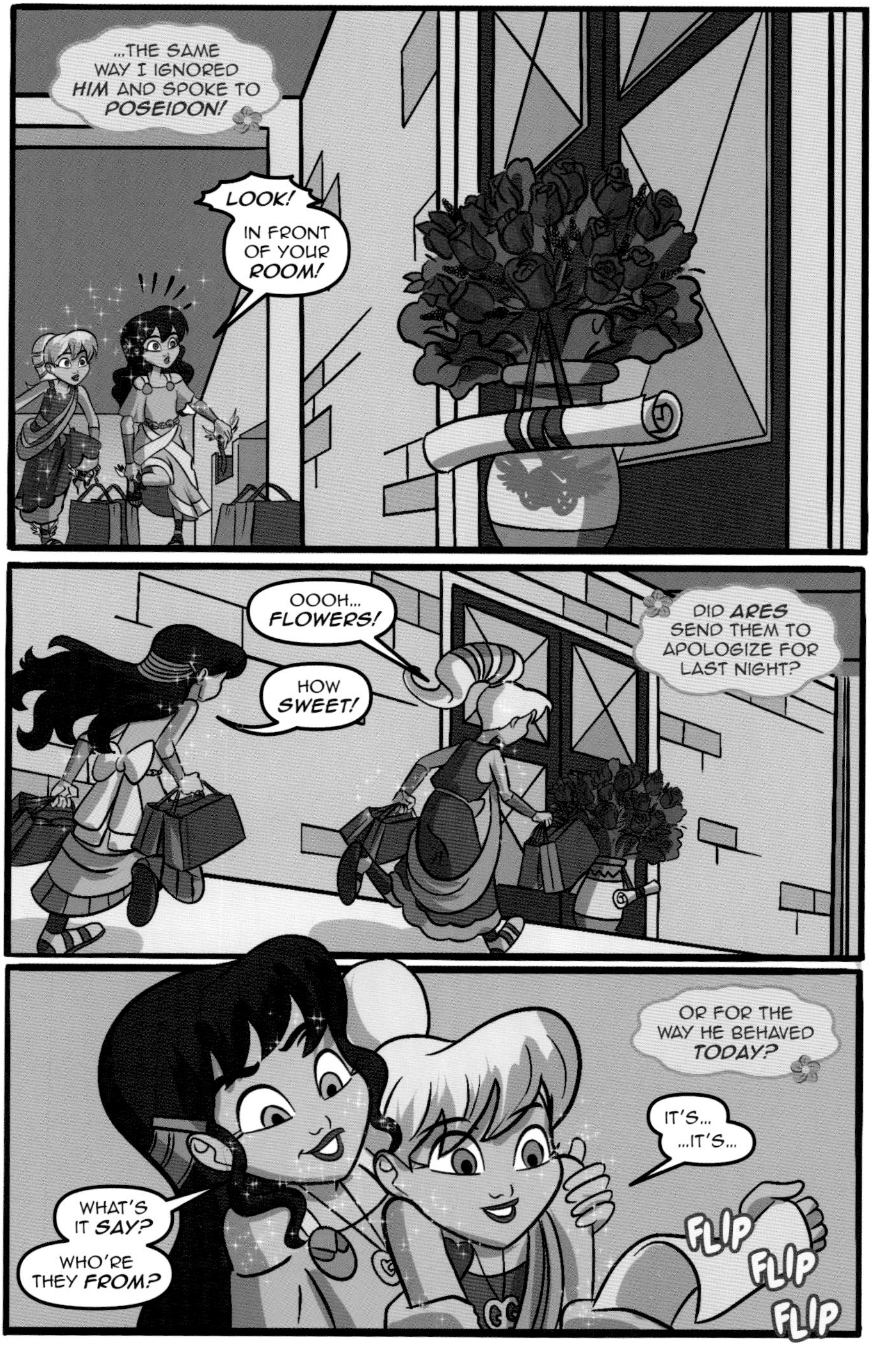
...THE SAME WAY I IGNORED HIM AND SPOKE TO POSEIDON!
LOOK!
IN FRONT OF YOUR ROOM!
OOOH... FLOWERS!
HOW SWEET!
DID ARES SEND THEM TO APOLOGIZE FOR LAST NIGHT?
OR FOR THE WAY HE BEHAVED TODAY?
WHAT'S IT SAY?
WHO'RE THEY FROM?
IT'S... ...IT'S...
FLIP
FLIP
FLIP

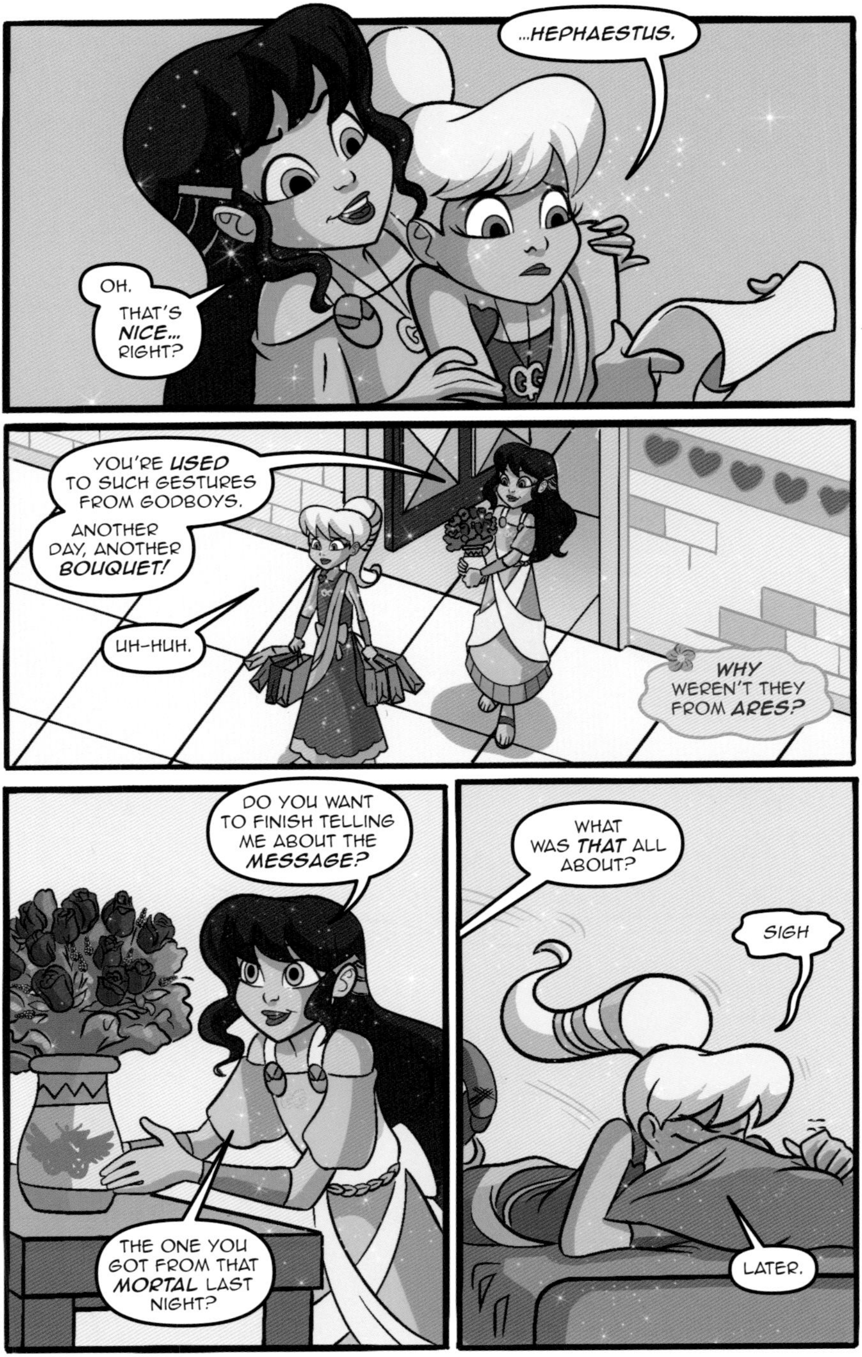

...HEPHAESTUS.
OH. THAT'S NICE... RIGHT?
YOU'RE USED TO SUCH GESTURES FROM GODBOYS.
ANOTHER DAY, ANOTHER BOUQUET!
UH-HUH.
WHY WEREN'T THEY FROM ARES?
DO YOU WANT TO FINISH TELLING ME ABOUT THE MESSAGE?
THE ONE YOU GOT FROM THAT MORTAL LAST NIGHT?
WHAT WAS THAT ALL ABOUT?
SIGH
LATER.

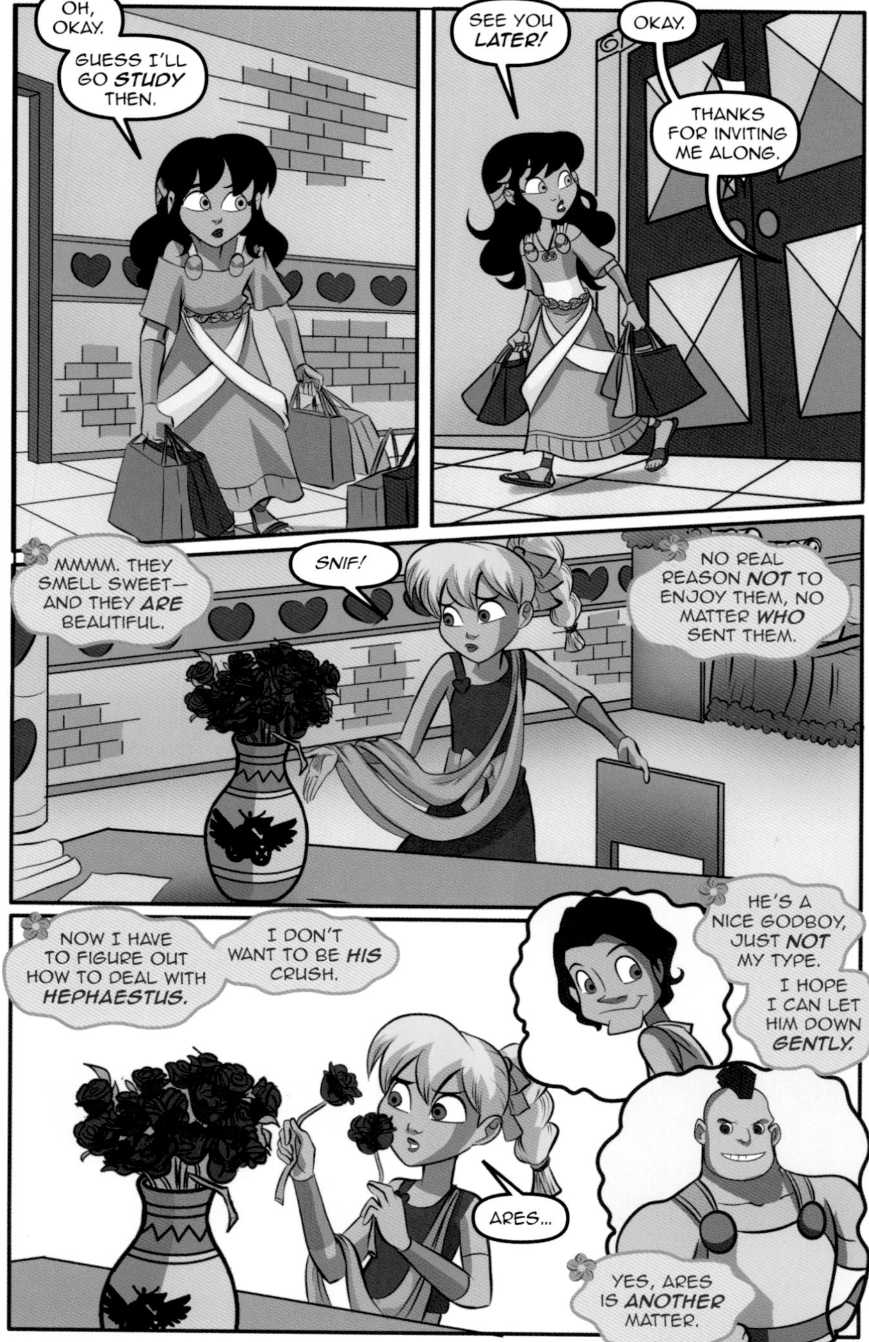

OH, OKAY.
GUESS I'LL GO STUDY THEN.
SEE YOU LATER!
OKAY.
THANKS FOR INVITING ME ALONG.
MMMM. THEY SMELL SWEET—AND THEY ARE BEAUTIFUL.
SNIF!
NO REAL REASON NOT TO ENJOY THEM, NO MATTER WHO SENT THEM.
NOW I HAVE TO FIGURE OUT HOW TO DEAL WITH HEPHAESTUS.
I DON'T WANT TO BE HIS CRUSH.
HE'S A NICE GODBOY, JUST NOT MY TYPE.
I HOPE I CAN LET HIM DOWN GENTLY.
ARES...
YES, ARES IS ANOTHER MATTER.

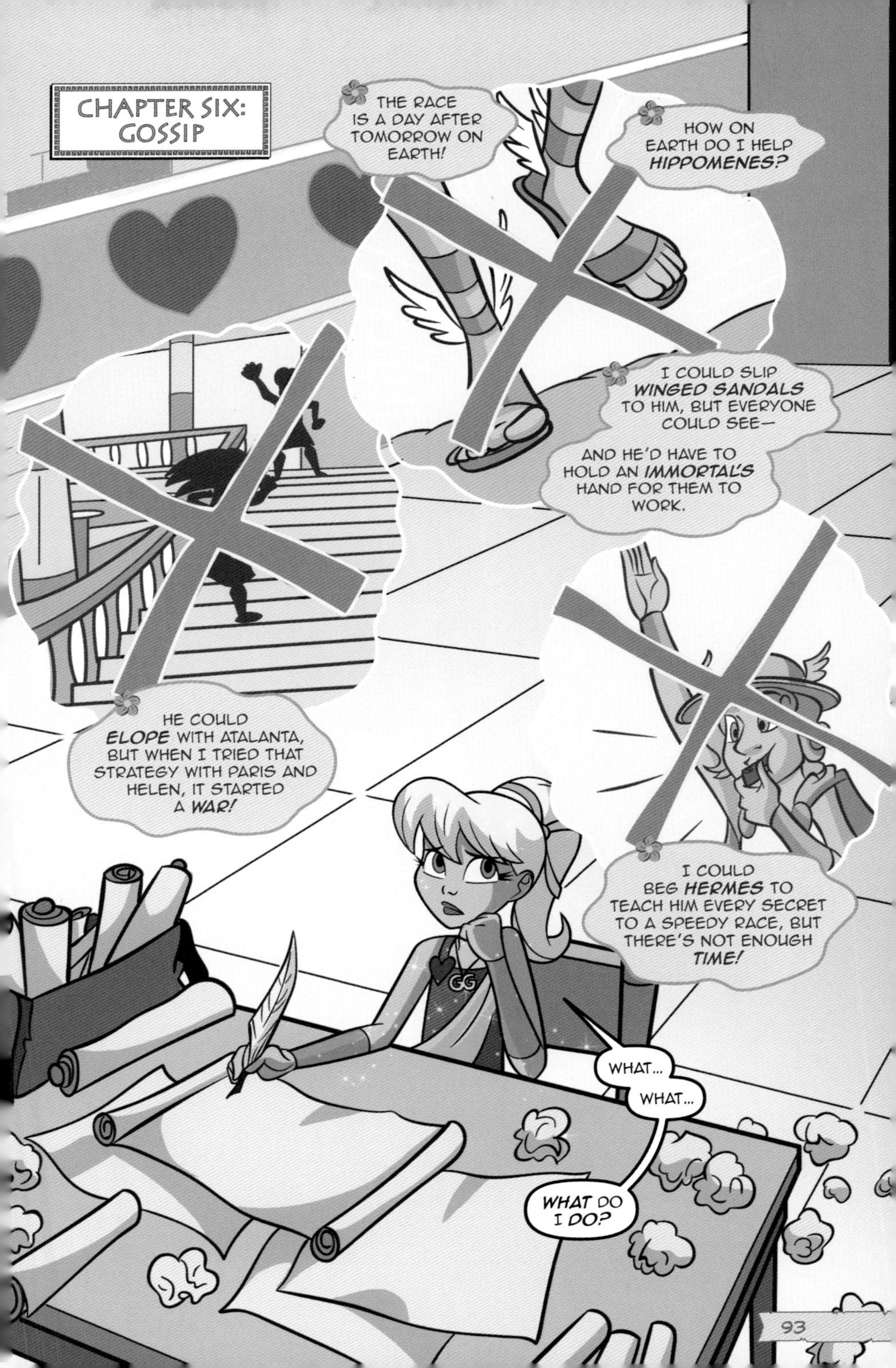
CHAPTER SIX: GOSSIP
THE RACE IS A DAY AFTER TOMORROW ON EARTH!
HOW ON EARTH DO I HELP HIPPOMENES?
I COULD SLIP WINGED SANDALS TO HIM, BUT EVERYONE COULD SEE—
AND HE'D HAVE TO HOLD AN IMMORTAL'S HAND FOR THEM TO WORK.
HE COULD ELOPE WITH ATALANTA, BUT WHEN I TRIED THAT STRATEGY WITH PARIS AND HELEN, IT STARTED A WAR!
I COULD BEG HERMES TO TEACH HIM EVERY SECRET TO A SPEEDY RACE, BUT THERE'S NOT ENOUGH TIME!
WHAT...
WHAT...
WHAT DO I DO?

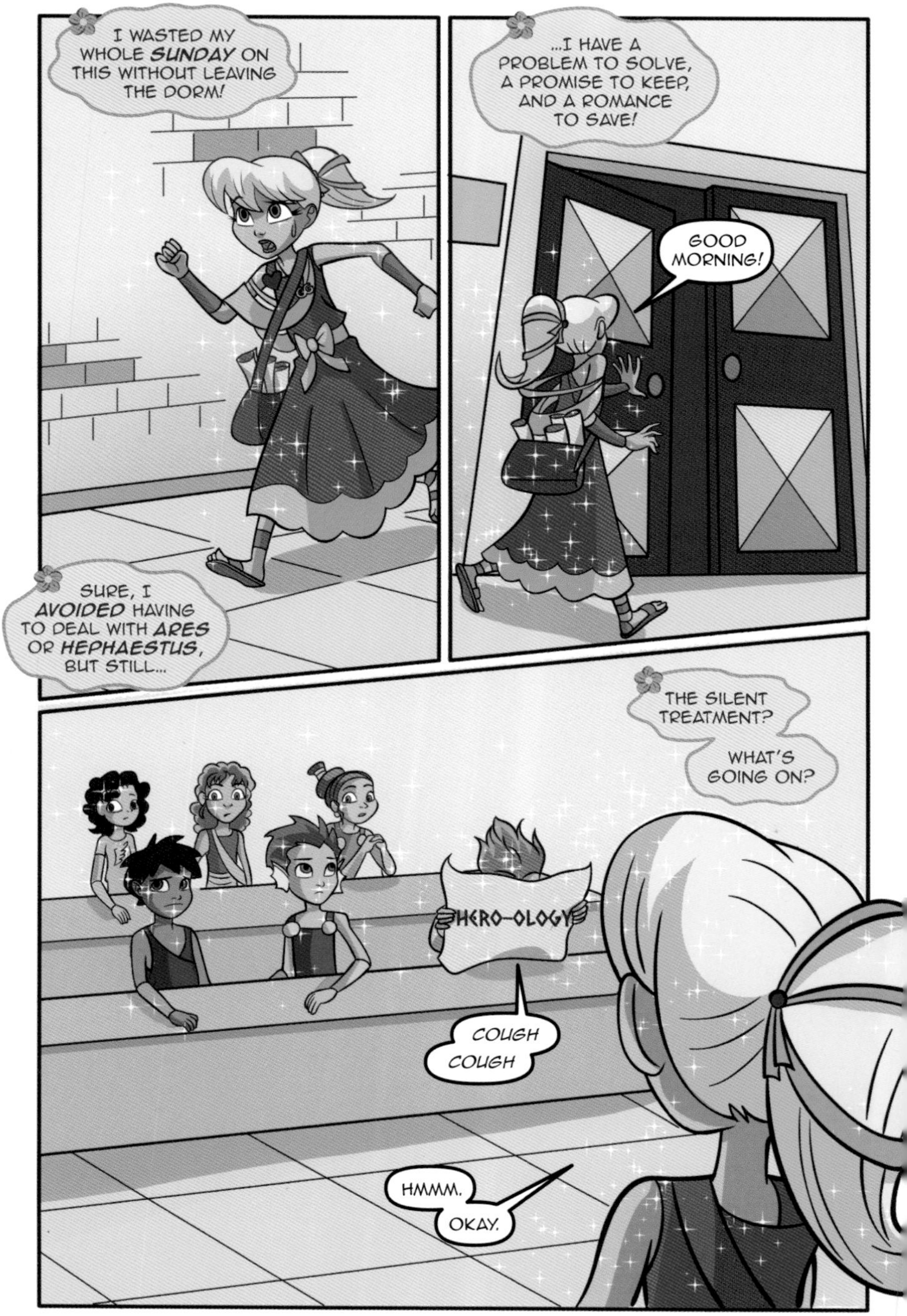
I WASTED MY WHOLE SUNDAY ON THIS WITHOUT LEAVING THE DORM!
SURE, I AVOIDED HAVING TO DEAL WITH ARES OR HEPHAESTUS, BUT STILL...
...I HAVE A PROBLEM TO SOLVE, A PROMISE TO KEEP, AND A ROMANCE TO SAVE!
GOOD MORNING!
THE SILENT TREATMENT?
WHAT'S GOING ON?
HERO-OLOGY
COUGH COUGH
HMMM.
OKAY.

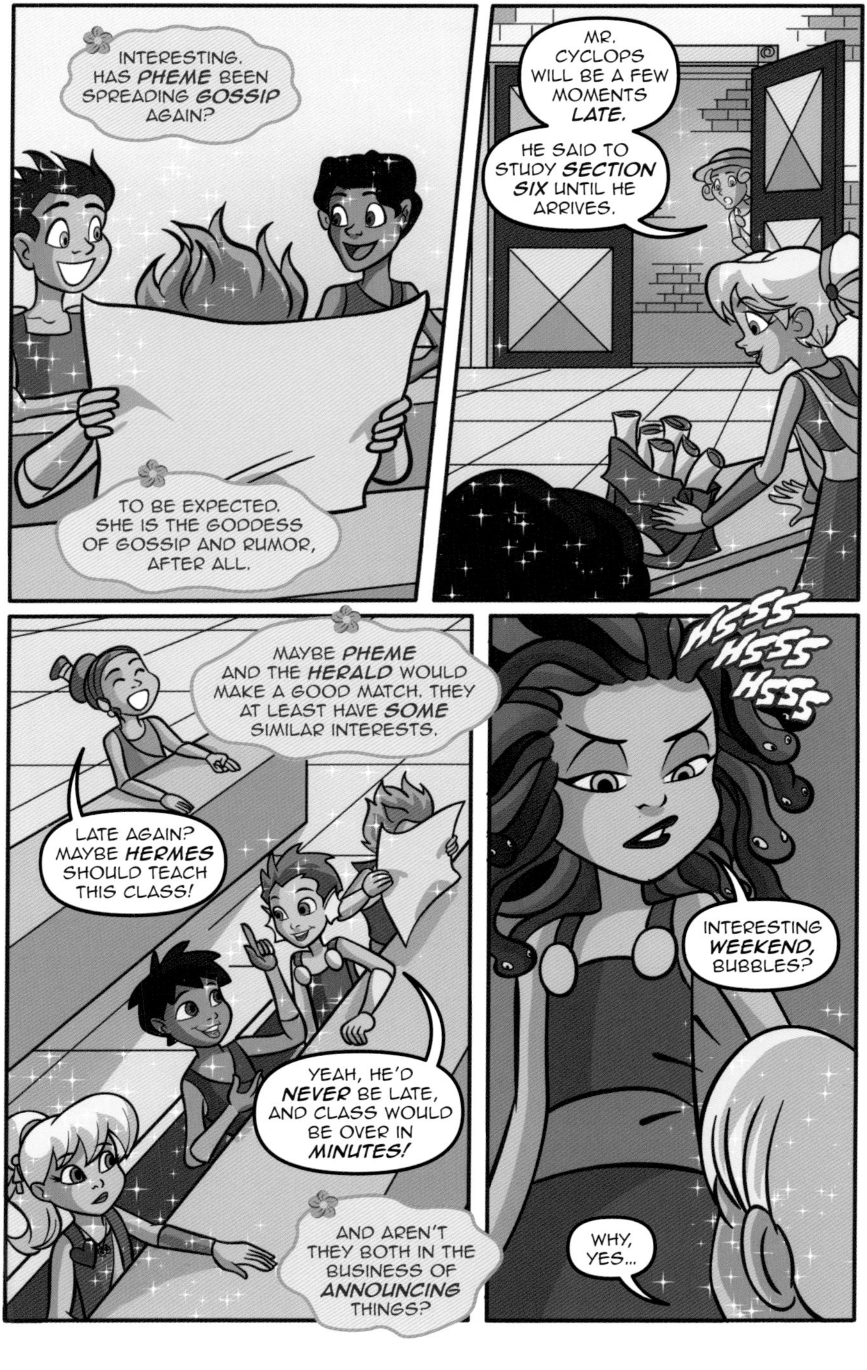
INTERESTING. HAS PHEME BEEN SPREADING GOSSIP AGAIN?
TO BE EXPECTED. SHE IS THE GODDESS OF GOSSIP AND RUMOR, AFTER ALL.
MR. CYCLOPS WILL BE A FEW MOMENTS LATE.
HE SAID TO STUDY SECTION SIX UNTIL HE ARRIVES.
MAYBE PHEME AND THE HERALD WOULD MAKE A GOOD MATCH. THEY AT LEAST HAVE SOME SIMILAR INTERESTS.
LATE AGAIN? MAYBE HERMES SHOULD TEACH THIS CLASS!
YEAH, HE'D NEVER BE LATE, AND CLASS WOULD BE OVER IN MINUTES!
AND AREN'T THEY BOTH IN THE BUSINESS OF ANNOUNCING THINGS?
HSSS HSSS HSSS
INTERESTING WEEKEND, BUBBLES?
WHY, YES...

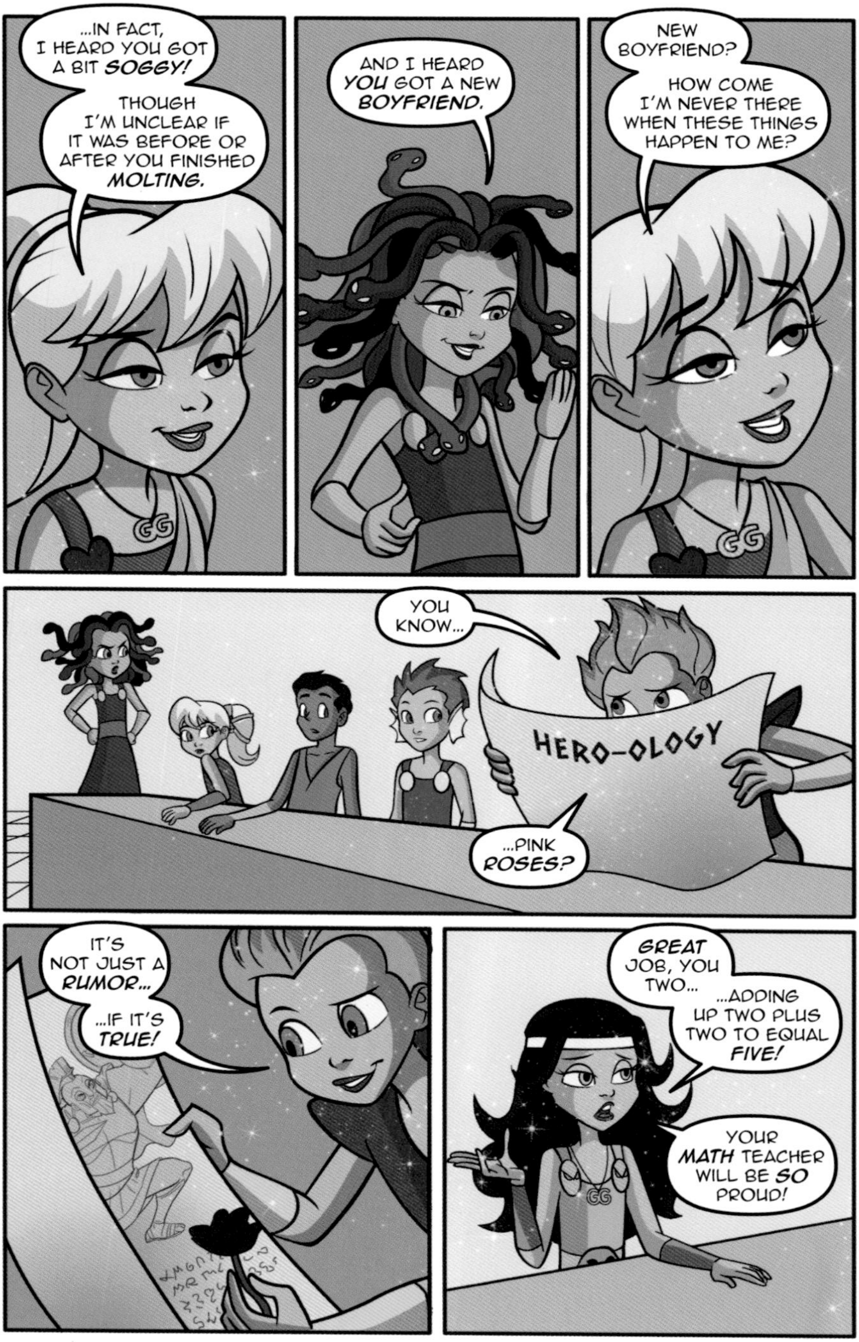

...IN FACT, I HEARD YOU GOT A BIT SOGGY!
THOUGH I'M UNCLEAR IF IT WAS BEFORE OR AFTER YOU FINISHED MOLTING.
AND I HEARD YOU GOT A NEW BOYFRIEND.
NEW BOYFRIEND?
HOW COME I'M NEVER THERE WHEN THESE THINGS HAPPEN TO ME?
YOU KNOW...
HERO-OLOGY
...PINK ROSES?
IT'S NOT JUST A RUMOR...
...IF IT'S TRUE!
GREAT JOB, YOU TWO...
...ADDING UP TWO PLUS TWO TO EQUAL FIVE!
YOUR MATH TEACHER WILL BE SO PROUD!

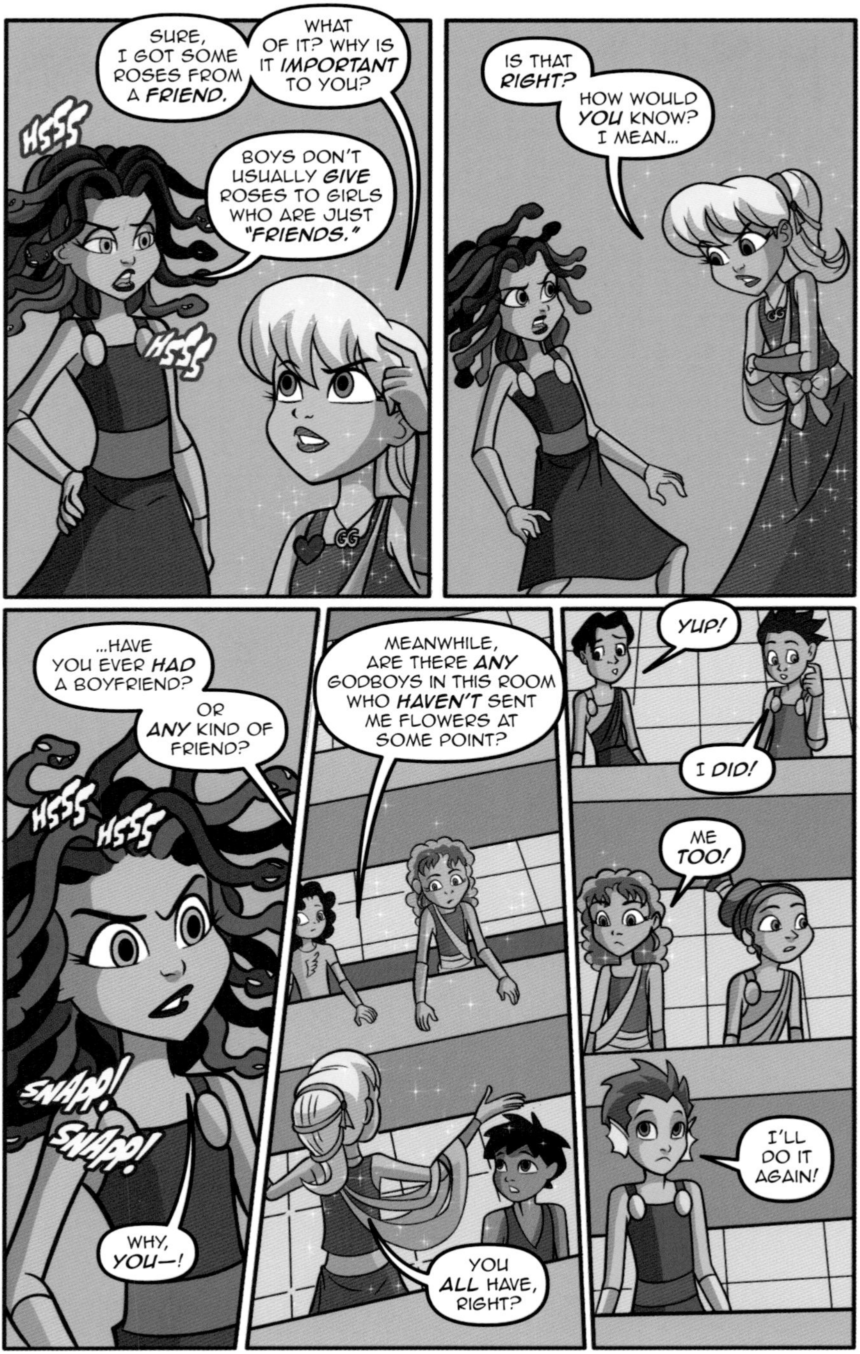
SURE, I GOT SOME ROSES FROM A FRIEND.
WHAT OF IT? WHY IS IT IMPORTANT TO YOU?
HSSS
BOYS DON'T USUALLY GIVE ROSES TO GIRLS WHO ARE JUST "FRIENDS."
HSSS
IS THAT RIGHT?
HOW WOULD YOU KNOW? I MEAN...
...HAVE YOU EVER HAD A BOYFRIEND?
OR ANY KIND OF FRIEND?
HSSS HSSS
SNAPP! SNAPP!
WHY, YOU—!
MEANWHILE, ARE THERE ANY GODBOYS IN THIS ROOM WHO HAVEN'T SENT ME FLOWERS AT SOME POINT?
YOU ALL HAVE, RIGHT?
YUP!
I DID!
ME TOO!
I'LL DO IT AGAIN!

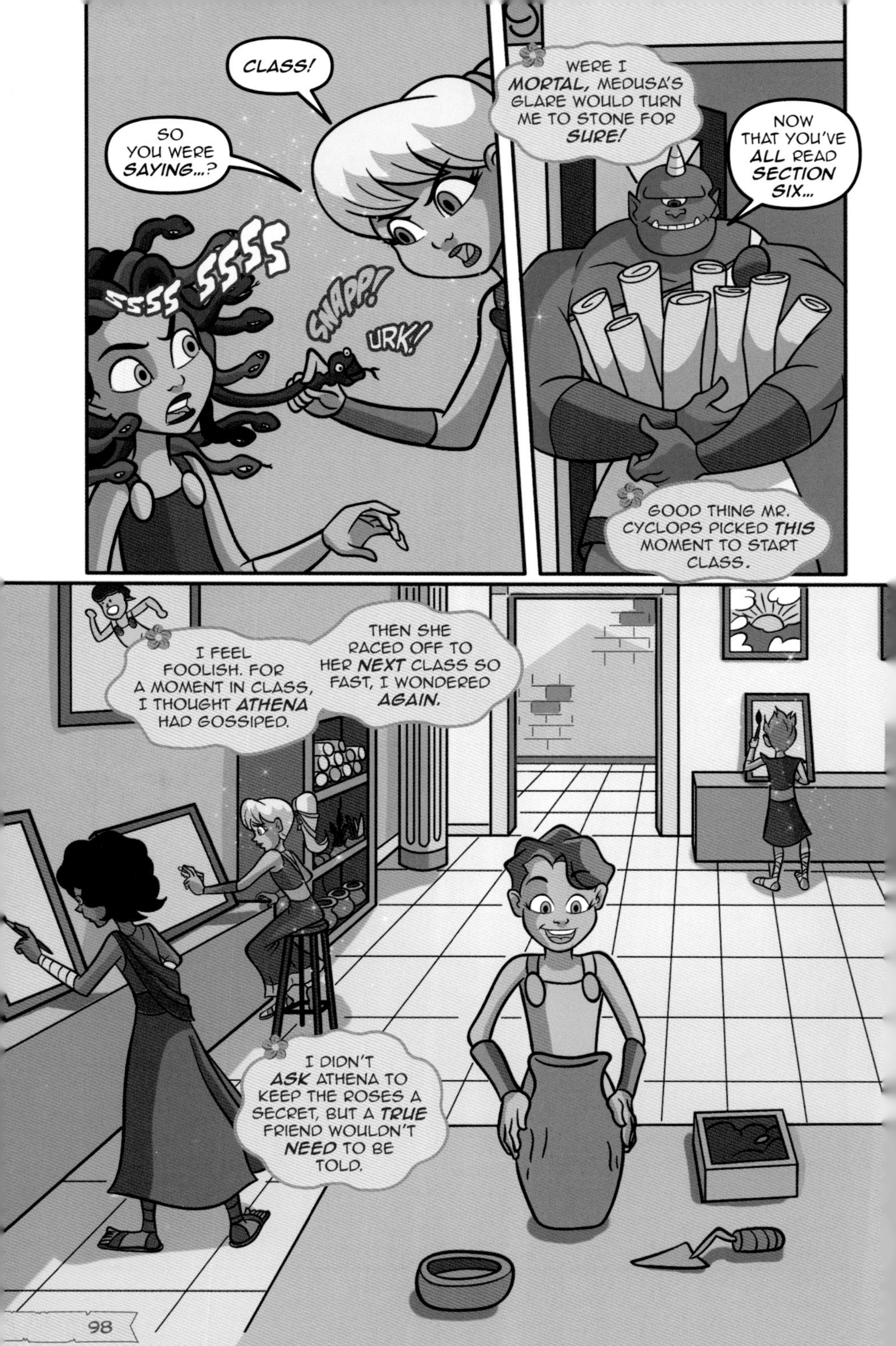
CLASS!
SO YOU WERE SAYING...?
SSSS SSSS
SNAPP!
URK!
WERE I MORTAL, MEDUSA'S GLARE WOULD TURN ME TO STONE FOR SURE!
NOW THAT YOU'VE ALL READ SECTION SIX...
GOOD THING MR. CYCLOPS PICKED THIS MOMENT TO START CLASS.
I FEEL FOOLISH. FOR A MOMENT IN CLASS, I THOUGHT ATHENA HAD GOSSIPED.
THEN SHE RACED OFF TO HER NEXT CLASS SO FAST, I WONDERED AGAIN.
I DIDN'T ASK ATHENA TO KEEP THE ROSES A SECRET, BUT A TRUE FRIEND WOULDN'T NEED TO BE TOLD.

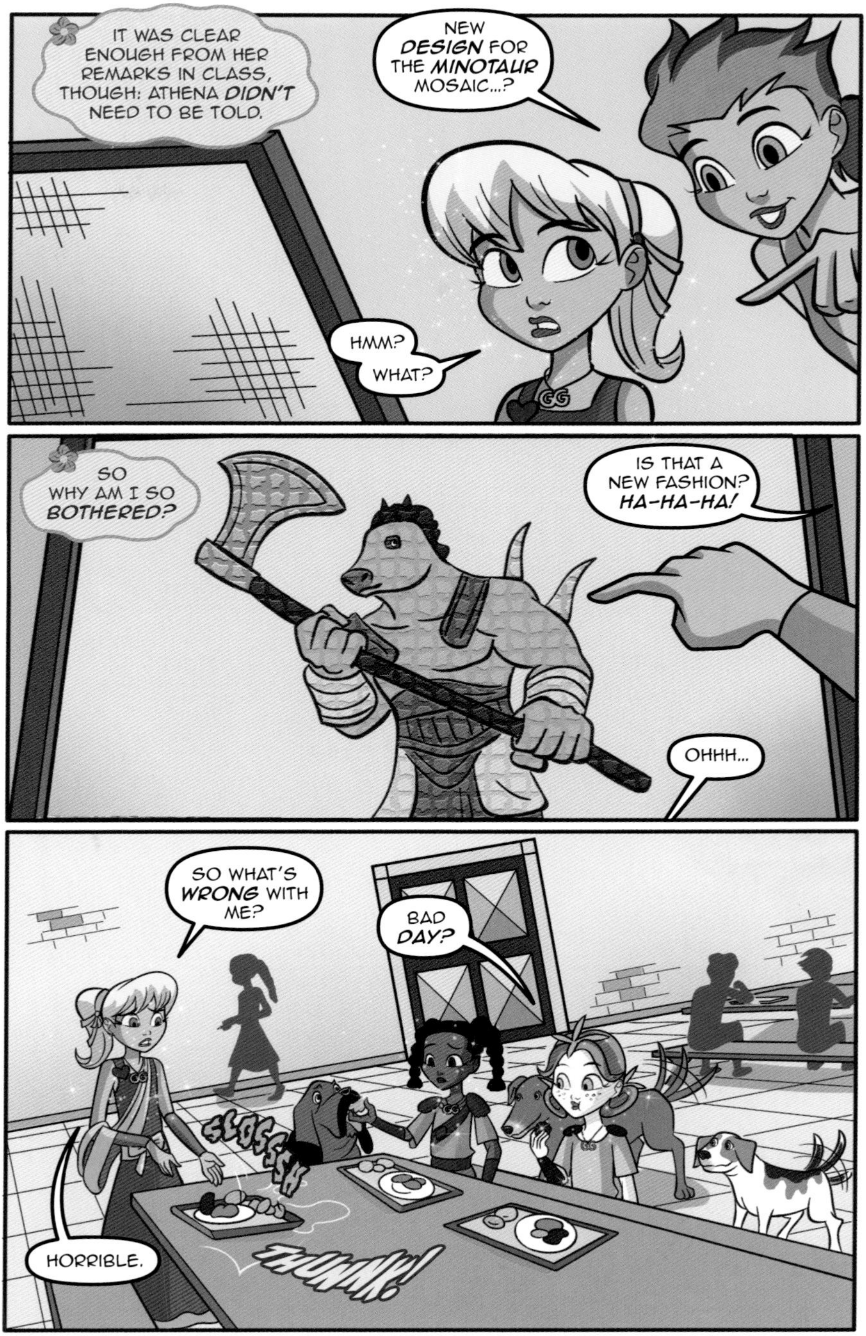
IT WAS CLEAR ENOUGH FROM HER REMARKS IN CLASS, THOUGH: ATHENA *DIDN'T* NEED TO BE TOLD.
NEW *DESIGN* FOR THE *MINOTAUR* MOSAIC...?
HMM? WHAT?
SO WHY AM I SO *BOTHERED?*
IS THAT A NEW FASHION? *HA-HA-HA!*
OHHH...
SO WHAT'S *WRONG* WITH ME?
BAD *DAY?*
SLOSSSH
HORRIBLE.
THUNK!

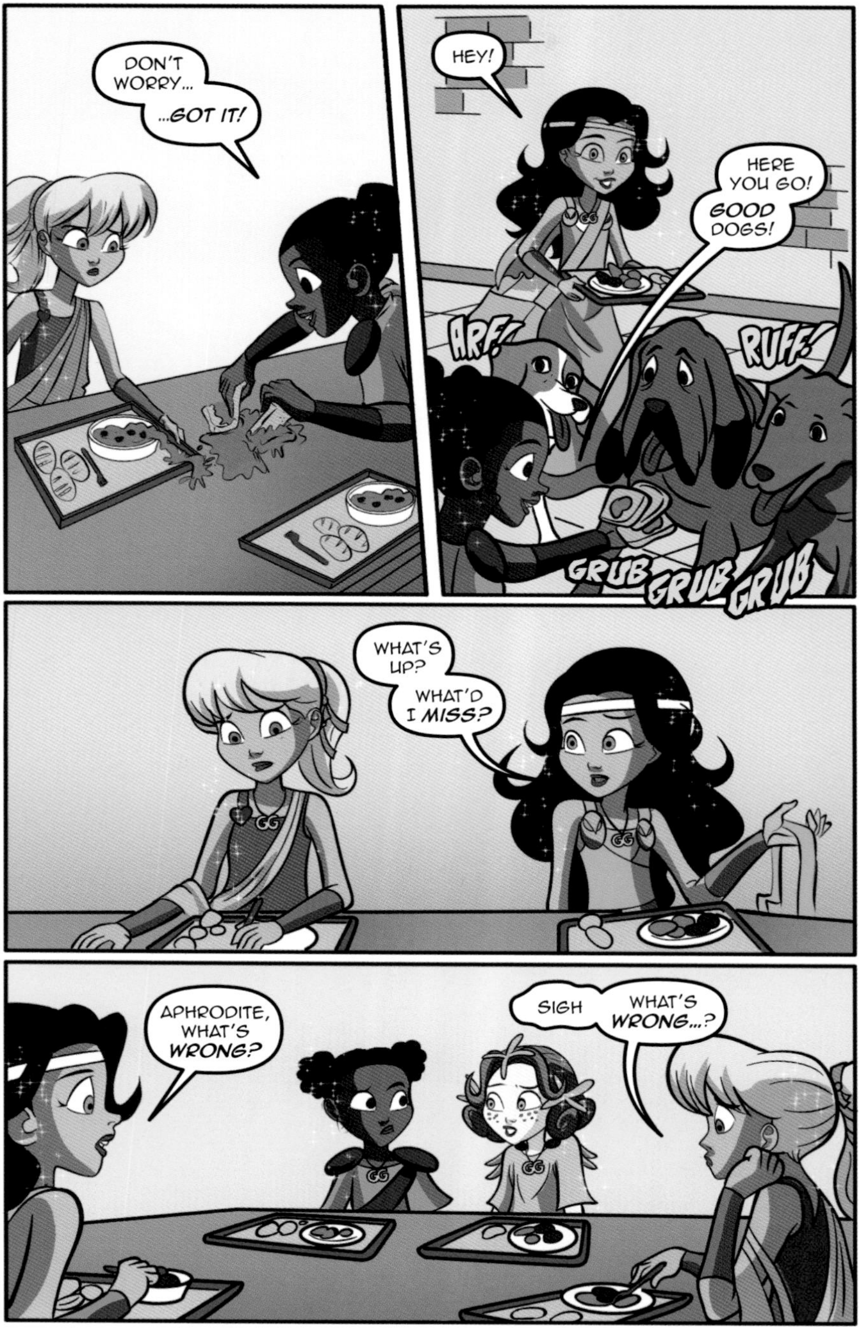
DON'T WORRY...
...GOT IT!
HEY!
HERE YOU GO! GOOD DOGS!
ARF!
RUFF!
GRUB GRUB GRUB
WHAT'S UP?
WHAT'D I MISS?
APHRODITE, WHAT'S WRONG?
SIGH
WHAT'S WRONG...?

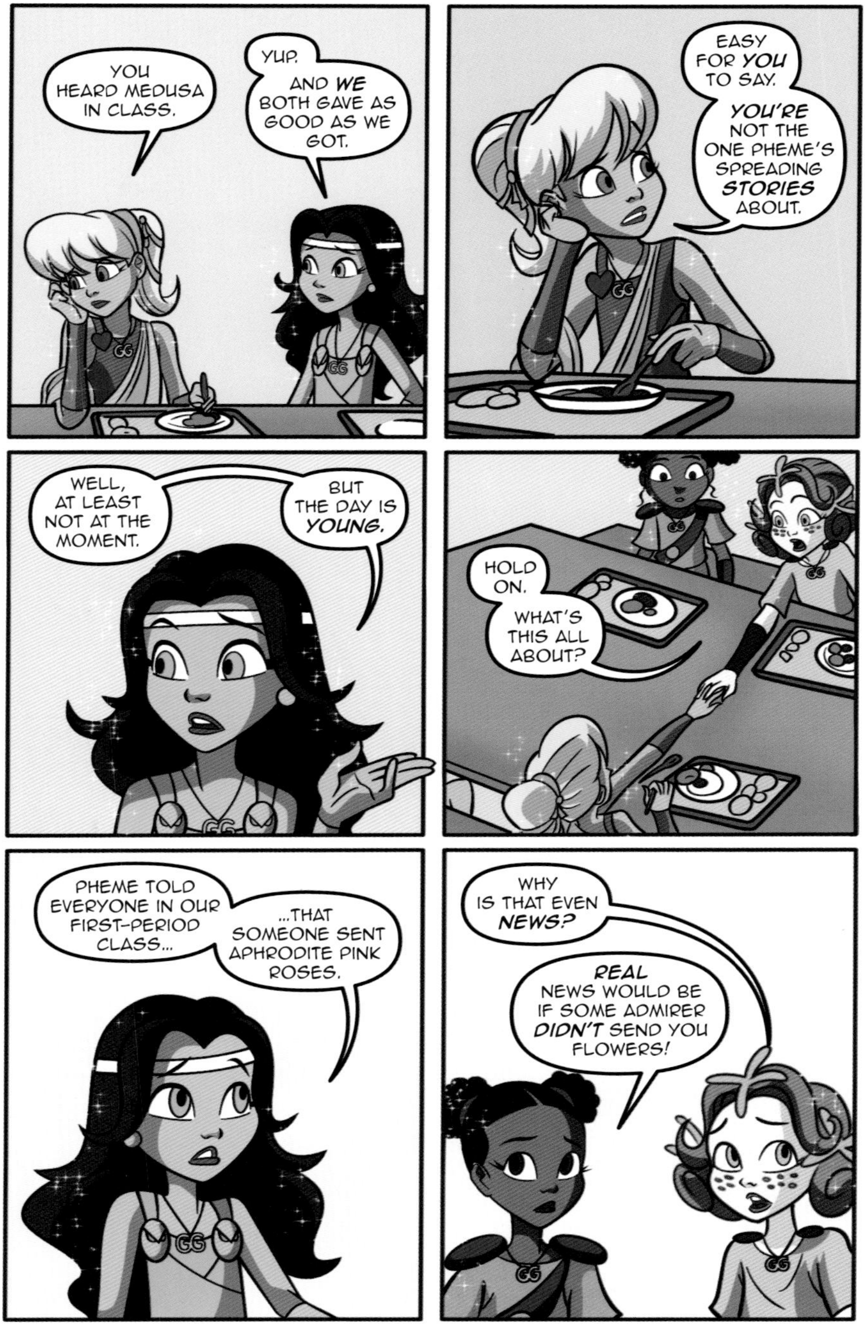
YOU HEARD MEDUSA IN CLASS.
YUP.
AND WE BOTH GAVE AS GOOD AS WE GOT.
EASY FOR YOU TO SAY.
YOU'RE NOT THE ONE PHEME'S SPREADING STORIES ABOUT.
WELL, AT LEAST NOT AT THE MOMENT.
BUT THE DAY IS YOUNG.
HOLD ON.
WHAT'S THIS ALL ABOUT?
PHEME TOLD EVERYONE IN OUR FIRST-PERIOD CLASS...
...THAT SOMEONE SENT APHRODITE PINK ROSES.
WHY IS THAT EVEN NEWS?
REAL NEWS WOULD BE IF SOME ADMIRER DIDN'T SEND YOU FLOWERS!

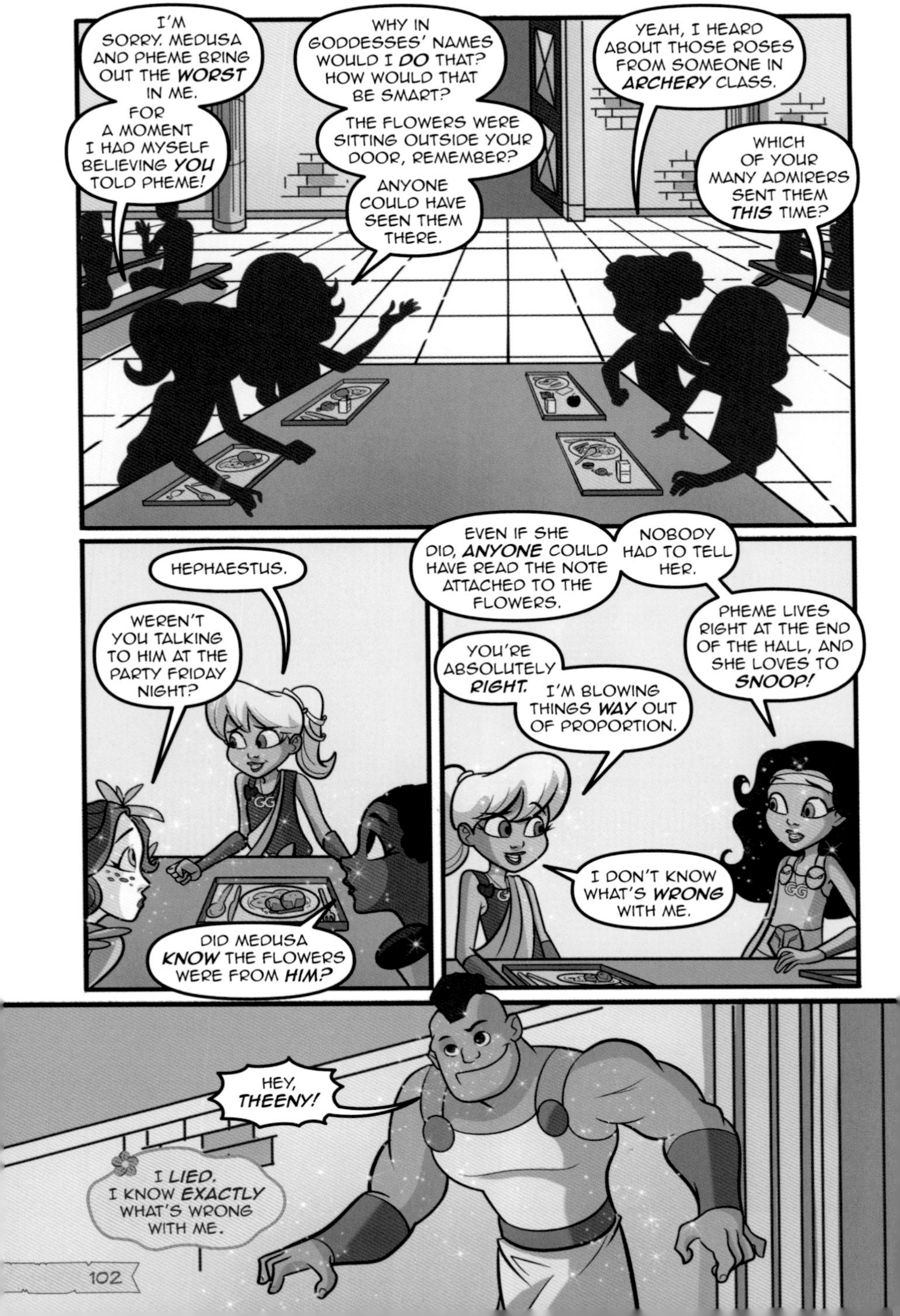
I'M SORRY. MEDUSA AND PHEME BRING OUT THE WORST IN ME.
FOR A MOMENT I HAD MYSELF BELIEVING YOU TOLD PHEME!
WHY IN GODDESSES' NAMES WOULD I DO THAT? HOW WOULD THAT BE SMART?
THE FLOWERS WERE SITTING OUTSIDE YOUR DOOR, REMEMBER?
ANYONE COULD HAVE SEEN THEM THERE.
YEAH, I HEARD ABOUT THOSE ROSES FROM SOMEONE IN ARCHERY CLASS.
WHICH OF YOUR MANY ADMIRERS SENT THEM THIS TIME?
HEPHAESTUS.
WEREN'T YOU TALKING TO HIM AT THE PARTY FRIDAY NIGHT?
DID MEDUSA KNOW THE FLOWERS WERE FROM HIM?
EVEN IF SHE DID, ANYONE COULD HAVE READ THE NOTE ATTACHED TO THE FLOWERS.
NOBODY HAD TO TELL HER.
PHEME LIVES RIGHT AT THE END OF THE HALL, AND SHE LOVES TO SNOOP!
YOU'RE ABSOLUTELY RIGHT.
I'M BLOWING THINGS WAY OUT OF PROPORTION.
I DON'T KNOW WHAT'S WRONG WITH ME.
HEY, THEENY!
I LIED. I KNOW EXACTLY WHAT'S WRONG WITH ME.

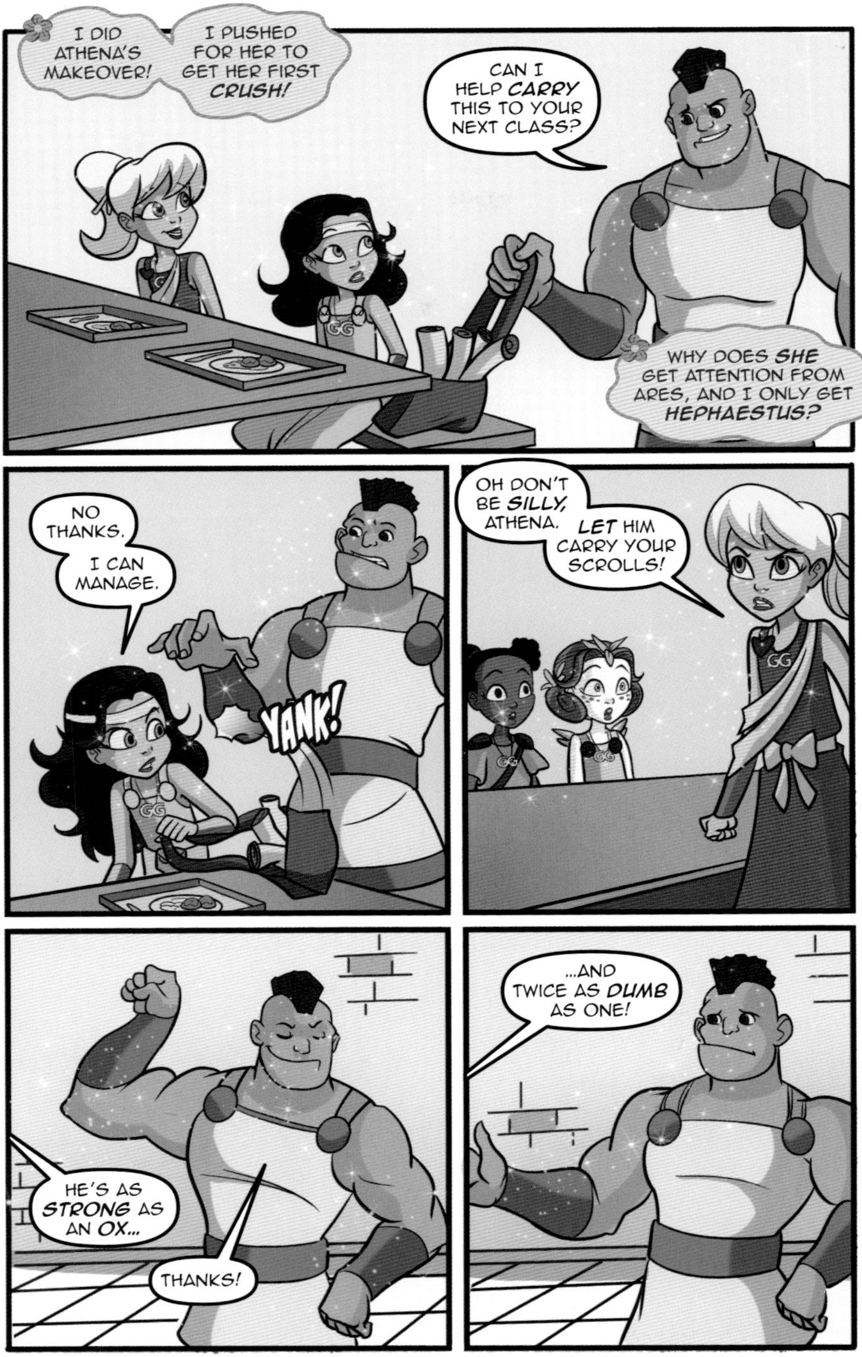

I DID ATHENA'S MAKEOVER!
I PUSHED FOR HER TO GET HER FIRST CRUSH!
CAN I HELP CARRY THIS TO YOUR NEXT CLASS?
WHY DOES SHE GET ATTENTION FROM ARES, AND I ONLY GET HEPHAESTUS?
NO THANKS.
I CAN MANAGE.
YANK!
OH DON'T BE SILLY, ATHENA.
LET HIM CARRY YOUR SCROLLS!
HE'S AS STRONG AS AN OX...
THANKS!
...AND TWICE AS DUMB AS ONE!

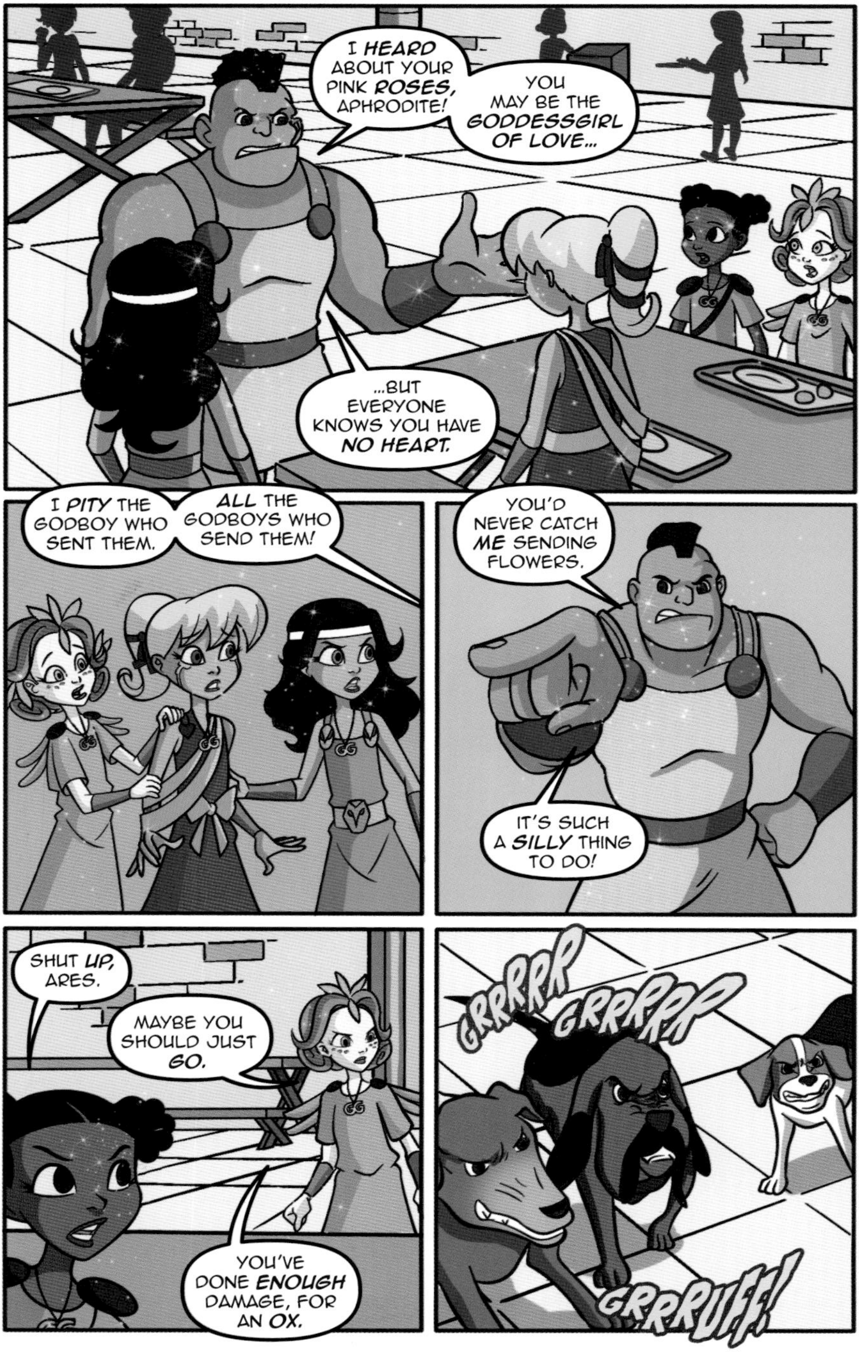
I HEARD ABOUT YOUR PINK ROSES, APHRODITE!
YOU MAY BE THE GODDESSGIRL OF LOVE...
...BUT EVERYONE KNOWS YOU HAVE NO HEART.
I PITY THE GODBOY WHO SENT THEM.
ALL THE GODBOYS WHO SEND THEM!
YOU'D NEVER CATCH ME SENDING FLOWERS.
IT'S SUCH A SILLY THING TO DO!
SHUT UP, ARES.
MAYBE YOU SHOULD JUST GO.
YOU'VE DONE ENOUGH DAMAGE, FOR AN OX.
GRRRRR
GRRRRRR
GRRRUFF!

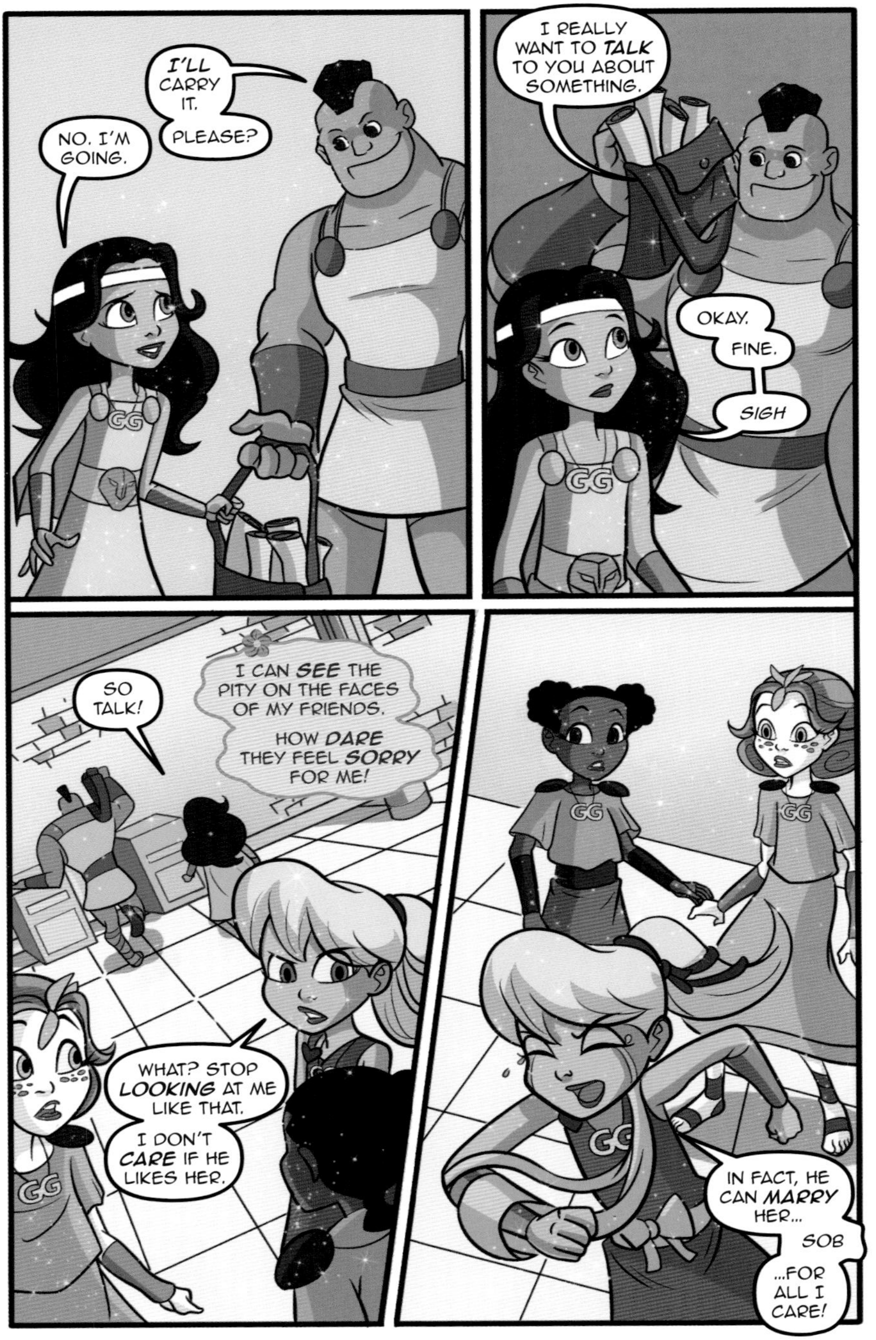

NO. I'M GOING.
I'LL CARRY IT.
PLEASE?
I REALLY WANT TO TALK TO YOU ABOUT SOMETHING.
OKAY.
FINE.
SIGH
SO TALK!
I CAN SEE THE PITY ON THE FACES OF MY FRIENDS.
HOW DARE THEY FEEL SORRY FOR ME!
WHAT? STOP LOOKING AT ME LIKE THAT.
I DON'T CARE IF HE LIKES HER.
IN FACT, HE CAN MARRY HER...
SOB
...FOR ALL I CARE!

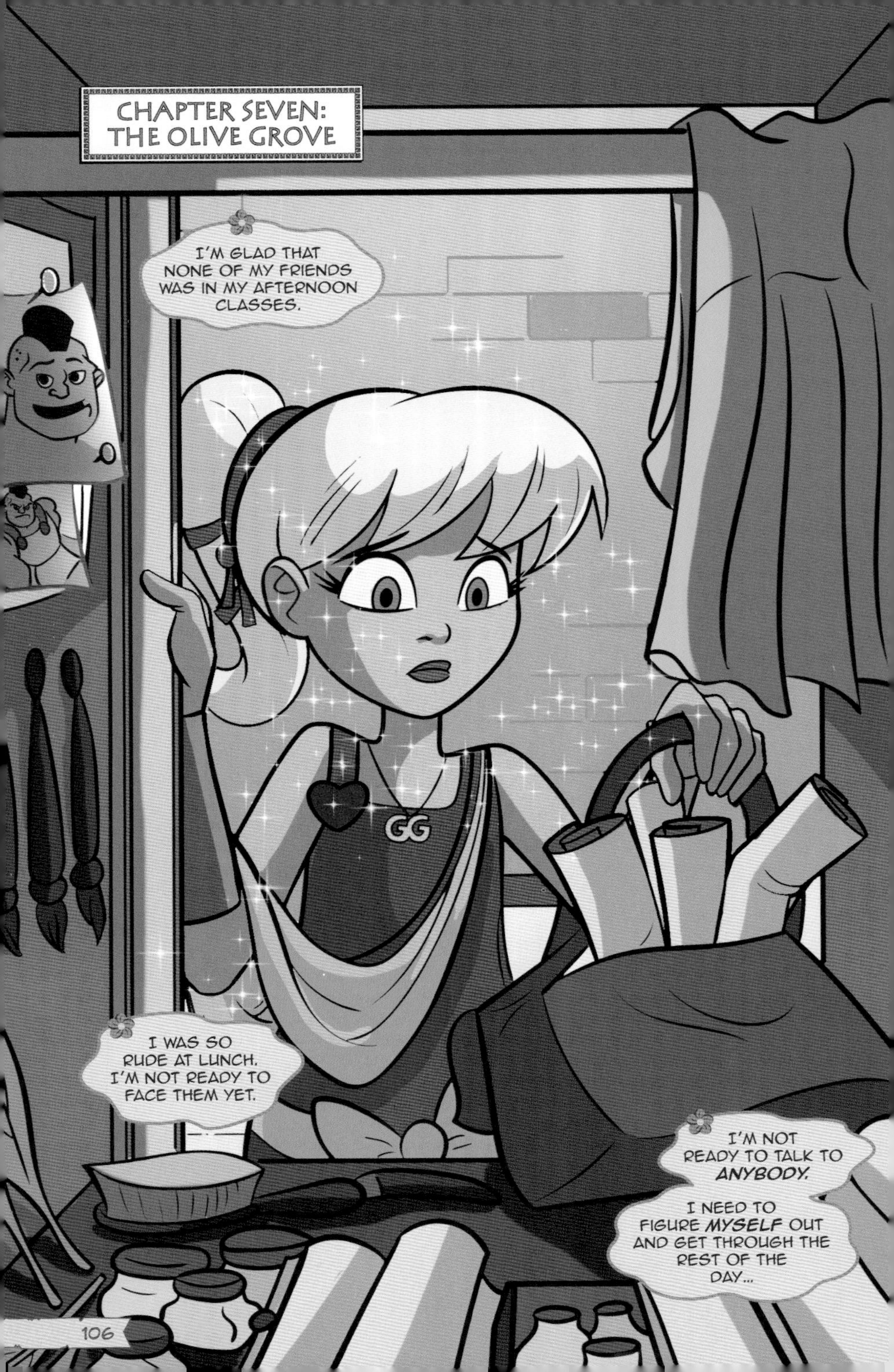
CHAPTER SEVEN:
THE OLIVE GROVE
I'M GLAD THAT NONE OF MY FRIENDS WAS IN MY AFTERNOON CLASSES.
GG
I WAS SO RUDE AT LUNCH. I'M NOT READY TO FACE THEM YET.
I'M NOT READY TO TALK TO *ANYBODY.*
I NEED TO FIGURE *MYSELF* OUT AND GET THROUGH THE REST OF THE DAY...

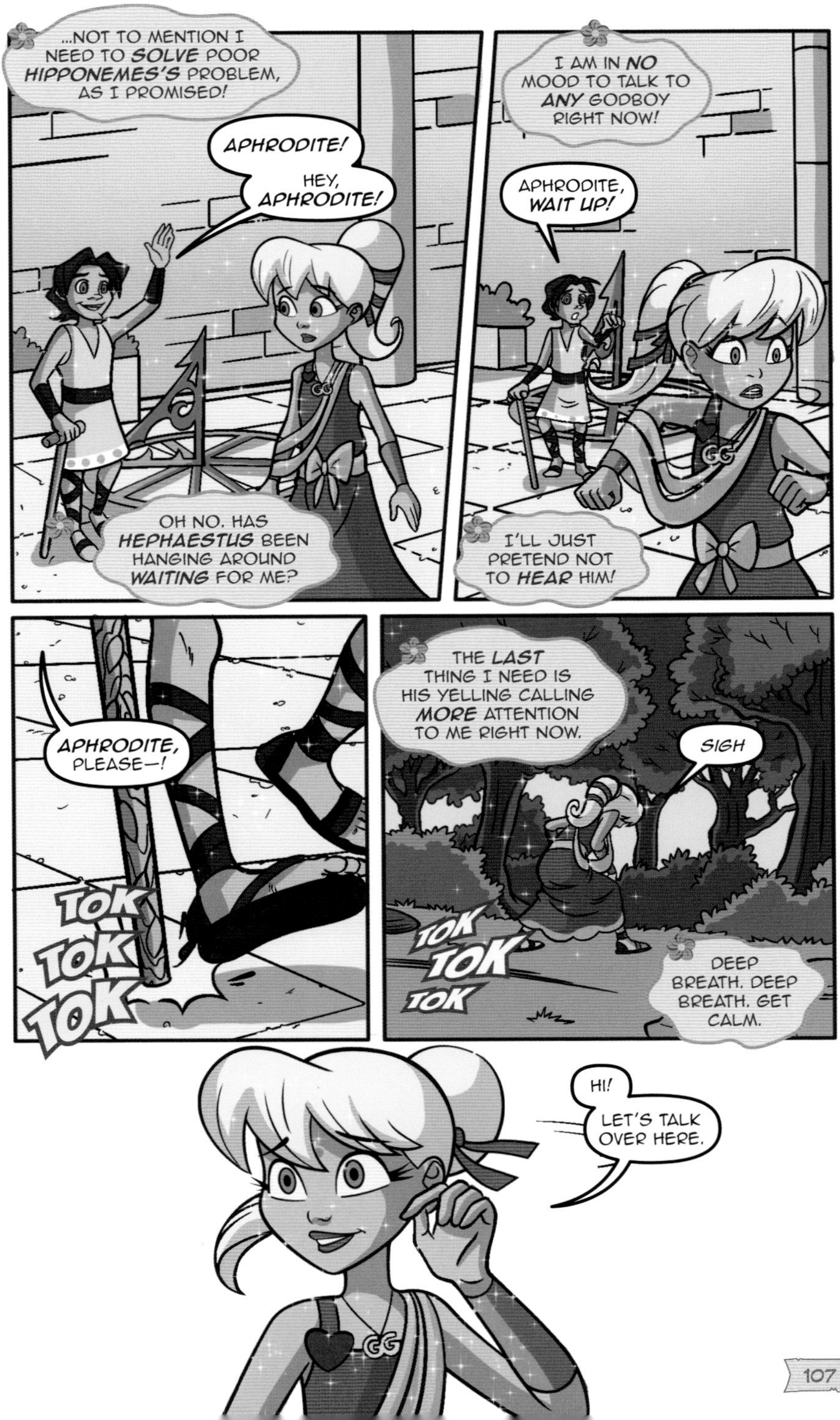

...NOT TO MENTION I NEED TO SOLVE POOR HIPPONEMES'S PROBLEM, AS I PROMISED!
APHRODITE!
HEY, APHRODITE!
OH NO. HAS HEPHAESTUS BEEN HANGING AROUND WAITING FOR ME?
I AM IN NO MOOD TO TALK TO ANY GODBOY RIGHT NOW!
APHRODITE, WAIT UP!
I'LL JUST PRETEND NOT TO HEAR HIM!
APHRODITE, PLEASE—!
TOK
TOK
TOK
THE LAST THING I NEED IS HIS YELLING CALLING MORE ATTENTION TO ME RIGHT NOW.
SIGH
TOK
TOK
TOK
DEEP BREATH. DEEP BREATH. GET CALM.
HI!
LET'S TALK OVER HERE.

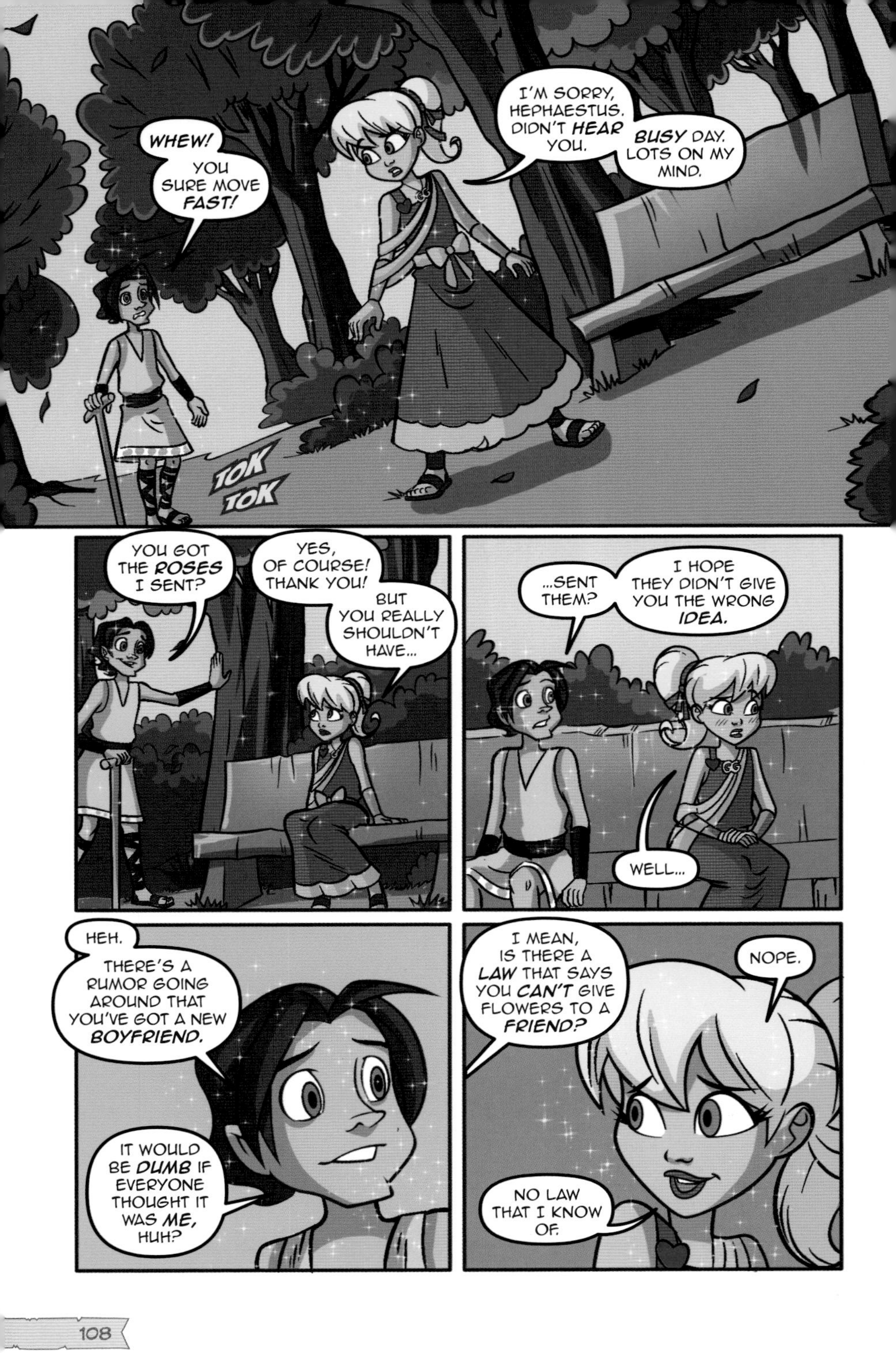
WHEW! YOU SURE MOVE FAST!
I'M SORRY, HEPHAESTUS. DIDN'T HEAR YOU.
BUSY DAY. LOTS ON MY MIND.
TOK TOK
YOU GOT THE ROSES I SENT?
YES, OF COURSE! THANK YOU!
BUT YOU REALLY SHOULDN'T HAVE...
...SENT THEM?
I HOPE THEY DIDN'T GIVE YOU THE WRONG IDEA.
WELL...
HEH.
THERE'S A RUMOR GOING AROUND THAT YOU'VE GOT A NEW BOYFRIEND.
IT WOULD BE DUMB IF EVERYONE THOUGHT IT WAS ME, HUH?
I MEAN, IS THERE A LAW THAT SAYS YOU CAN'T GIVE FLOWERS TO A FRIEND?
NOPE.
NO LAW THAT I KNOW OF.

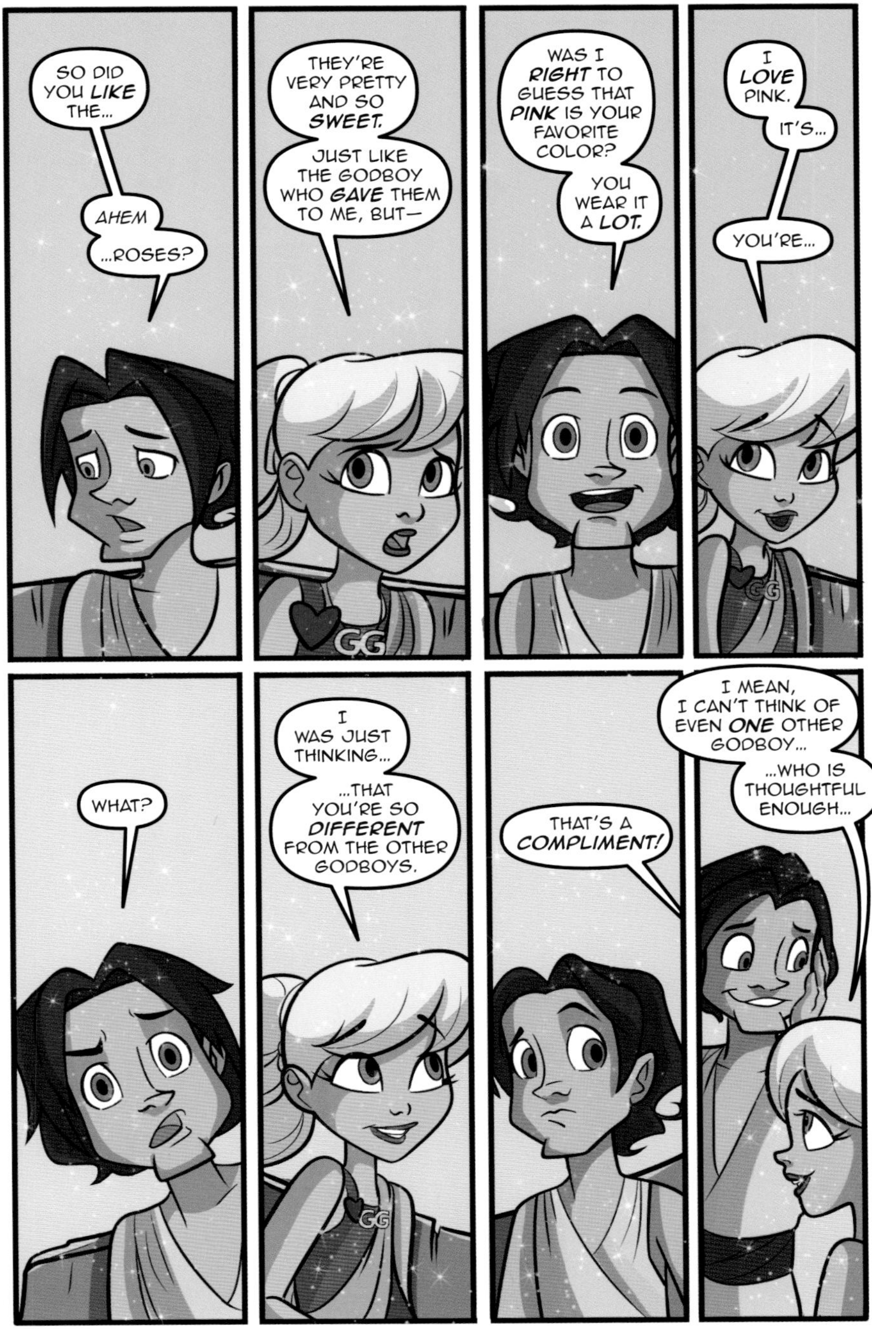

SO DID YOU LIKE THE...
AHEM
...ROSES?
THEY'RE VERY PRETTY AND SO SWEET.
JUST LIKE THE GODBOY WHO GAVE THEM TO ME, BUT—
WAS I RIGHT TO GUESS THAT PINK IS YOUR FAVORITE COLOR?
YOU WEAR IT A LOT.
I LOVE PINK.
IT'S...
YOU'RE...
WHAT?
I WAS JUST THINKING...
...THAT YOU'RE SO DIFFERENT FROM THE OTHER GODBOYS.
THAT'S A COMPLIMENT!
I MEAN, I CAN'T THINK OF EVEN ONE OTHER GODBOY...
...WHO IS THOUGHTFUL ENOUGH...

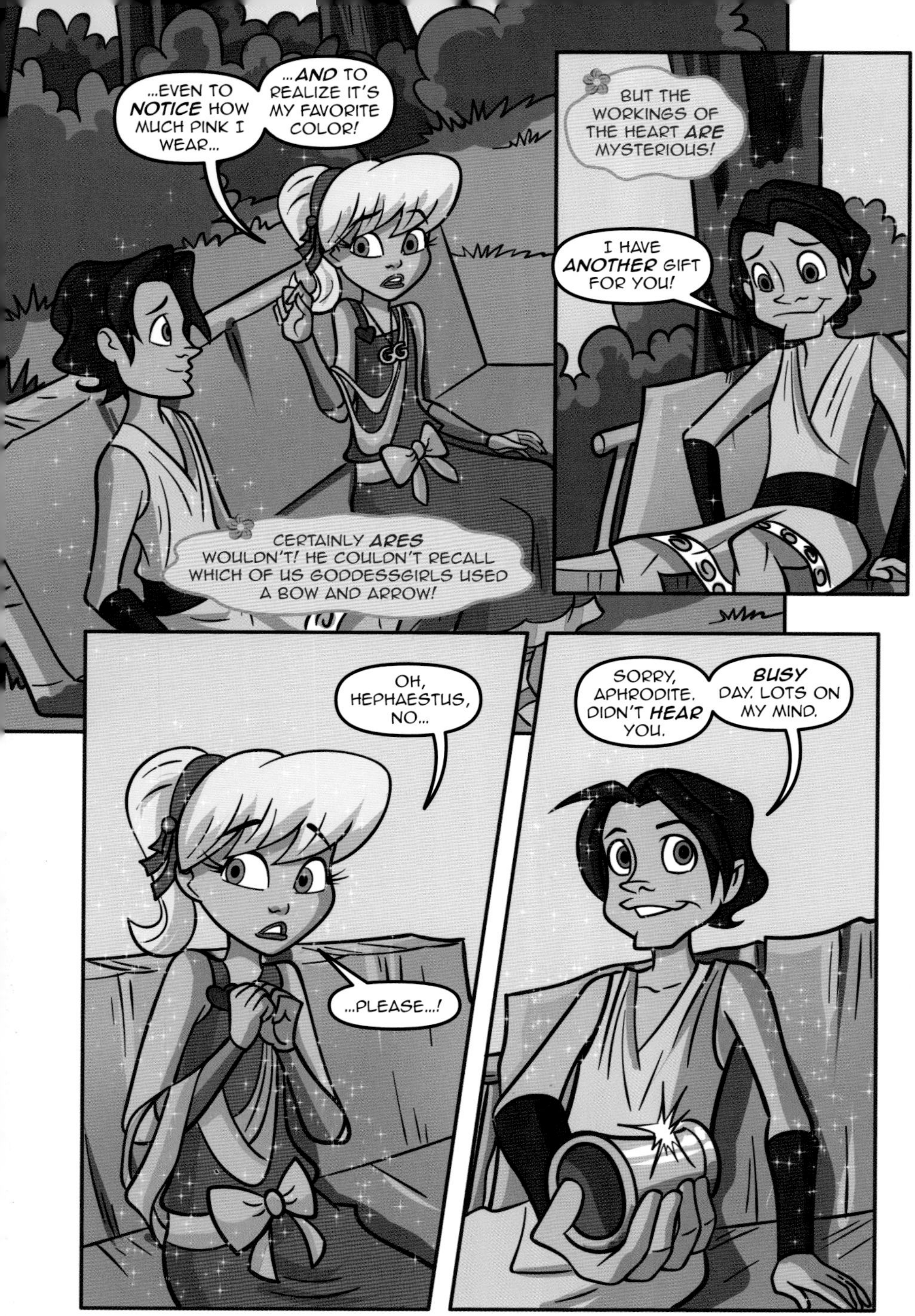
...EVEN TO NOTICE HOW MUCH PINK I WEAR...
...AND TO REALIZE IT'S MY FAVORITE COLOR!
CERTAINLY ARES WOULDN'T! HE COULDN'T RECALL WHICH OF US GODDESSGIRLS USED A BOW AND ARROW!
BUT THE WORKINGS OF THE HEART ARE MYSTERIOUS!
I HAVE ANOTHER GIFT FOR YOU!
OH, HEPHAESTUS, NO...
...PLEASE...!
SORRY, APHRODITE. DIDN'T HEAR YOU.
BUSY DAY. LOTS ON MY MIND.

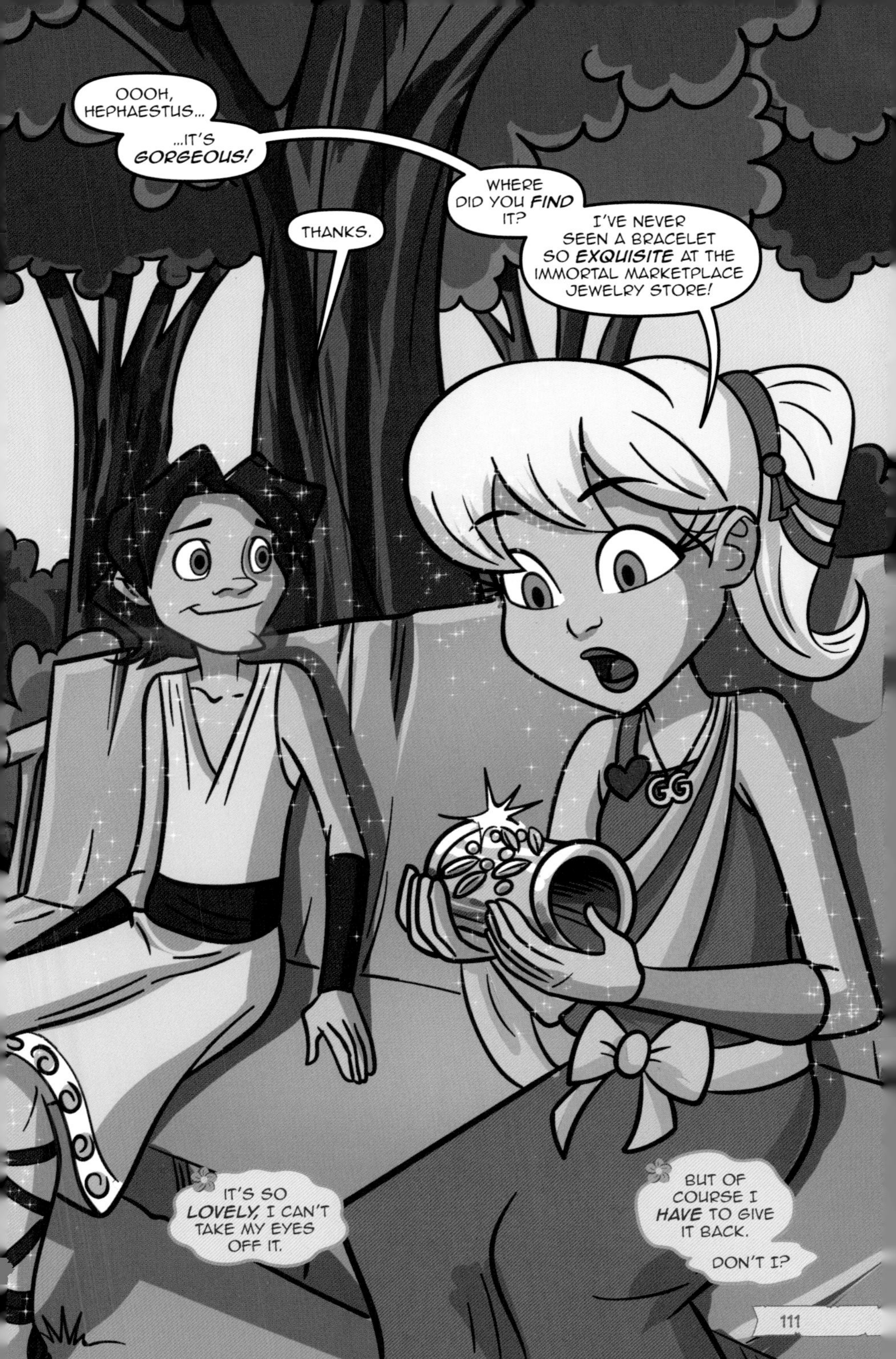
OOOH, HEPHAESTUS...
...IT'S GORGEOUS!
WHERE DID YOU FIND IT?
THANKS.
I'VE NEVER SEEN A BRACELET SO EXQUISITE AT THE IMMORTAL MARKETPLACE JEWELRY STORE!
GG
IT'S SO LOVELY, I CAN'T TAKE MY EYES OFF IT.
BUT OF COURSE I HAVE TO GIVE IT BACK.
DON'T I?

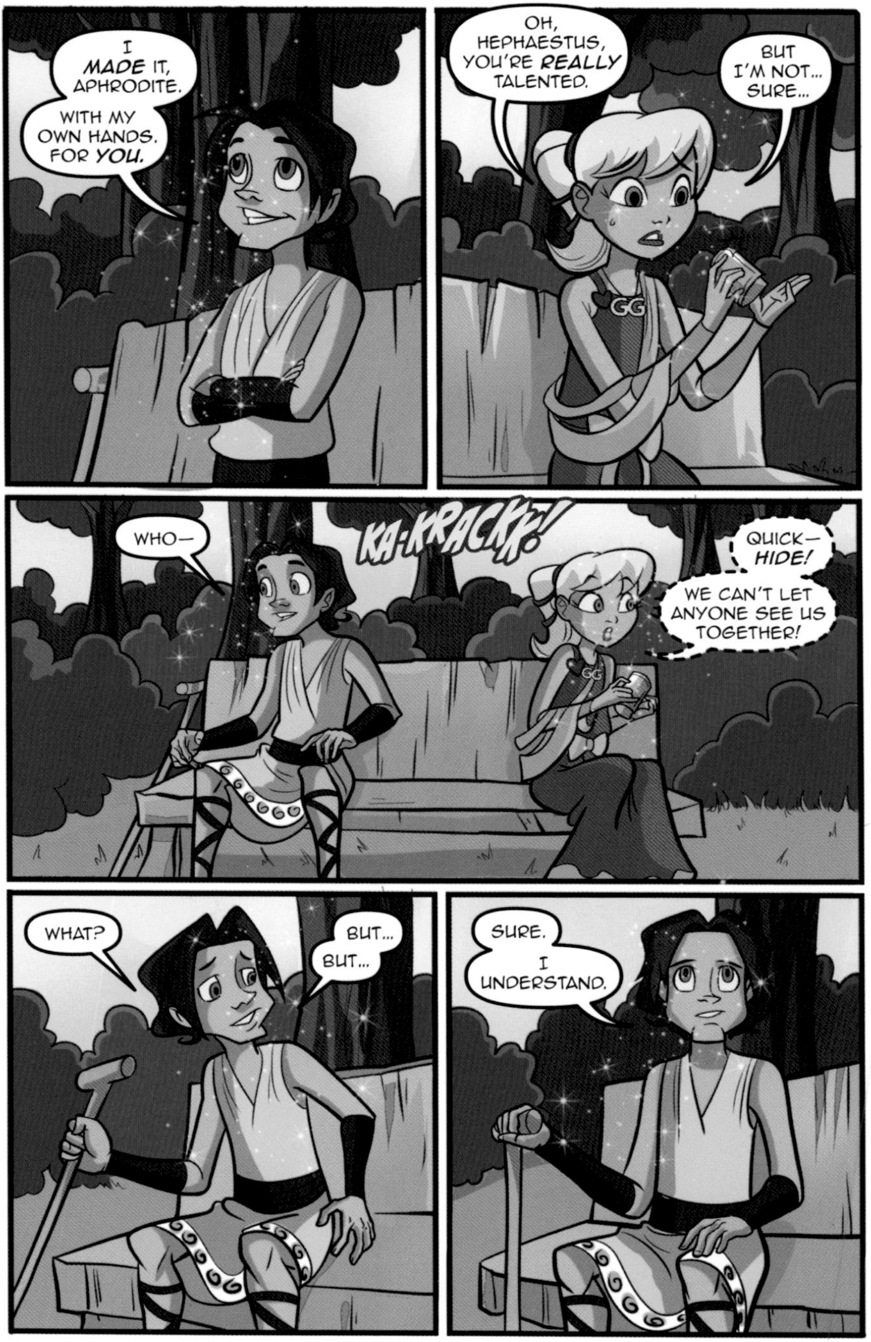

I MADE IT, APHRODITE.
WITH MY OWN HANDS. FOR YOU.
OH, HEPHAESTUS, YOU'RE REALLY TALENTED.
BUT I'M NOT... SURE...
WHO—
KA-KRACKK!
QUICK— HIDE!
WE CAN'T LET ANYONE SEE US TOGETHER!
WHAT?
BUT... BUT...
SURE.
I UNDERSTAND.

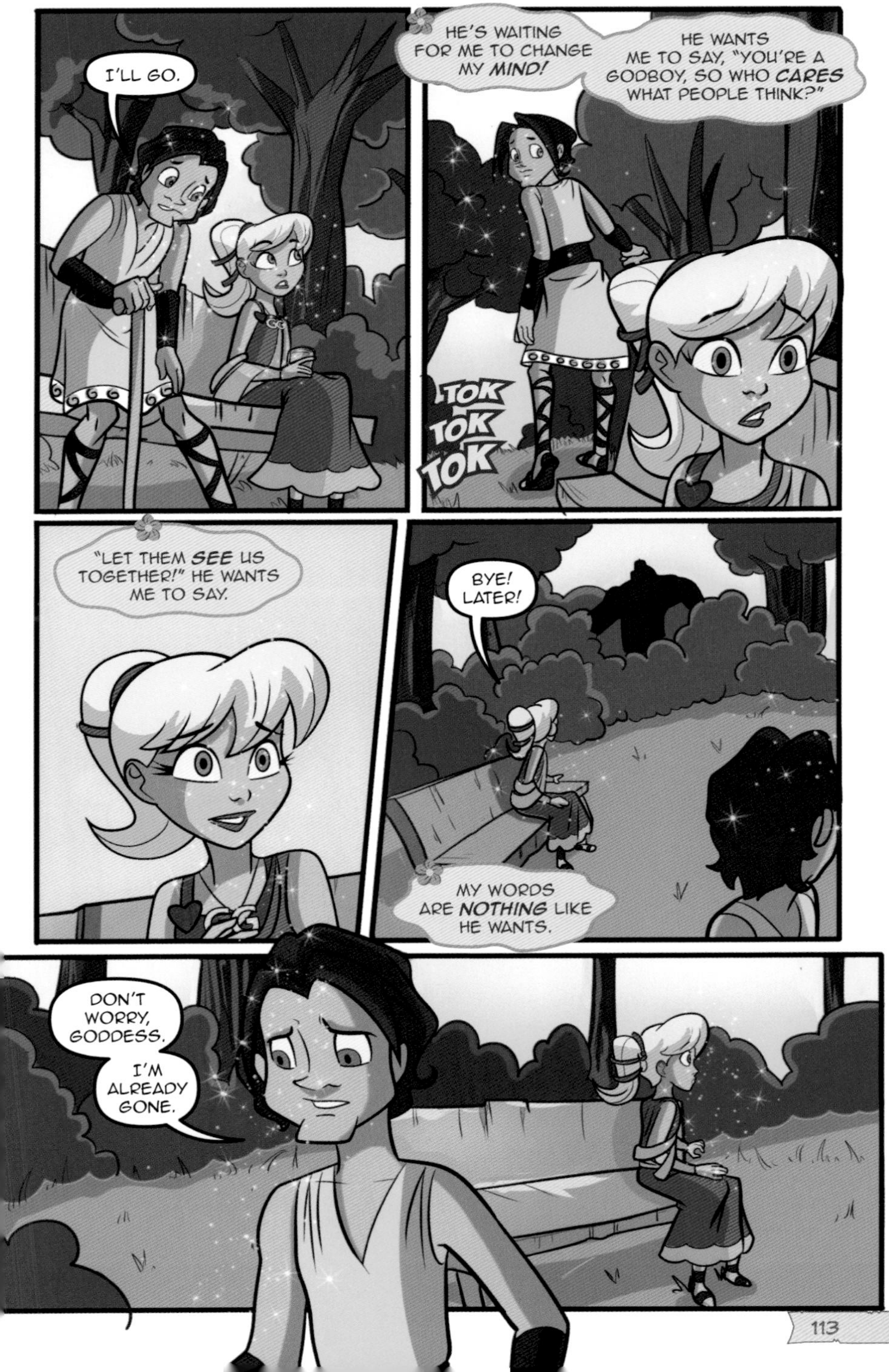
I'LL GO.
HE'S WAITING FOR ME TO CHANGE MY *MIND!*
HE WANTS ME TO SAY, "YOU'RE A GODBOY, SO WHO *CARES* WHAT PEOPLE THINK?"
TOK TOK TOK
"LET THEM *SEE* US TOGETHER!" HE WANTS ME TO SAY.
BYE! LATER!
MY WORDS ARE *NOTHING* LIKE HE WANTS.
DON'T WORRY, GODDESS.
I'M ALREADY GONE.

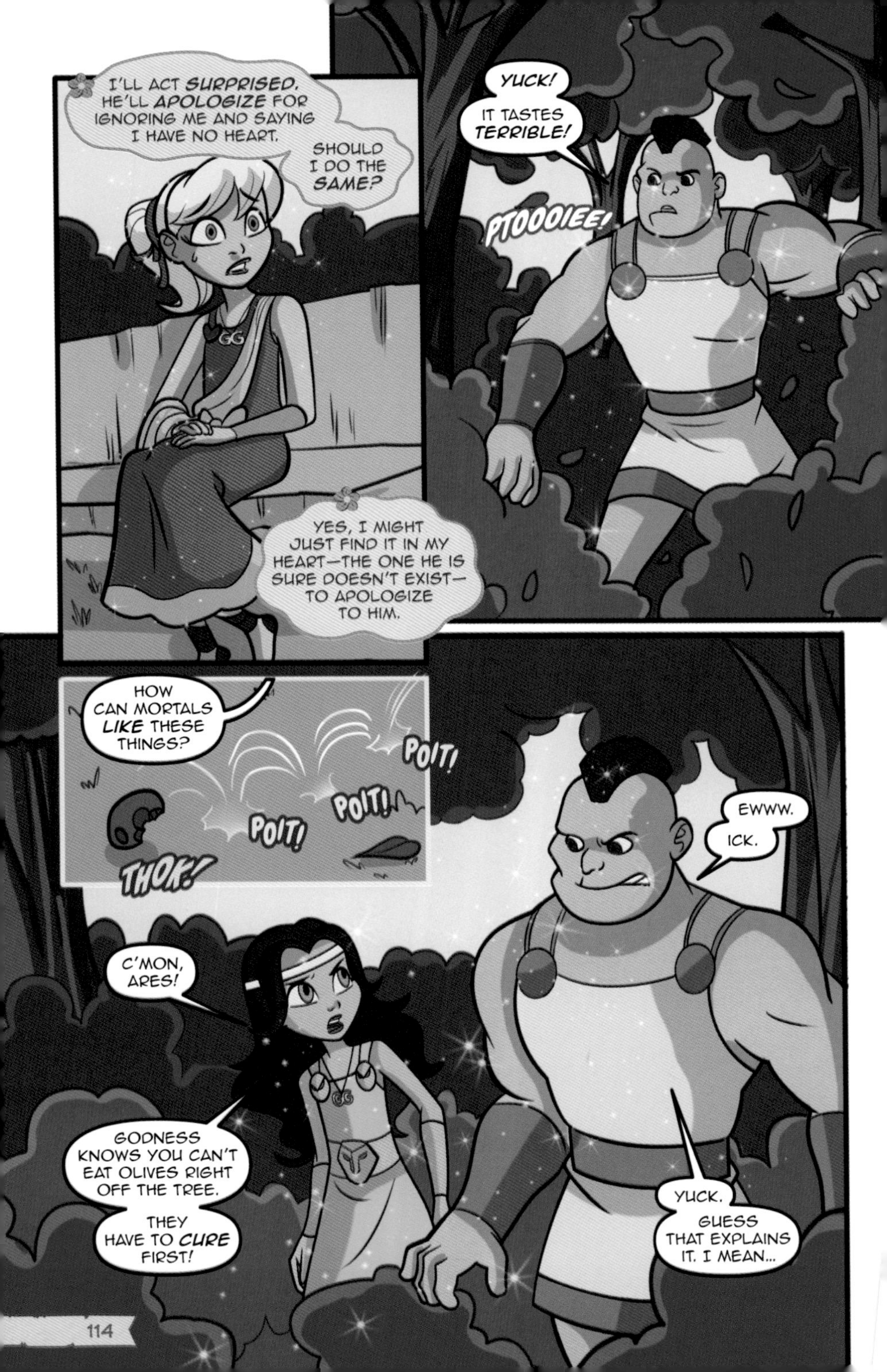
I'LL ACT SURPRISED. HE'LL APOLOGIZE FOR IGNORING ME AND SAYING I HAVE NO HEART.
SHOULD I DO THE SAME?
YES, I MIGHT JUST FIND IT IN MY HEART—THE ONE HE IS SURE DOESN'T EXIST—TO APOLOGIZE TO HIM.
YUCK!
IT TASTES TERRIBLE!
PTOOOIEE!
HOW CAN MORTALS LIKE THESE THINGS?
POIT!
POIT!
POIT!
THOK!
EWWW.
ICK.
C'MON, ARES!
GODNESS KNOWS YOU CAN'T EAT OLIVES RIGHT OFF THE TREE.
THEY HAVE TO CURE FIRST!
YUCK.
GUESS THAT EXPLAINS IT. I MEAN...

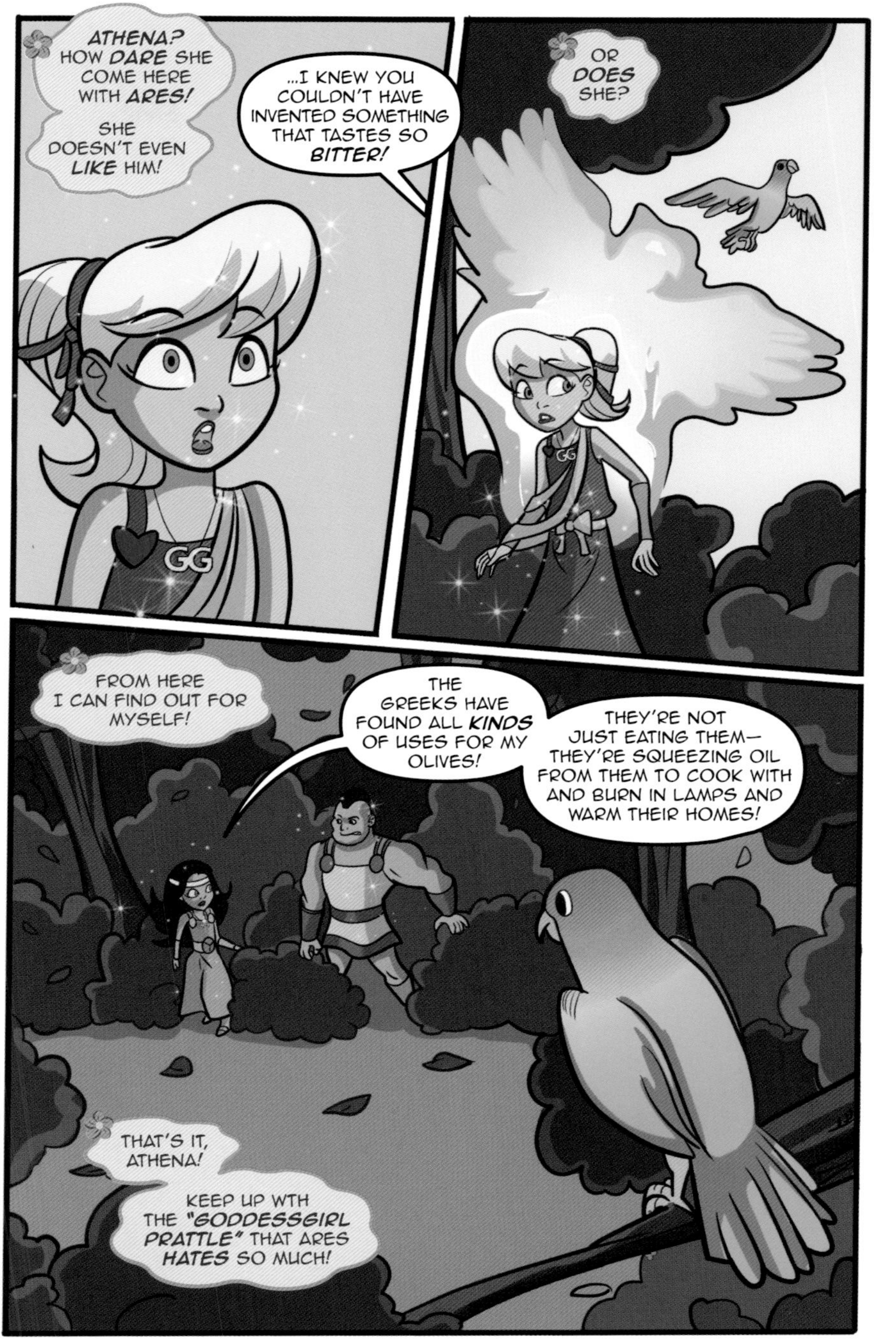
ATHENA? HOW DARE SHE COME HERE WITH ARES!
SHE DOESN'T EVEN LIKE HIM!
...I KNEW YOU COULDN'T HAVE INVENTED SOMETHING THAT TASTES SO BITTER!
OR DOES SHE?
FROM HERE I CAN FIND OUT FOR MYSELF!
THE GREEKS HAVE FOUND ALL KINDS OF USES FOR MY OLIVES!
THEY'RE NOT JUST EATING THEM—THEY'RE SQUEEZING OIL FROM THEM TO COOK WITH AND BURN IN LAMPS AND WARM THEIR HOMES!
THAT'S IT, ATHENA!
KEEP UP WTH THE "GODDESSGIRL PRATTLE" THAT ARES HATES SO MUCH!

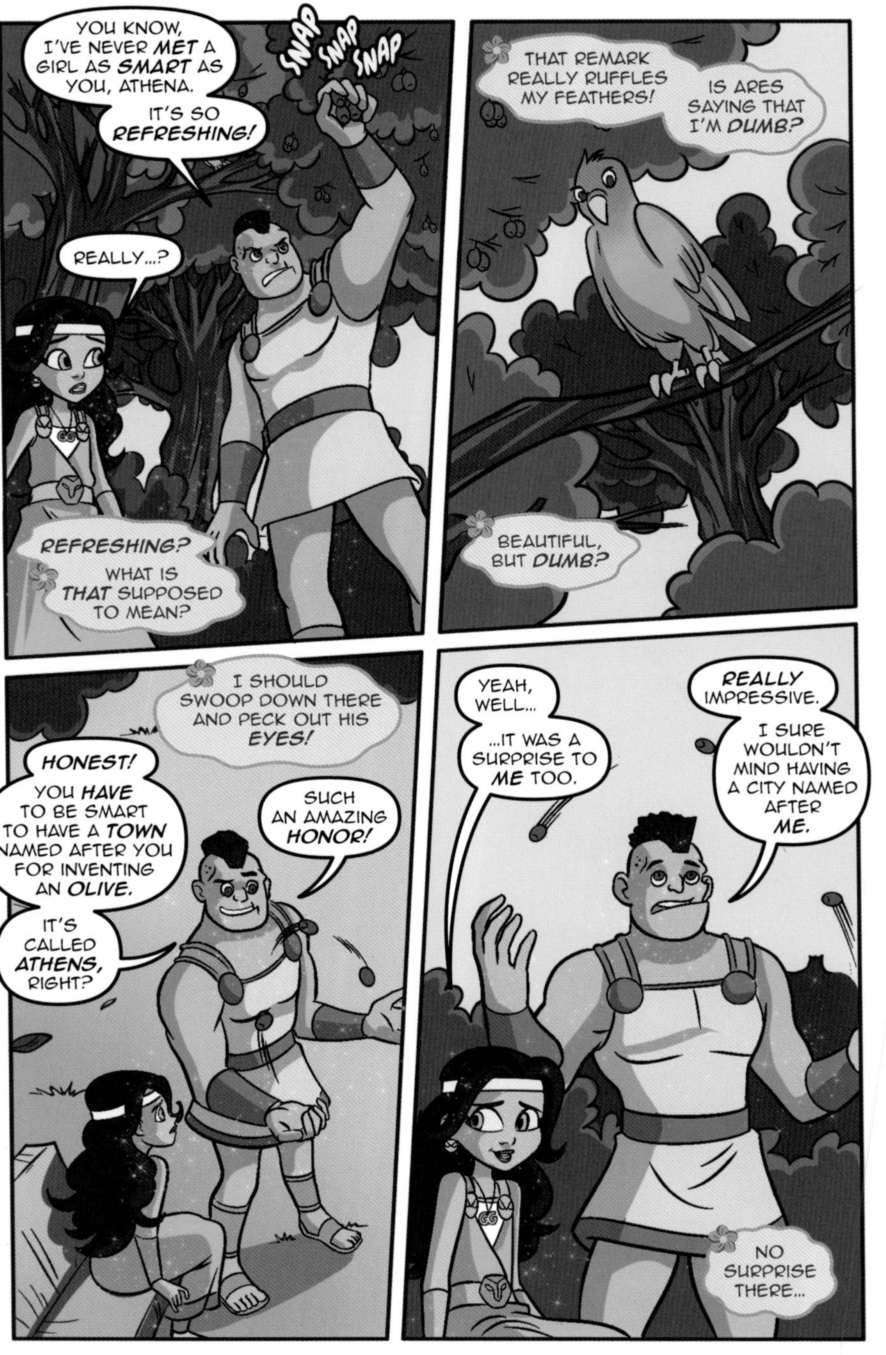
YOU KNOW, I'VE NEVER MET A GIRL AS SMART AS YOU, ATHENA.
IT'S SO REFRESHING!
SNAP SNAP SNAP
REALLY...?
REFRESHING? WHAT IS THAT SUPPOSED TO MEAN?
THAT REMARK REALLY RUFFLES MY FEATHERS!
IS ARES SAYING THAT I'M DUMB?
BEAUTIFUL, BUT DUMB?
I SHOULD SWOOP DOWN THERE AND PECK OUT HIS EYES!
HONEST!
YOU HAVE TO BE SMART TO HAVE A TOWN NAMED AFTER YOU FOR INVENTING AN OLIVE.
SUCH AN AMAZING HONOR!
IT'S CALLED ATHENS, RIGHT?
YEAH, WELL...
...IT WAS A SURPRISE TO ME TOO.
REALLY IMPRESSIVE.
I SURE WOULDN'T MIND HAVING A CITY NAMED AFTER ME.
NO SURPRISE THERE...

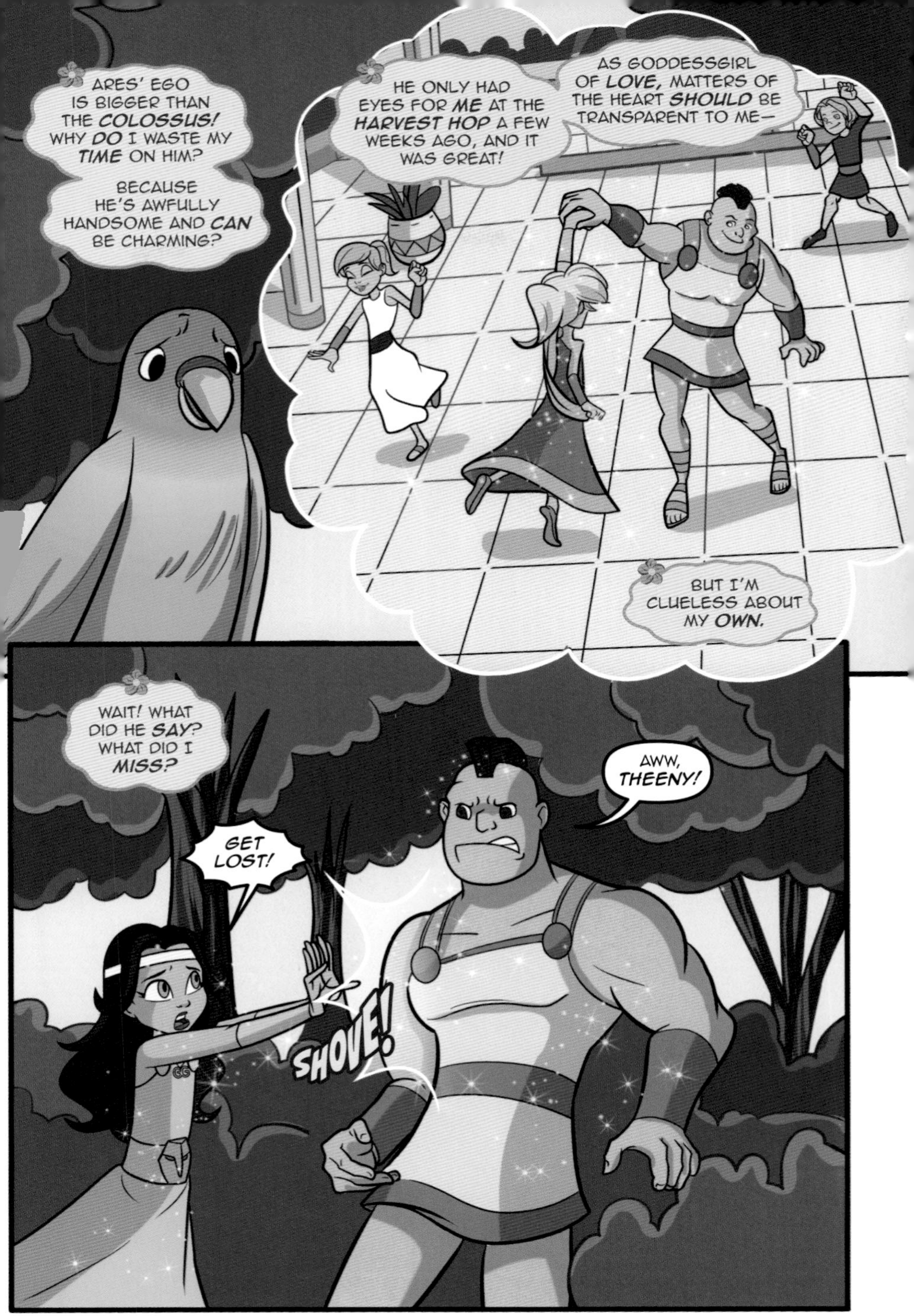
ARES' EGO IS BIGGER THAN THE COLOSSUS! WHY DO I WASTE MY TIME ON HIM?
BECAUSE HE'S AWFULLY HANDSOME AND CAN BE CHARMING?
HE ONLY HAD EYES FOR ME AT THE HARVEST HOP A FEW WEEKS AGO, AND IT WAS GREAT!
AS GODDESSGIRL OF LOVE, MATTERS OF THE HEART SHOULD BE TRANSPARENT TO ME—
BUT I'M CLUELESS ABOUT MY OWN.
WAIT! WHAT DID HE SAY? WHAT DID I MISS?
AWW, THEENY!
GET LOST!
SHOVE!

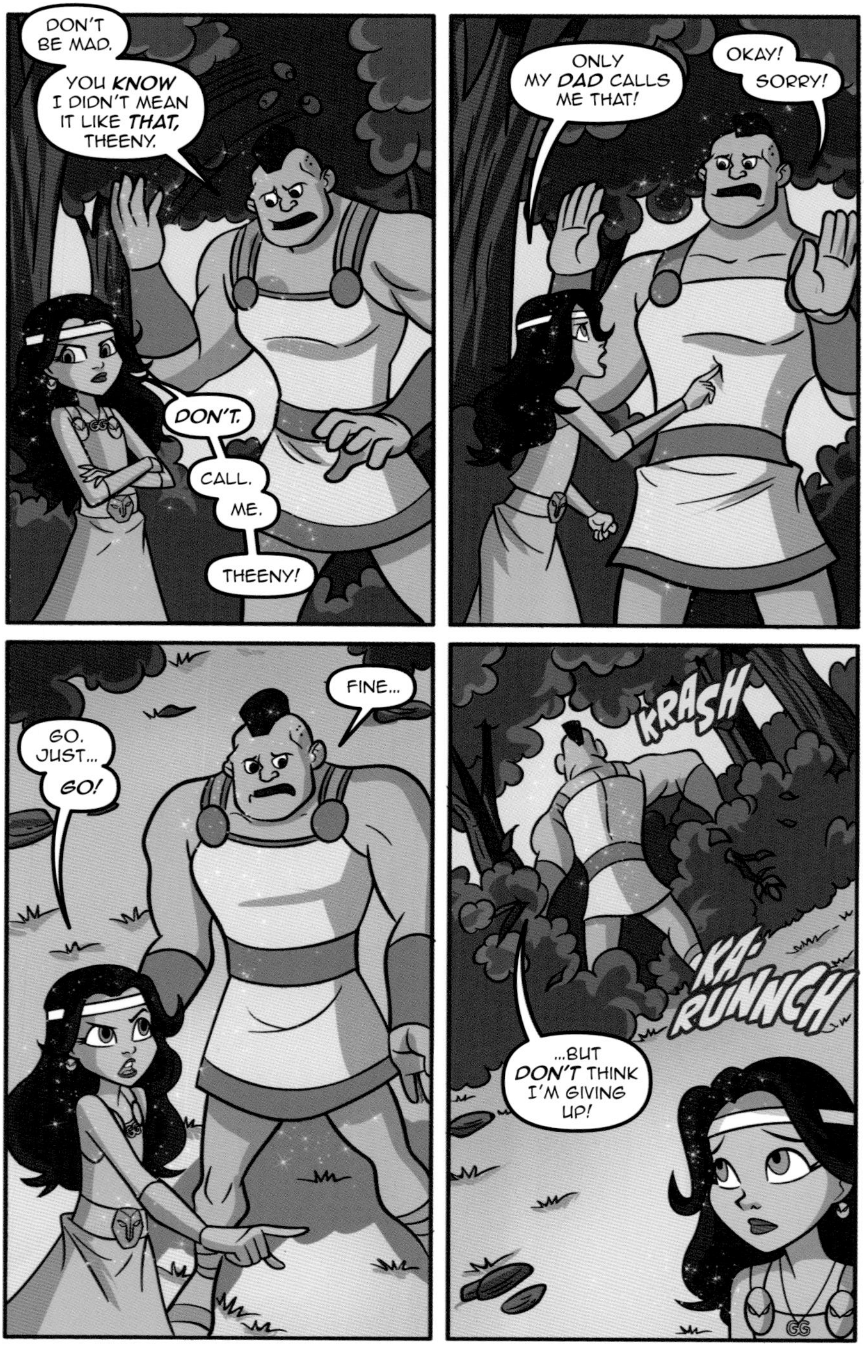
DON'T BE MAD.
YOU KNOW I DIDN'T MEAN IT LIKE THAT, THEENY.
DON'T.
CALL.
ME.
THEENY!
ONLY MY DAD CALLS ME THAT!
OKAY!
SORRY!
GO. JUST... GO!
FINE...
KRASH
KA-RUNNCH
...BUT DON'T THINK I'M GIVING UP!

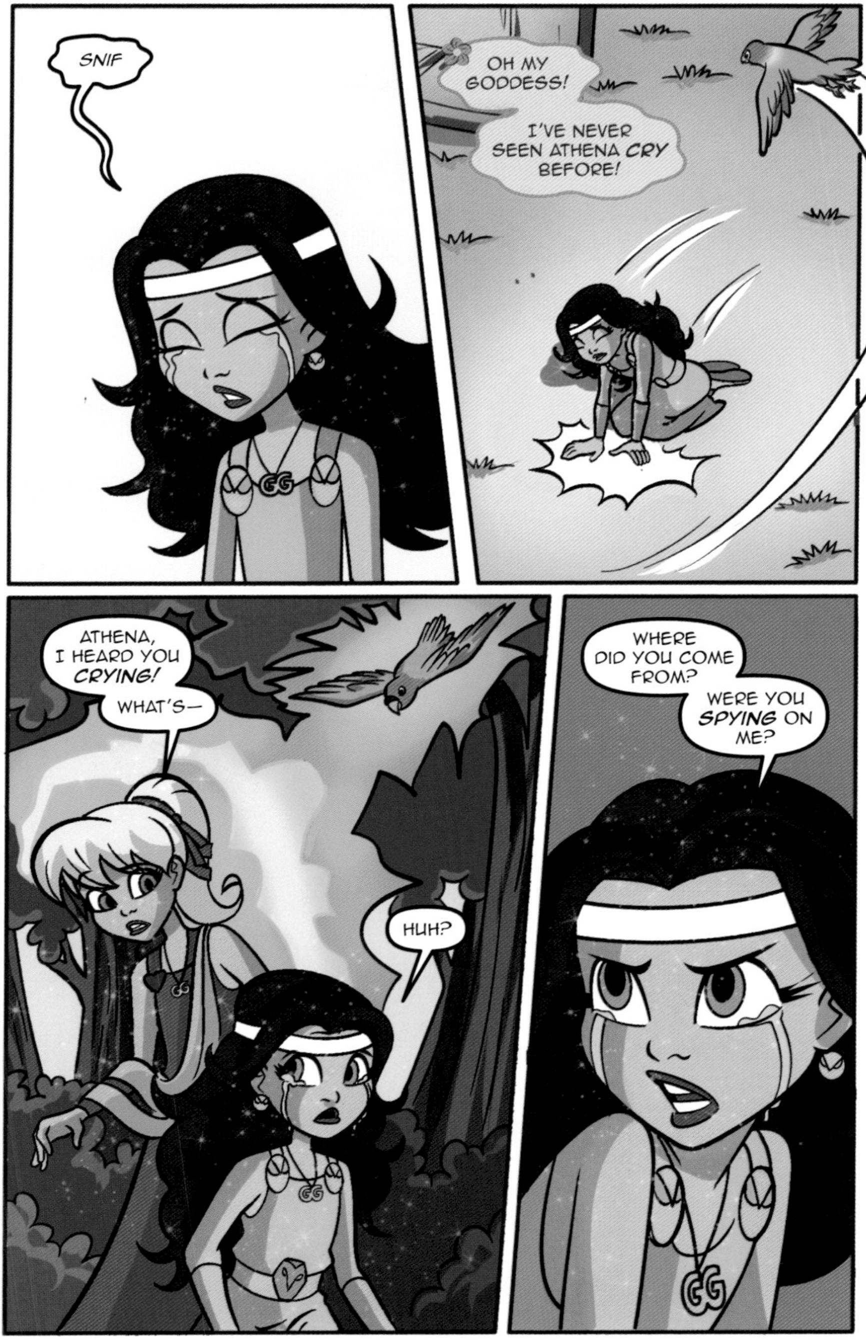
SNIF
OH MY GODDESS!
I'VE NEVER SEEN ATHENA CRY BEFORE!
ATHENA, I HEARD YOU CRYING!
WHAT'S—
HUH?
WHERE DID YOU COME FROM?
WERE YOU SPYING ON ME?

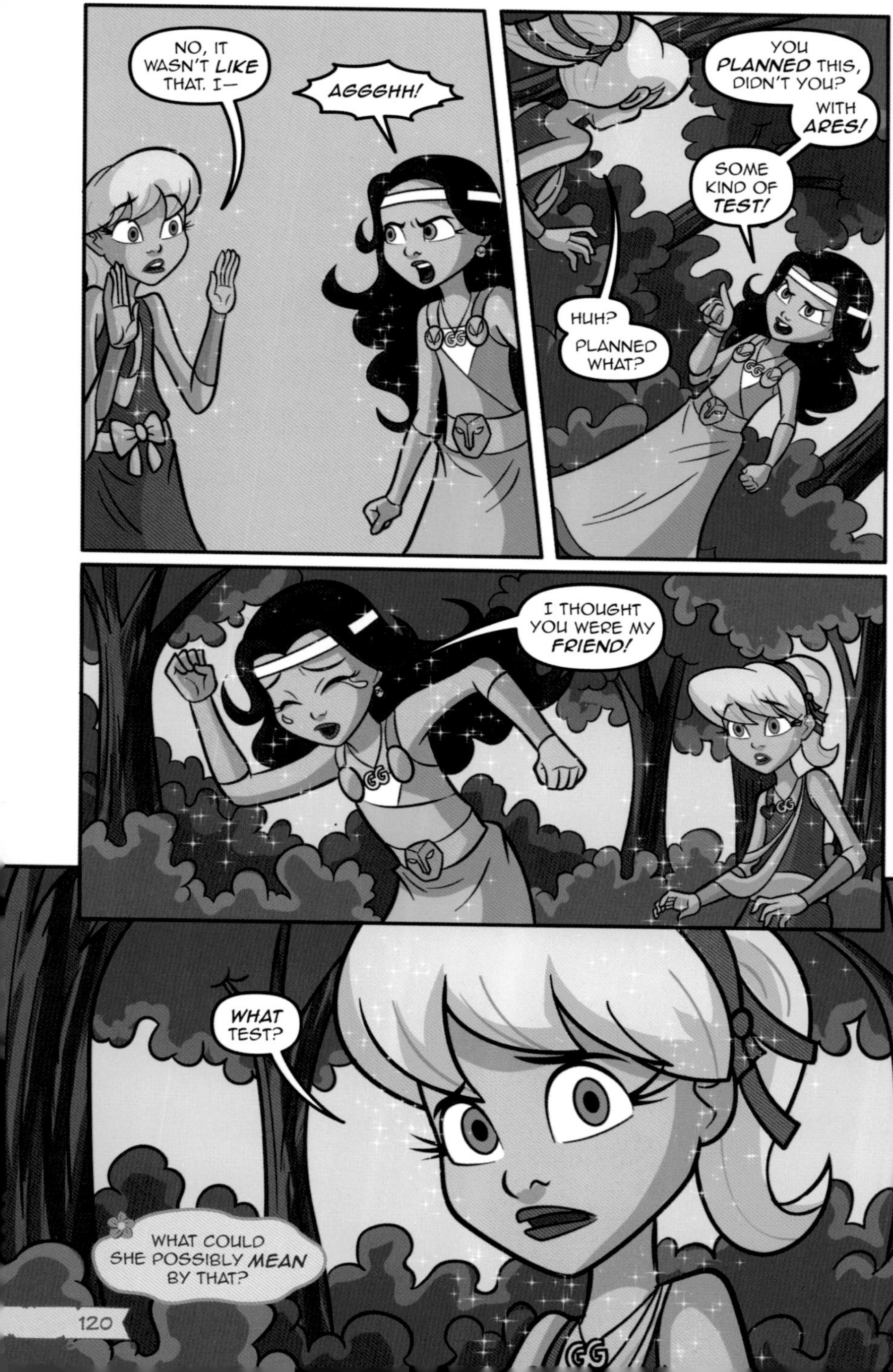
NO, IT WASN'T *LIKE* THAT. I—
AGGGHH!
YOU *PLANNED* THIS, DIDN'T YOU?
WITH *ARES!*
SOME KIND OF *TEST!*
HUH?
PLANNED WHAT?
I THOUGHT YOU WERE MY *FRIEND!*
WHAT TEST?
WHAT COULD SHE POSSIBLY *MEAN* BY THAT?

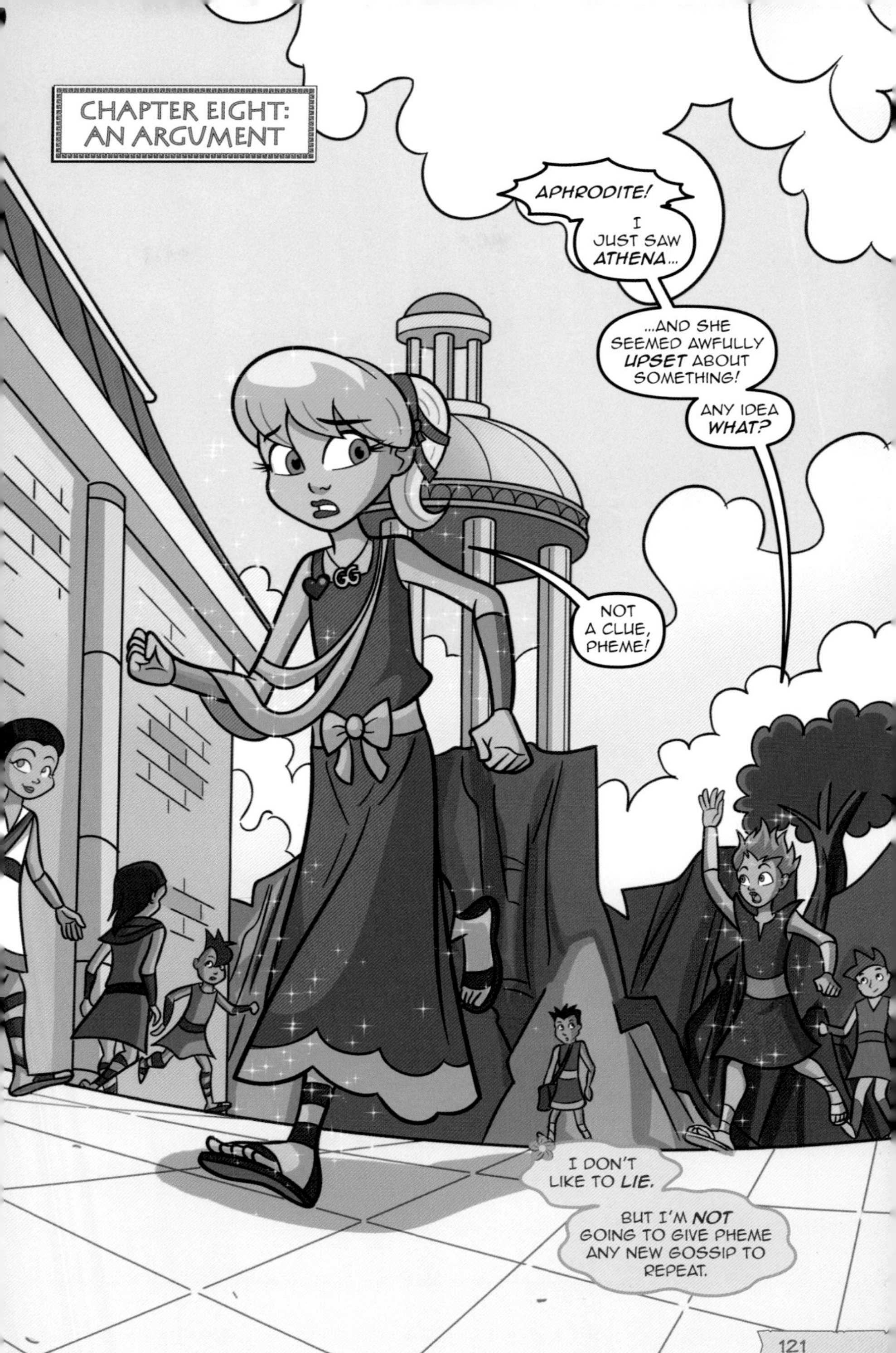
CHAPTER EIGHT: AN ARGUMENT
APHRODITE!
I JUST SAW ATHENA...
...AND SHE SEEMED AWFULLY UPSET ABOUT SOMETHING!
ANY IDEA WHAT?
NOT A CLUE, PHEME!
I DON'T LIKE TO LIE.
BUT I'M NOT GOING TO GIVE PHEME ANY NEW GOSSIP TO REPEAT.

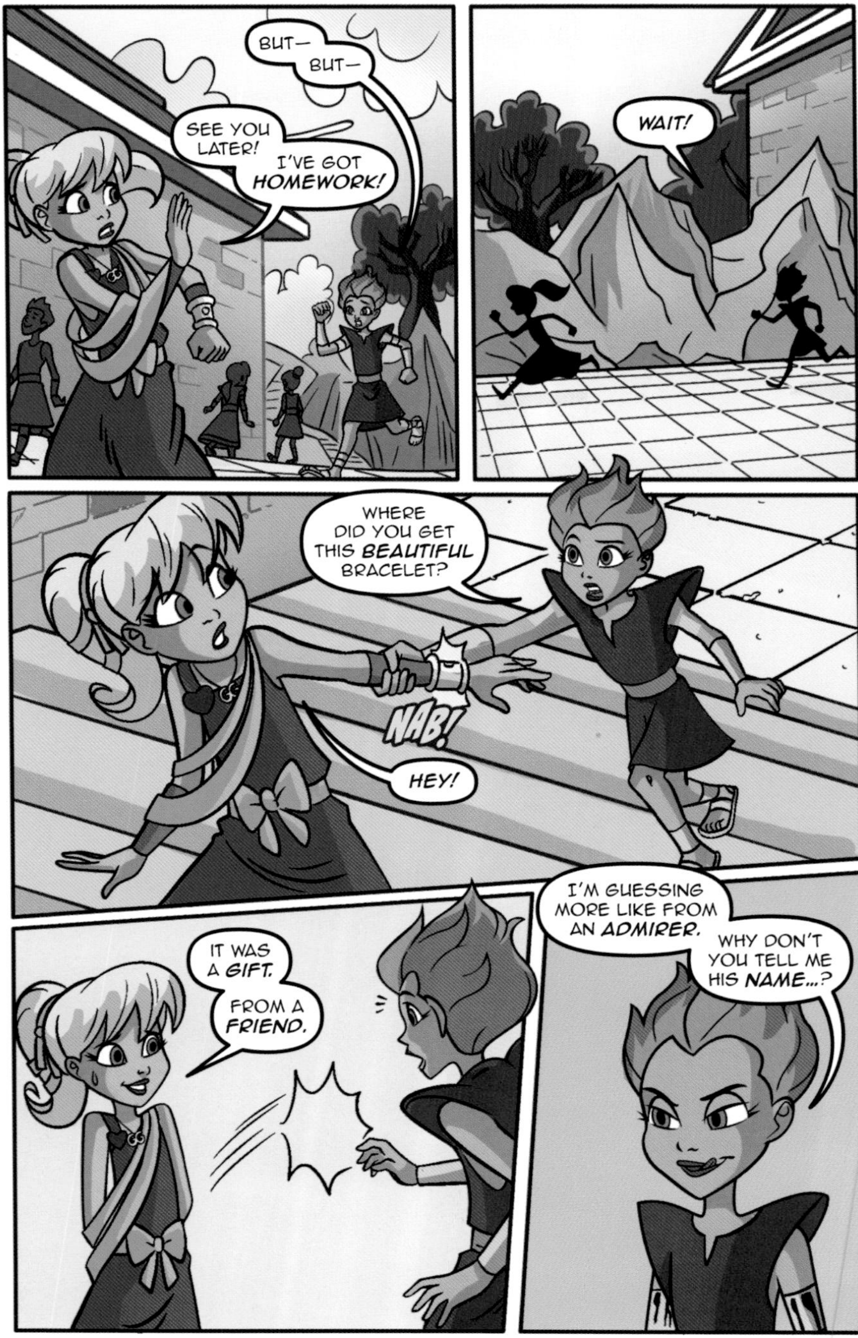

BUT— BUT—
SEE YOU LATER!
I'VE GOT HOMEWORK!
WAIT!
WHERE DID YOU GET THIS BEAUTIFUL BRACELET?
NAB!
HEY!
IT WAS A GIFT.
FROM A FRIEND.
I'M GUESSING MORE LIKE FROM AN ADMIRER.
WHY DON'T YOU TELL ME HIS NAME...?

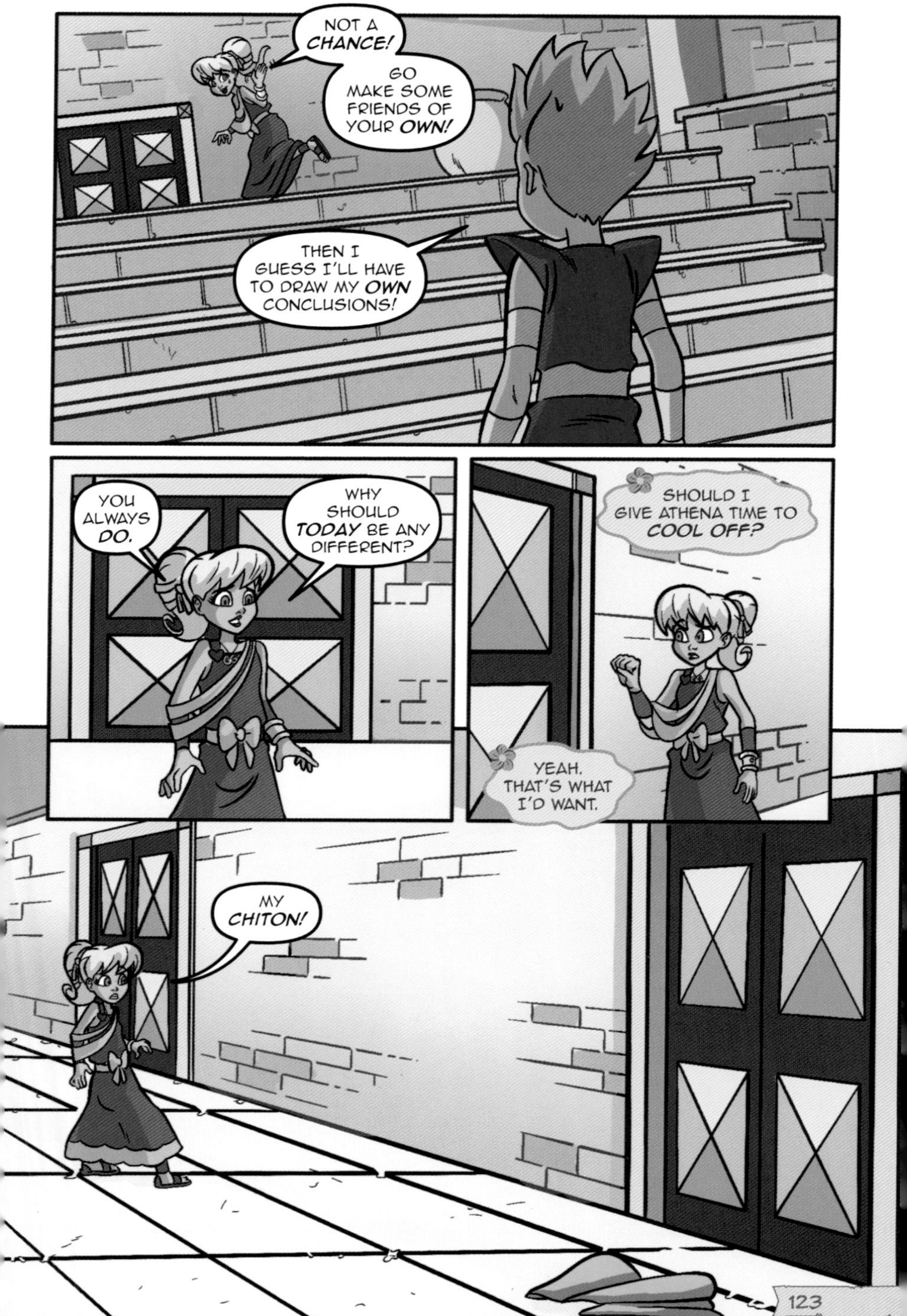
NOT A CHANCE!
GO MAKE SOME FRIENDS OF YOUR OWN!
THEN I GUESS I'LL HAVE TO DRAW MY OWN CONCLUSIONS!
YOU ALWAYS DO.
WHY SHOULD TODAY BE ANY DIFFERENT?
SHOULD I GIVE ATHENA TIME TO COOL OFF?
YEAH. THAT'S WHAT I'D WANT.
MY CHITON!

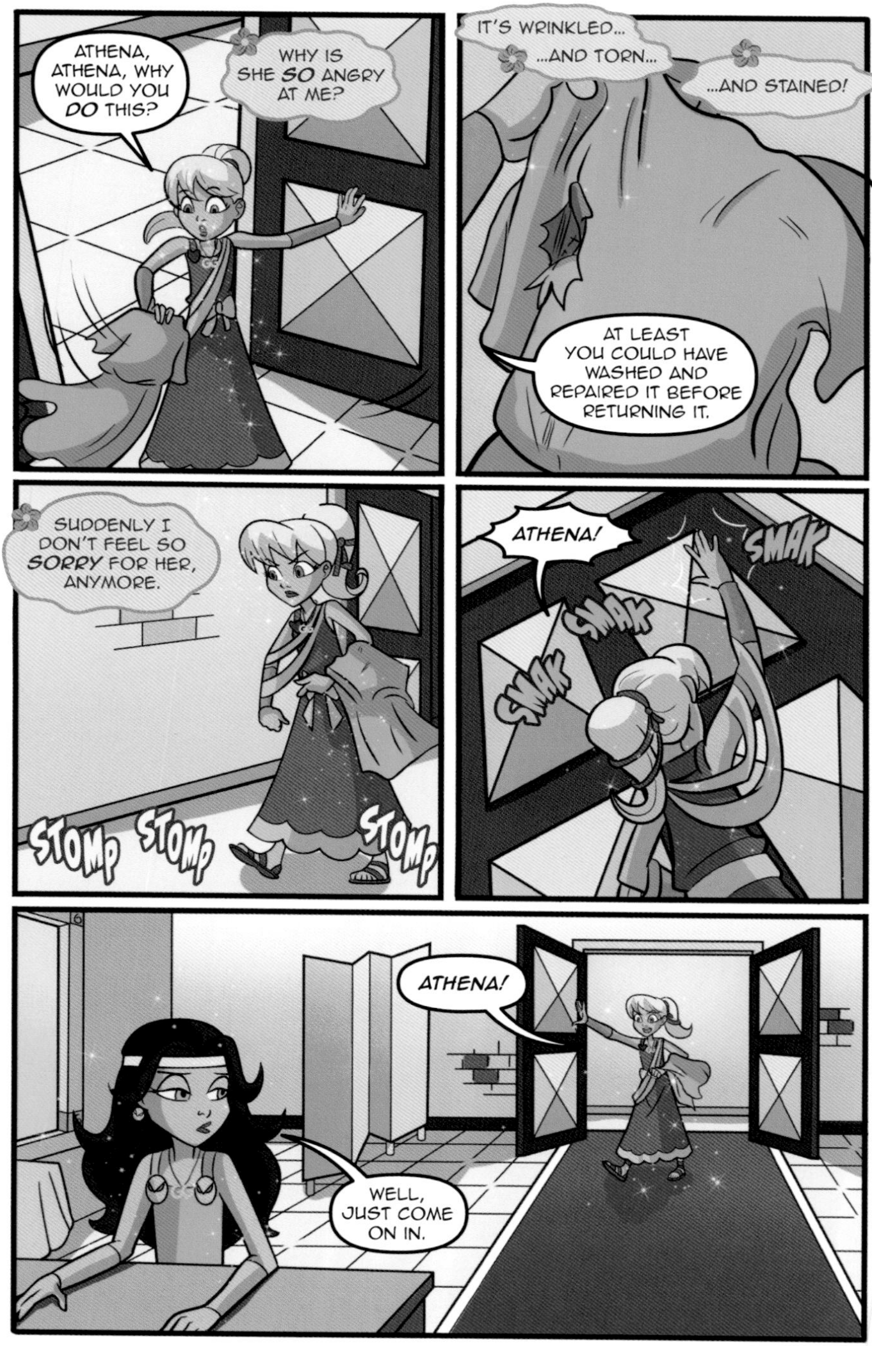
ATHENA, ATHENA, WHY WOULD YOU DO THIS?
WHY IS SHE SO ANGRY AT ME?
IT'S WRINKLED...
...AND TORN...
...AND STAINED!
AT LEAST YOU COULD HAVE WASHED AND REPAIRED IT BEFORE RETURNING IT.
SUDDENLY I DON'T FEEL SO SORRY FOR HER, ANYMORE.
STOMP STOMP STOMP
ATHENA!
SMAK SMAK SMAK
ATHENA!
WELL, JUST COME ON IN.

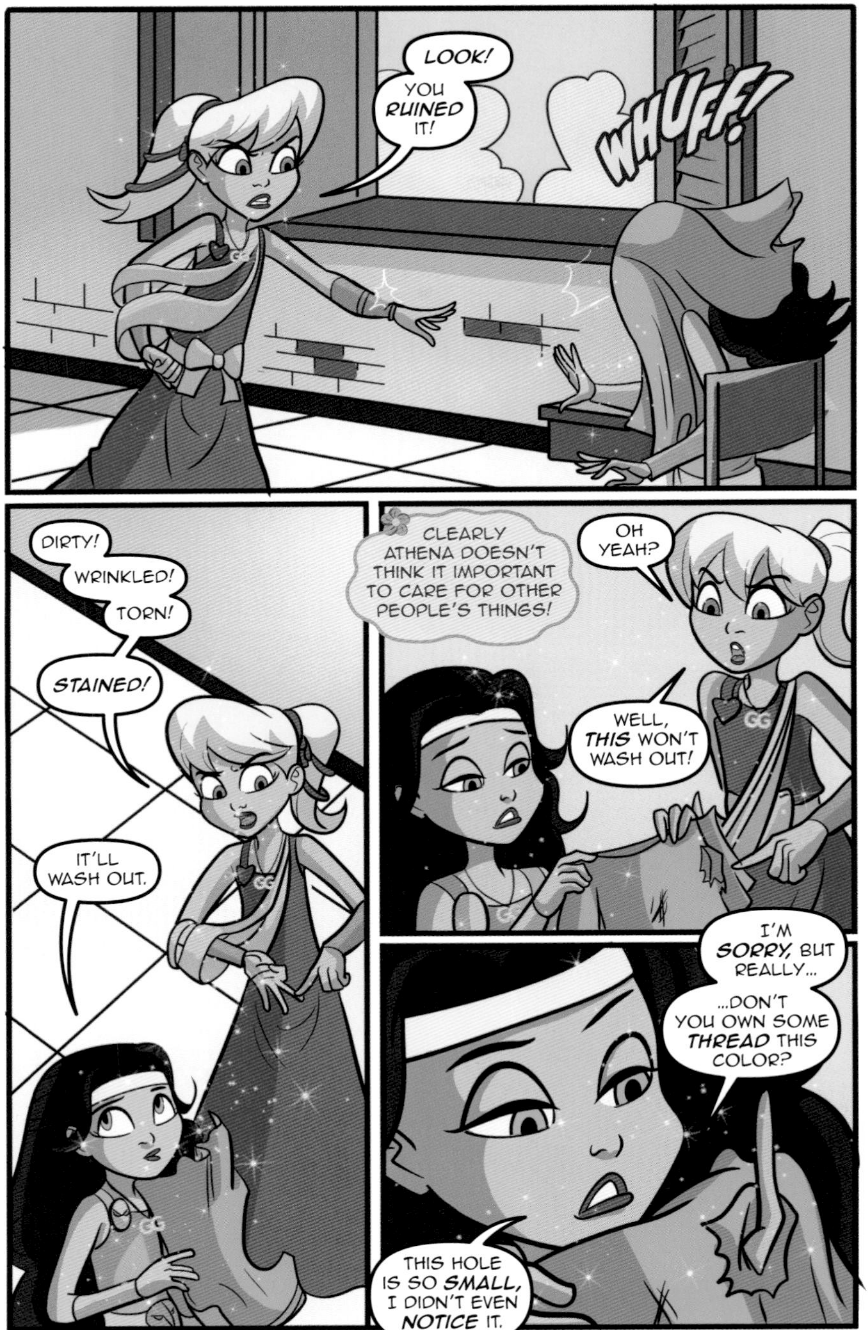
LOOK!
YOU RUINED IT!
WHUFF!
DIRTY!
WRINKLED!
TORN!
STAINED!
IT'LL WASH OUT.
CLEARLY ATHENA DOESN'T THINK IT IMPORTANT TO CARE FOR OTHER PEOPLE'S THINGS!
OH YEAH?
WELL, THIS WON'T WASH OUT!
I'M SORRY, BUT REALLY...
...DON'T YOU OWN SOME THREAD THIS COLOR?
THIS HOLE IS SO SMALL, I DIDN'T EVEN NOTICE IT.

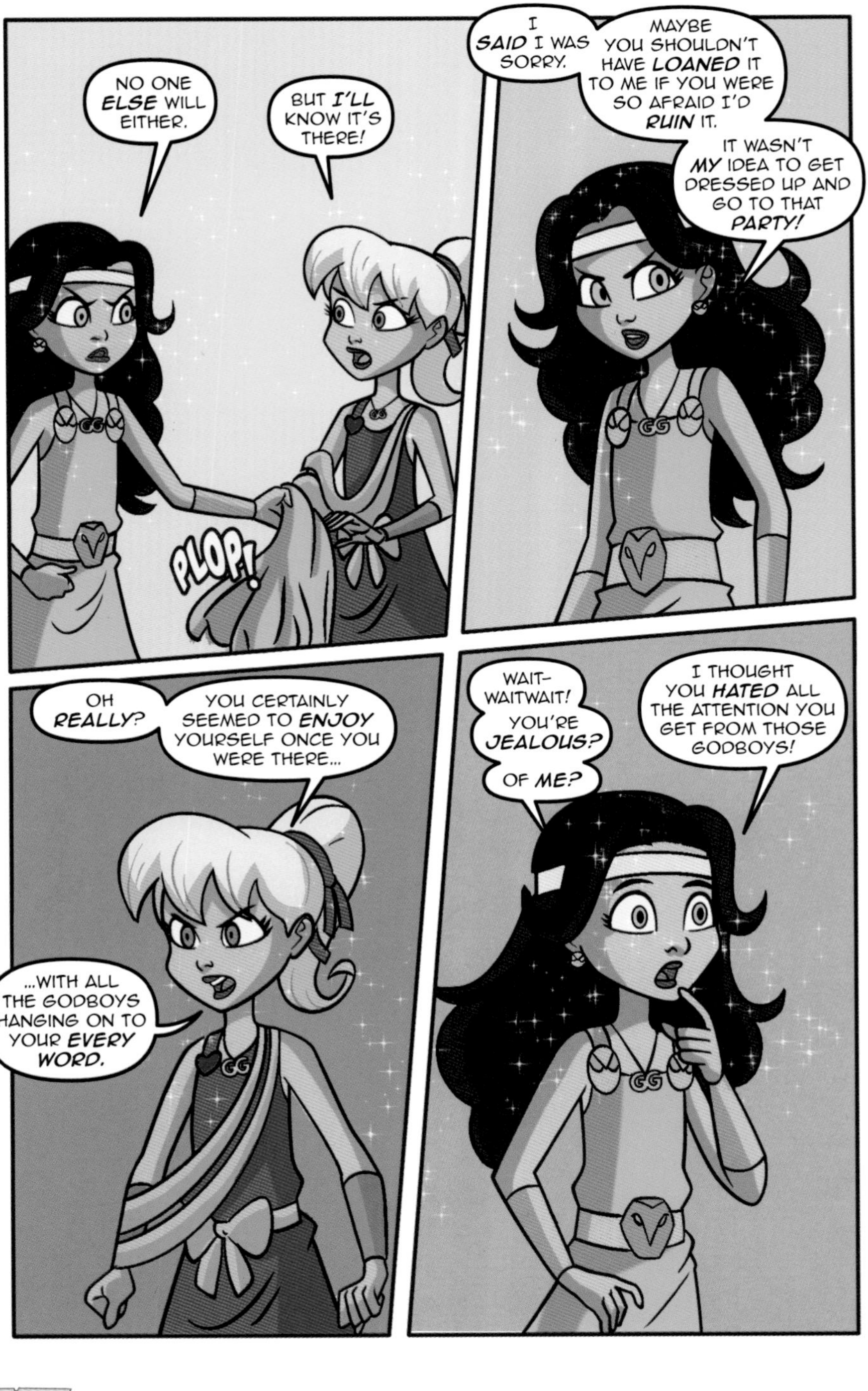
NO ONE ELSE WILL EITHER.
BUT I'LL KNOW IT'S THERE!
PLOP!
I SAID I WAS SORRY.
MAYBE YOU SHOULDN'T HAVE LOANED IT TO ME IF YOU WERE SO AFRAID I'D RUIN IT.
IT WASN'T MY IDEA TO GET DRESSED UP AND GO TO THAT PARTY!
OH REALLY?
YOU CERTAINLY SEEMED TO ENJOY YOURSELF ONCE YOU WERE THERE...
...WITH ALL THE GODBOYS HANGING ON TO YOUR EVERY WORD.
WAIT-WAITWAIT!
YOU'RE JEALOUS?
OF ME?
I THOUGHT YOU HATED ALL THE ATTENTION YOU GET FROM THOSE GODBOYS!

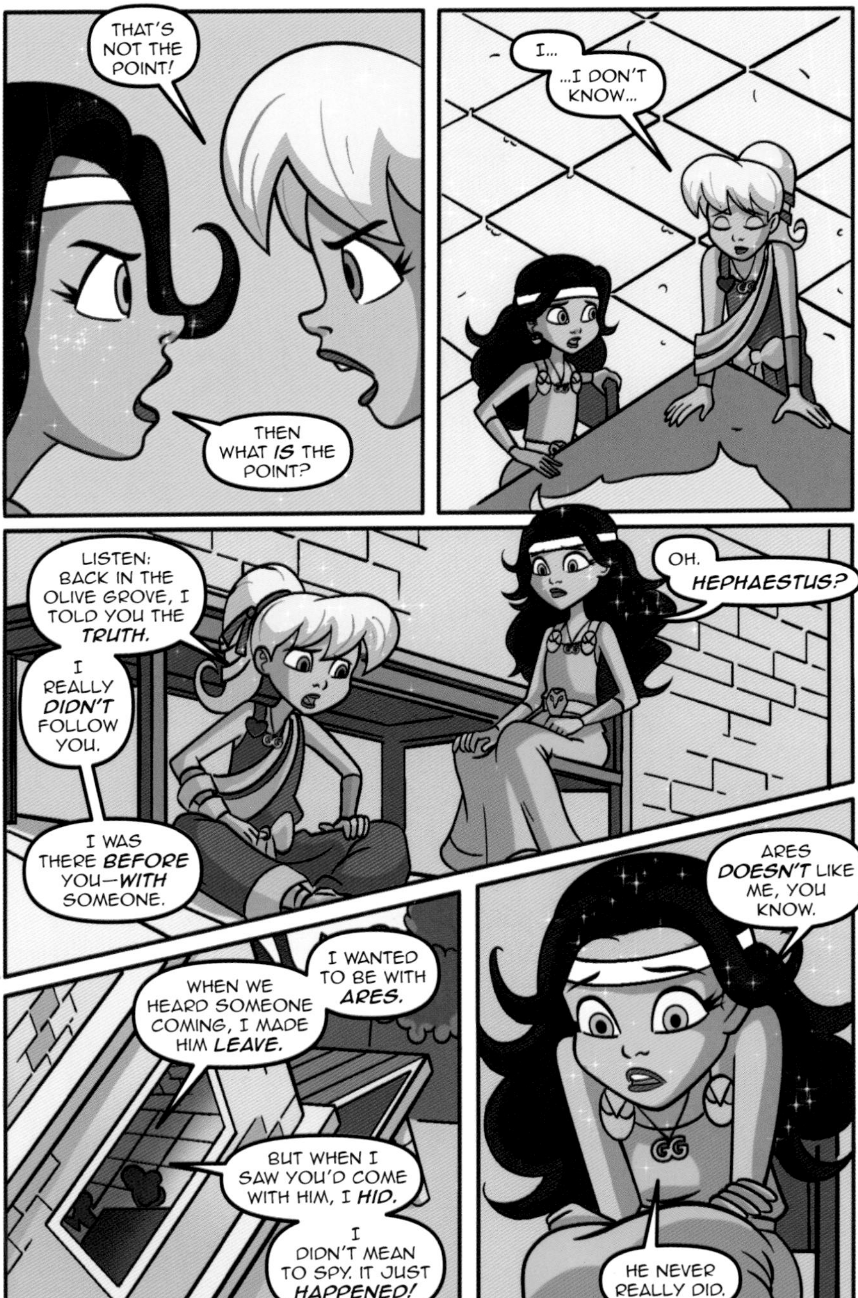
THAT'S NOT THE POINT!
THEN WHAT *IS* THE POINT?
I...
...I DON'T KNOW...
LISTEN: BACK IN THE OLIVE GROVE, I TOLD YOU THE *TRUTH.*
I REALLY *DIDN'T* FOLLOW YOU.
I WAS THERE *BEFORE* YOU—*WITH* SOMEONE.
OH. *HEPHAESTUS?*
I WANTED TO BE WITH *ARES.*
WHEN WE HEARD SOMEONE COMING, I MADE HIM *LEAVE.*
BUT WHEN I SAW YOU'D COME WITH HIM, I *HID.*
I DIDN'T MEAN TO SPY. IT JUST *HAPPENED!*
ARES *DOESN'T* LIKE ME, YOU KNOW.
HE NEVER REALLY DID.

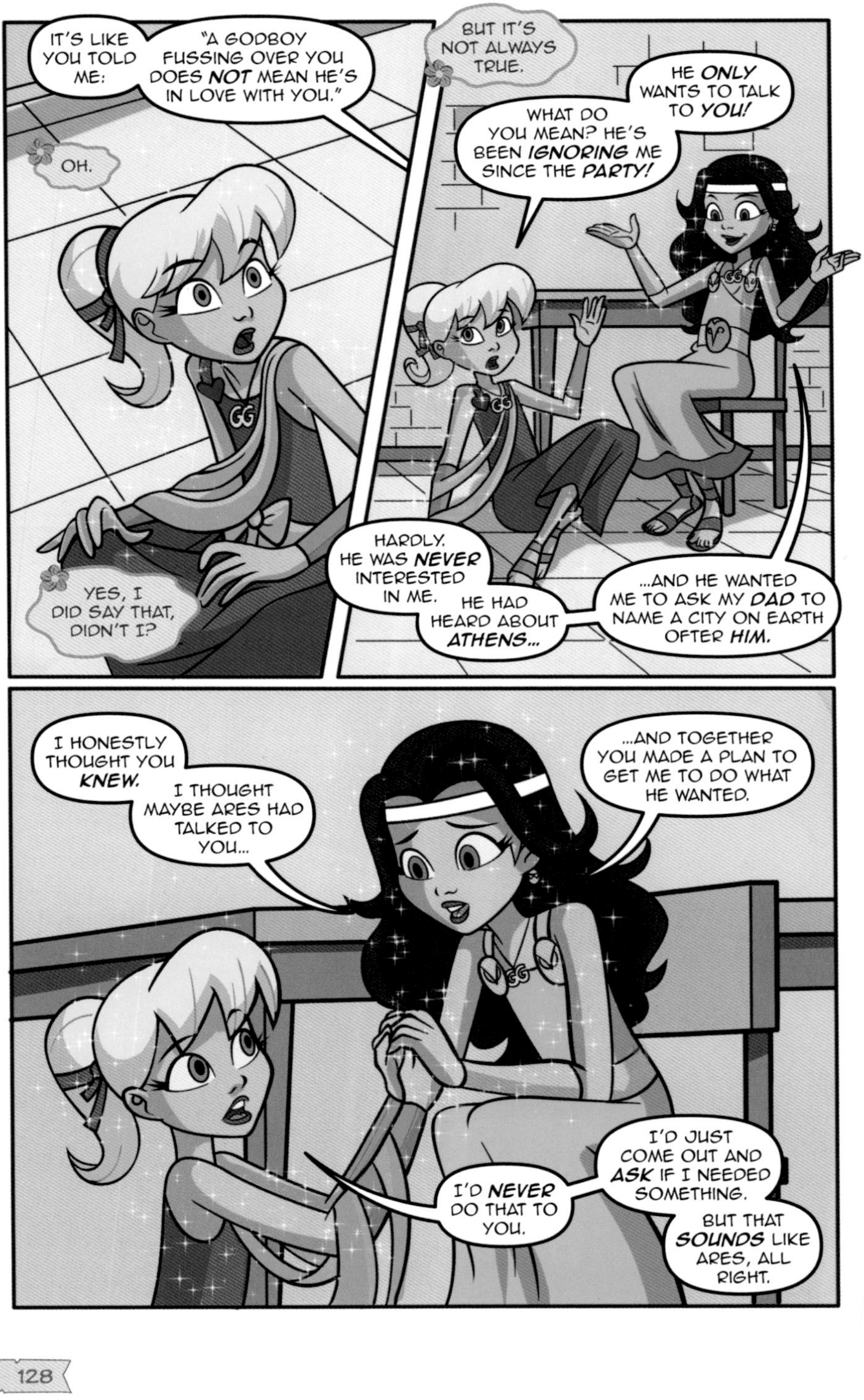
IT'S LIKE YOU TOLD ME:
"A GODBOY FUSSING OVER YOU DOES **NOT** MEAN HE'S IN LOVE WITH YOU."
OH.
YES, I DID SAY THAT, DIDN'T I?
BUT IT'S NOT ALWAYS TRUE.
HE **ONLY** WANTS TO TALK TO **YOU!**
WHAT DO YOU MEAN? HE'S BEEN **IGNORING** ME SINCE THE **PARTY!**
HARDLY. HE WAS **NEVER** INTERESTED IN ME.
HE HAD HEARD ABOUT **ATHENS...**
...AND HE WANTED ME TO ASK MY **DAD** TO NAME A CITY ON EARTH OFTER **HIM.**
I HONESTLY THOUGHT YOU **KNEW.**
I THOUGHT MAYBE ARES HAD TALKED TO YOU...
...AND TOGETHER YOU MADE A PLAN TO GET ME TO DO WHAT HE WANTED.
I'D **NEVER** DO THAT TO YOU.
I'D JUST COME OUT AND **ASK** IF I NEEDED SOMETHING.
BUT THAT **SOUNDS** LIKE ARES, ALL RIGHT.

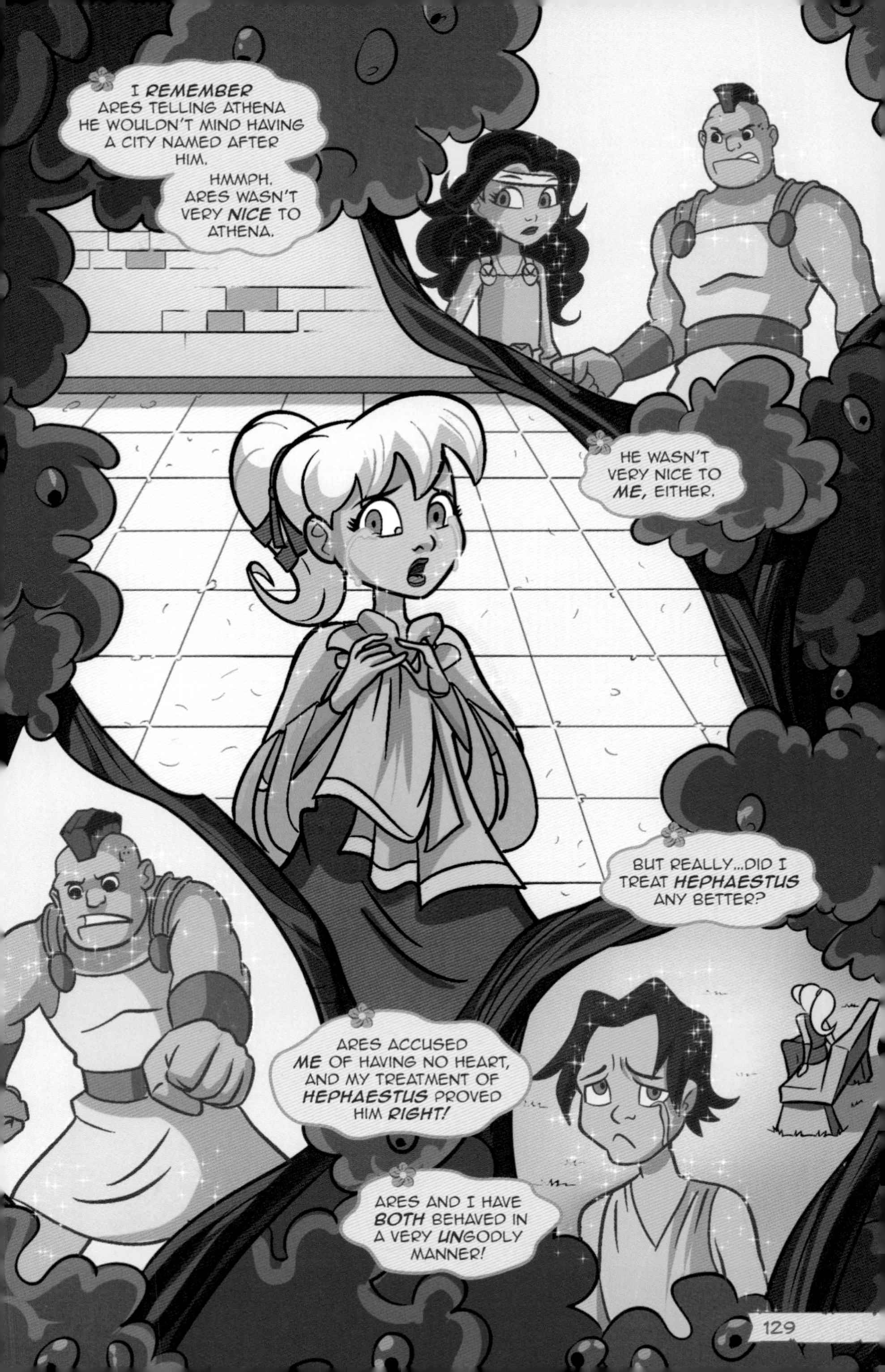
I REMEMBER ARES TELLING ATHENA HE WOULDN'T MIND HAVING A CITY NAMED AFTER HIM.
HMMPH. ARES WASN'T VERY NICE TO ATHENA.
HE WASN'T VERY NICE TO ME, EITHER.
BUT REALLY...DID I TREAT HEPHAESTUS ANY BETTER?
ARES ACCUSED ME OF HAVING NO HEART, AND MY TREATMENT OF HEPHAESTUS PROVED HIM RIGHT!
ARES AND I HAVE BOTH BEHAVED IN A VERY UNGODLY MANNER!

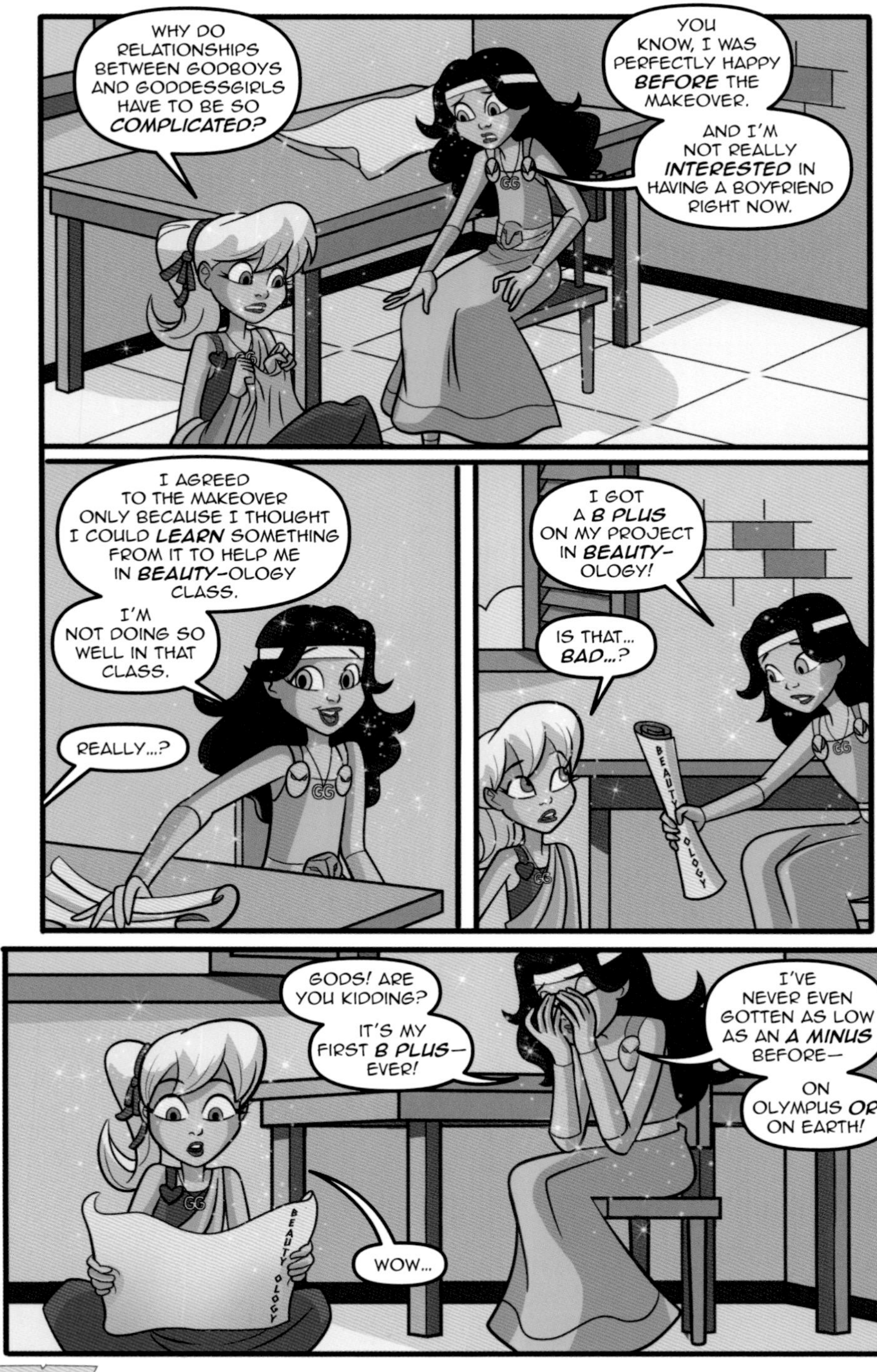
WHY DO RELATIONSHIPS BETWEEN GODBOYS AND GODDESSGIRLS HAVE TO BE SO COMPLICATED?
YOU KNOW, I WAS PERFECTLY HAPPY BEFORE THE MAKEOVER.
AND I'M NOT REALLY INTERESTED IN HAVING A BOYFRIEND RIGHT NOW.
I AGREED TO THE MAKEOVER ONLY BECAUSE I THOUGHT I COULD LEARN SOMETHING FROM IT TO HELP ME IN BEAUTY-OLOGY CLASS.
I'M NOT DOING SO WELL IN THAT CLASS.
REALLY...?
I GOT A B PLUS ON MY PROJECT IN BEAUTY-OLOGY!
IS THAT... BAD...?
BEAUTY-OLOGY
GODS! ARE YOU KIDDING?
IT'S MY FIRST B PLUS—EVER!
I'VE NEVER EVEN GOTTEN AS LOW AS AN A MINUS BEFORE—
ON OLYMPUS OR ON EARTH!
BEAUTY-OLOGY
WOW...

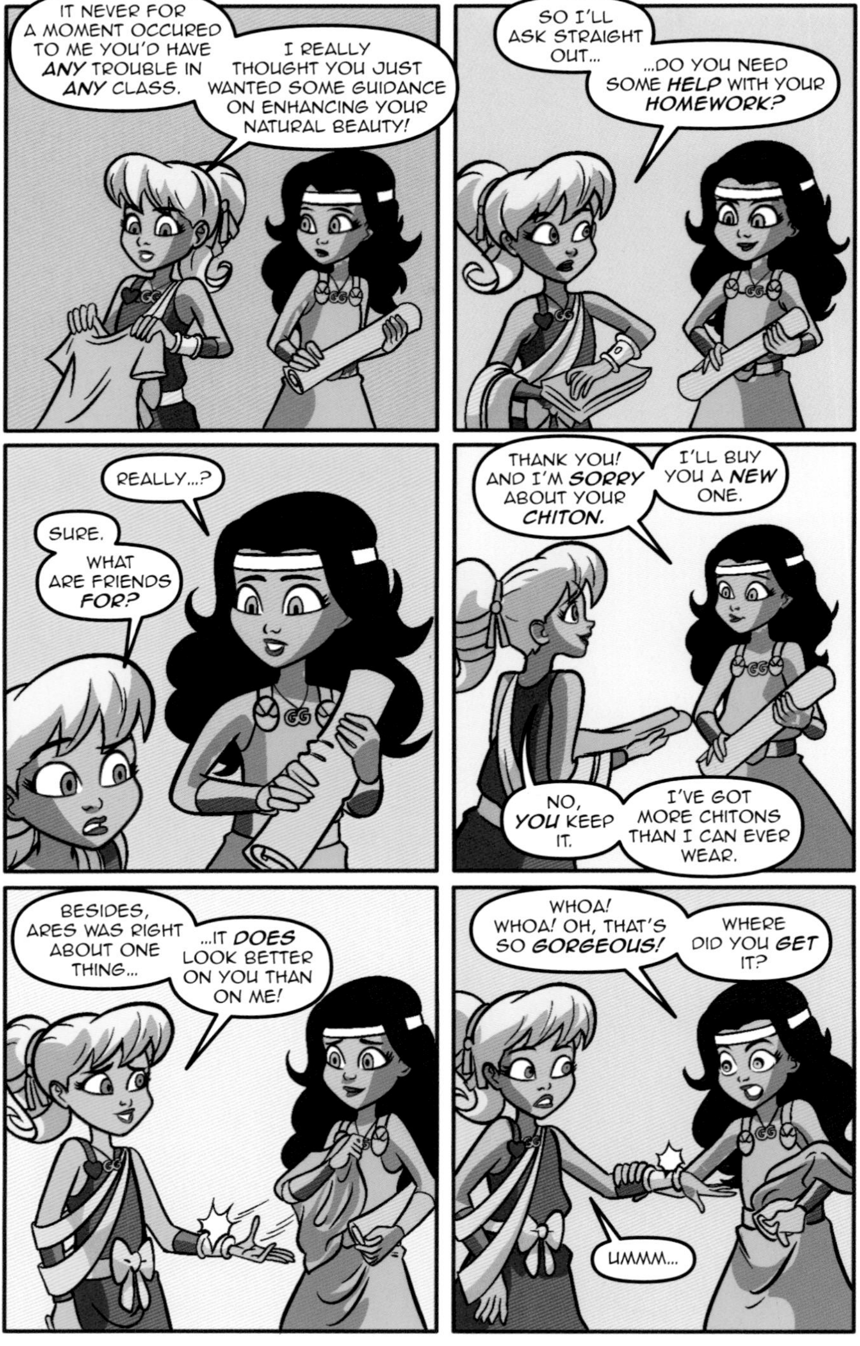
IT NEVER FOR A MOMENT OCCURED TO ME YOU'D HAVE ANY TROUBLE IN ANY CLASS.
I REALLY THOUGHT YOU JUST WANTED SOME GUIDANCE ON ENHANCING YOUR NATURAL BEAUTY!
SO I'LL ASK STRAIGHT OUT...
...DO YOU NEED SOME HELP WITH YOUR HOMEWORK?
REALLY...?
SURE.
WHAT ARE FRIENDS FOR?
THANK YOU! AND I'M SORRY ABOUT YOUR CHITON.
I'LL BUY YOU A NEW ONE.
NO, YOU KEEP IT.
I'VE GOT MORE CHITONS THAN I CAN EVER WEAR.
BESIDES, ARES WAS RIGHT ABOUT ONE THING...
...IT DOES LOOK BETTER ON YOU THAN ON ME!
WHOA! WHOA! OH, THAT'S SO GORGEOUS!
WHERE DID YOU GET IT?
UMMM...

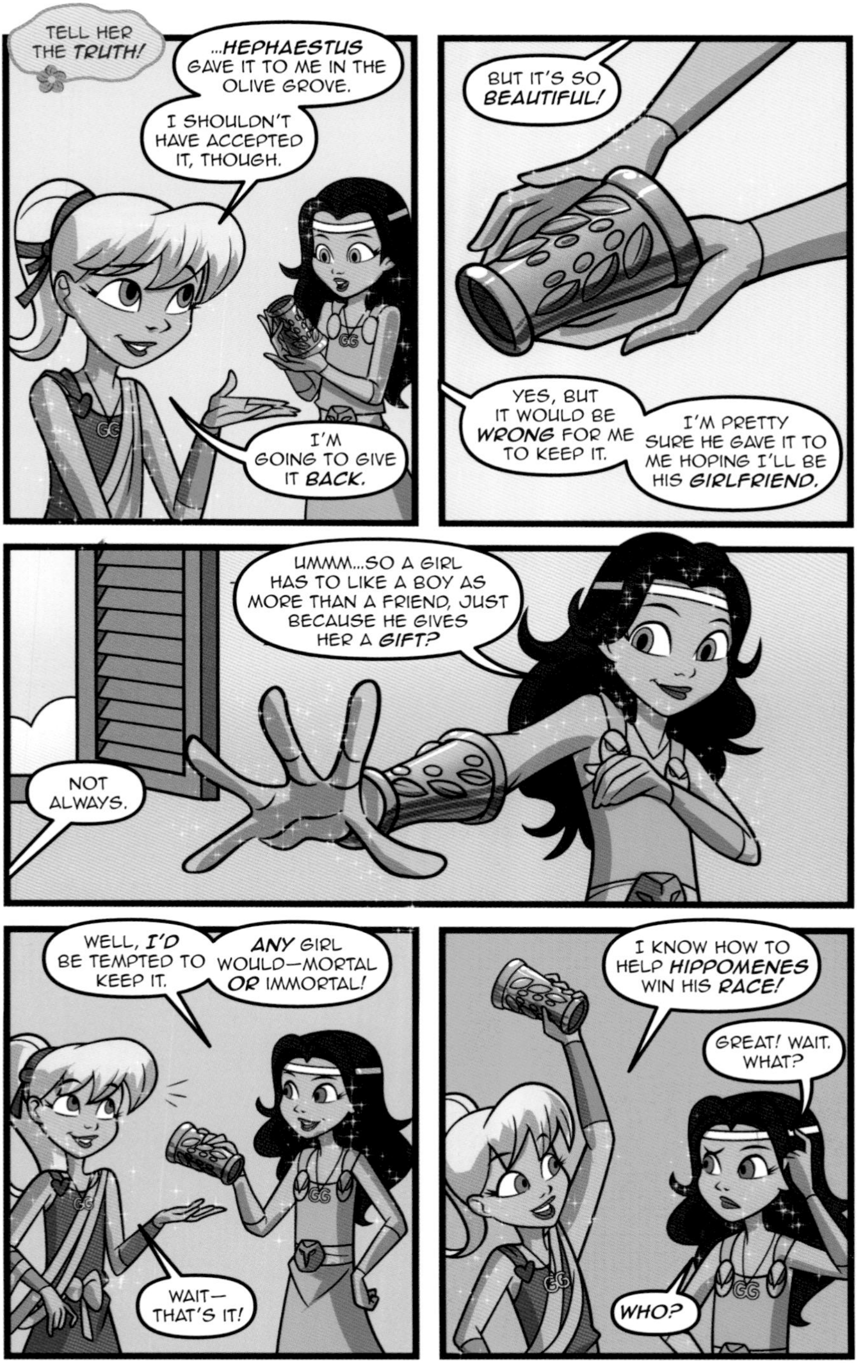
TELL HER THE TRUTH!
...HEPHAESTUS GAVE IT TO ME IN THE OLIVE GROVE.
I SHOULDN'T HAVE ACCEPTED IT, THOUGH.
I'M GOING TO GIVE IT BACK.
BUT IT'S SO BEAUTIFUL!
YES, BUT IT WOULD BE WRONG FOR ME TO KEEP IT.
I'M PRETTY SURE HE GAVE IT TO ME HOPING I'LL BE HIS GIRLFRIEND.
UMMM...SO A GIRL HAS TO LIKE A BOY AS MORE THAN A FRIEND, JUST BECAUSE HE GIVES HER A GIFT?
NOT ALWAYS.
WELL, I'D BE TEMPTED TO KEEP IT.
ANY GIRL WOULD—MORTAL OR IMMORTAL!
WAIT—THAT'S IT!
I KNOW HOW TO HELP HIPPOMENES WIN HIS RACE!
GREAT! WAIT. WHAT?
WHO?

CHAPTER NINE: THE APPLES

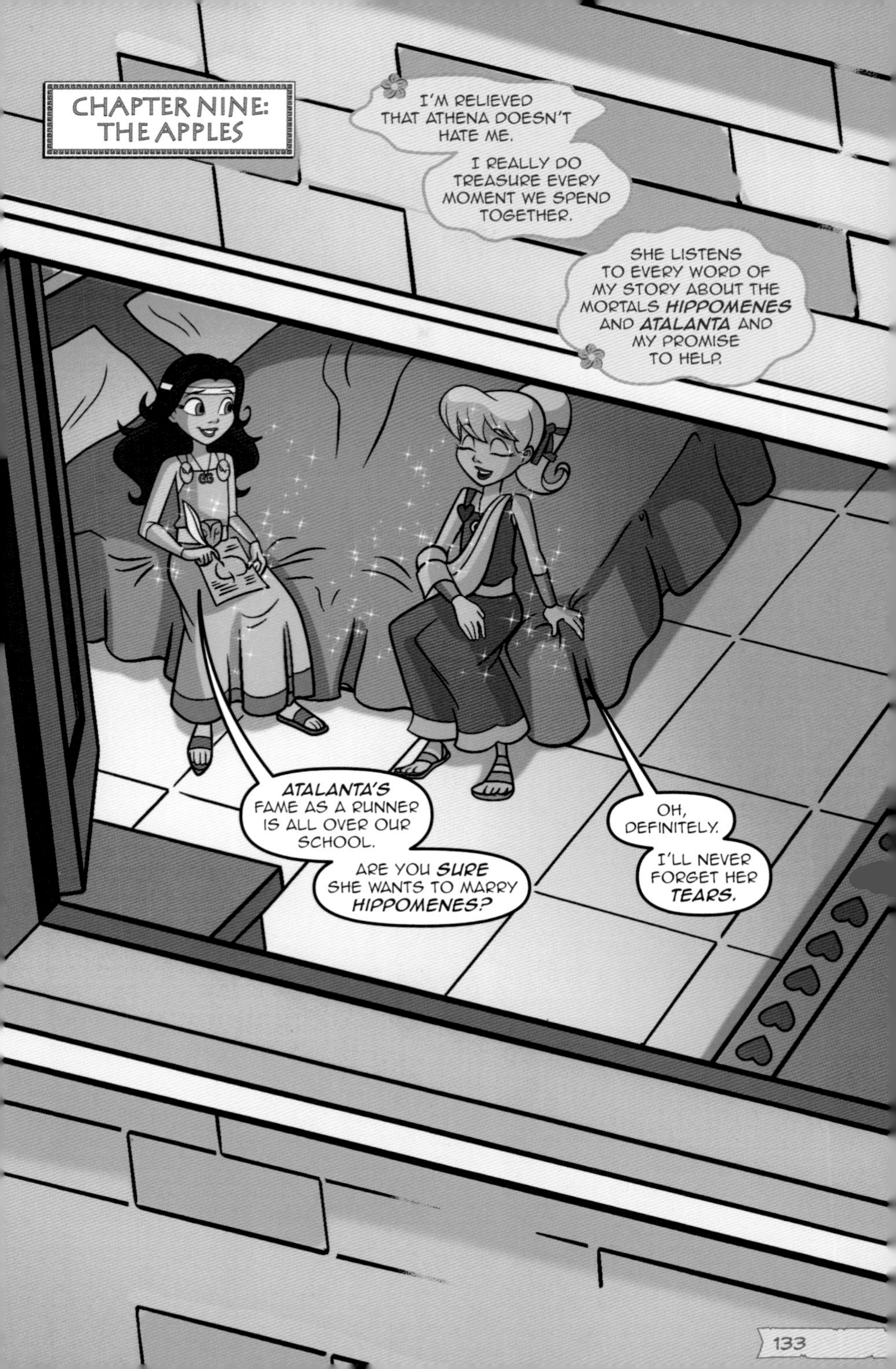

I'M RELIEVED THAT ATHENA DOESN'T HATE ME.
I REALLY DO TREASURE EVERY MOMENT WE SPEND TOGETHER.
SHE LISTENS TO EVERY WORD OF MY STORY ABOUT THE MORTALS HIPPOMENES AND ATALANTA AND MY PROMISE TO HELP.
ATALANTA'S FAME AS A RUNNER IS ALL OVER OUR SCHOOL.
ARE YOU SURE SHE WANTS TO MARRY HIPPOMENES?
OH, DEFINITELY.
I'LL NEVER FORGET HER TEARS.

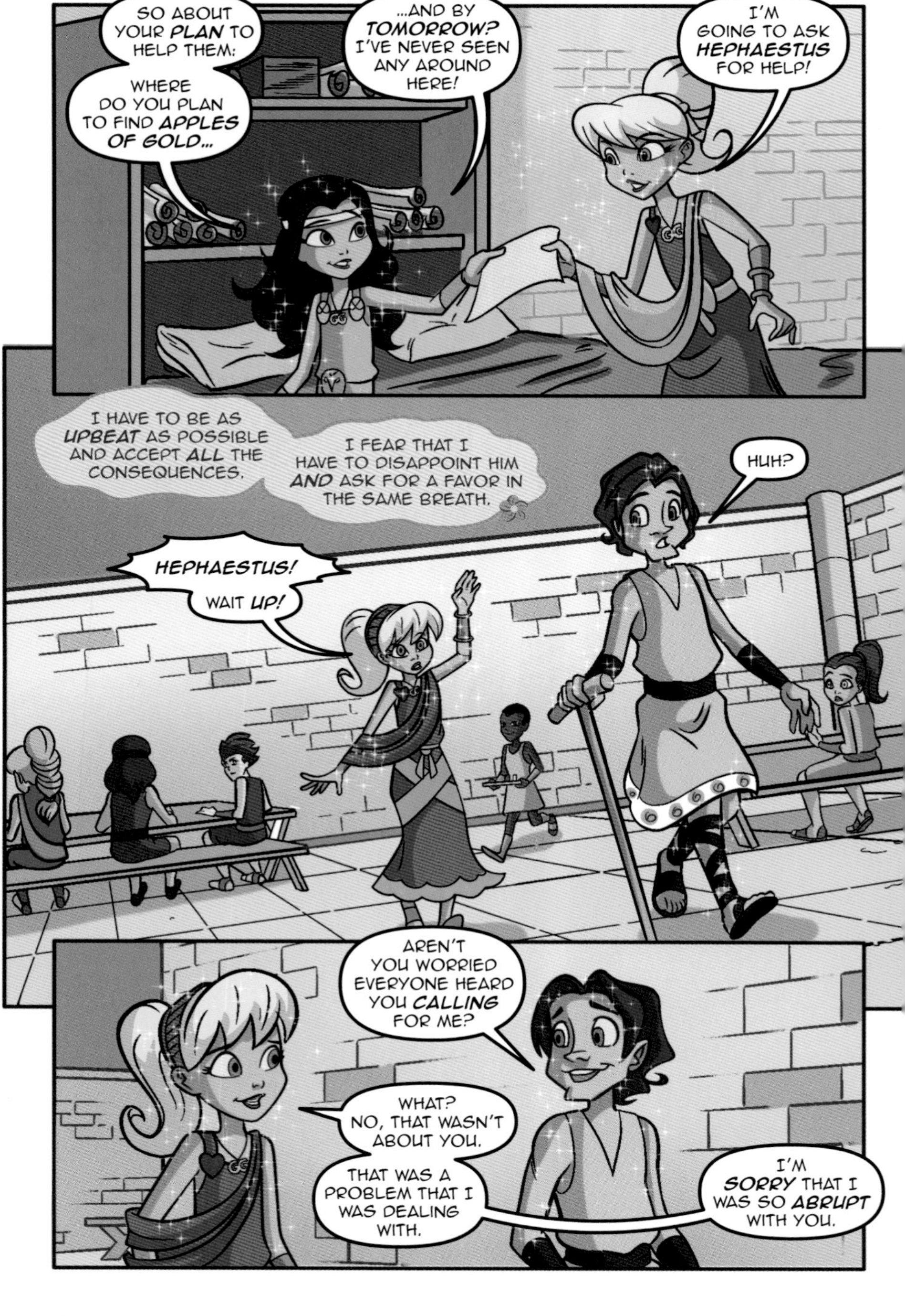
SO ABOUT YOUR PLAN TO HELP THEM:
WHERE DO YOU PLAN TO FIND APPLES OF GOLD...
...AND BY TOMORROW? I'VE NEVER SEEN ANY AROUND HERE!
I'M GOING TO ASK HEPHAESTUS FOR HELP!
I HAVE TO BE AS UPBEAT AS POSSIBLE AND ACCEPT ALL THE CONSEQUENCES.
I FEAR THAT I HAVE TO DISAPPOINT HIM AND ASK FOR A FAVOR IN THE SAME BREATH.
HUH?
HEPHAESTUS!
WAIT UP!
AREN'T YOU WORRIED EVERYONE HEARD YOU CALLING FOR ME?
WHAT? NO, THAT WASN'T ABOUT YOU.
THAT WAS A PROBLEM THAT I WAS DEALING WITH.
I'M SORRY THAT I WAS SO ABRUPT WITH YOU.

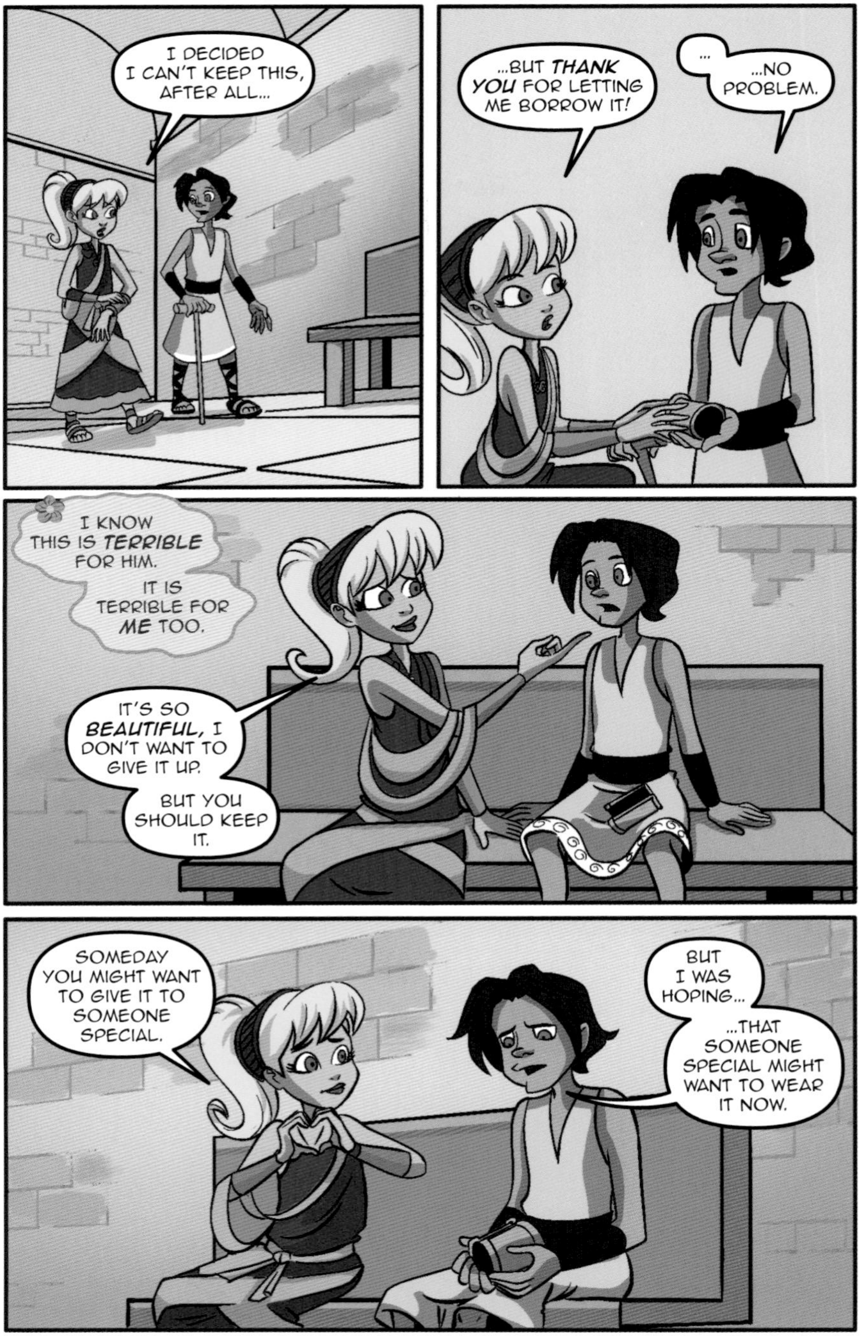
I DECIDED I CAN'T KEEP THIS, AFTER ALL...
...BUT **THANK YOU** FOR LETTING ME BORROW IT!
...
...NO PROBLEM.
I KNOW THIS IS **TERRIBLE** FOR HIM.
IT IS TERRIBLE FOR **ME** TOO.
IT'S SO **BEAUTIFUL,** I DON'T WANT TO GIVE IT UP.
BUT YOU SHOULD KEEP IT.
SOMEDAY YOU MIGHT WANT TO GIVE IT TO SOMEONE SPECIAL.
BUT I WAS HOPING...
...THAT SOMEONE SPECIAL MIGHT WANT TO WEAR IT NOW.

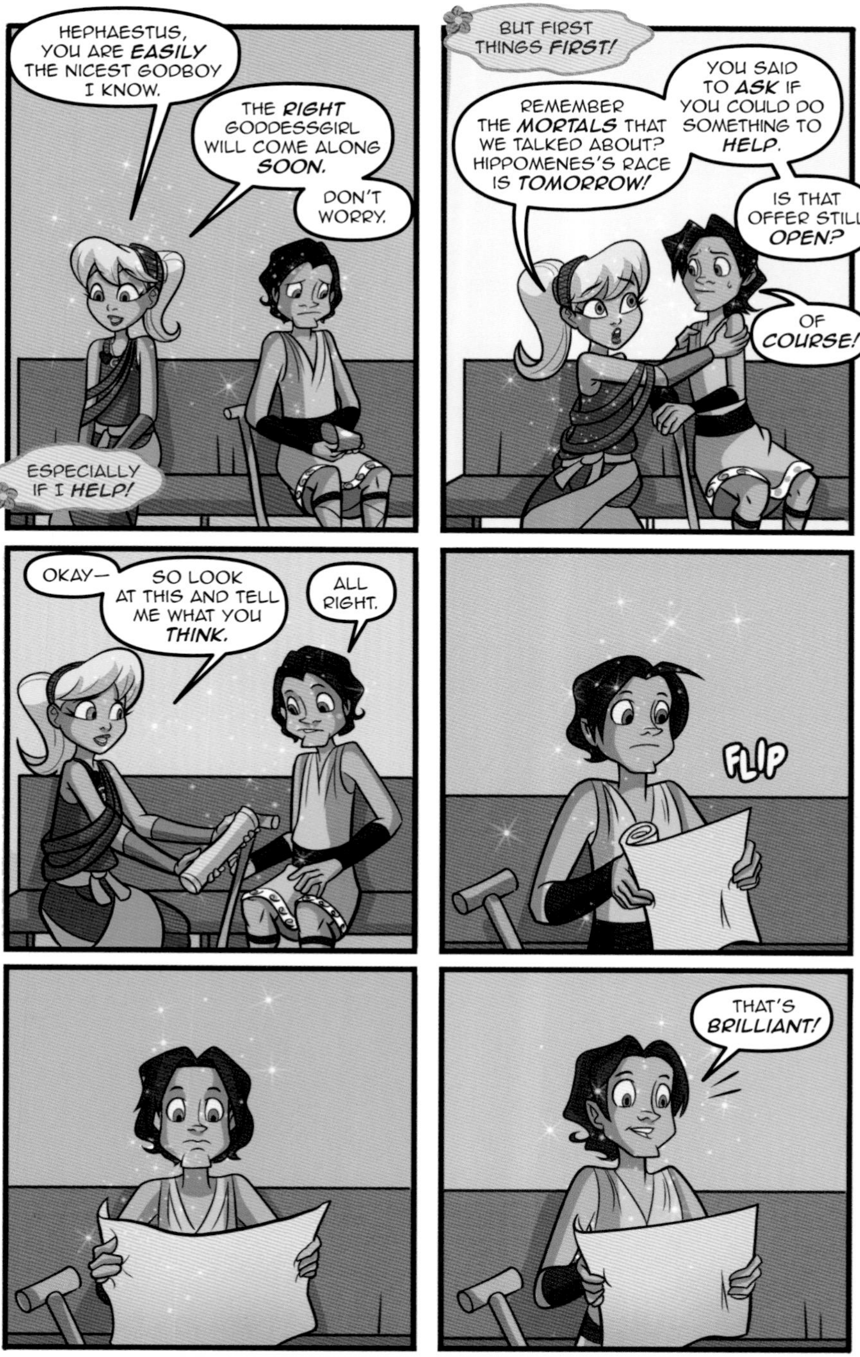
HEPHAESTUS, YOU ARE EASILY THE NICEST GODBOY I KNOW.
THE RIGHT GODDESSGIRL WILL COME ALONG SOON.
DON'T WORRY.
ESPECIALLY IF I HELP!
BUT FIRST THINGS FIRST!
REMEMBER THE MORTALS THAT WE TALKED ABOUT? HIPPOMENES'S RACE IS TOMORROW!
YOU SAID TO ASK IF YOU COULD DO SOMETHING TO HELP.
IS THAT OFFER STILL OPEN?
OF COURSE!
OKAY—
SO LOOK AT THIS AND TELL ME WHAT YOU THINK.
ALL RIGHT.
FLIP
THAT'S BRILLIANT!

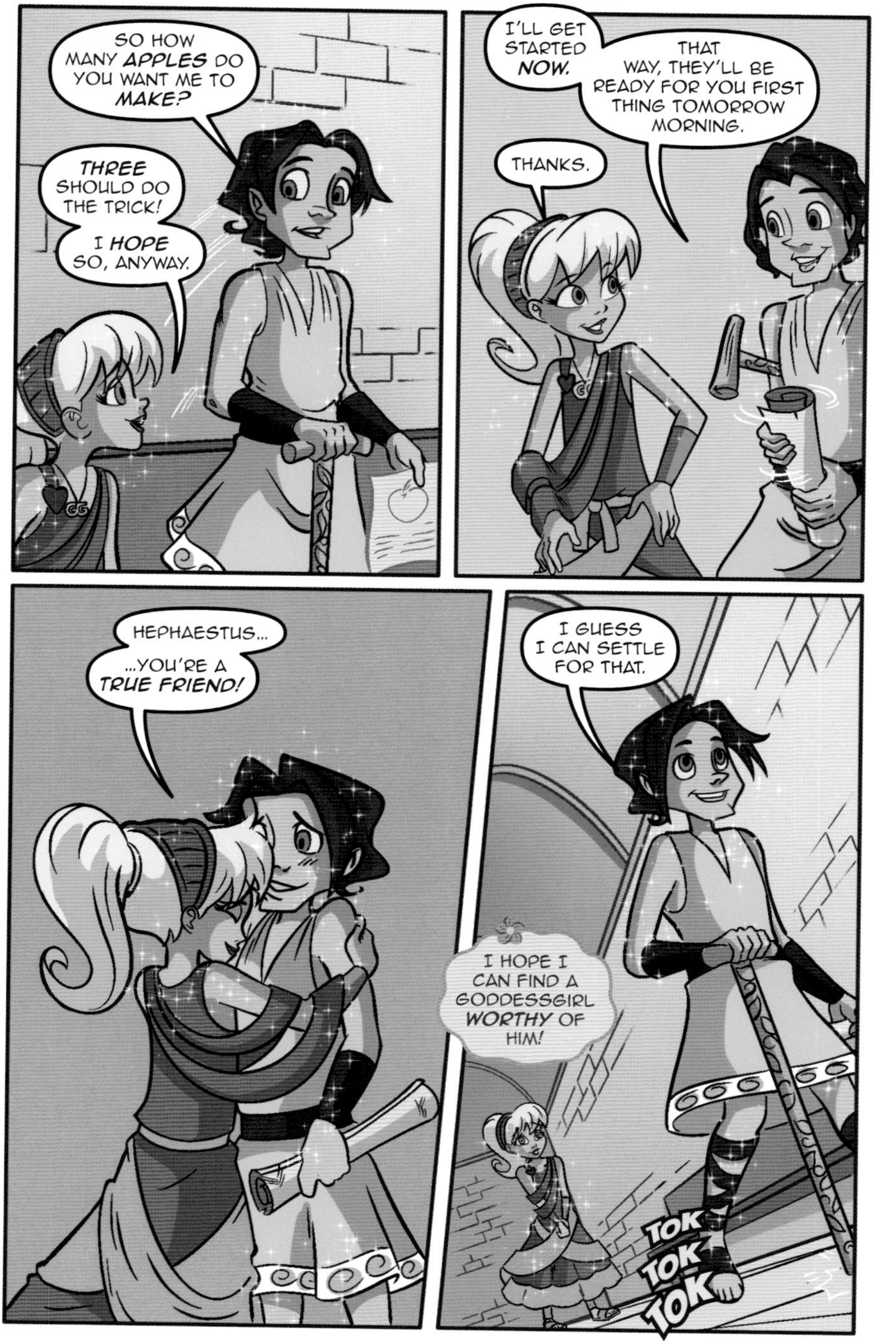
SO HOW MANY APPLES DO YOU WANT ME TO MAKE?
THREE SHOULD DO THE TRICK!
I HOPE SO, ANYWAY.
I'LL GET STARTED NOW.
THAT WAY, THEY'LL BE READY FOR YOU FIRST THING TOMORROW MORNING.
THANKS.
HEPHAESTUS...
...YOU'RE A TRUE FRIEND!
I GUESS I CAN SETTLE FOR THAT.
I HOPE I CAN FIND A GODDESSGIRL WORTHY OF HIM!
TOK TOK TOK

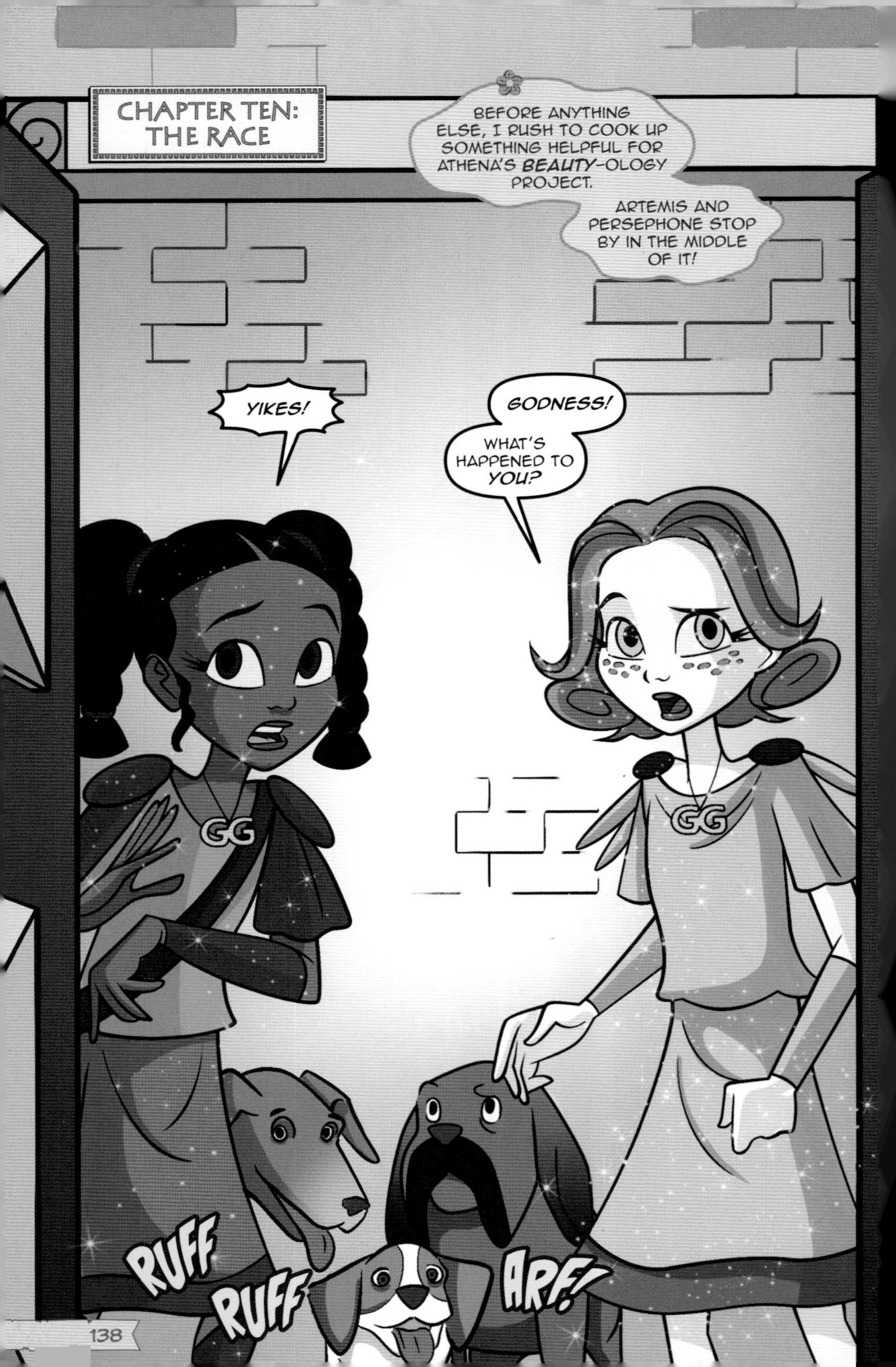
CHAPTER TEN: THE RACE
BEFORE ANYTHING ELSE, I RUSH TO COOK UP SOMETHING HELPFUL FOR ATHENA'S *BEAUTY*-OLOGY PROJECT.
ARTEMIS AND PERSEPHONE STOP BY IN THE MIDDLE OF IT!
YIKES!
GODNESS!
WHAT'S HAPPENED TO *YOU?*
RUFF
RUFF
ARF!

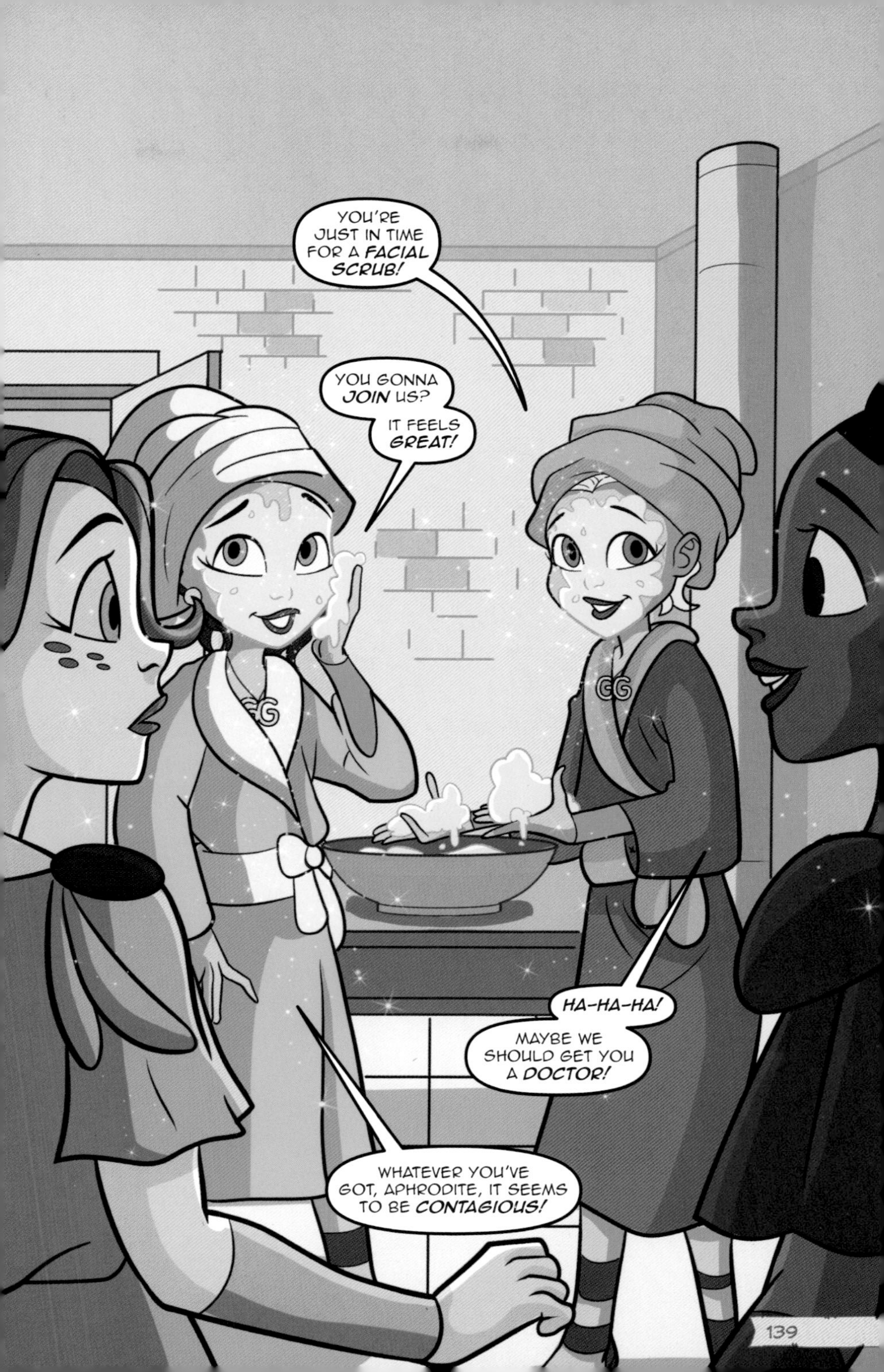
YOU'RE JUST IN TIME FOR A *FACIAL SCRUB!*
YOU GONNA *JOIN* US?
IT FEELS *GREAT!*
HA-HA-HA!
MAYBE WE SHOULD GET YOU A *DOCTOR!*
WHATEVER YOU'VE GOT, APHRODITE, IT SEEMS TO BE *CONTAGIOUS!*

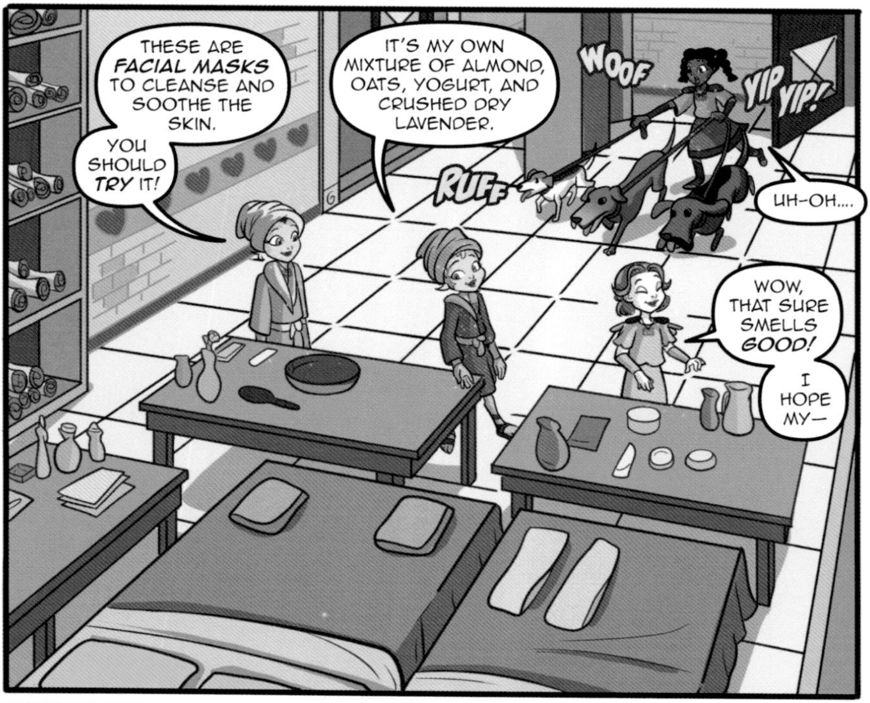
THESE ARE FACIAL MASKS TO CLEANSE AND SOOTHE THE SKIN.
YOU SHOULD TRY IT!
IT'S MY OWN MIXTURE OF ALMOND, OATS, YOGURT, AND CRUSHED DRY LAVENDER.
WOOF
YIP YIP!
RUFF
UH-OH....
WOW, THAT SURE SMELLS GOOD!
I HOPE MY—

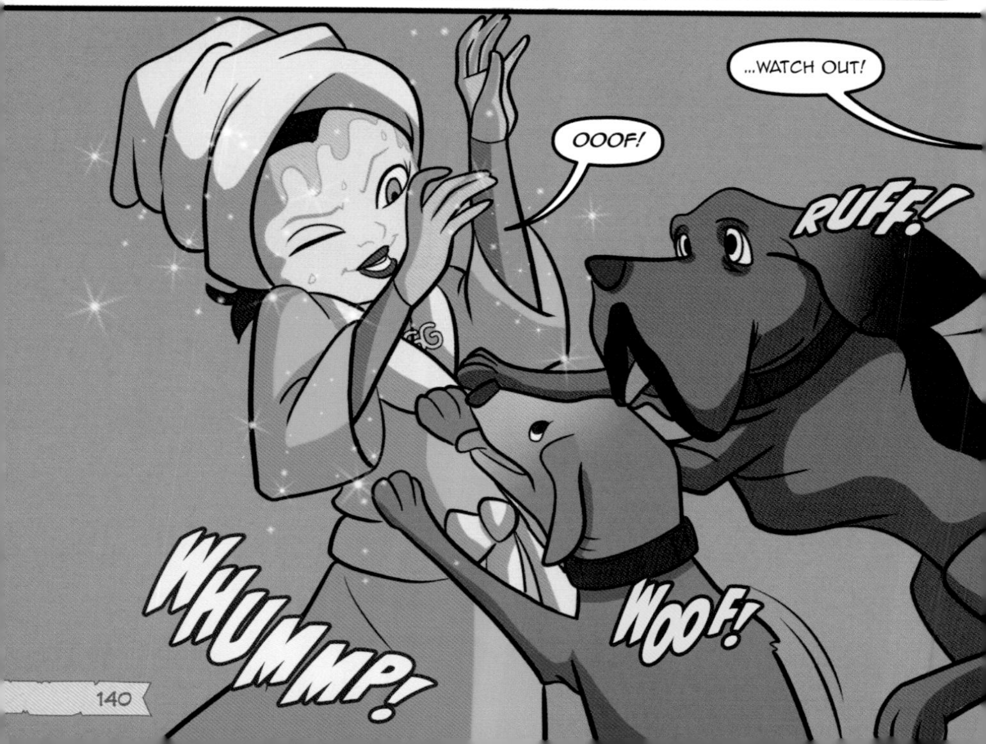
...WATCH OUT!
OOOF!
RUFF!
WHUMMP!
WOOF!

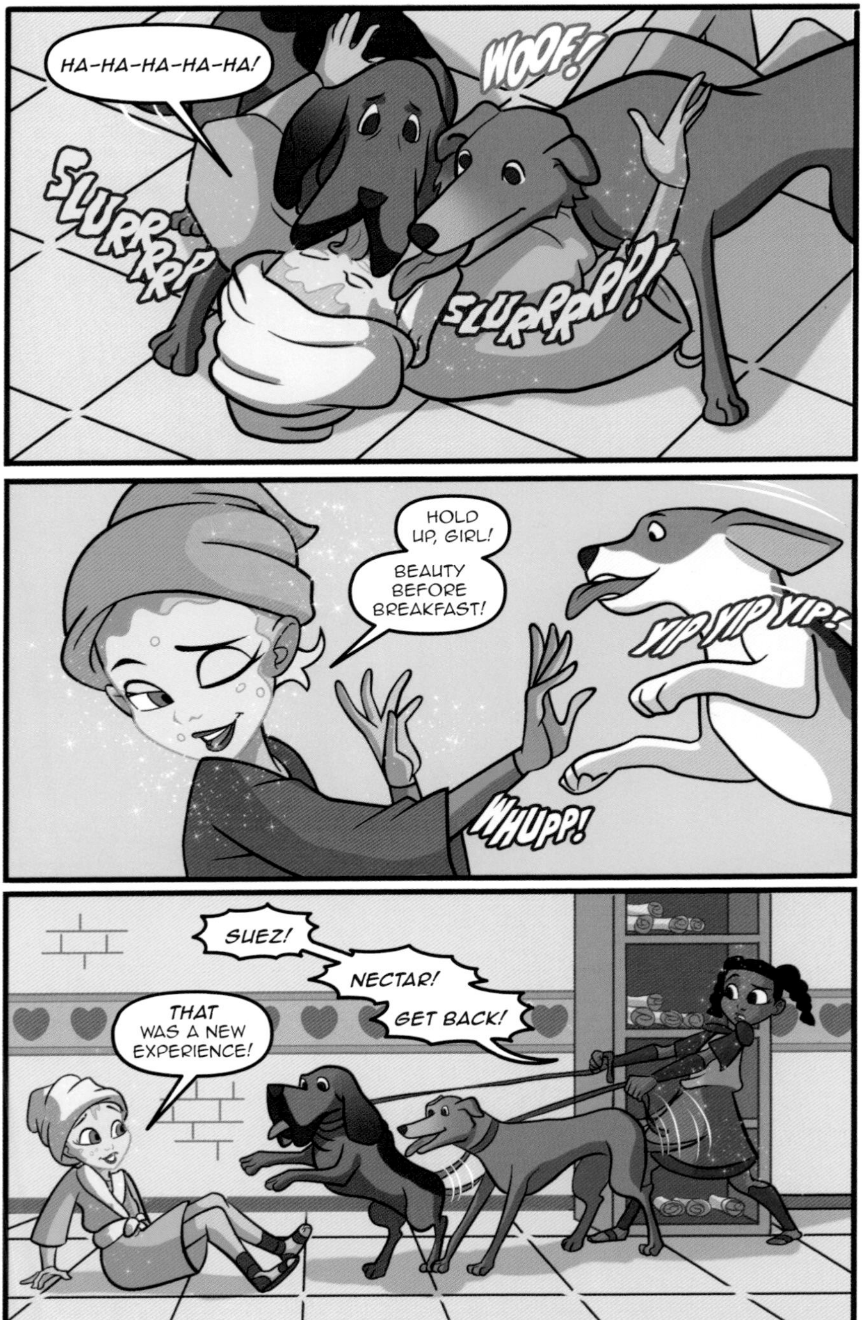
HA-HA-HA-HA-HA!
WOOF!
SLURRRRRP
SLURRRRP!
HOLD UP, GIRL!
BEAUTY BEFORE BREAKFAST!
YIP YIP YIP!
WHUPP!
SUEZ!
NECTAR!
GET BACK!
THAT WAS A NEW EXPERIENCE!

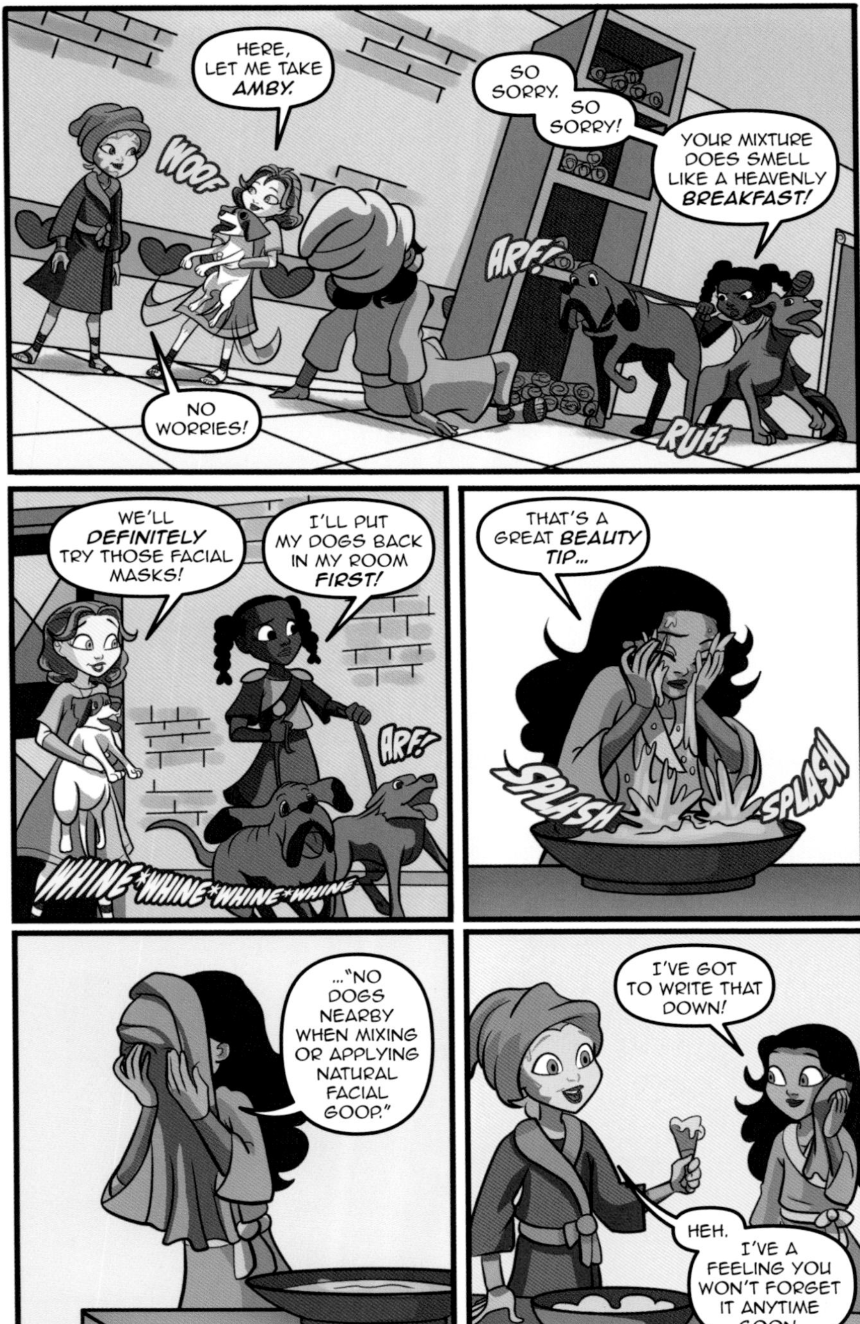
HERE, LET ME TAKE AMBY.
WOOF
SO SORRY.
SO SORRY!
YOUR MIXTURE DOES SMELL LIKE A HEAVENLY BREAKFAST!
ARF!
NO WORRIES!
RUFF
WE'LL DEFINITELY TRY THOSE FACIAL MASKS!
I'LL PUT MY DOGS BACK IN MY ROOM FIRST!
ARF!
WHINE*WHINE*WHINE*WHINE
THAT'S A GREAT BEAUTY TIP...
SPLASH
SPLASH
..."NO DOGS NEARBY WHEN MIXING OR APPLYING NATURAL FACIAL GOOP."
I'VE GOT TO WRITE THAT DOWN!
HEH. I'VE A FEELING YOU WON'T FORGET IT ANYTIME SOON.

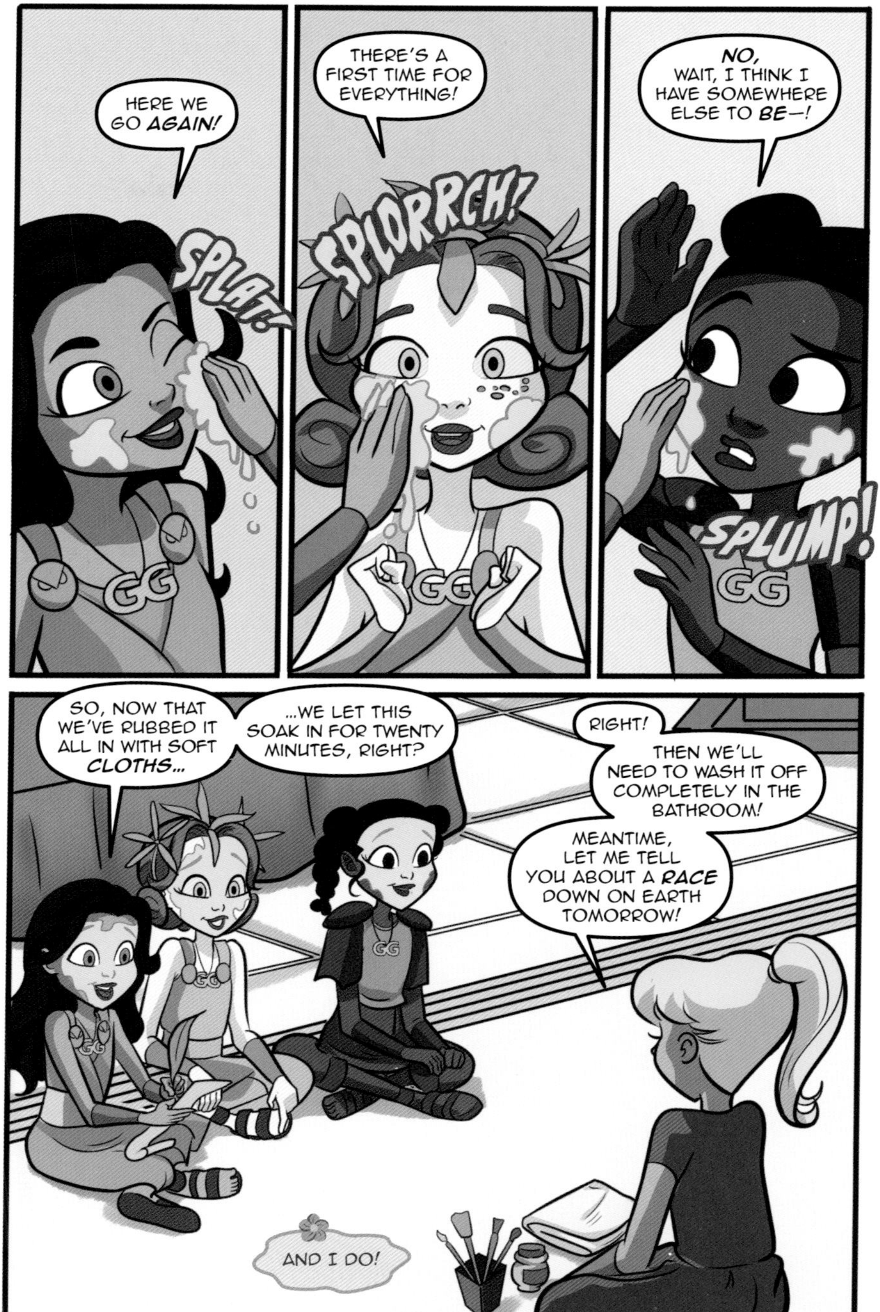
HERE WE GO AGAIN!
SPLAT!
THERE'S A FIRST TIME FOR EVERYTHING!
SPLORRCH!
NO, WAIT, I THINK I HAVE SOMEWHERE ELSE TO BE—!
SPLUMP!
SO, NOW THAT WE'VE RUBBED IT ALL IN WITH SOFT CLOTHS...
...WE LET THIS SOAK IN FOR TWENTY MINUTES, RIGHT?
RIGHT!
THEN WE'LL NEED TO WASH IT OFF COMPLETELY IN THE BATHROOM!
MEANTIME, LET ME TELL YOU ABOUT A RACE DOWN ON EARTH TOMORROW!
AND I DO!

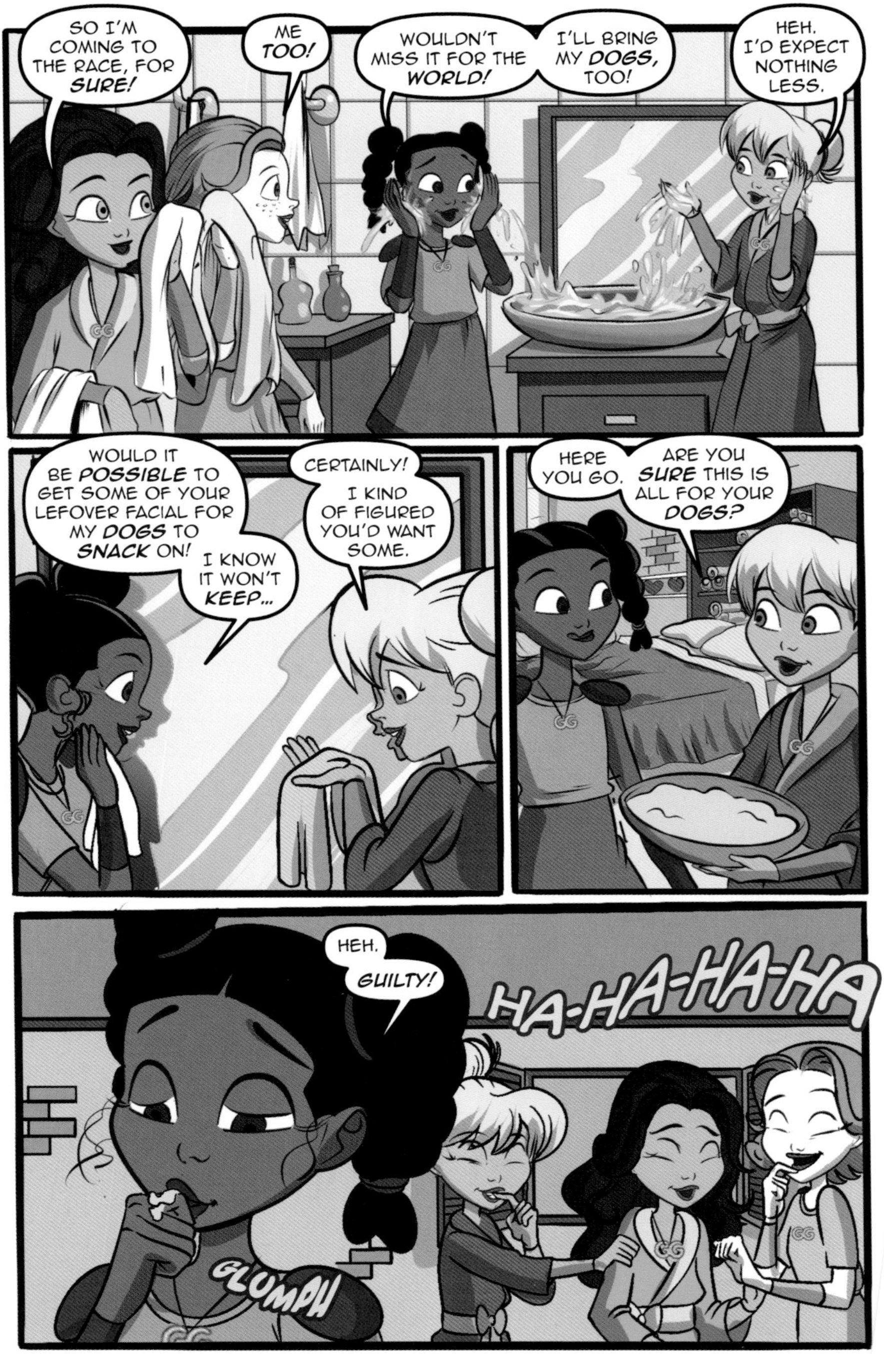
SO I'M COMING TO THE RACE, FOR SURE!
ME TOO!
WOULDN'T MISS IT FOR THE WORLD!
I'LL BRING MY DOGS, TOO!
HEH. I'D EXPECT NOTHING LESS.
WOULD IT BE POSSIBLE TO GET SOME OF YOUR LEFOVER FACIAL FOR MY DOGS TO SNACK ON!
I KNOW IT WON'T KEEP...
CERTAINLY!
I KIND OF FIGURED YOU'D WANT SOME.
HERE YOU GO.
ARE YOU SURE THIS IS ALL FOR YOUR DOGS?
HEH. GUILTY!
HA-HA-HA-HA-HA
GLUMPH

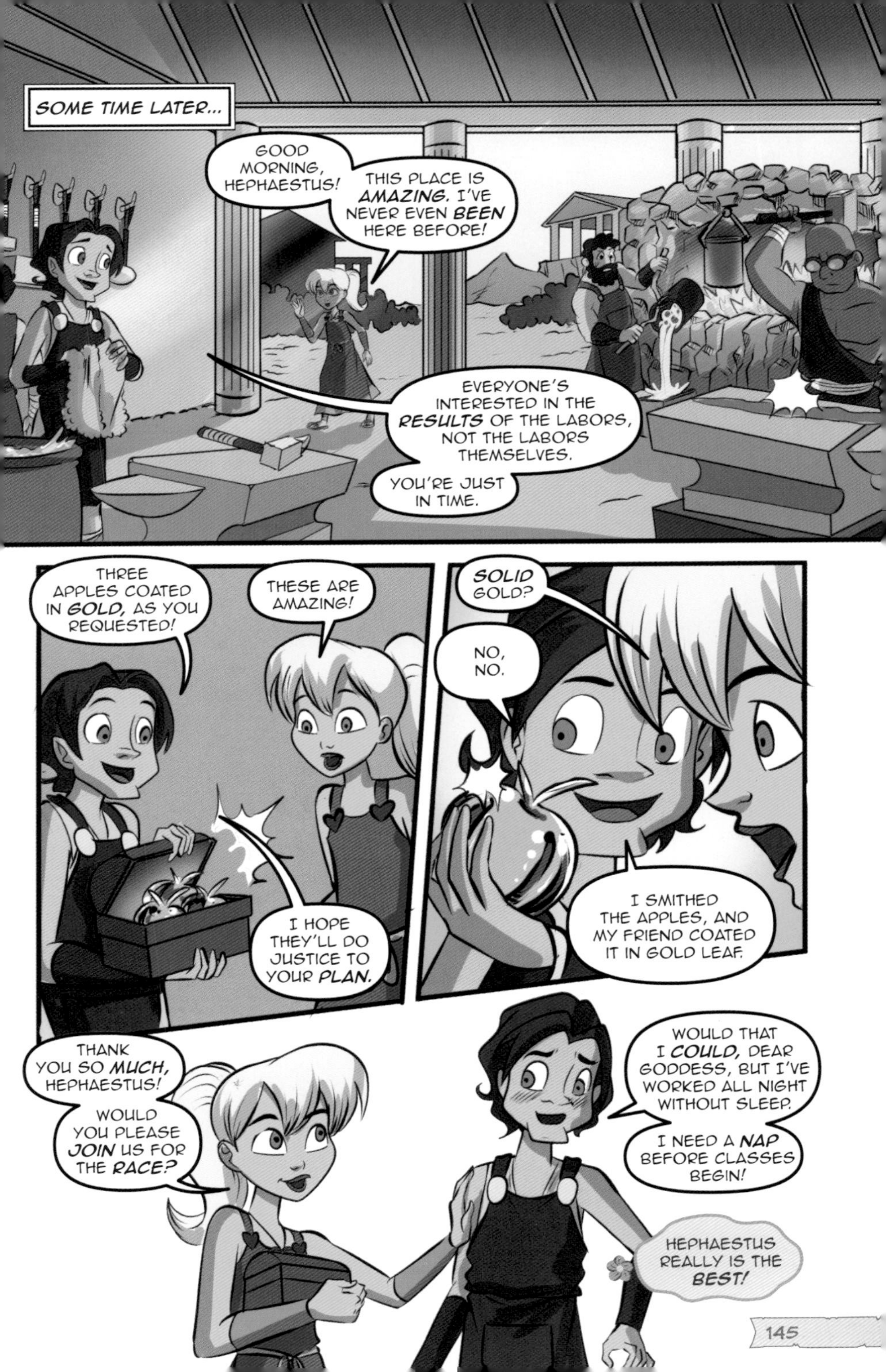
SOME TIME LATER...
GOOD MORNING, HEPHAESTUS!
THIS PLACE IS AMAZING. I'VE NEVER EVEN BEEN HERE BEFORE!
EVERYONE'S INTERESTED IN THE RESULTS OF THE LABORS, NOT THE LABORS THEMSELVES.
YOU'RE JUST IN TIME.
THREE APPLES COATED IN GOLD, AS YOU REQUESTED!
THESE ARE AMAZING!
I HOPE THEY'LL DO JUSTICE TO YOUR PLAN.
SOLID GOLD?
NO, NO.
I SMITHED THE APPLES, AND MY FRIEND COATED IT IN GOLD LEAF.
THANK YOU SO MUCH, HEPHAESTUS!
WOULD YOU PLEASE JOIN US FOR THE RACE?
WOULD THAT I COULD, DEAR GODDESS, BUT I'VE WORKED ALL NIGHT WITHOUT SLEEP.
I NEED A NAP BEFORE CLASSES BEGIN!
HEPHAESTUS REALLY IS THE BEST!

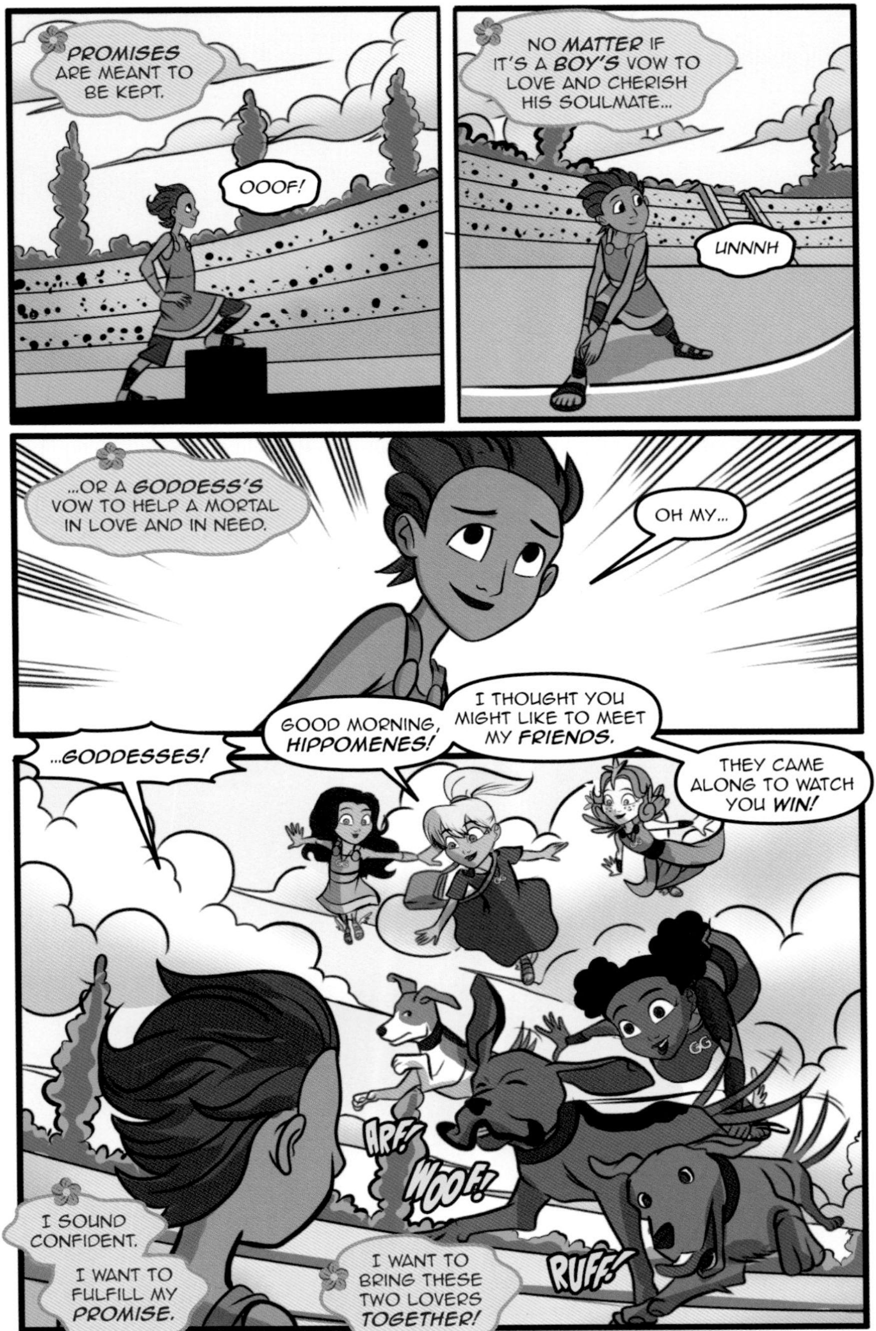
PROMISES ARE MEANT TO BE KEPT.
OOOF!
NO MATTER IF IT'S A BOY'S VOW TO LOVE AND CHERISH HIS SOULMATE...
UNNNH
...OR A GODDESS'S VOW TO HELP A MORTAL IN LOVE AND IN NEED.
OH MY...
...GODDESSES!
GOOD MORNING, HIPPOMENES!
I THOUGHT YOU MIGHT LIKE TO MEET MY FRIENDS.
THEY CAME ALONG TO WATCH YOU WIN!
ARF!
WOOF!
RUFF!
I SOUND CONFIDENT.
I WANT TO FULFILL MY PROMISE.
I WANT TO BRING THESE TWO LOVERS TOGETHER!

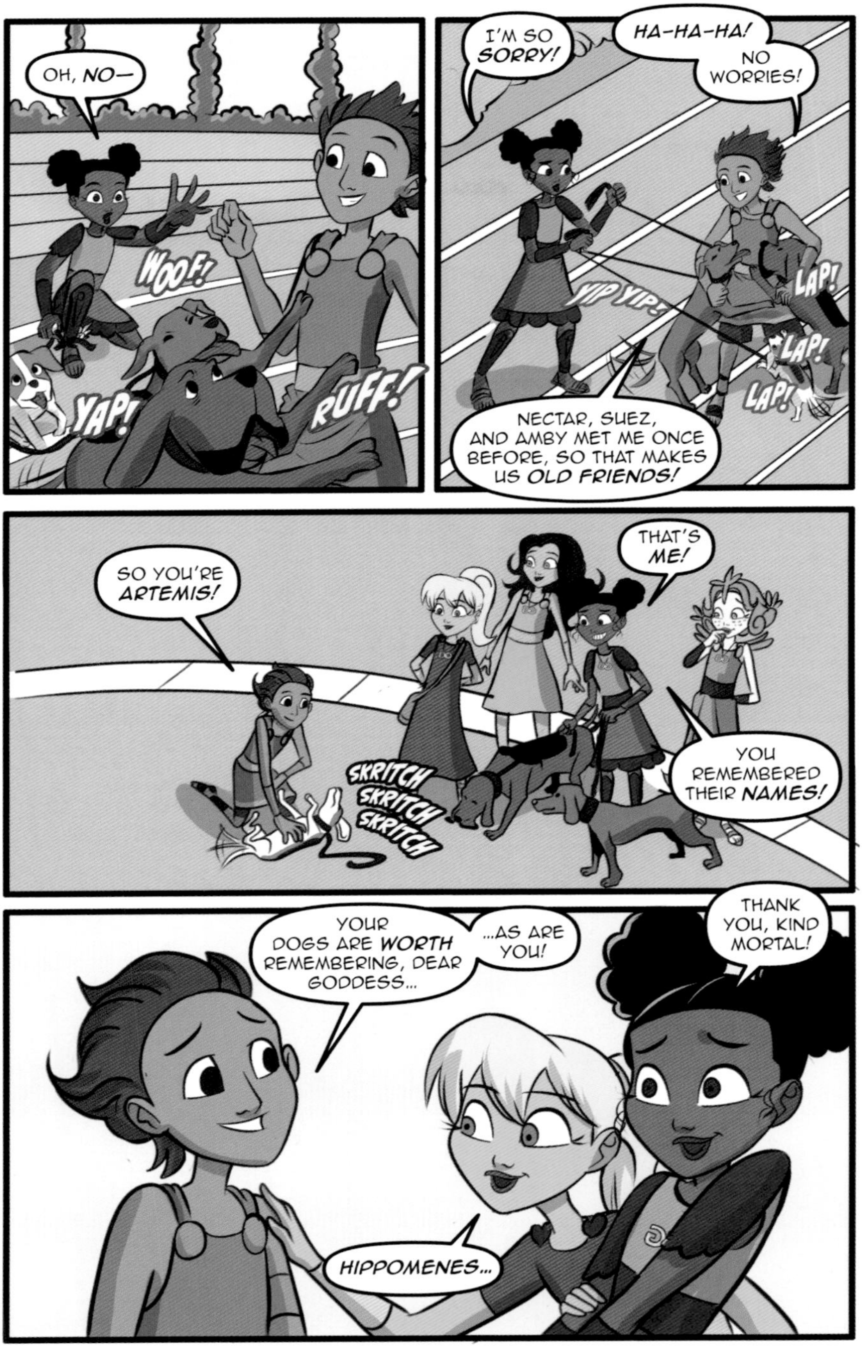
OH, NO—
WOOF!
YAP!
RUFF!
I'M SO SORRY!
HA-HA-HA! NO WORRIES!
YIP YIP!
LAP!
LAP!
LAP!
NECTAR, SUEZ, AND AMBY MET ME ONCE BEFORE, SO THAT MAKES US OLD FRIENDS!
SO YOU'RE ARTEMIS!
THAT'S ME!
SKRITCH SKRITCH SKRITCH
YOU REMEMBERED THEIR NAMES!
YOUR DOGS ARE WORTH REMEMBERING, DEAR GODDESS...
...AS ARE YOU!
THANK YOU, KIND MORTAL!
HIPPOMENES...

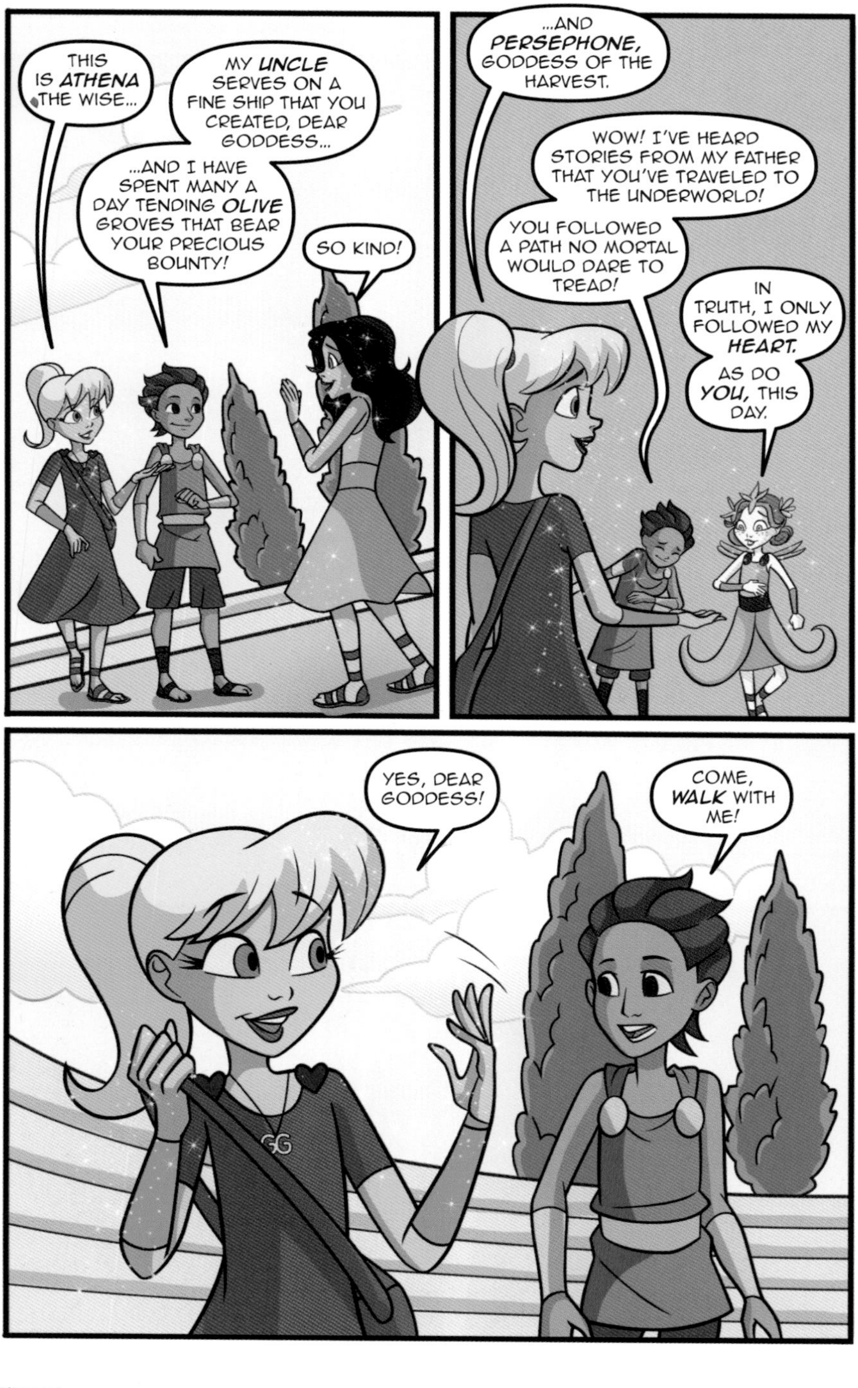
THIS IS ATHENA THE WISE...
MY UNCLE SERVES ON A FINE SHIP THAT YOU CREATED, DEAR GODDESS...
...AND I HAVE SPENT MANY A DAY TENDING OLIVE GROVES THAT BEAR YOUR PRECIOUS BOUNTY!
SO KIND!
...AND PERSEPHONE, GODDESS OF THE HARVEST.
WOW! I'VE HEARD STORIES FROM MY FATHER THAT YOU'VE TRAVELED TO THE UNDERWORLD!
YOU FOLLOWED A PATH NO MORTAL WOULD DARE TO TREAD!
IN TRUTH, I ONLY FOLLOWED MY HEART.
AS DO YOU, THIS DAY.
COME, WALK WITH ME!
YES, DEAR GODDESS!

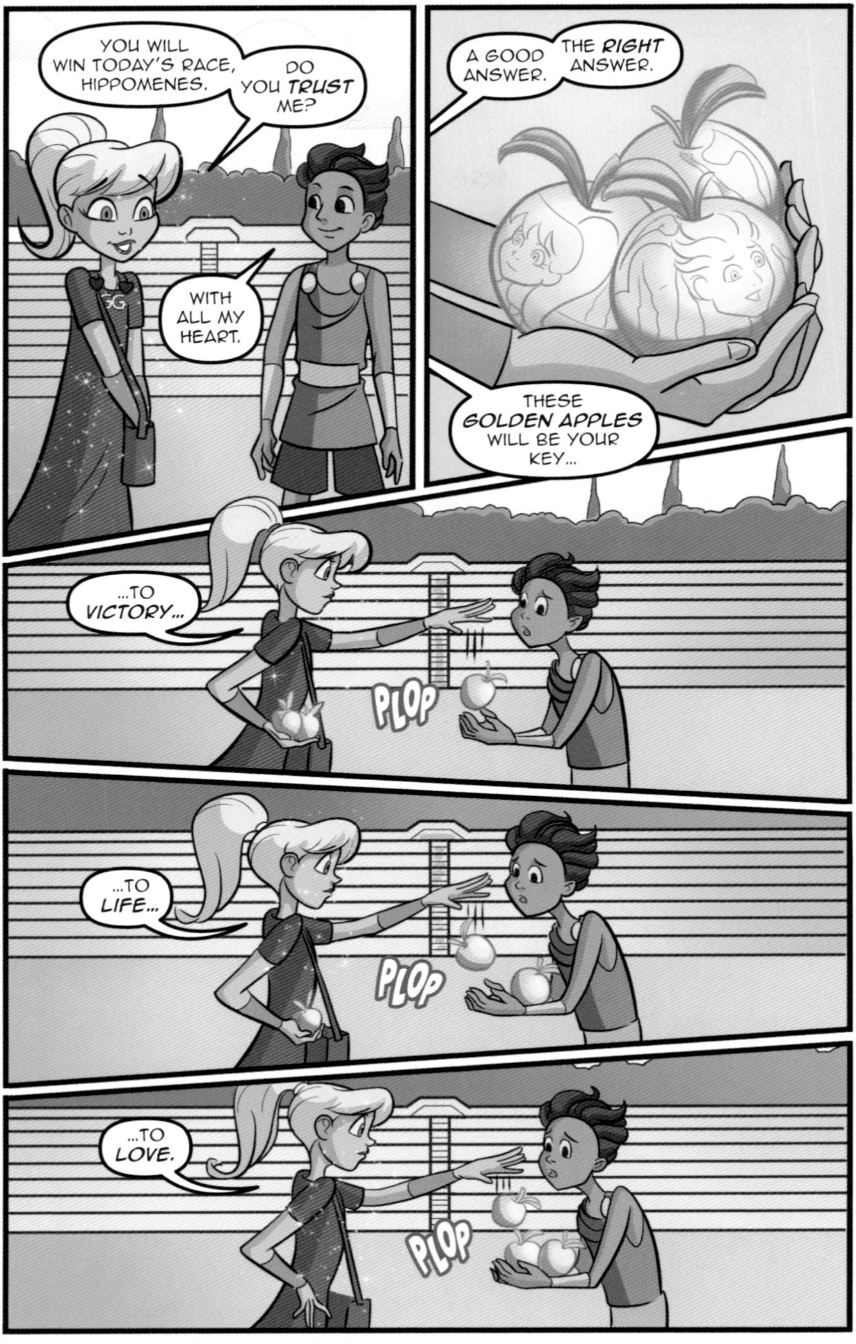
YOU WILL WIN TODAY'S RACE, HIPPOMENES.
DO YOU TRUST ME?
WITH ALL MY HEART.
A GOOD ANSWER.
THE RIGHT ANSWER.
THESE GOLDEN APPLES WILL BE YOUR KEY...
...TO VICTORY...
PLOP
...TO LIFE...
PLOP
...TO LOVE.
PLOP

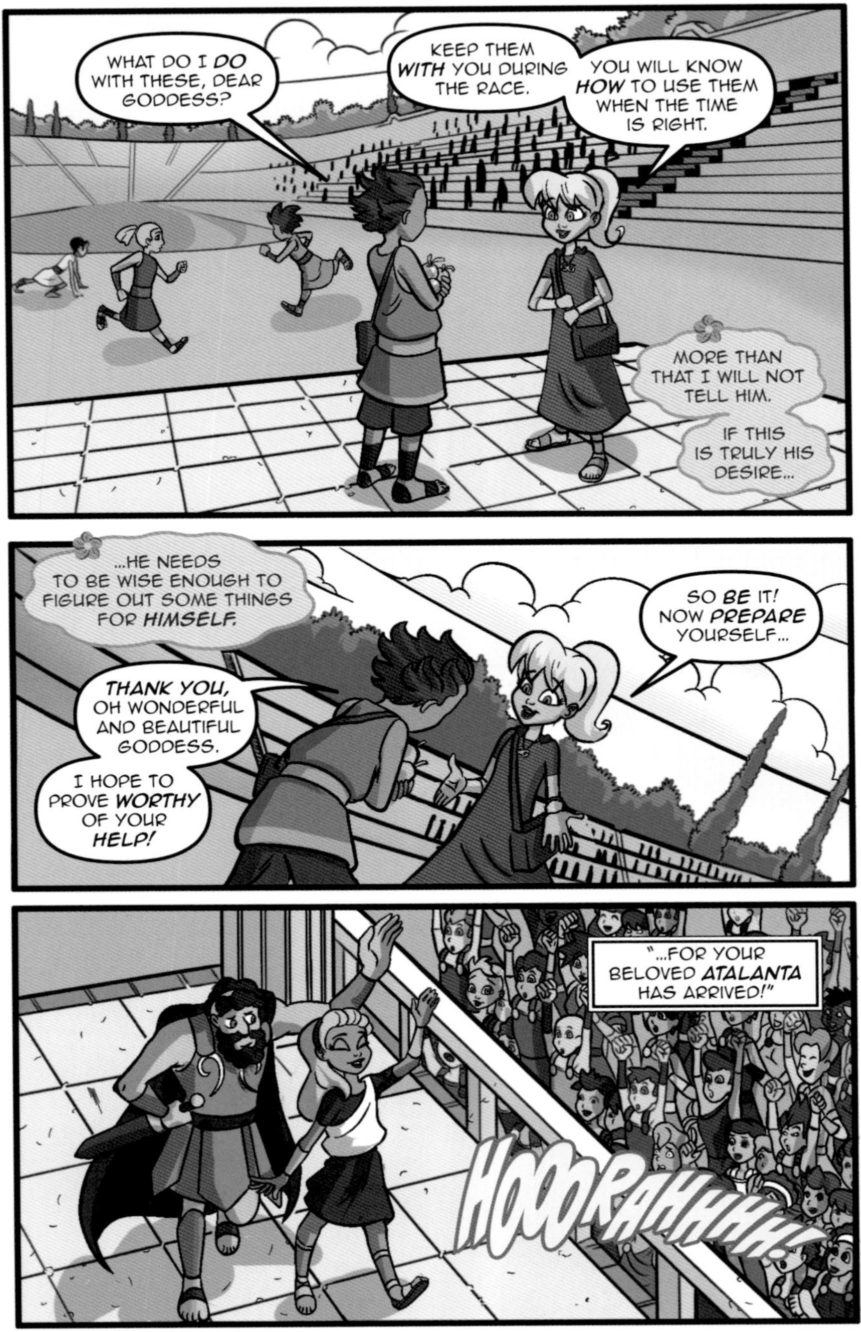

WHAT DO I DO WITH THESE, DEAR GODDESS?
KEEP THEM WITH YOU DURING THE RACE.
YOU WILL KNOW HOW TO USE THEM WHEN THE TIME IS RIGHT.
MORE THAN THAT I WILL NOT TELL HIM.
IF THIS IS TRULY HIS DESIRE...
...HE NEEDS TO BE WISE ENOUGH TO FIGURE OUT SOME THINGS FOR HIMSELF.
THANK YOU, OH WONDERFUL AND BEAUTIFUL GODDESS.
I HOPE TO PROVE WORTHY OF YOUR HELP!
SO BE IT! NOW PREPARE YOURSELF...
"...FOR YOUR BELOVED ATALANTA HAS ARRIVED!"
HOOORAHHHH!

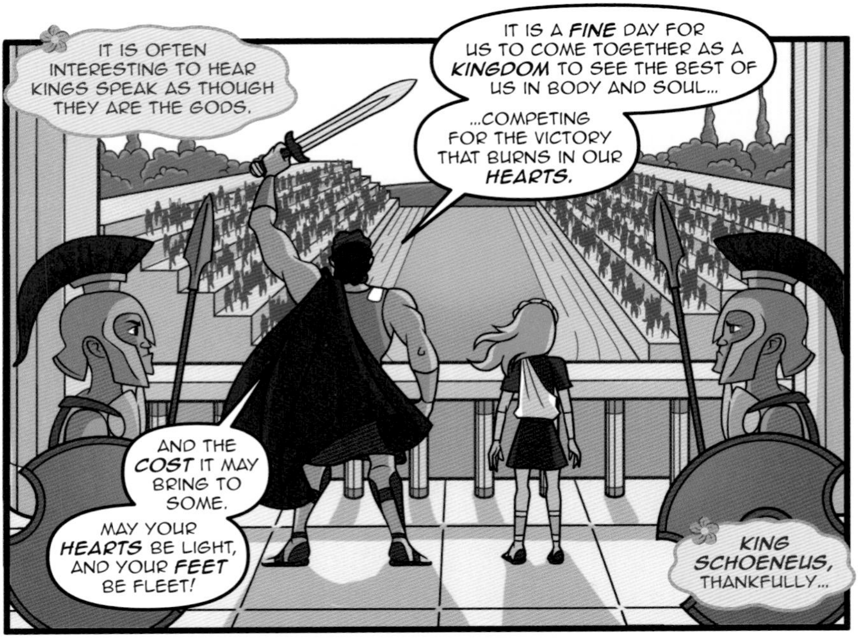
IT IS OFTEN INTERESTING TO HEAR KINGS SPEAK AS THOUGH THEY ARE THE GODS.
IT IS A FINE DAY FOR US TO COME TOGETHER AS A KINGDOM TO SEE THE BEST OF US IN BODY AND SOUL...
...COMPETING FOR THE VICTORY THAT BURNS IN OUR HEARTS.
AND THE COST IT MAY BRING TO SOME.
MAY YOUR HEARTS BE LIGHT, AND YOUR FEET BE FLEET!
KING SCHOENEUS, THANKFULLY...

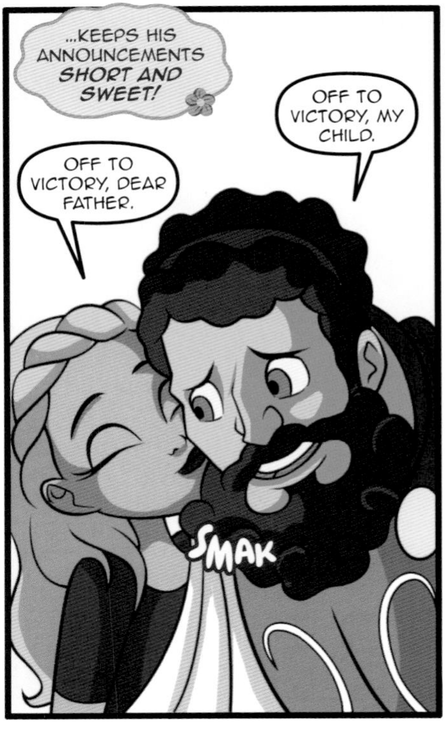
...KEEPS HIS ANNOUNCEMENTS SHORT AND SWEET!
OFF TO VICTORY, DEAR FATHER.
OFF TO VICTORY, MY CHILD.
SMAK

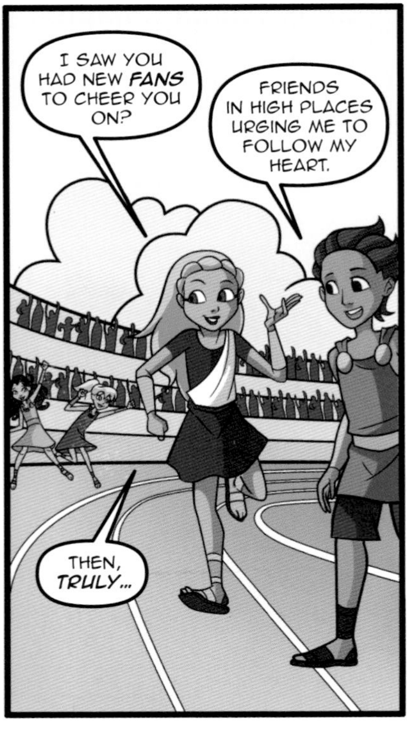
I SAW YOU HAD NEW FANS TO CHEER YOU ON?
FRIENDS IN HIGH PLACES URGING ME TO FOLLOW MY HEART.
THEN, TRULY...

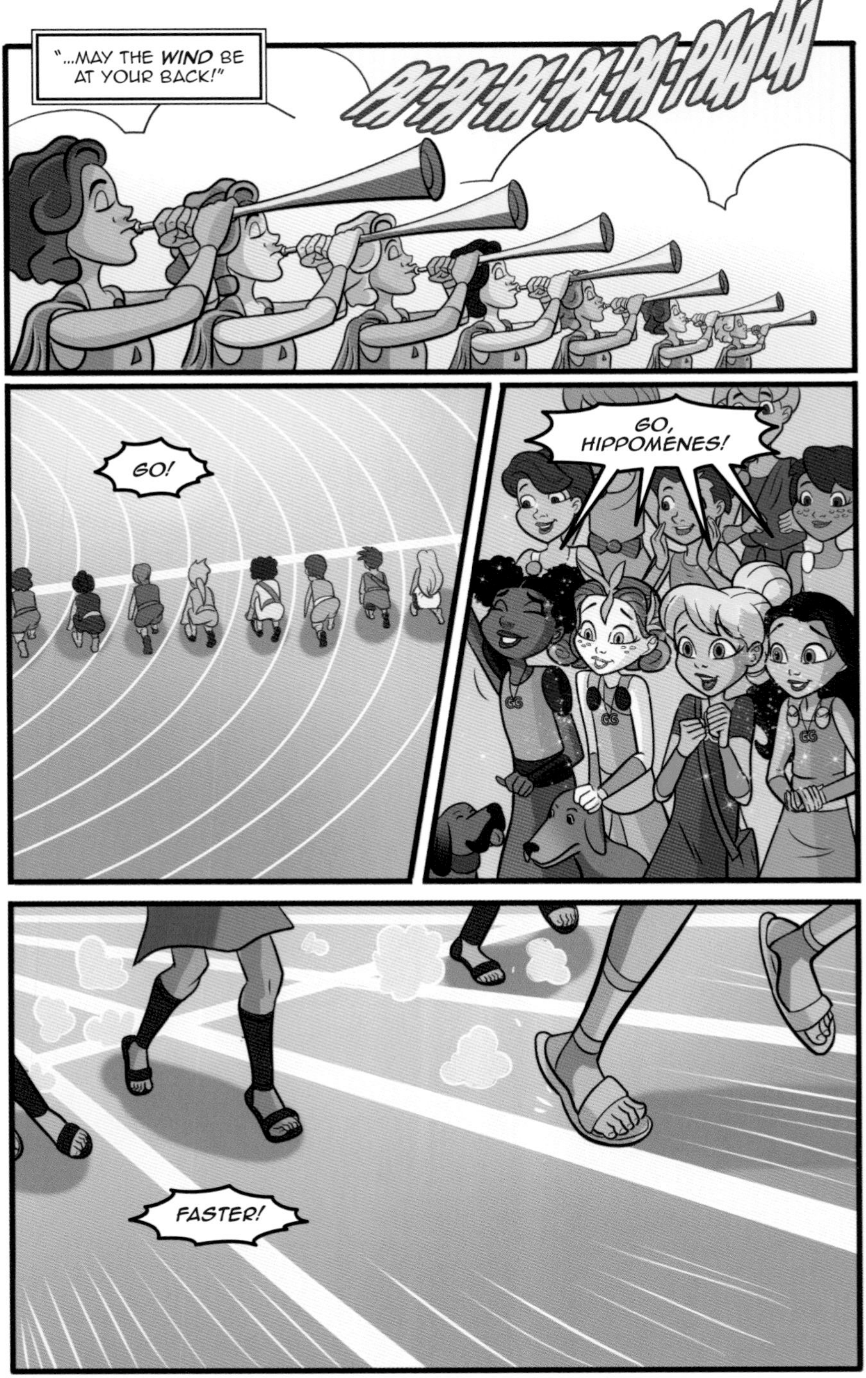
"...MAY THE *WIND* BE AT YOUR BACK!"
PA-PA-PA-PA-PA-PAAAA
GO!
GO, HIPPOMENES!
FASTER!

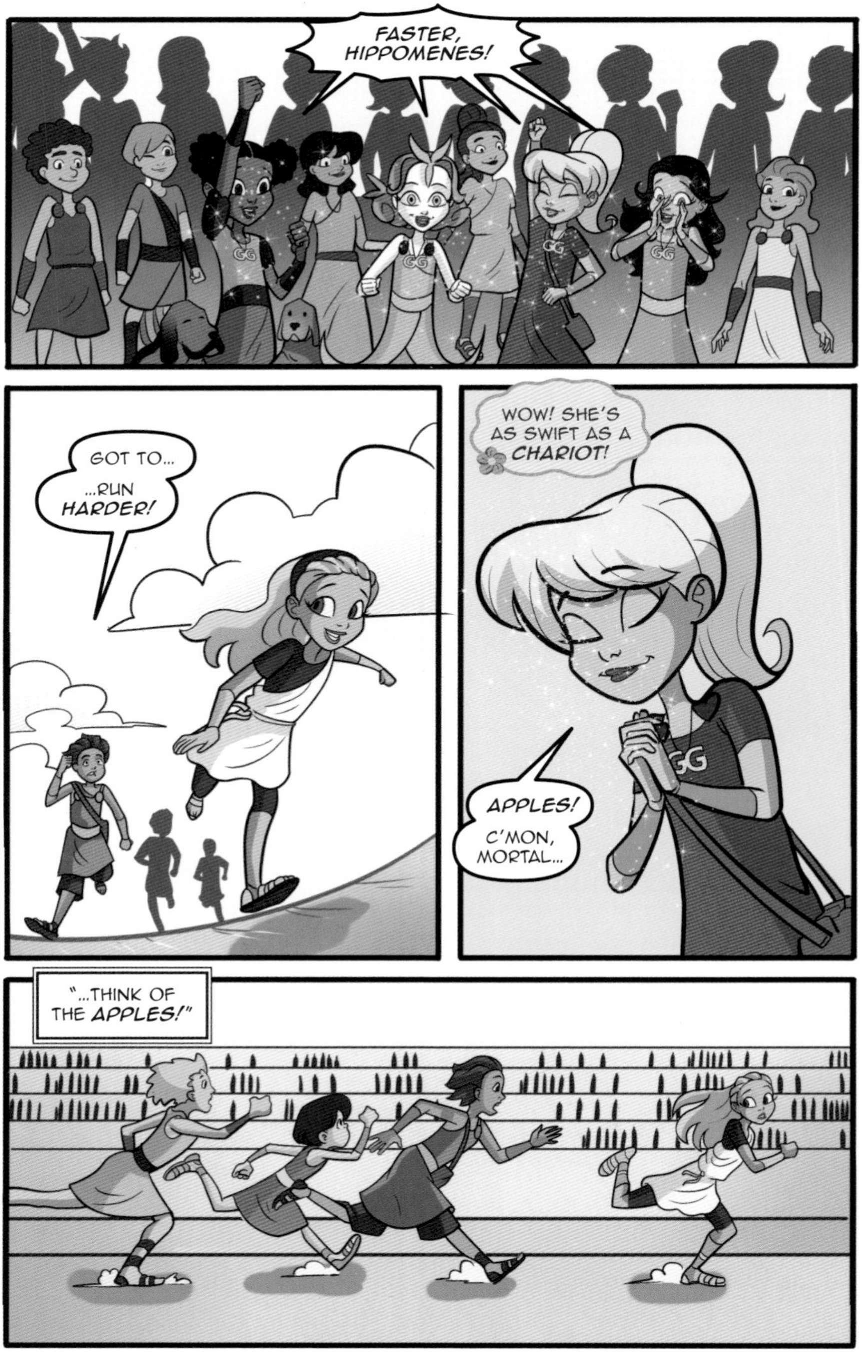
FASTER, HIPPOMENES!
GOT TO... ...RUN HARDER!
WOW! SHE'S AS SWIFT AS A CHARIOT!
APPLES! C'MON, MORTAL...
"...THINK OF THE APPLES!"

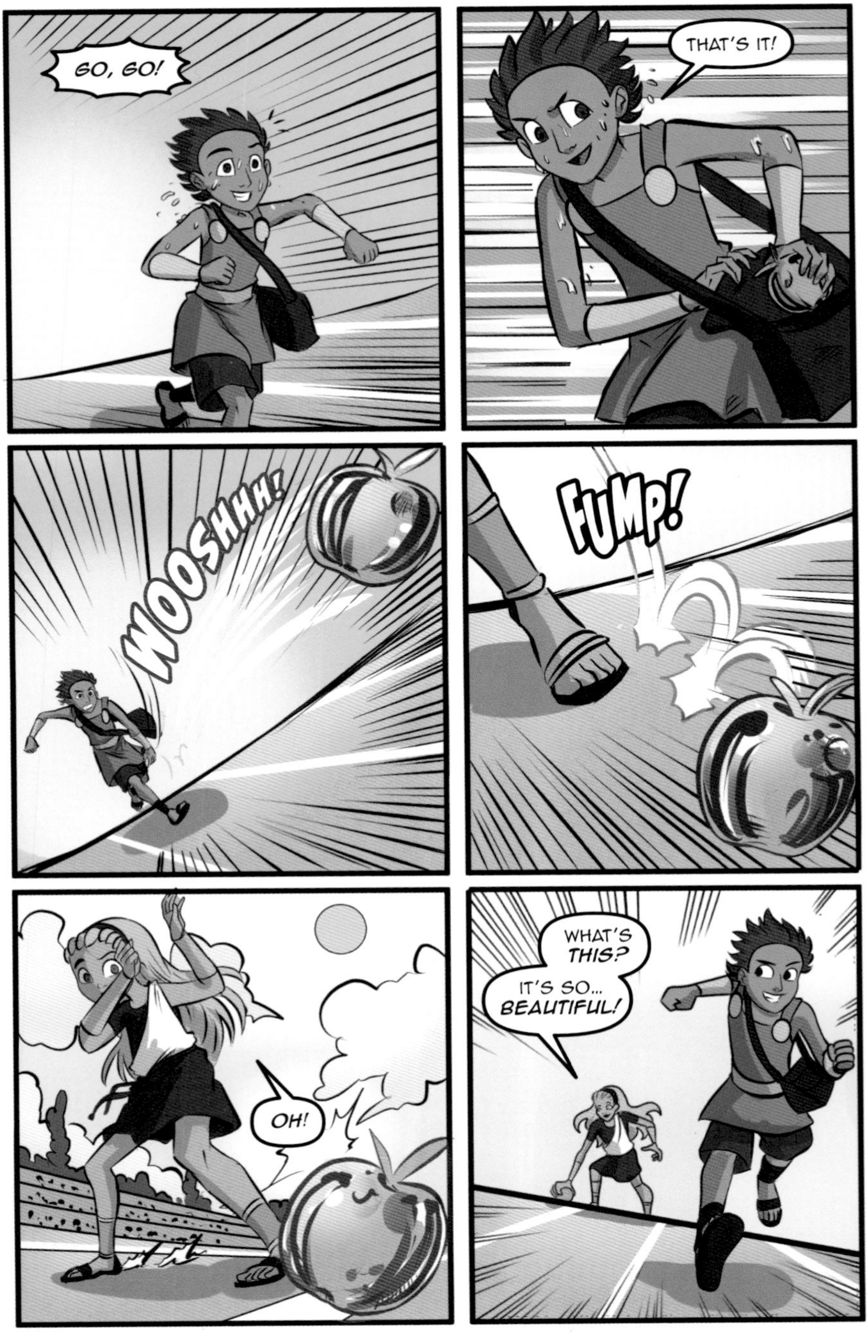
GO, GO!
THAT'S IT!
WOOSHHH!
FUMP!
OH!
WHAT'S THIS?
IT'S SO... BEAUTIFUL!

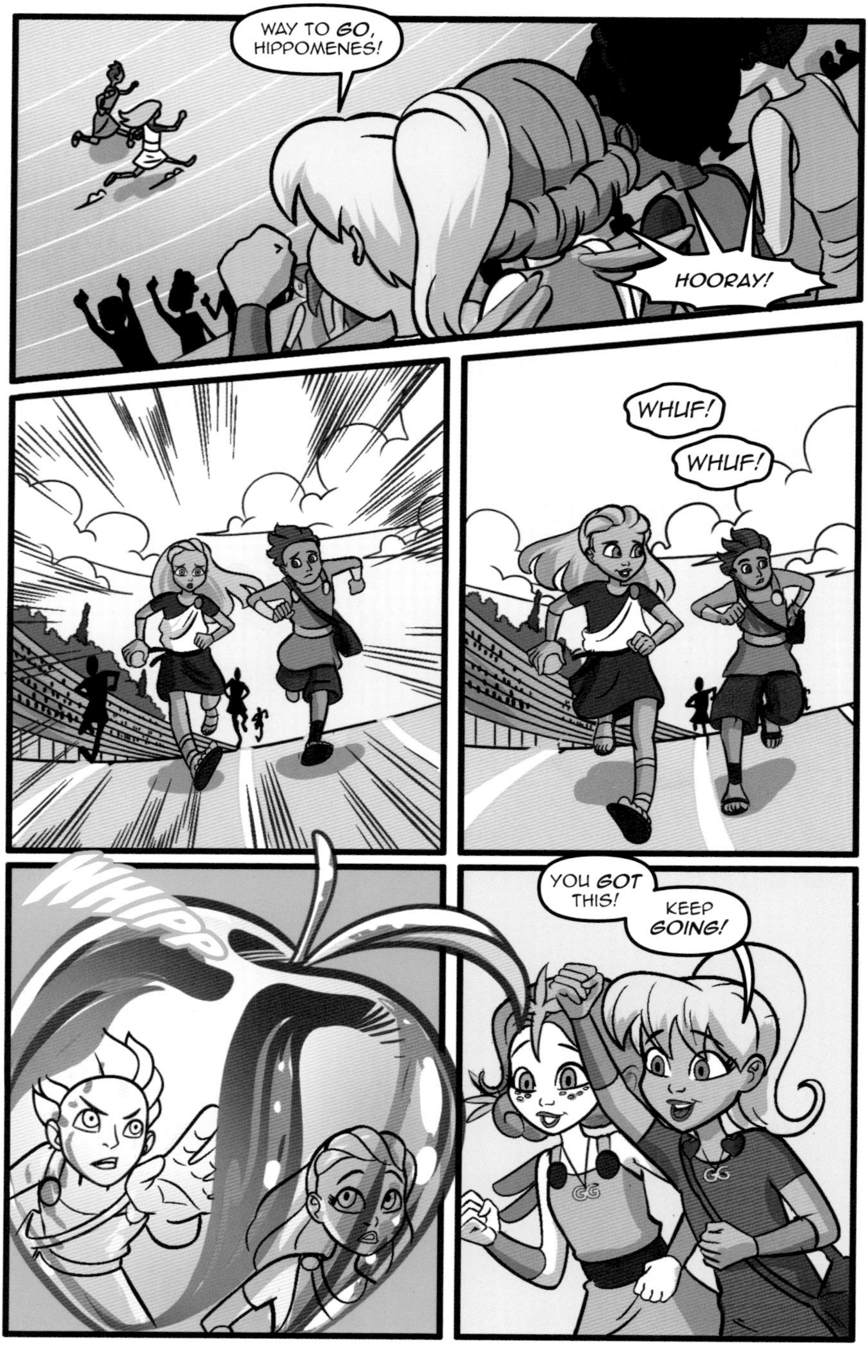
WAY TO GO, HIPPOMENES!
HOORAY!
WHUF!
WHUF!
WHIPP
YOU GOT THIS!
KEEP GOING!

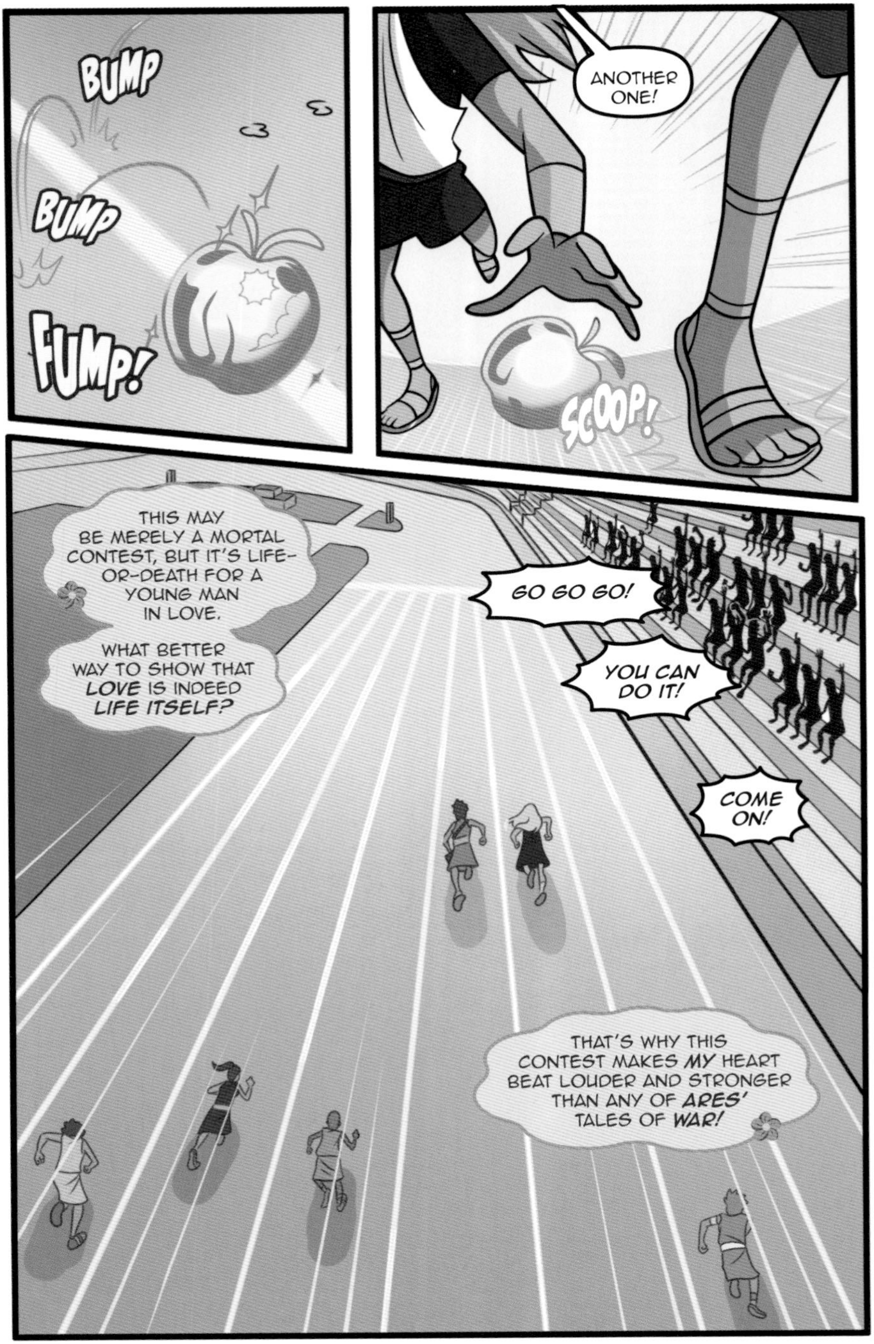
BUMP
BUMP
FUMP!
ANOTHER ONE!
SCOOP!
THIS MAY BE MERELY A MORTAL CONTEST, BUT IT'S LIFE-OR-DEATH FOR A YOUNG MAN IN LOVE.
WHAT BETTER WAY TO SHOW THAT LOVE IS INDEED LIFE ITSELF?
GO GO GO!
YOU CAN DO IT!
COME ON!
THAT'S WHY THIS CONTEST MAKES MY HEART BEAT LOUDER AND STRONGER THAN ANY OF ARES' TALES OF WAR!

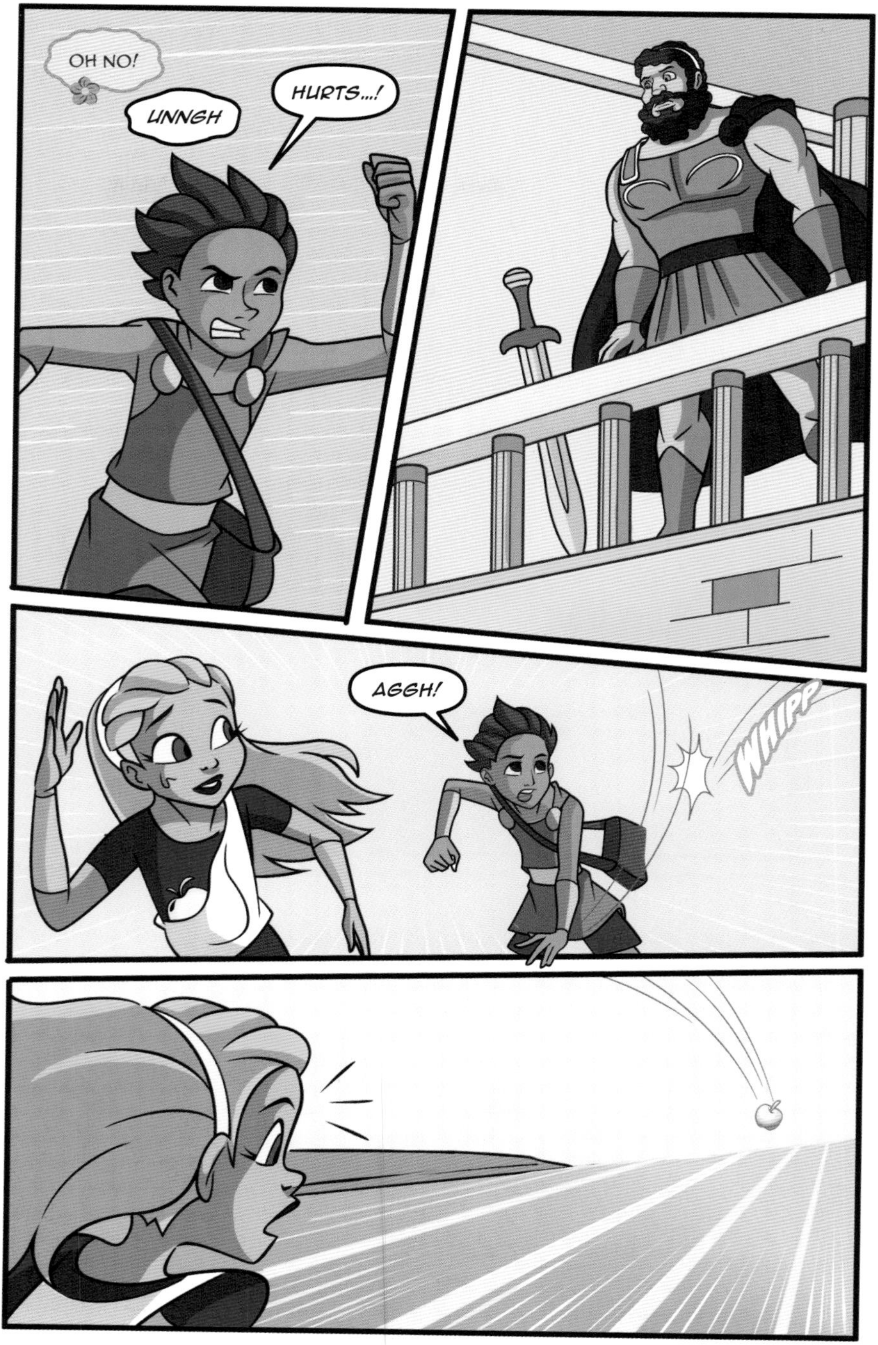
OH NO!
UNNGH
HURTS...!
AGGH!
WHIPP

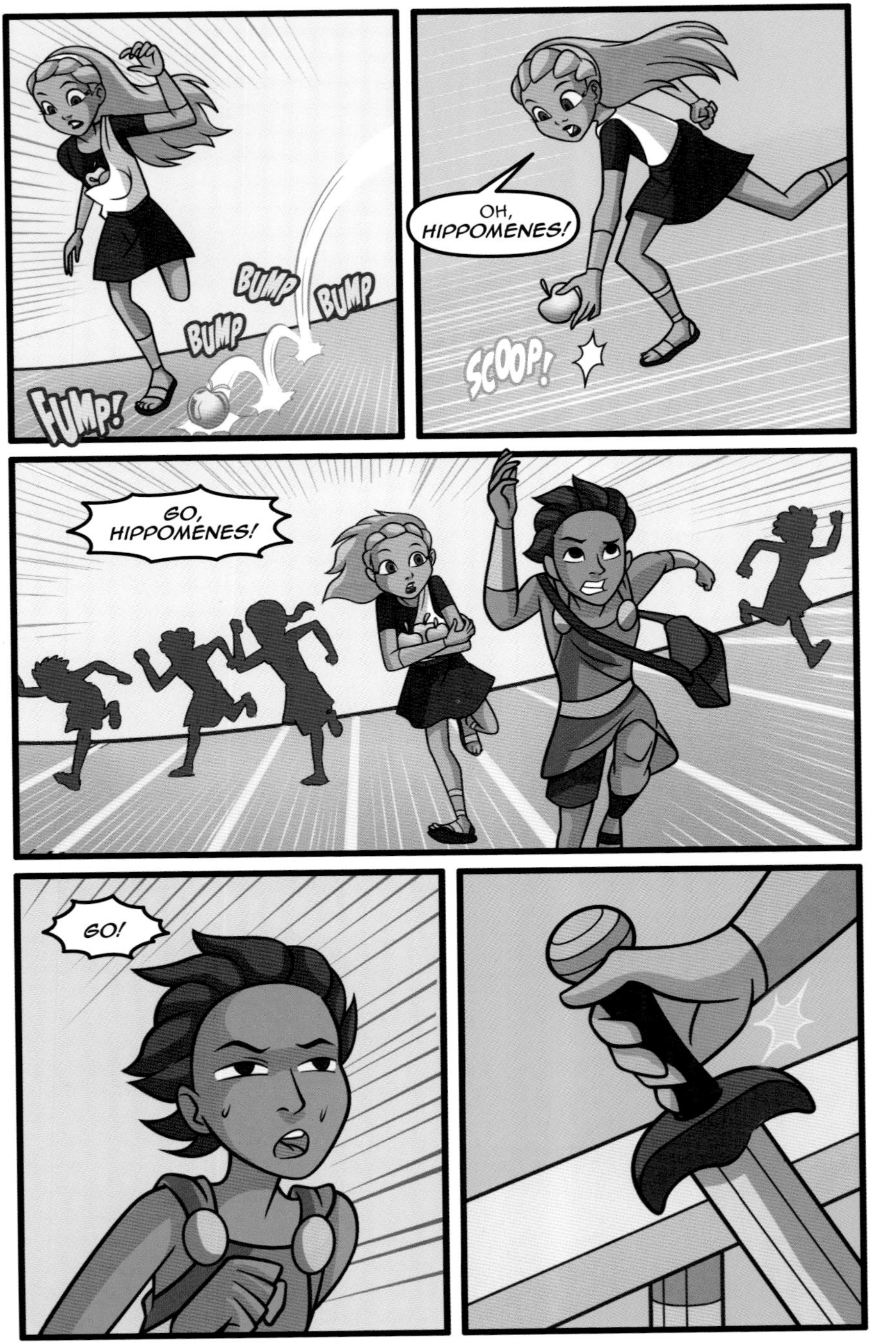
BUMP
BUMP
BUMP
FUMP!
OH, HIPPOMENES!
SCOOP!
GO, HIPPOMENES!
GO!

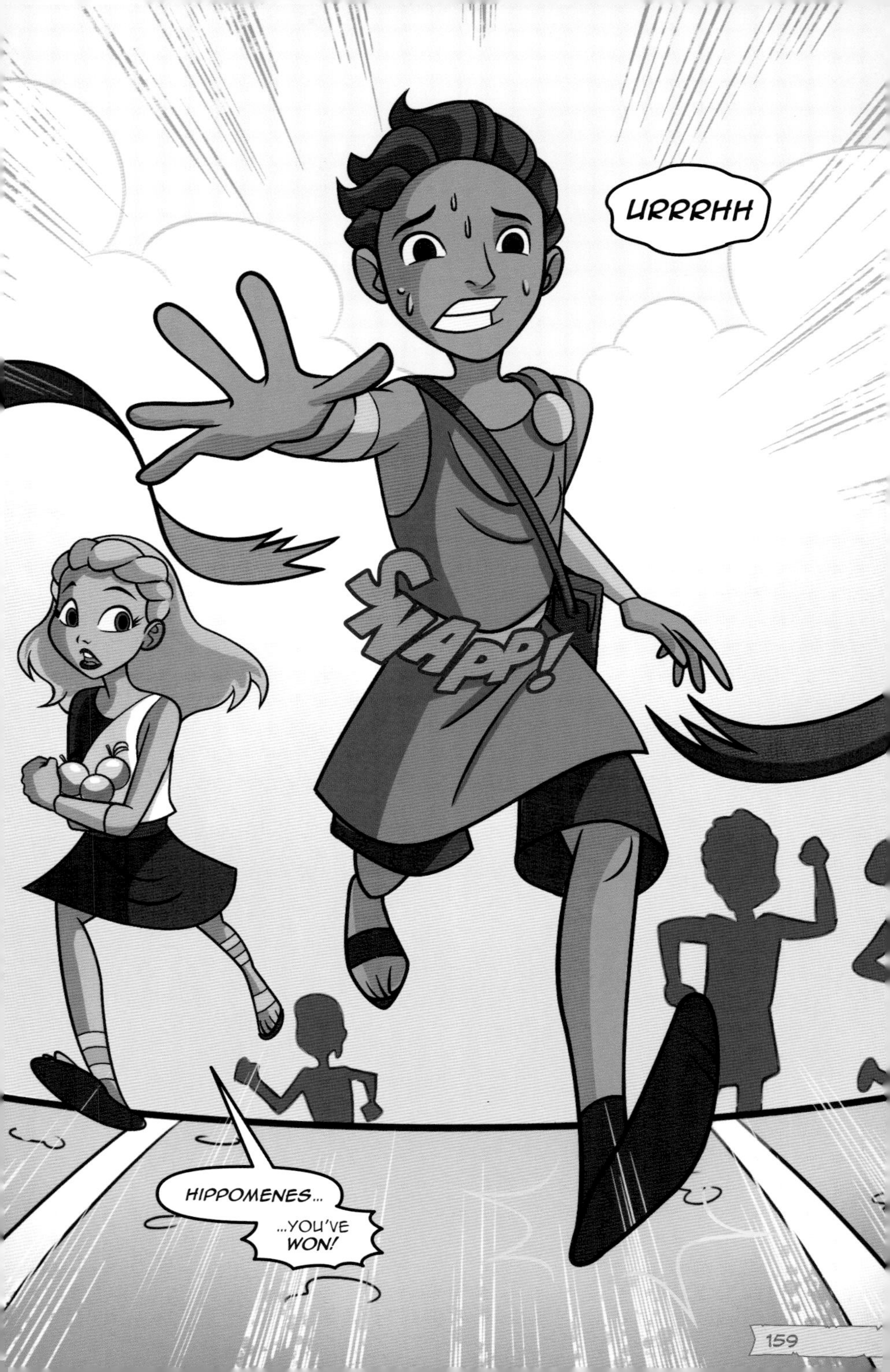
URRRHH
WHAPP!
HIPPOMENES...
...YOU'VE WON!

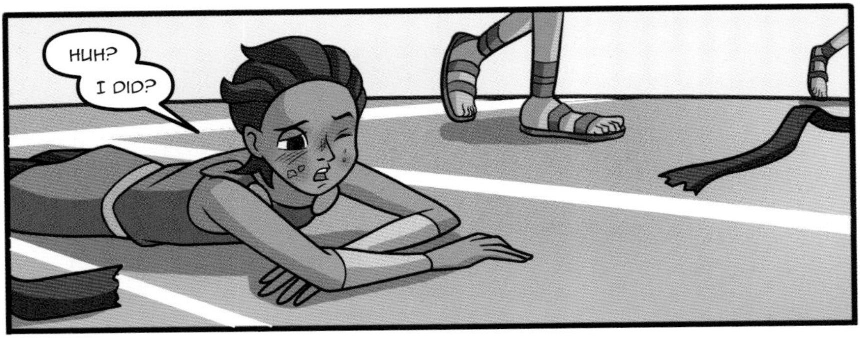
HUH?
I DID?

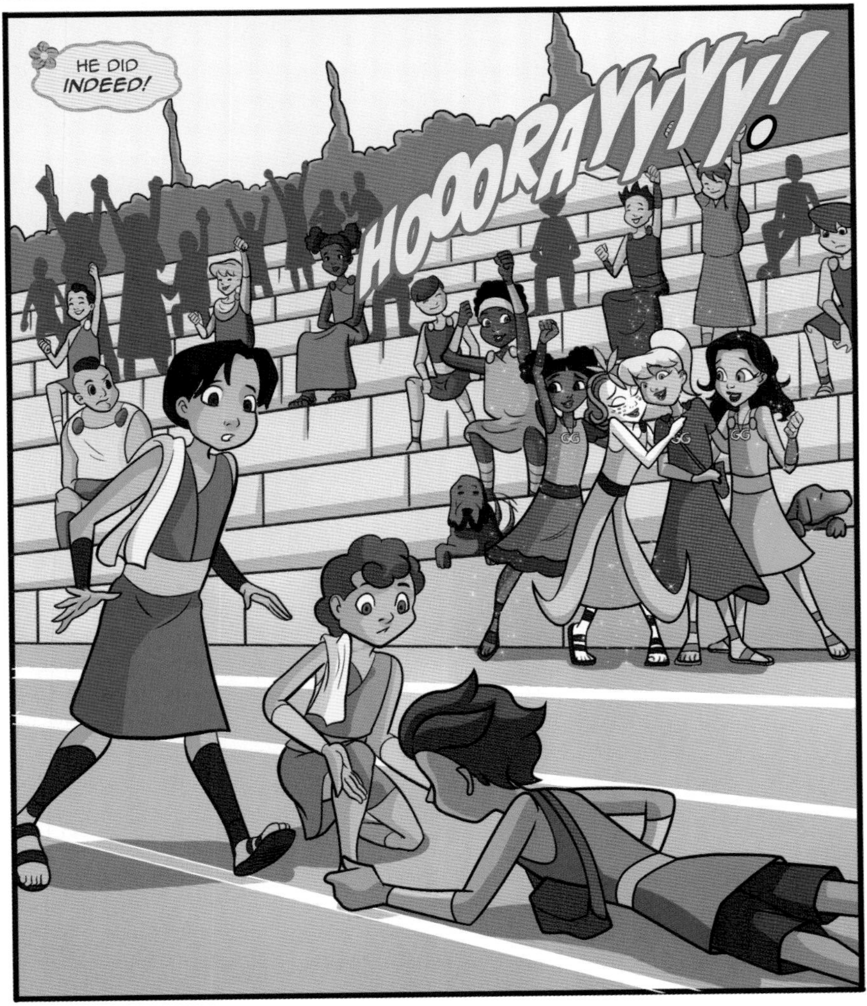
HE DID INDEED!
HOOORAYYYY!

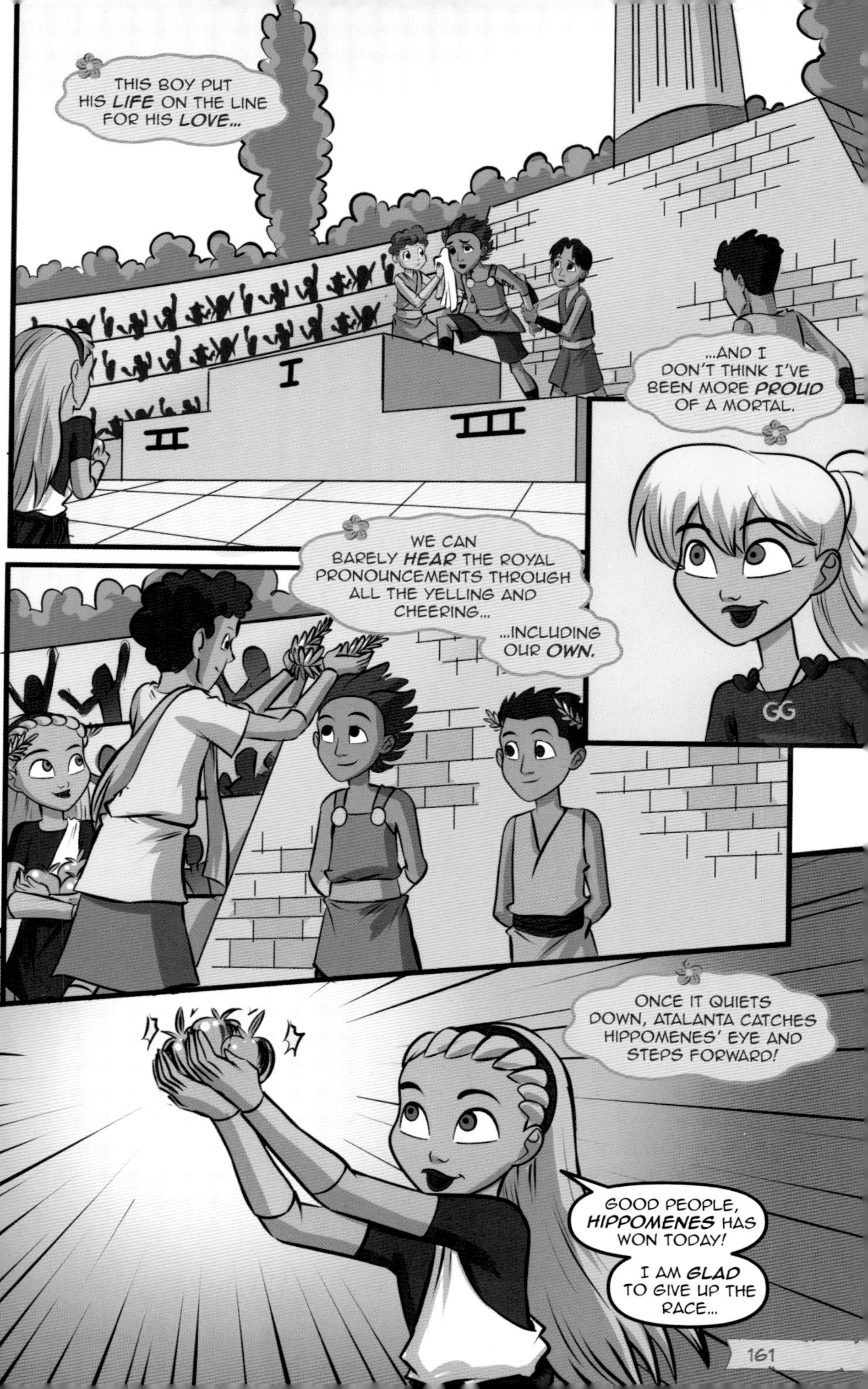

THIS BOY PUT HIS LIFE ON THE LINE FOR HIS LOVE...
...AND I DON'T THINK I'VE BEEN MORE PROUD OF A MORTAL.
I
II
III
GG
WE CAN BARELY HEAR THE ROYAL PRONOUNCEMENTS THROUGH ALL THE YELLING AND CHEERING...
...INCLUDING OUR OWN.
ONCE IT QUIETS DOWN, ATALANTA CATCHES HIPPOMENES' EYE AND STEPS FORWARD!
GOOD PEOPLE, HIPPOMENES HAS WON TODAY!
I AM GLAD TO GIVE UP THE RACE...

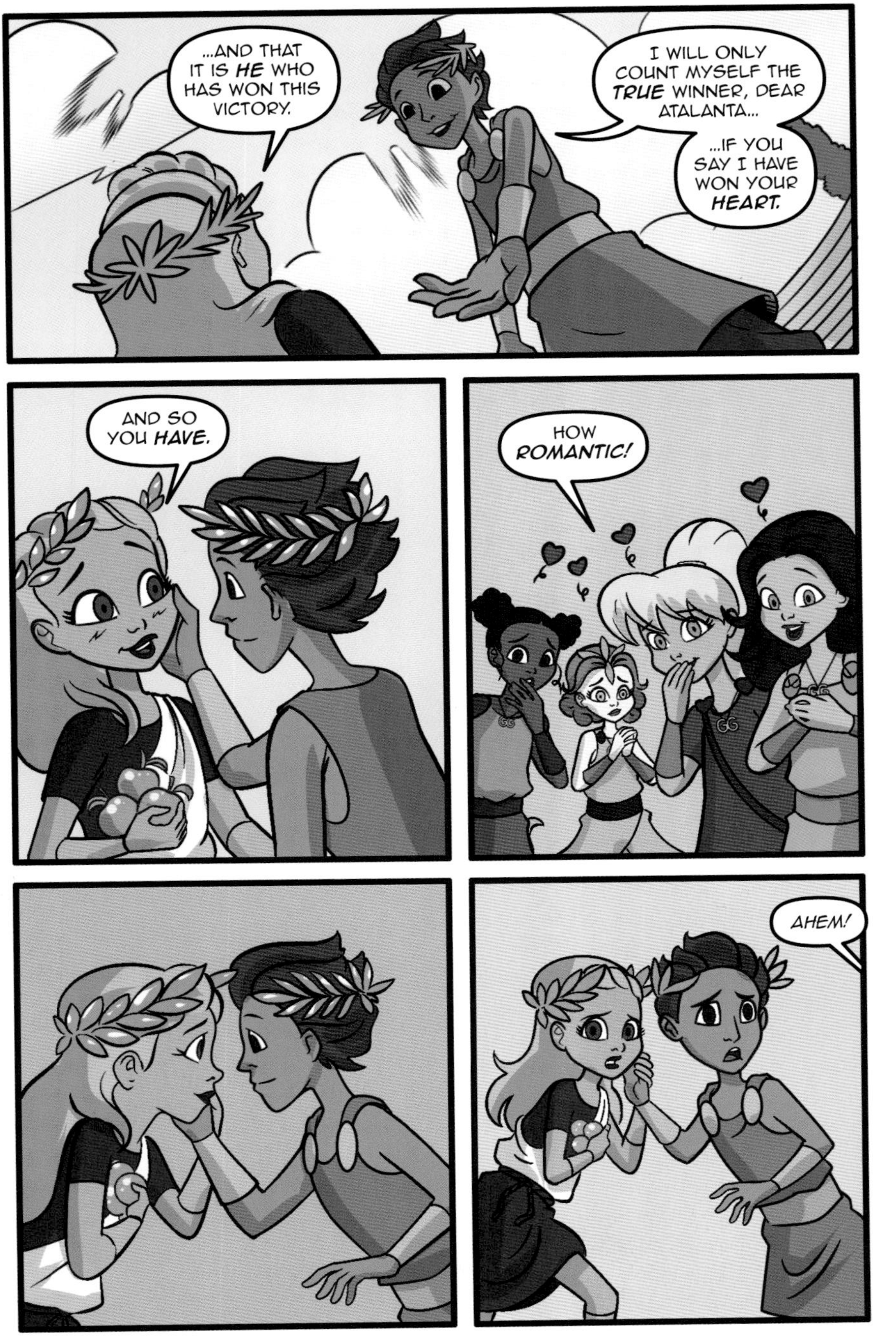
...AND THAT IT IS *HE* WHO HAS WON THIS VICTORY.
I WILL ONLY COUNT MYSELF THE *TRUE* WINNER, DEAR ATALANTA...
...IF YOU SAY I HAVE WON YOUR *HEART.*
AND SO YOU *HAVE.*
HOW *ROMANTIC!*
AHEM!

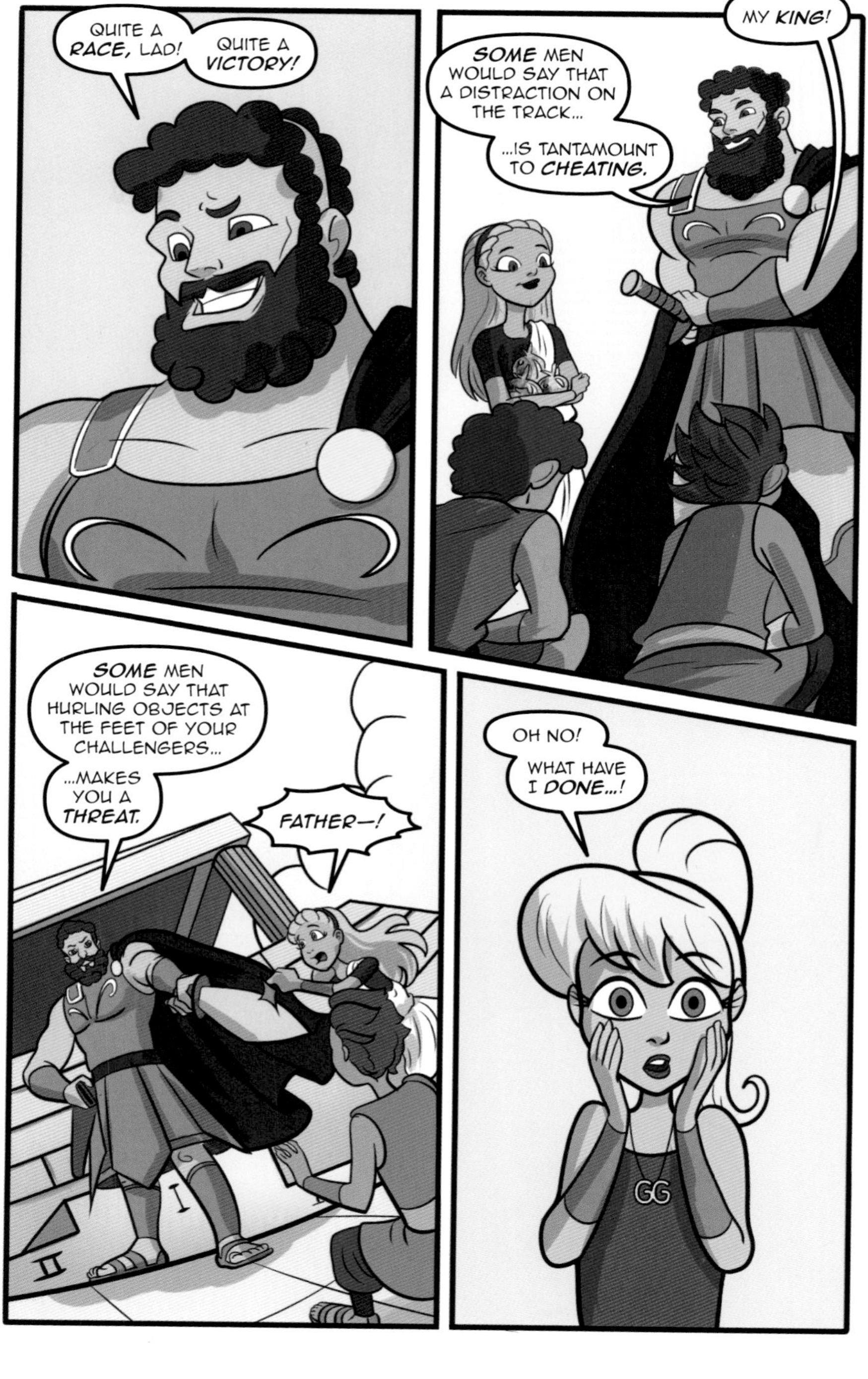
QUITE A RACE, LAD!
QUITE A VICTORY!
MY KING!
SOME MEN WOULD SAY THAT A DISTRACTION ON THE TRACK...
...IS TANTAMOUNT TO CHEATING.
SOME MEN WOULD SAY THAT HURLING OBJECTS AT THE FEET OF YOUR CHALLENGERS...
...MAKES YOU A THREAT.
FATHER—!
OH NO!
WHAT HAVE I DONE...!
GG

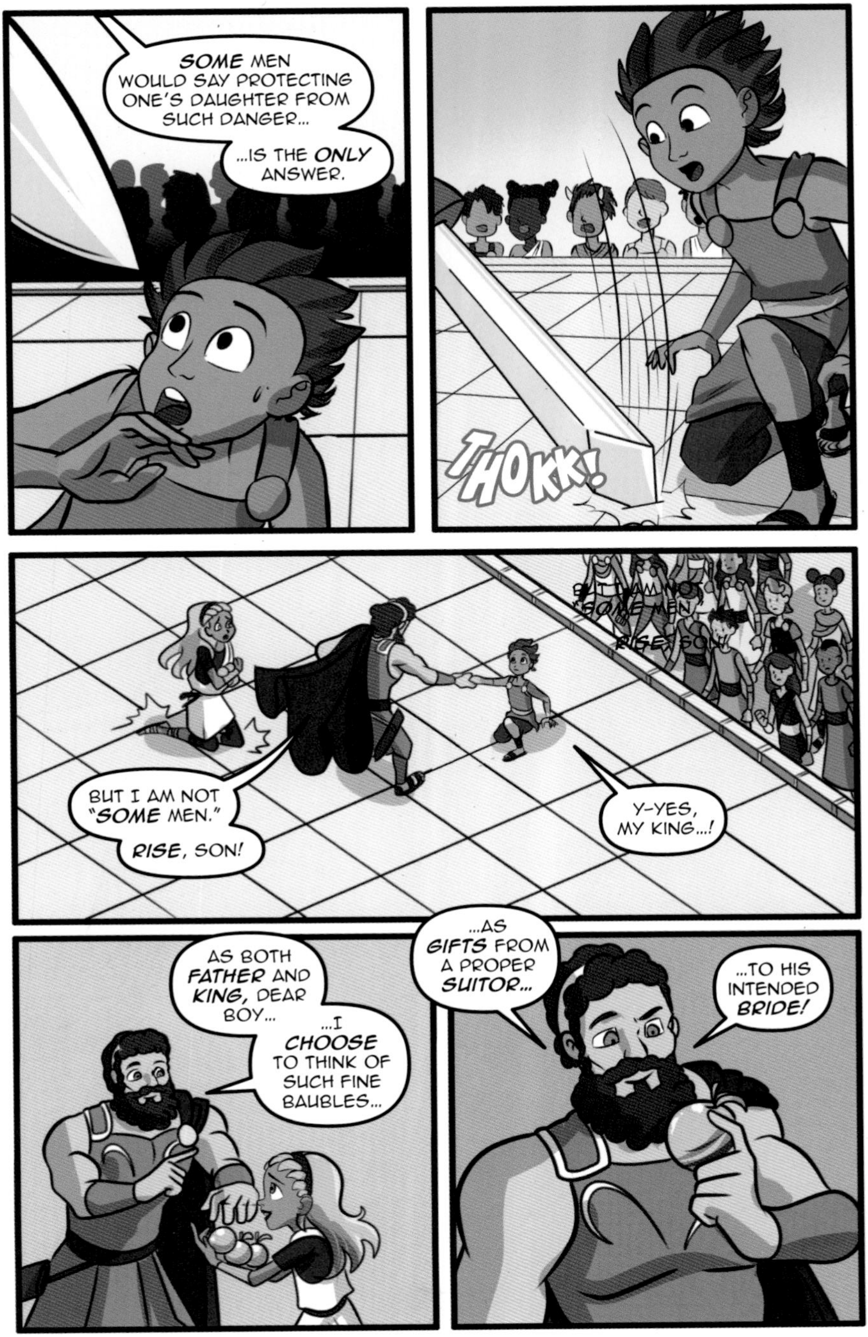
SOME MEN WOULD SAY PROTECTING ONE'S DAUGHTER FROM SUCH DANGER...
...IS THE ONLY ANSWER.
THOKK!
BUT I AM NOT "SOME MEN."
RISE, SON!
Y-YES, MY KING...!
AS BOTH FATHER AND KING, DEAR BOY...
...I CHOOSE TO THINK OF SUCH FINE BAUBLES...
...AS GIFTS FROM A PROPER SUITOR...
...TO HIS INTENDED BRIDE!

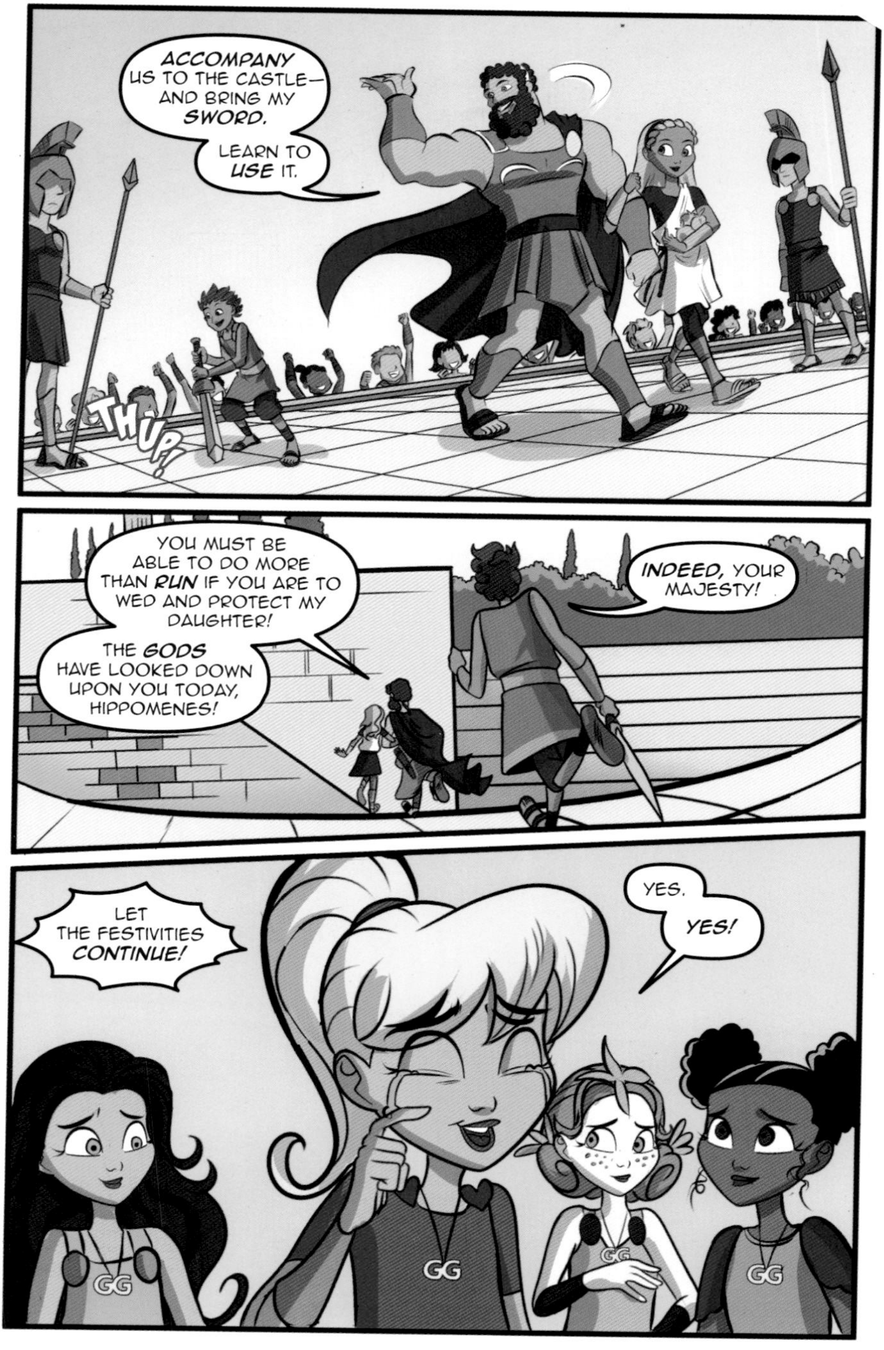
ACCOMPANY US TO THE CASTLE— AND BRING MY SWORD.
LEARN TO USE IT.
THUP!
YOU MUST BE ABLE TO DO MORE THAN RUN IF YOU ARE TO WED AND PROTECT MY DAUGHTER!
THE GODS HAVE LOOKED DOWN UPON YOU TODAY, HIPPOMENES!
INDEED, YOUR MAJESTY!
LET THE FESTIVITIES CONTINUE!
YES.
YES!
GG
GG
GG
GG

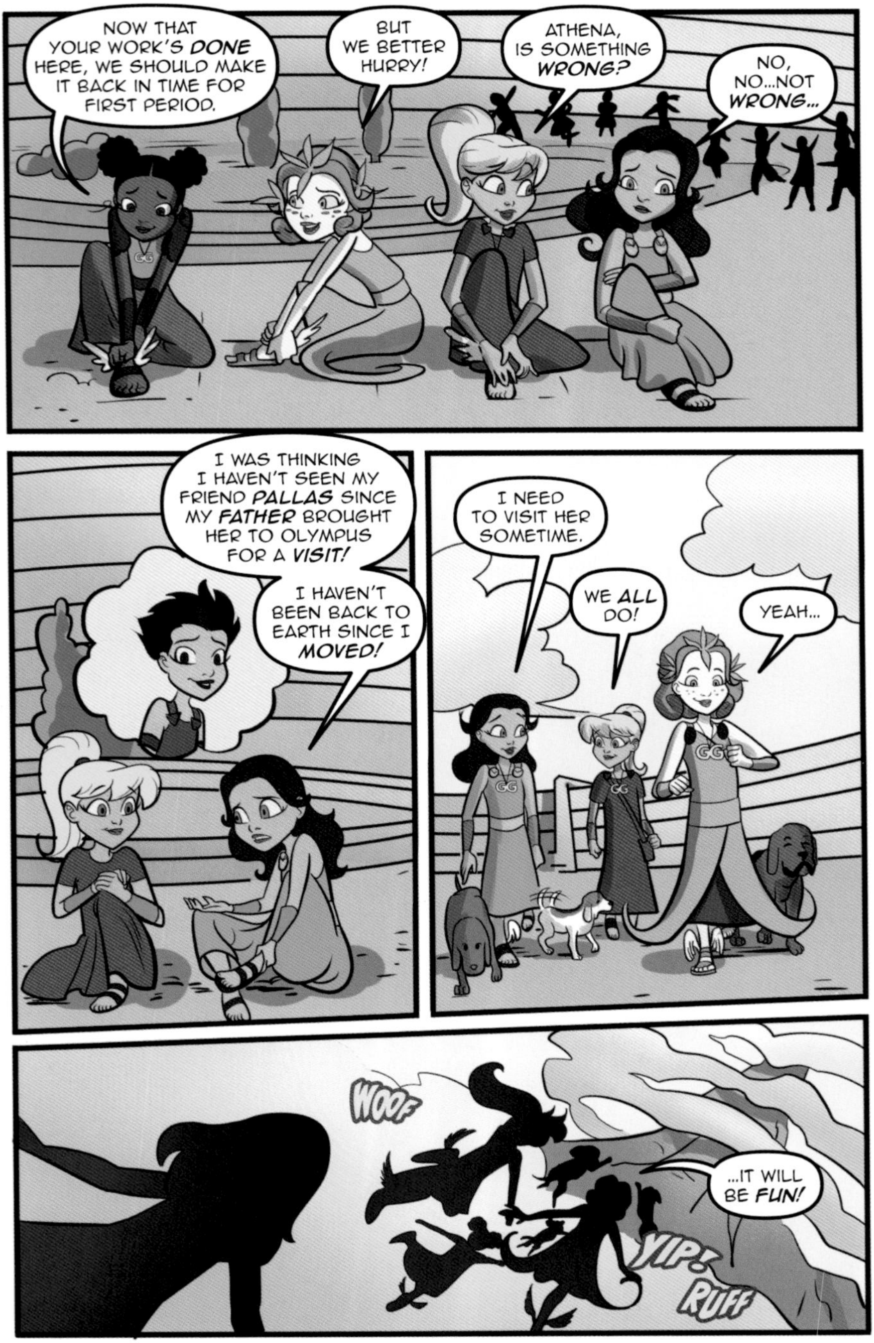
NOW THAT YOUR WORK'S DONE HERE, WE SHOULD MAKE IT BACK IN TIME FOR FIRST PERIOD.
BUT WE BETTER HURRY!
ATHENA, IS SOMETHING WRONG?
NO, NO...NOT WRONG...
I WAS THINKING I HAVEN'T SEEN MY FRIEND PALLAS SINCE MY FATHER BROUGHT HER TO OLYMPUS FOR A VISIT!
I HAVEN'T BEEN BACK TO EARTH SINCE I MOVED!
I NEED TO VISIT HER SOMETIME.
WE ALL DO!
YEAH...
WOOF
...IT WILL BE FUN!
YIP!
RUFF

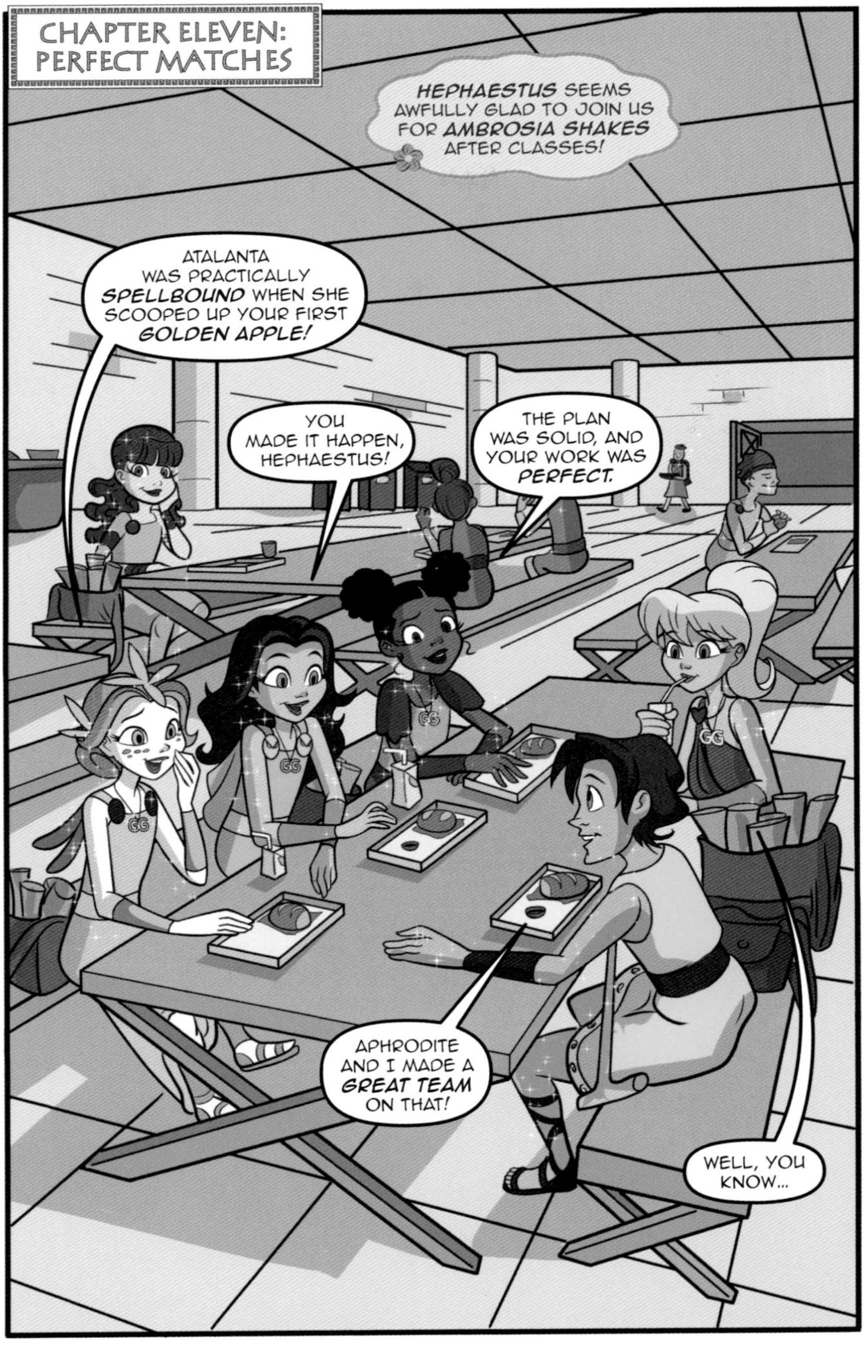
CHAPTER ELEVEN: PERFECT MATCHES
HEPHAESTUS SEEMS AWFULLY GLAD TO JOIN US FOR AMBROSIA SHAKES AFTER CLASSES!
ATALANTA WAS PRACTICALLY SPELLBOUND WHEN SHE SCOOPED UP YOUR FIRST GOLDEN APPLE!
YOU MADE IT HAPPEN, HEPHAESTUS!
THE PLAN WAS SOLID, AND YOUR WORK WAS PERFECT.
APHRODITE AND I MADE A GREAT TEAM ON THAT!
WELL, YOU KNOW...

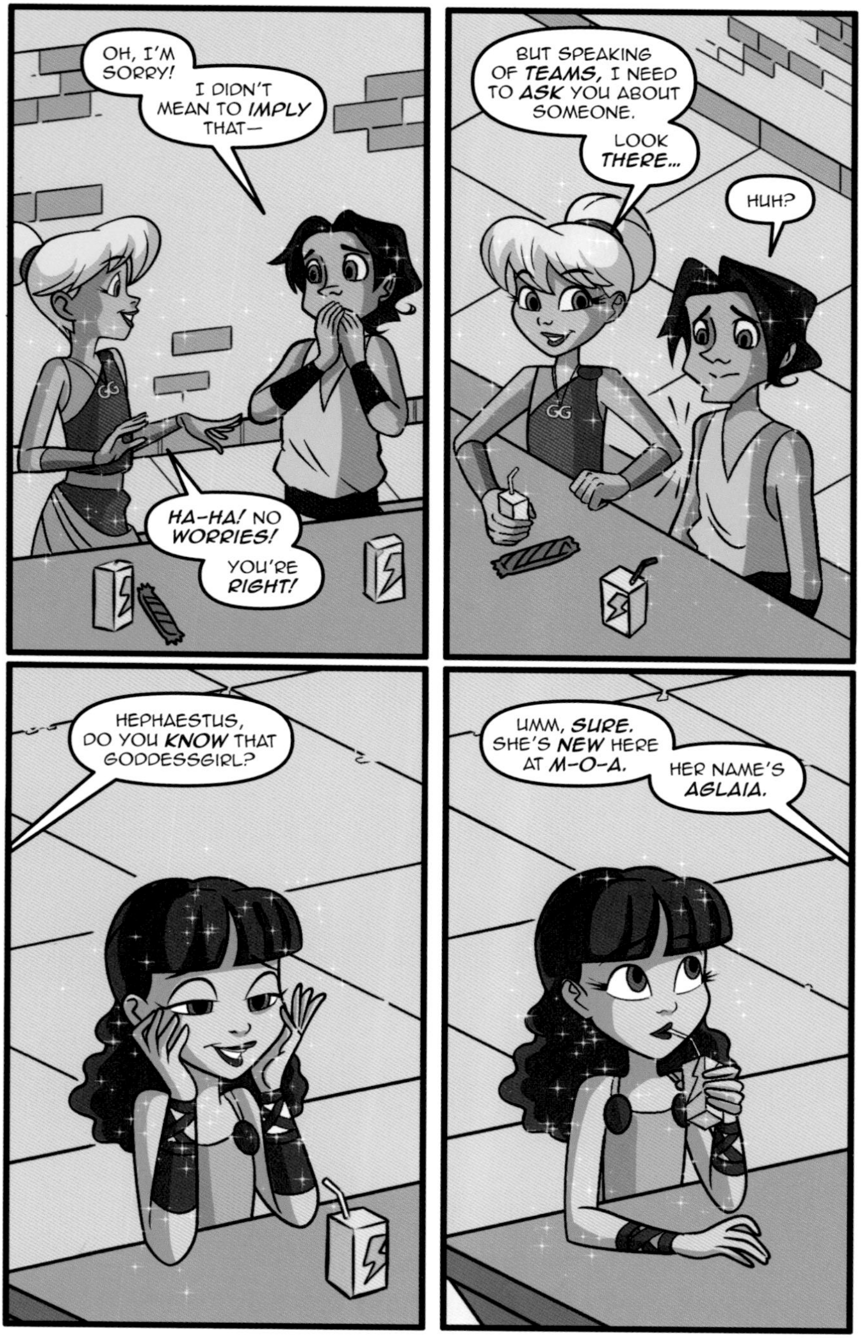
OH, I'M SORRY!
I DIDN'T MEAN TO *IMPLY* THAT—
HA-HA! NO *WORRIES!*
YOU'RE *RIGHT!*
BUT SPEAKING OF *TEAMS,* I NEED TO *ASK* YOU ABOUT SOMEONE.
LOOK *THERE...*
HUH?
HEPHAESTUS, DO YOU *KNOW* THAT GODDESSGIRL?
UMM, *SURE.* SHE'S *NEW* HERE AT *M-O-A.*
HER NAME'S *AGLAIA.*

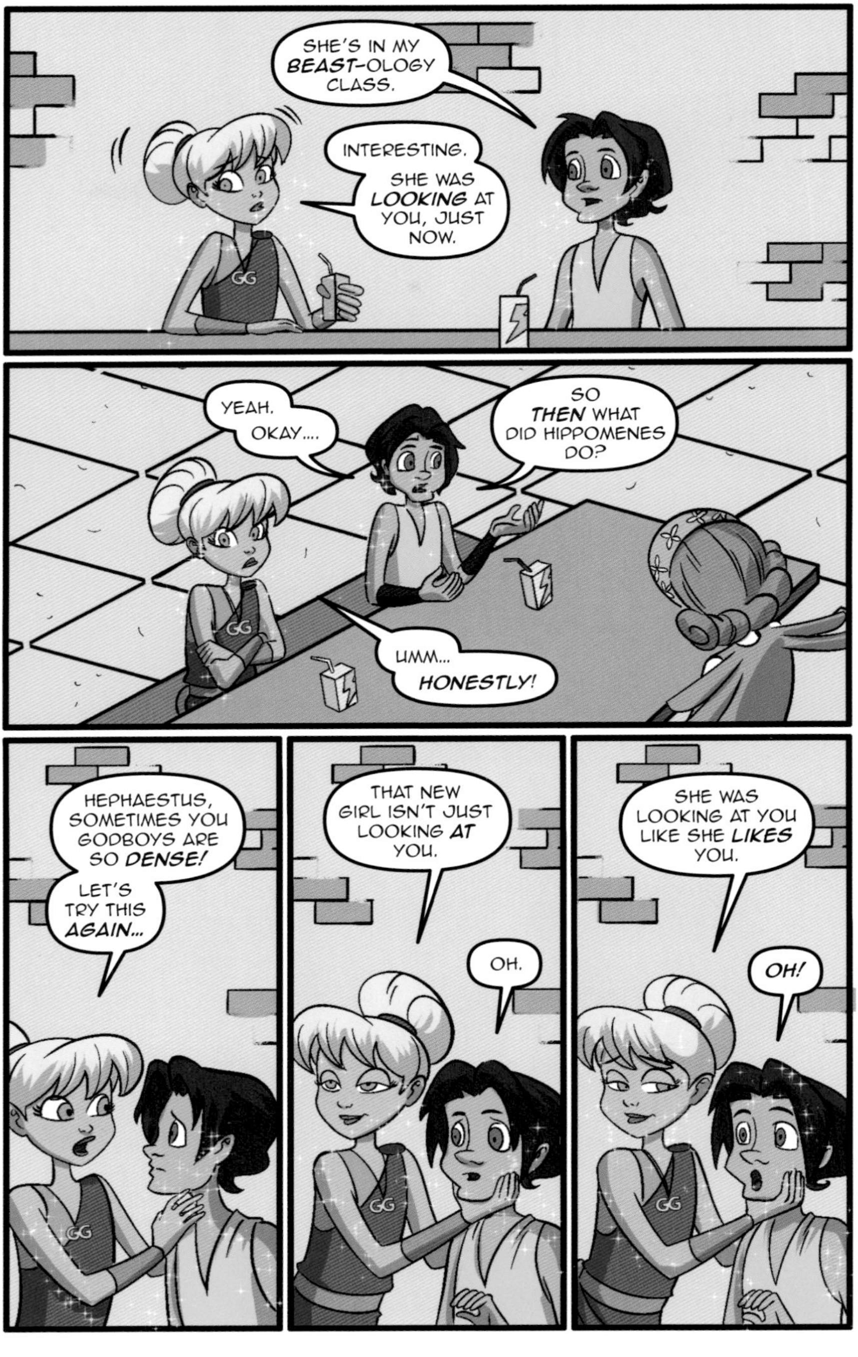
SHE'S IN MY BEAST-OLOGY CLASS.
INTERESTING.
SHE WAS LOOKING AT YOU, JUST NOW.
YEAH.
OKAY....
SO THEN WHAT DID HIPPOMENES DO?
UMM... HONESTLY!
HEPHAESTUS, SOMETIMES YOU GODBOYS ARE SO DENSE!
LET'S TRY THIS AGAIN...
THAT NEW GIRL ISN'T JUST LOOKING AT YOU.
OH.
SHE WAS LOOKING AT YOU LIKE SHE LIKES YOU.
OH!

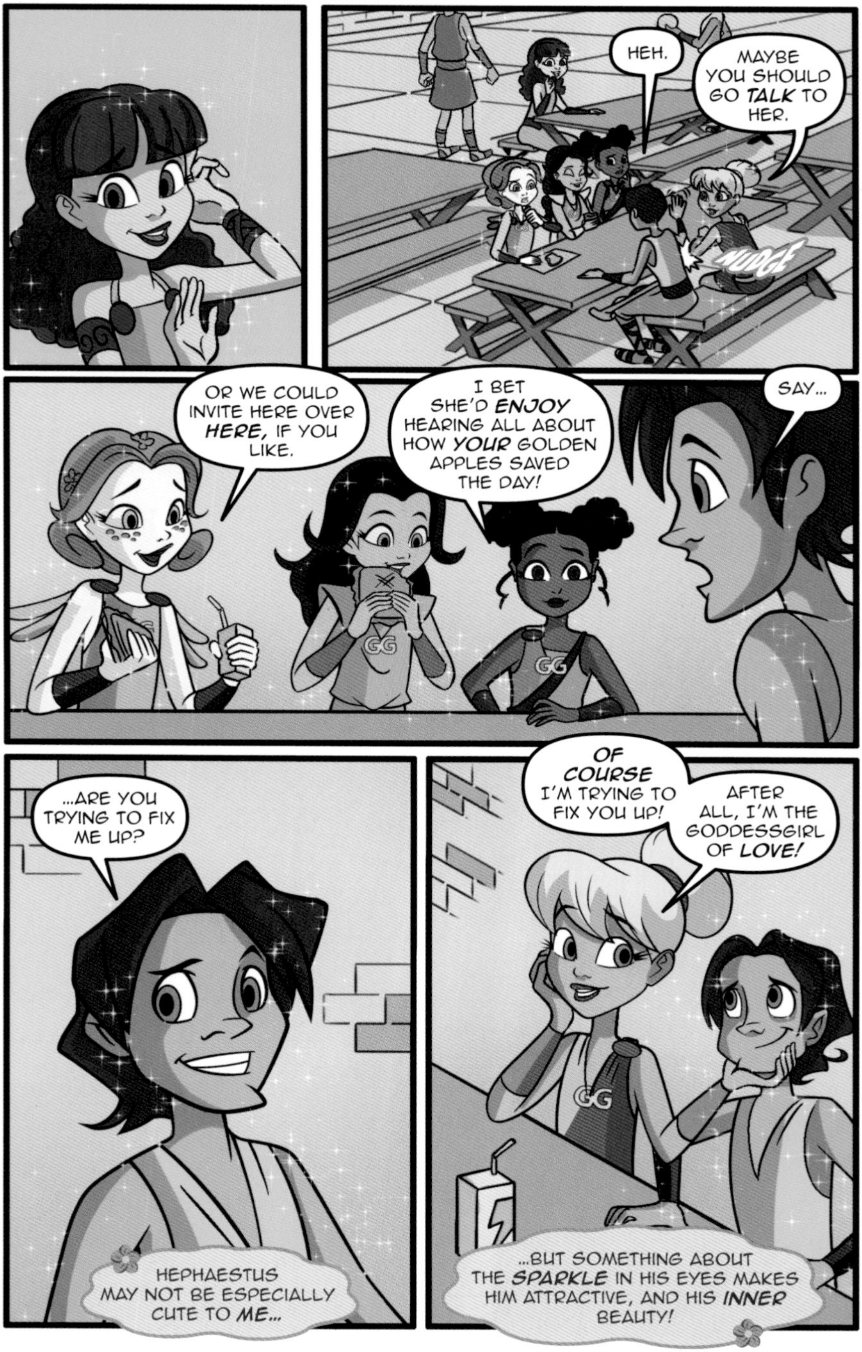
HEH.
MAYBE YOU SHOULD GO TALK TO HER.
NUDGE
OR WE COULD INVITE HERE OVER HERE, IF YOU LIKE.
I BET SHE'D ENJOY HEARING ALL ABOUT HOW YOUR GOLDEN APPLES SAVED THE DAY!
SAY...
...ARE YOU TRYING TO FIX ME UP?
HEPHAESTUS MAY NOT BE ESPECIALLY CUTE TO ME...
OF COURSE I'M TRYING TO FIX YOU UP!
AFTER ALL, I'M THE GODDESSGIRL OF LOVE!
...BUT SOMETHING ABOUT THE SPARKLE IN HIS EYES MAKES HIM ATTRACTIVE, AND HIS INNER BEAUTY!

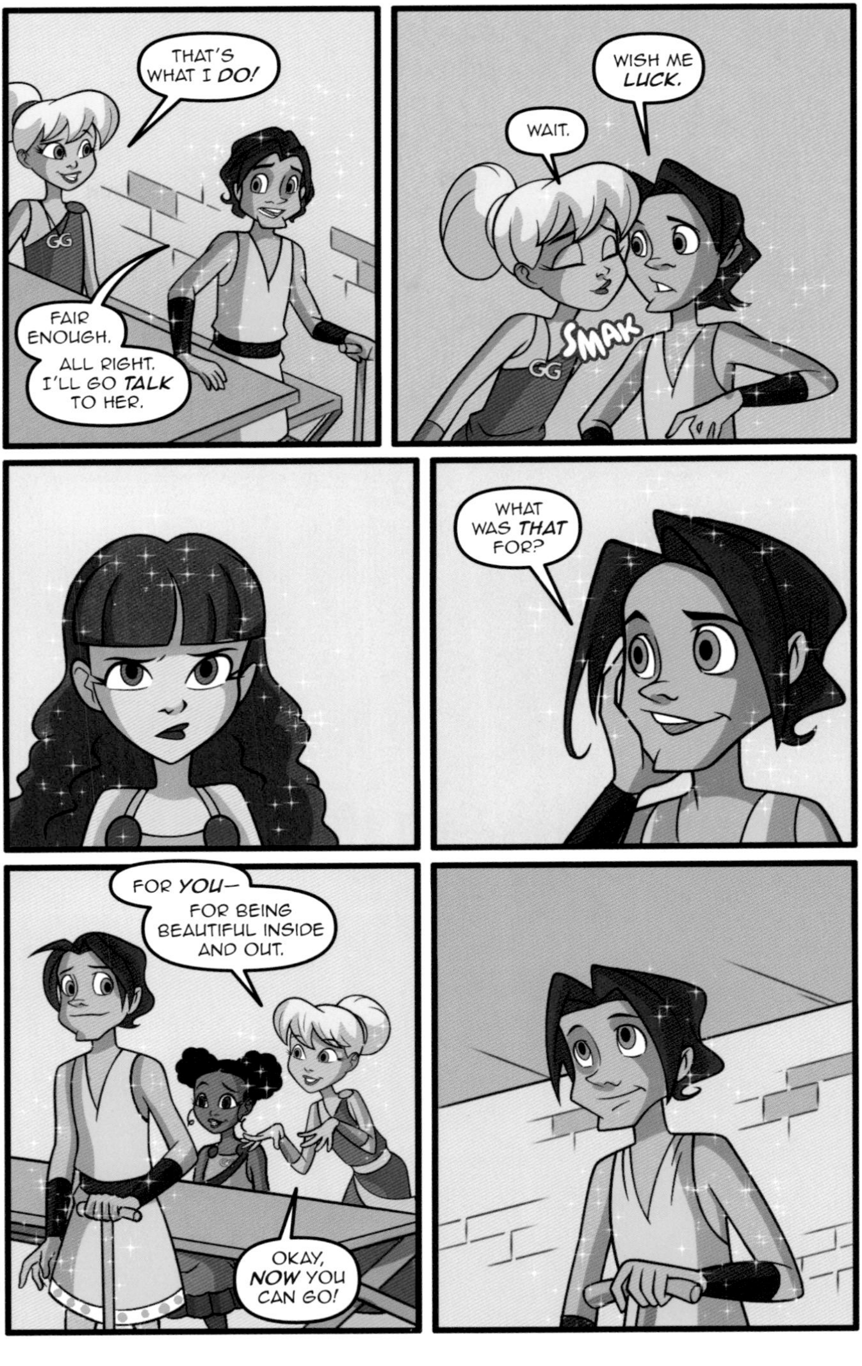
THAT'S WHAT I DO!
FAIR ENOUGH.
ALL RIGHT. I'LL GO TALK TO HER.
WISH ME LUCK.
WAIT.
SMAK
WHAT WAS THAT FOR?
FOR YOU—
FOR BEING BEAUTIFUL INSIDE AND OUT.
OKAY, NOW YOU CAN GO!

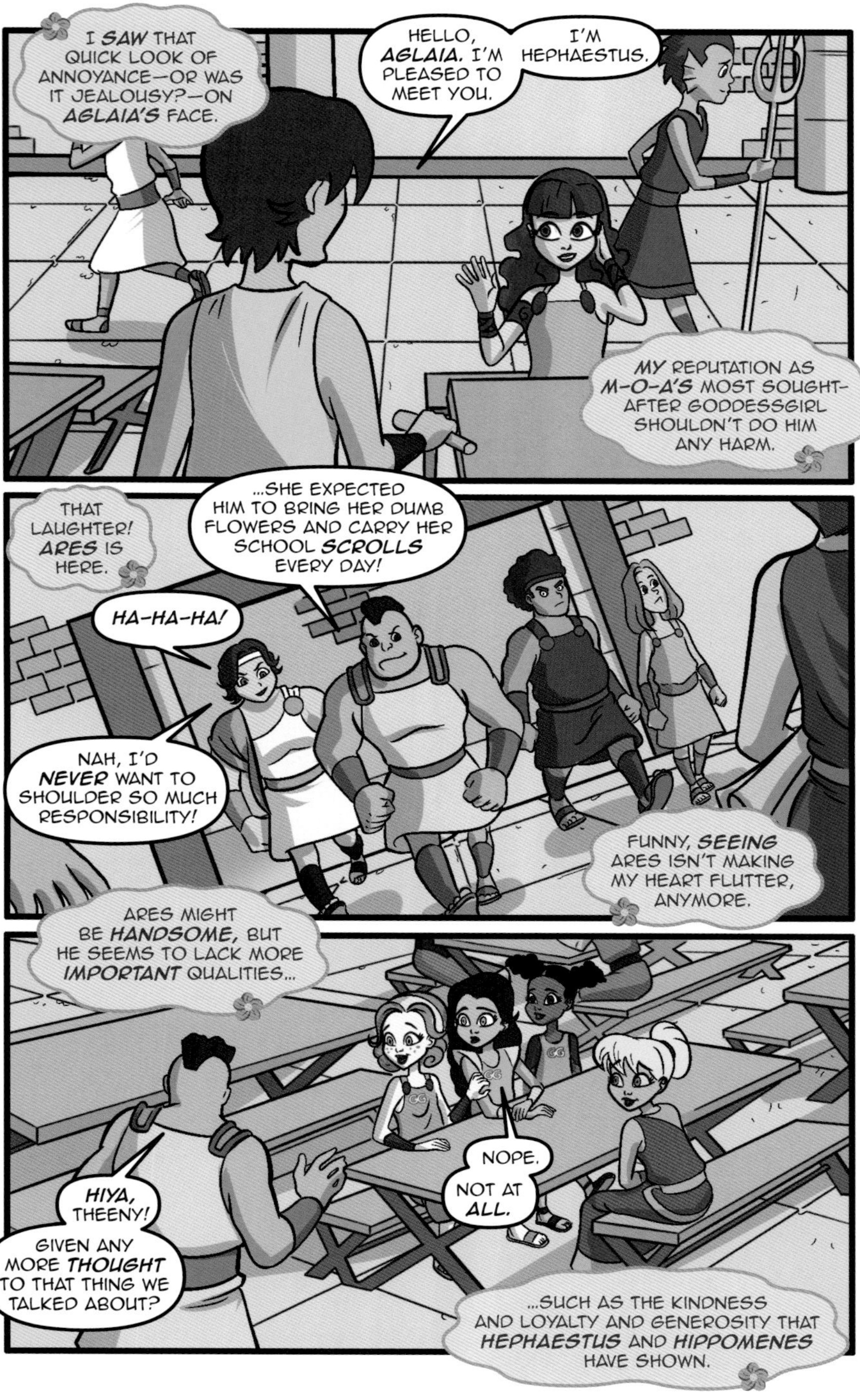

I *SAW* THAT QUICK LOOK OF ANNOYANCE—OR WAS IT JEALOUSY?—ON *AGLAIA'S* FACE.
HELLO, *AGLAIA.* I'M PLEASED TO MEET YOU.
I'M HEPHAESTUS.
MY REPUTATION AS *M-O-A'S* MOST SOUGHT-AFTER GODDESSGIRL SHOULDN'T DO HIM ANY HARM.
THAT LAUGHTER! *ARES* IS HERE.
...SHE EXPECTED HIM TO BRING HER DUMB FLOWERS AND CARRY HER SCHOOL *SCROLLS* EVERY DAY!
HA-HA-HA!
NAH, I'D *NEVER* WANT TO SHOULDER SO MUCH RESPONSIBILITY!
FUNNY, *SEEING* ARES ISN'T MAKING MY HEART FLUTTER, ANYMORE.
ARES MIGHT BE *HANDSOME,* BUT HE SEEMS TO LACK MORE *IMPORTANT* QUALITIES...
HIYA, THEENY!
GIVEN ANY MORE *THOUGHT* TO THAT THING WE TALKED ABOUT?
NOPE.
NOT AT *ALL.*
...SUCH AS THE KINDNESS AND LOYALTY AND GENEROSITY THAT *HEPHAESTUS* AND *HIPPOMENES* HAVE SHOWN.

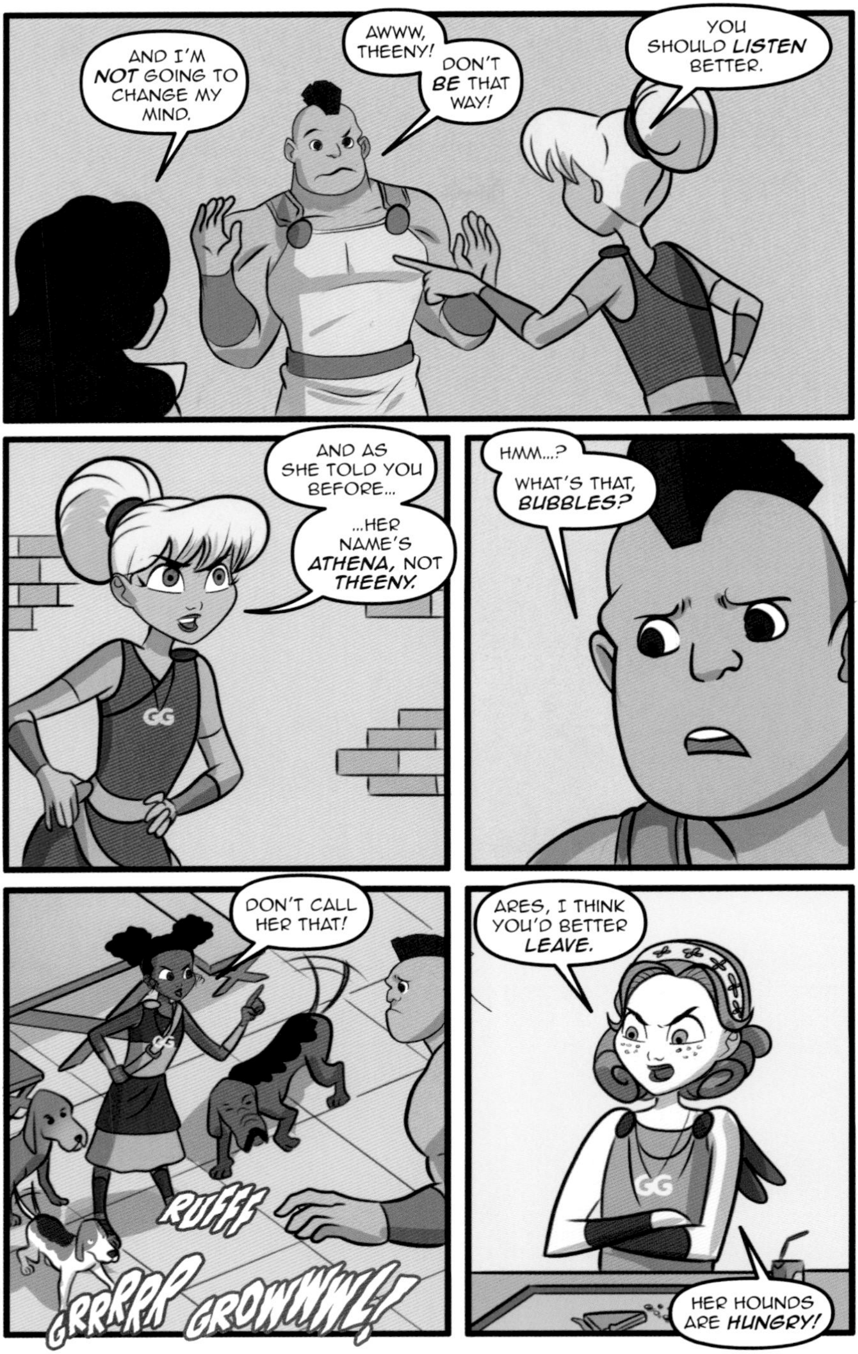
AND I'M NOT GOING TO CHANGE MY MIND.
AWWW, THEENY!
DON'T BE THAT WAY!
YOU SHOULD LISTEN BETTER.
AND AS SHE TOLD YOU BEFORE...
...HER NAME'S ATHENA, NOT THEENY.
HMM...?
WHAT'S THAT, BUBBLES?
DON'T CALL HER THAT!
RUFF!
GRRRRR
GROWWWL!
ARES, I THINK YOU'D BETTER LEAVE.
HER HOUNDS ARE HUNGRY!

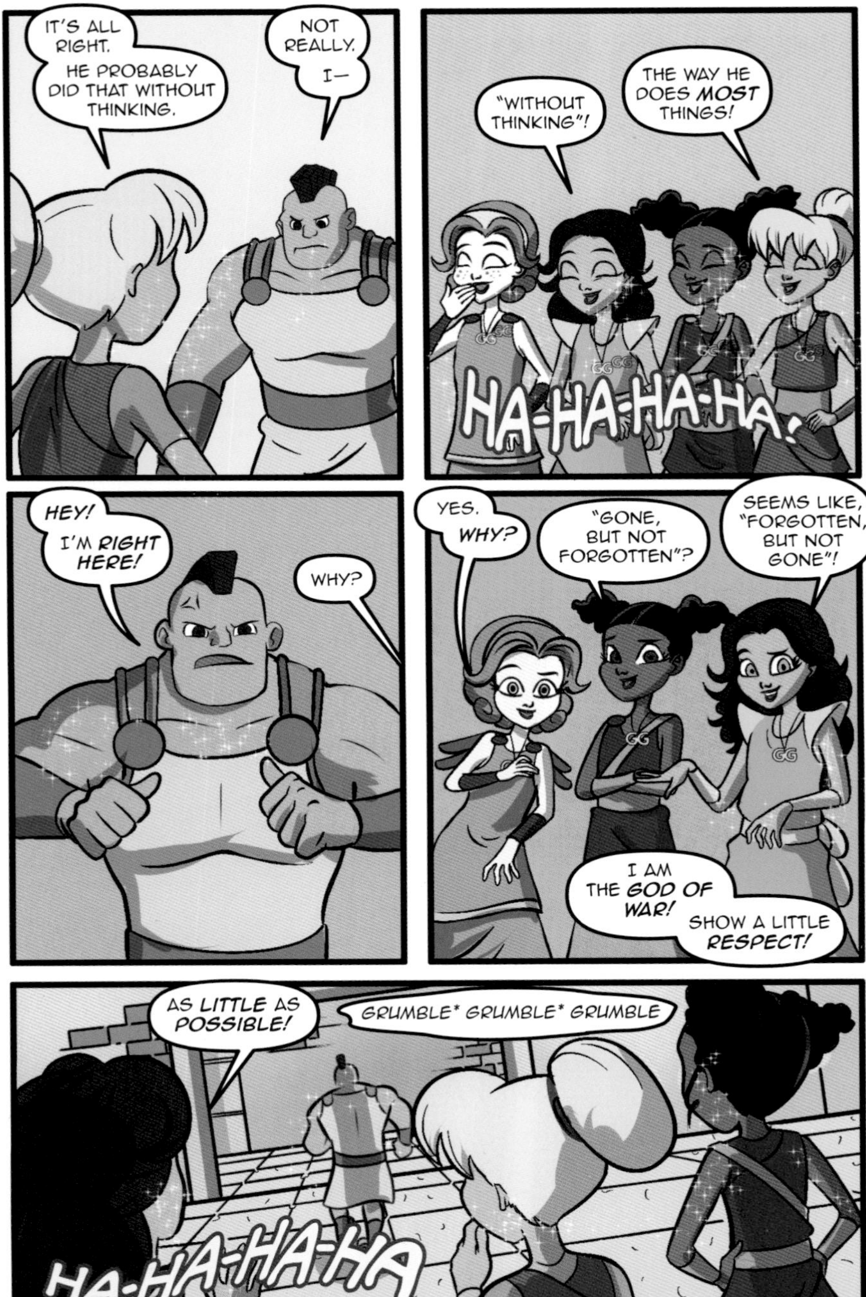
IT'S ALL RIGHT.
HE PROBABLY DID THAT WITHOUT THINKING.
NOT REALLY.
I—
"WITHOUT THINKING"!
THE WAY HE DOES MOST THINGS!
HA-HA-HA-HA!
HEY!
I'M RIGHT HERE!
WHY?
YES. WHY?
"GONE, BUT NOT FORGOTTEN"?
SEEMS LIKE, "FORGOTTEN, BUT NOT GONE"!
I AM THE GOD OF WAR!
SHOW A LITTLE RESPECT!
AS LITTLE AS POSSIBLE!
GRUMBLE* GRUMBLE* GRUMBLE
HA-HA-HA-HA-HA

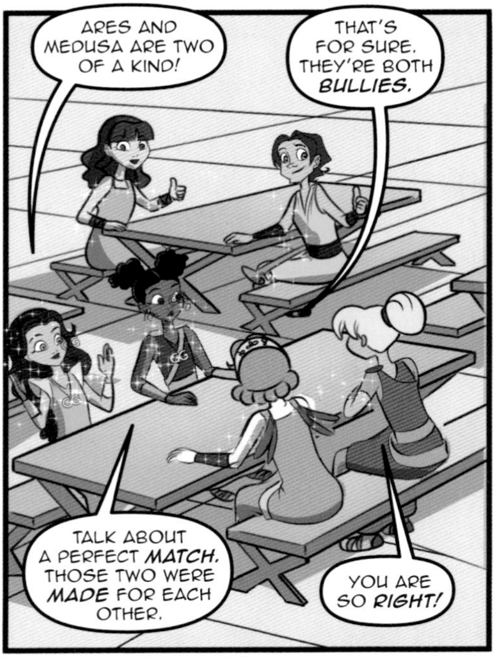
ARES AND MEDUSA ARE TWO OF A KIND!
THAT'S FOR SURE. THEY'RE BOTH BULLIES.
TALK ABOUT A PERFECT MATCH. THOSE TWO WERE MADE FOR EACH OTHER.
YOU ARE SO RIGHT!

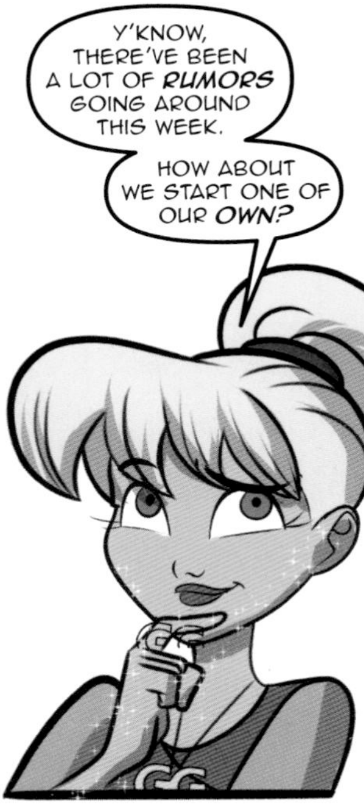
Y'KNOW, THERE'VE BEEN A LOT OF RUMORS GOING AROUND THIS WEEK.
HOW ABOUT WE START ONE OF OUR OWN?

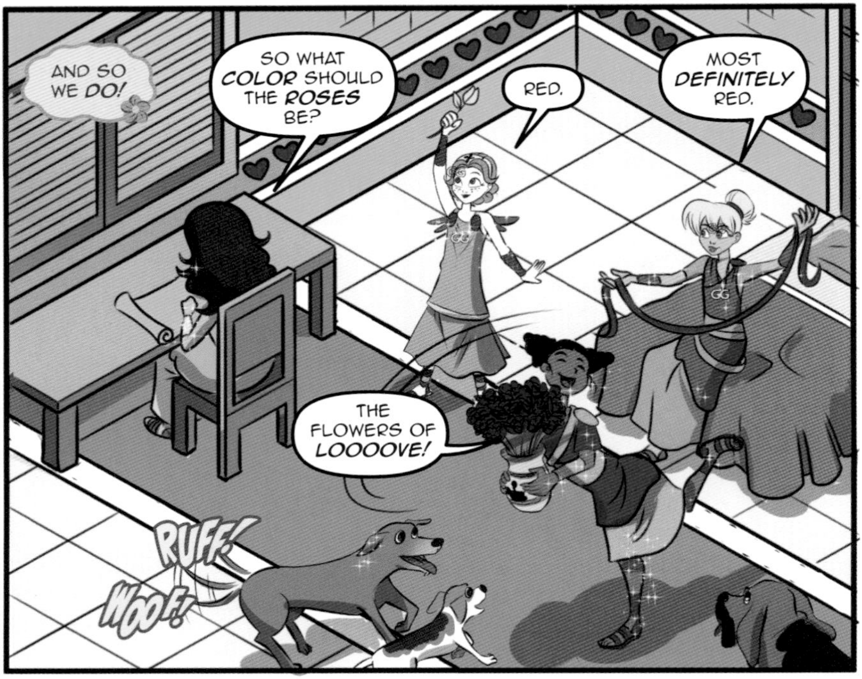
AND SO WE DO!
SO WHAT COLOR SHOULD THE ROSES BE?
RED.
MOST DEFINITELY RED.
THE FLOWERS OF LOOOOVE!
RUFF!
WOOF!

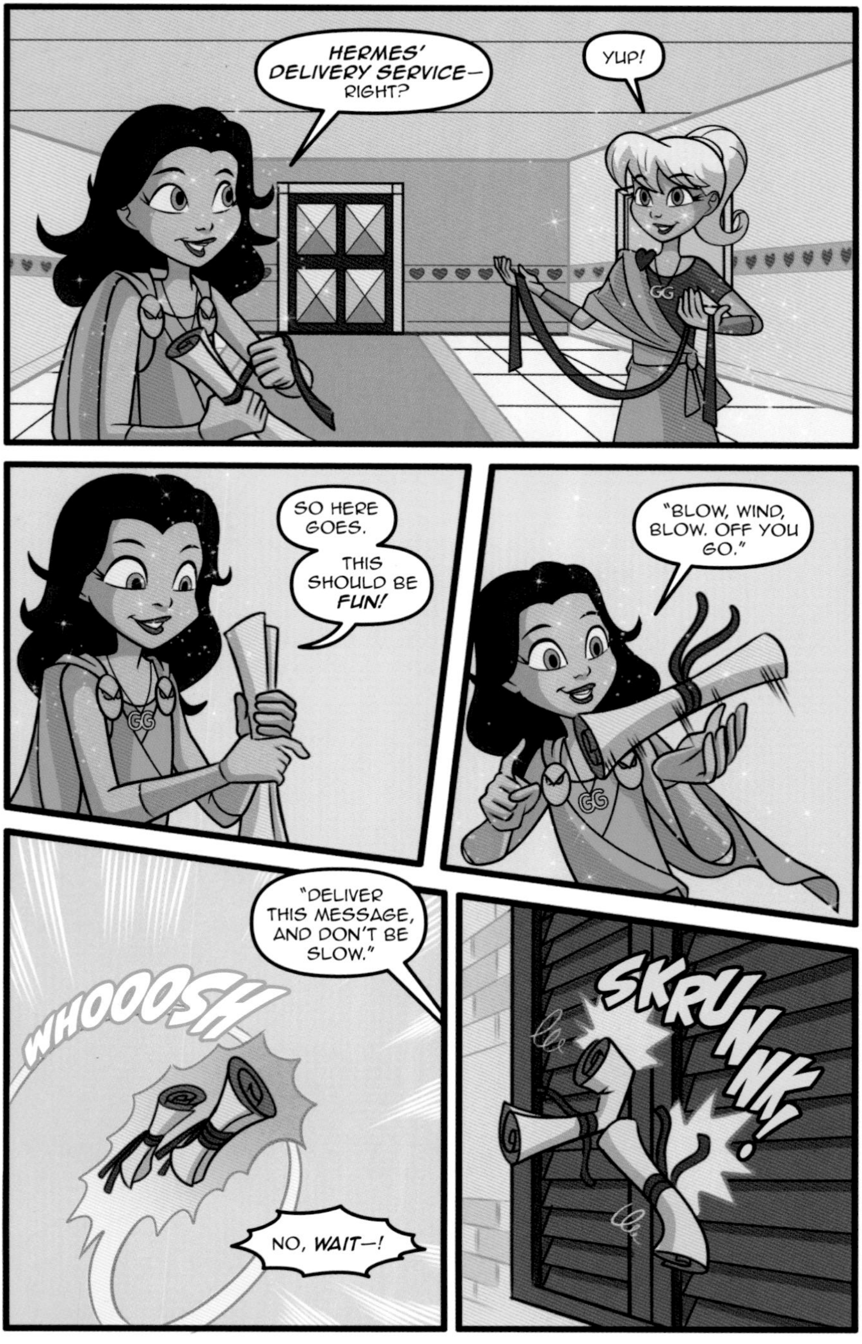
HERMES' DELIVERY SERVICE— RIGHT?
YUP!
SO HERE GOES.
THIS SHOULD BE FUN!
"BLOW, WIND, BLOW. OFF YOU GO."
"DELIVER THIS MESSAGE, AND DON'T BE SLOW."
WHOOOSH
NO, WAIT—!
SKRUNK!

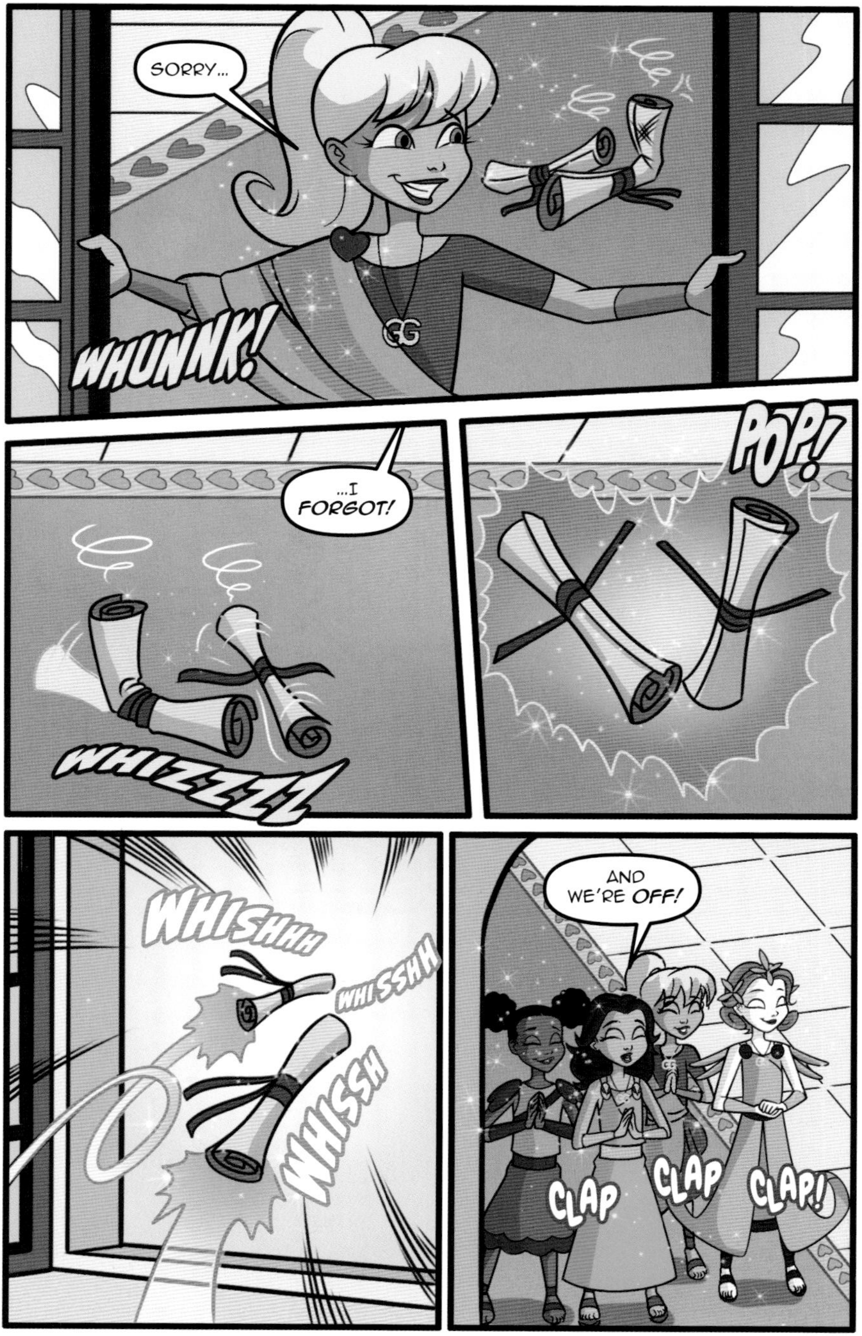
SORRY...
WHUNNK!
...I FORGOT!
WHIZZZZ
POP!
WHISHHH
WHISSHH
WHISSH
AND WE'RE OFF!
CLAP
CLAP
CLAP!

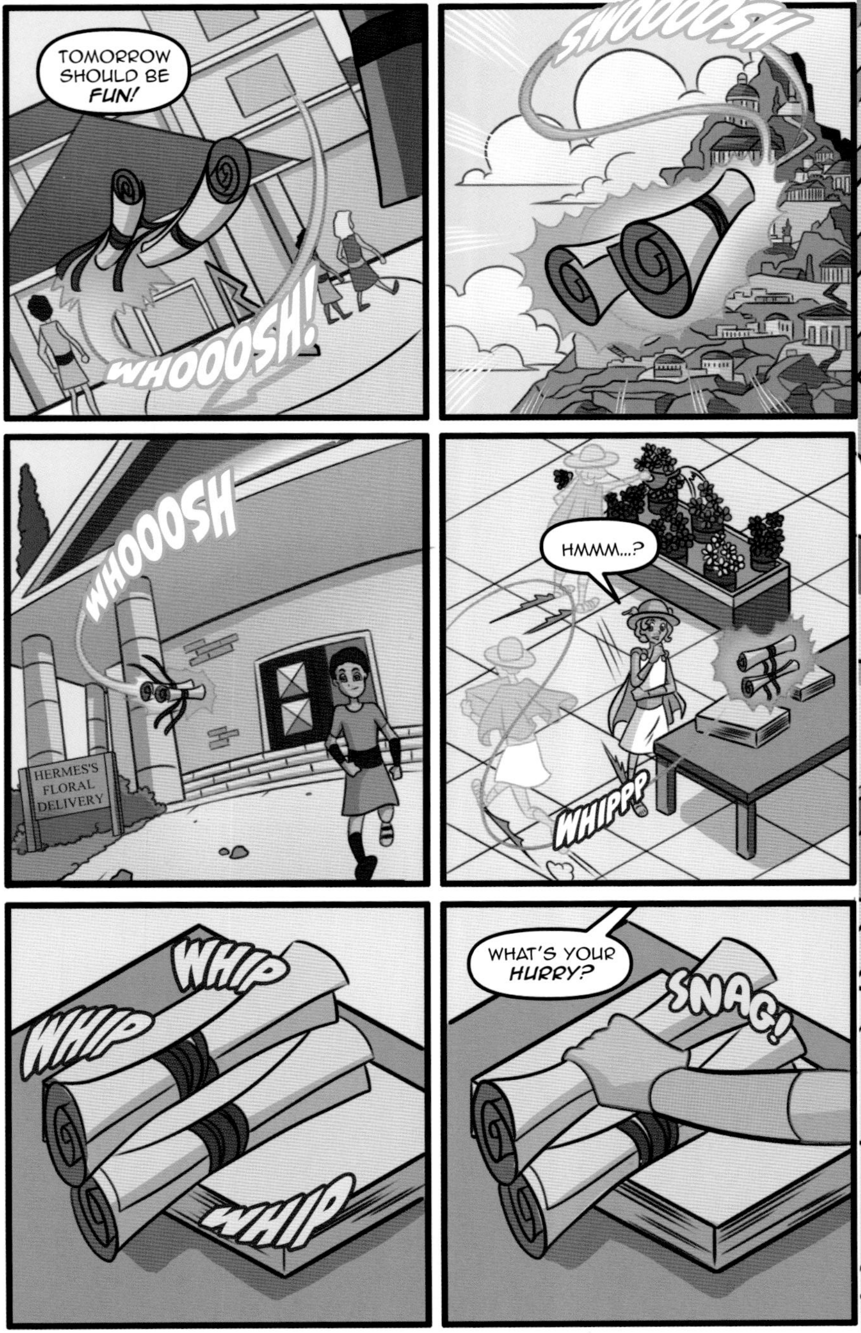
TOMORROW SHOULD BE FUN!
WHOOOSH!
SWOOOOSH
WHOOOSH
HERMES'S FLORAL DELIVERY
HMMM...?
WHIPPP
WHIP
WHIP
WHIP
WHAT'S YOUR HURRY?
SNAG!

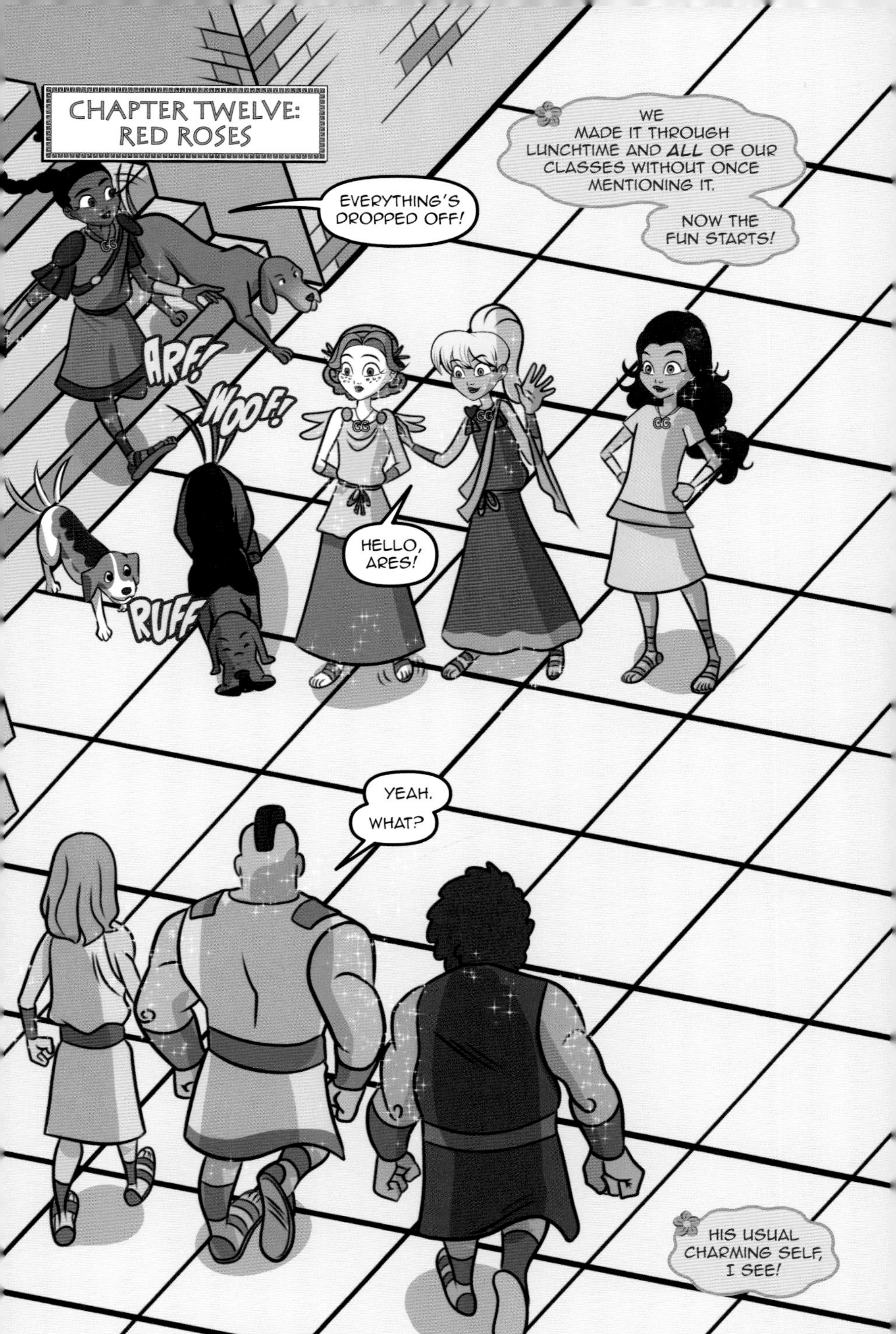
CHAPTER TWELVE: RED ROSES
WE MADE IT THROUGH LUNCHTIME AND ALL OF OUR CLASSES WITHOUT ONCE MENTIONING IT.
NOW THE FUN STARTS!
EVERYTHING'S DROPPED OFF!
ARF!
WOOF!
RUFF
HELLO, ARES!
YEAH. WHAT?
HIS USUAL CHARMING SELF, I SEE!

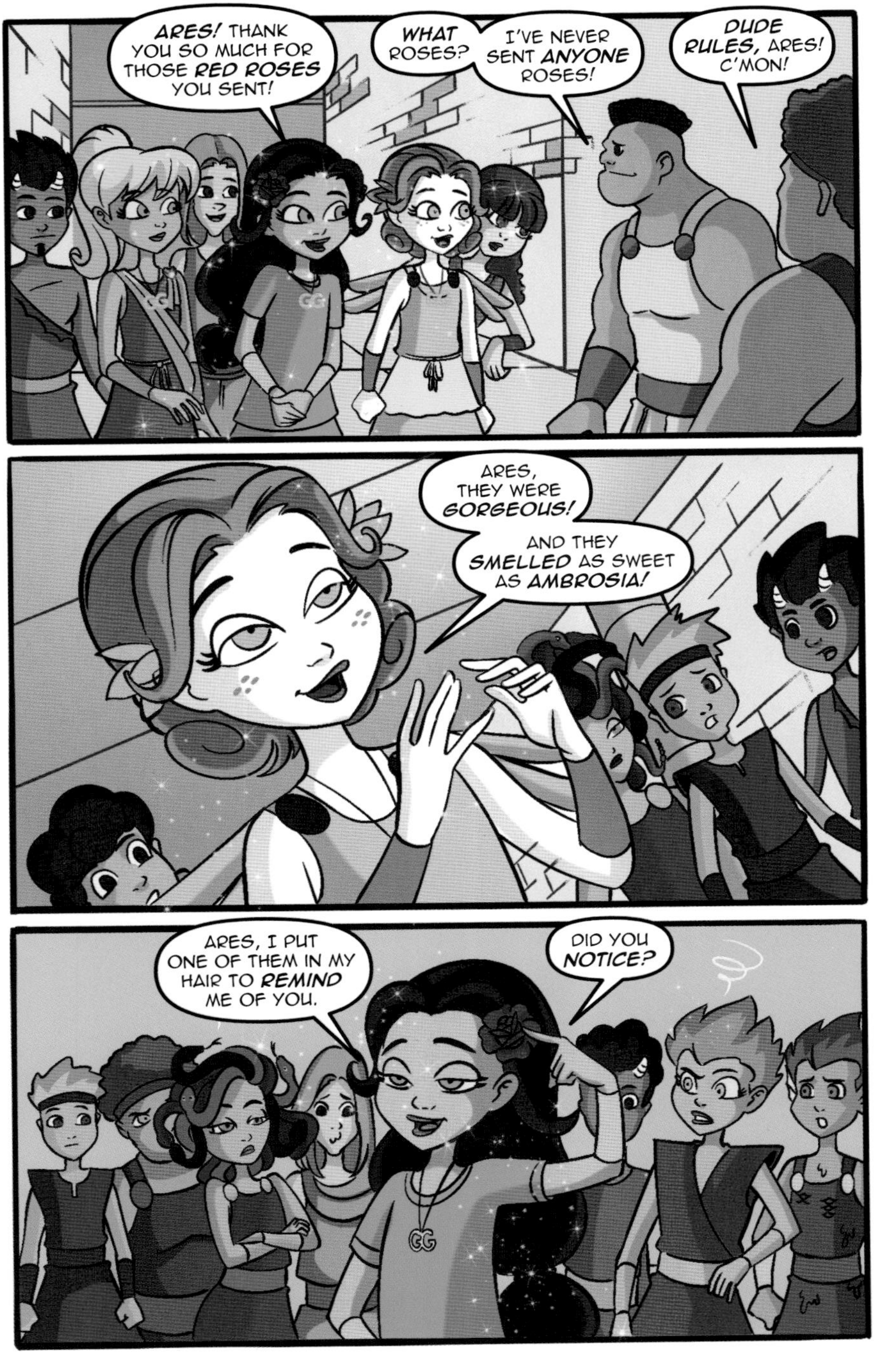
ARES! THANK YOU SO MUCH FOR THOSE RED ROSES YOU SENT!
WHAT ROSES?
I'VE NEVER SENT ANYONE ROSES!
DUDE RULES, ARES! C'MON!
ARES, THEY WERE GORGEOUS!
AND THEY SMELLED AS SWEET AS AMBROSIA!
ARES, I PUT ONE OF THEM IN MY HAIR TO REMIND ME OF YOU.
DID YOU NOTICE?

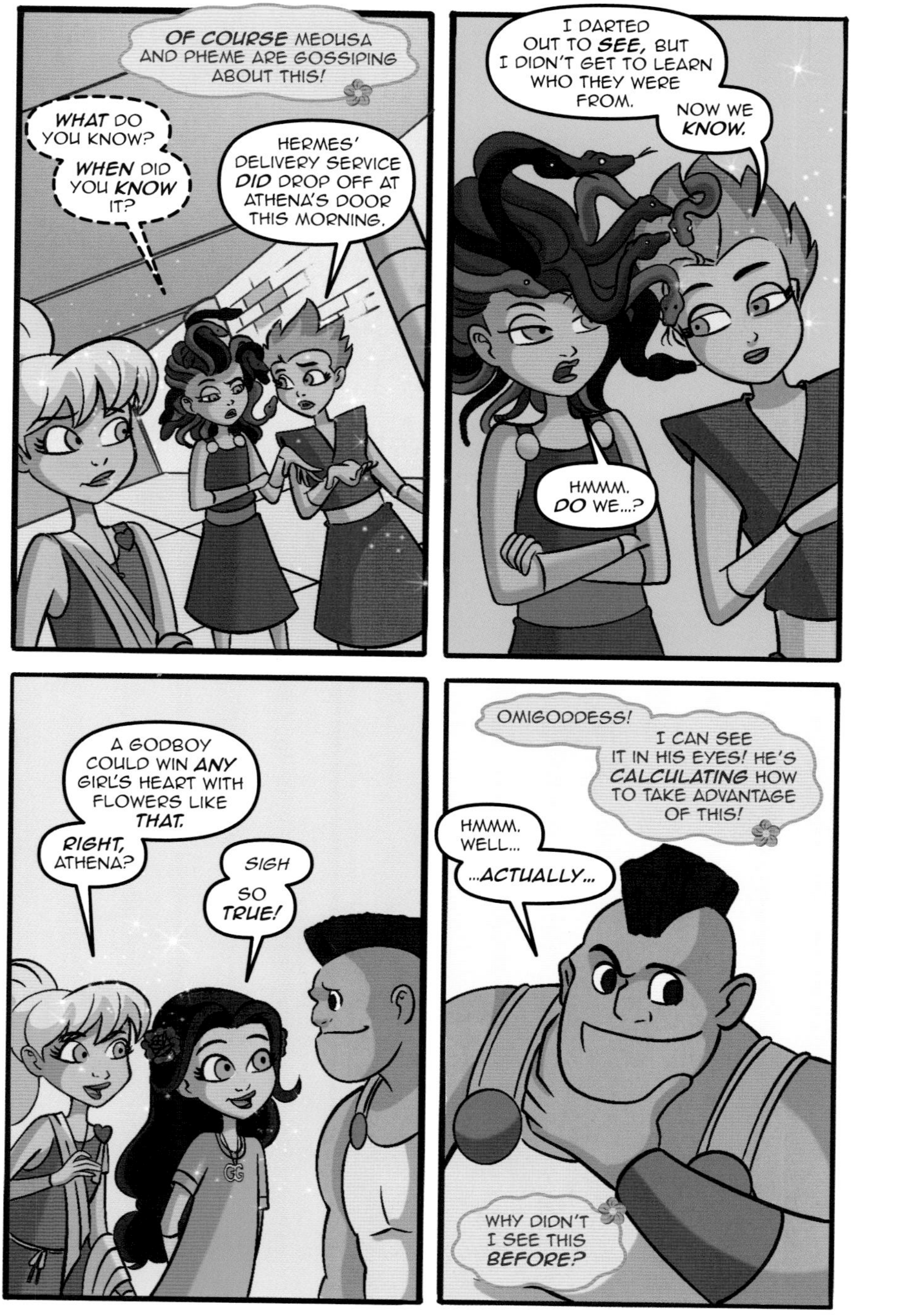
OF COURSE MEDUSA AND PHEME ARE GOSSIPING ABOUT THIS!
WHAT DO YOU KNOW? WHEN DID YOU KNOW IT?
HERMES' DELIVERY SERVICE DID DROP OFF AT ATHENA'S DOOR THIS MORNING.
I DARTED OUT TO SEE, BUT I DIDN'T GET TO LEARN WHO THEY WERE FROM.
NOW WE KNOW.
HMMM. DO WE...?
A GODBOY COULD WIN ANY GIRL'S HEART WITH FLOWERS LIKE THAT.
RIGHT, ATHENA?
SIGH
SO TRUE!
OMIGODDESS!
I CAN SEE IT IN HIS EYES! HE'S CALCULATING HOW TO TAKE ADVANTAGE OF THIS!
HMMM. WELL...
...ACTUALLY...
WHY DIDN'T I SEE THIS BEFORE?

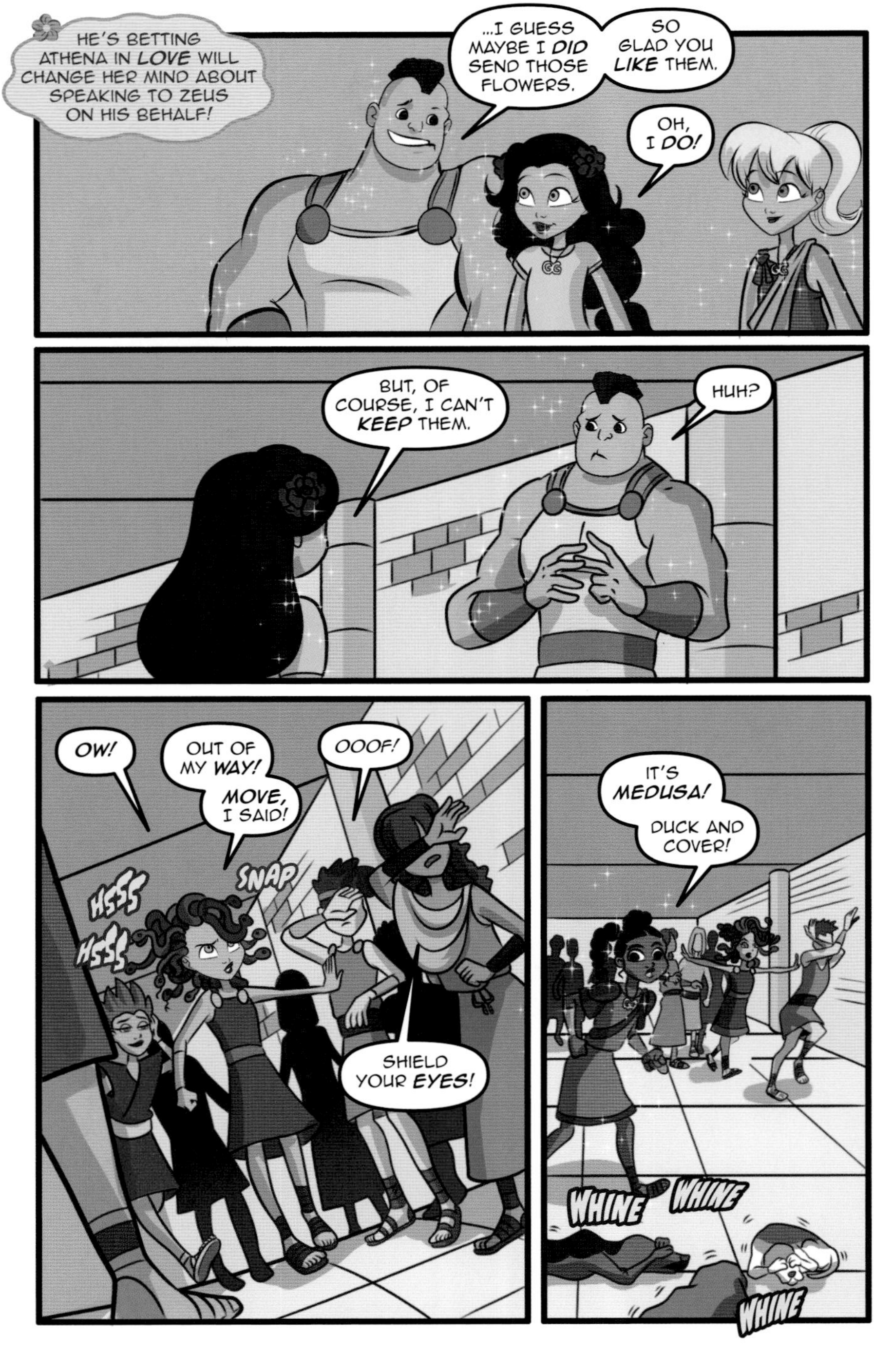
HE'S BETTING ATHENA IN LOVE WILL CHANGE HER MIND ABOUT SPEAKING TO ZEUS ON HIS BEHALF!
...I GUESS MAYBE I DID SEND THOSE FLOWERS.
SO GLAD YOU LIKE THEM.
OH, I DO!
BUT, OF COURSE, I CAN'T KEEP THEM.
HUH?
OW!
OUT OF MY WAY! MOVE, I SAID!
OOOF!
HSSS
HSSS
SNAP
SHIELD YOUR EYES!
IT'S MEDUSA! DUCK AND COVER!
WHINE
WHINE
WHINE

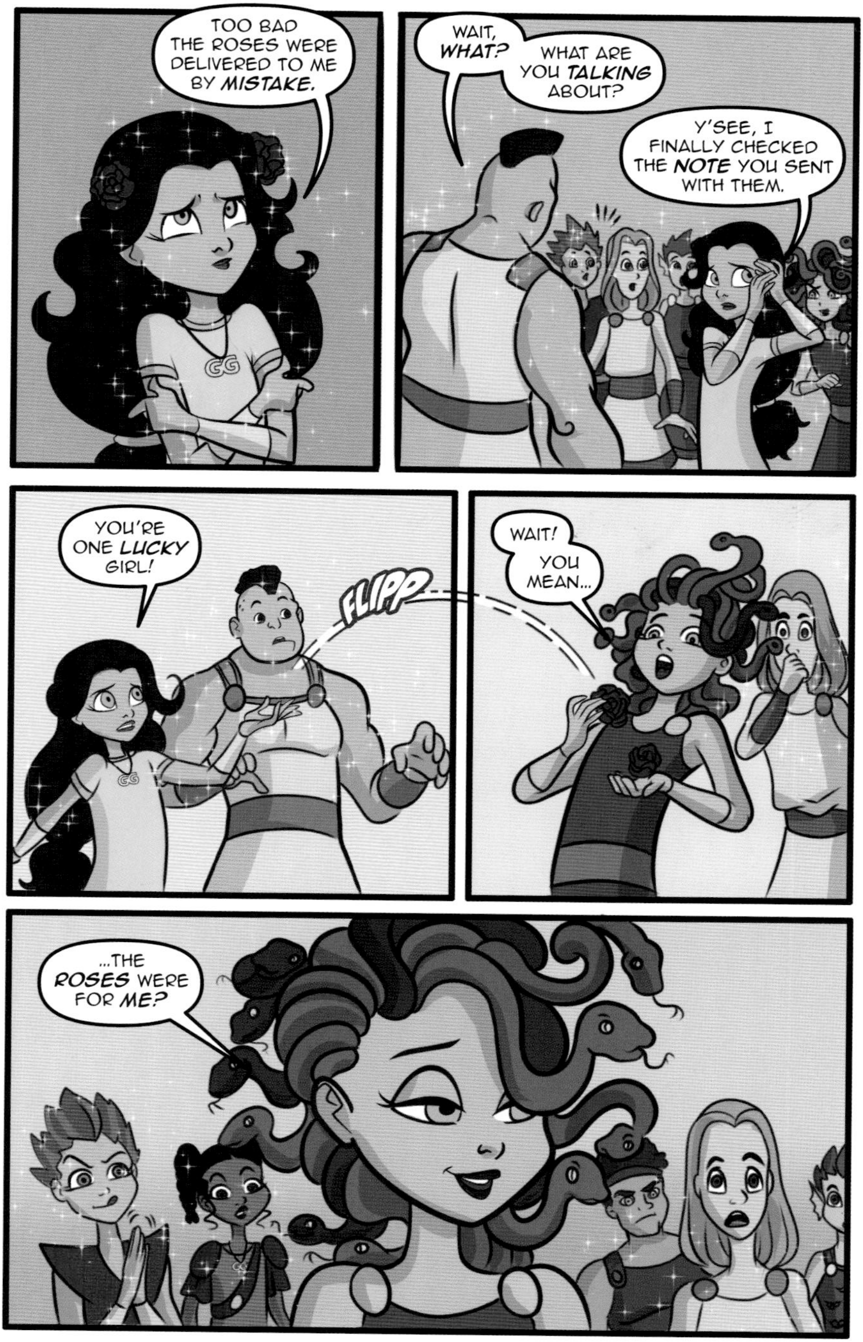
TOO BAD THE ROSES WERE DELIVERED TO ME BY *MISTAKE.*
WAIT, *WHAT?*
WHAT ARE YOU *TALKING* ABOUT?
Y'SEE, I FINALLY CHECKED THE *NOTE* YOU SENT WITH THEM.
YOU'RE ONE *LUCKY* GIRL!
FLIPP
WAIT!
YOU MEAN...
...THE *ROSES* WERE FOR *ME?*

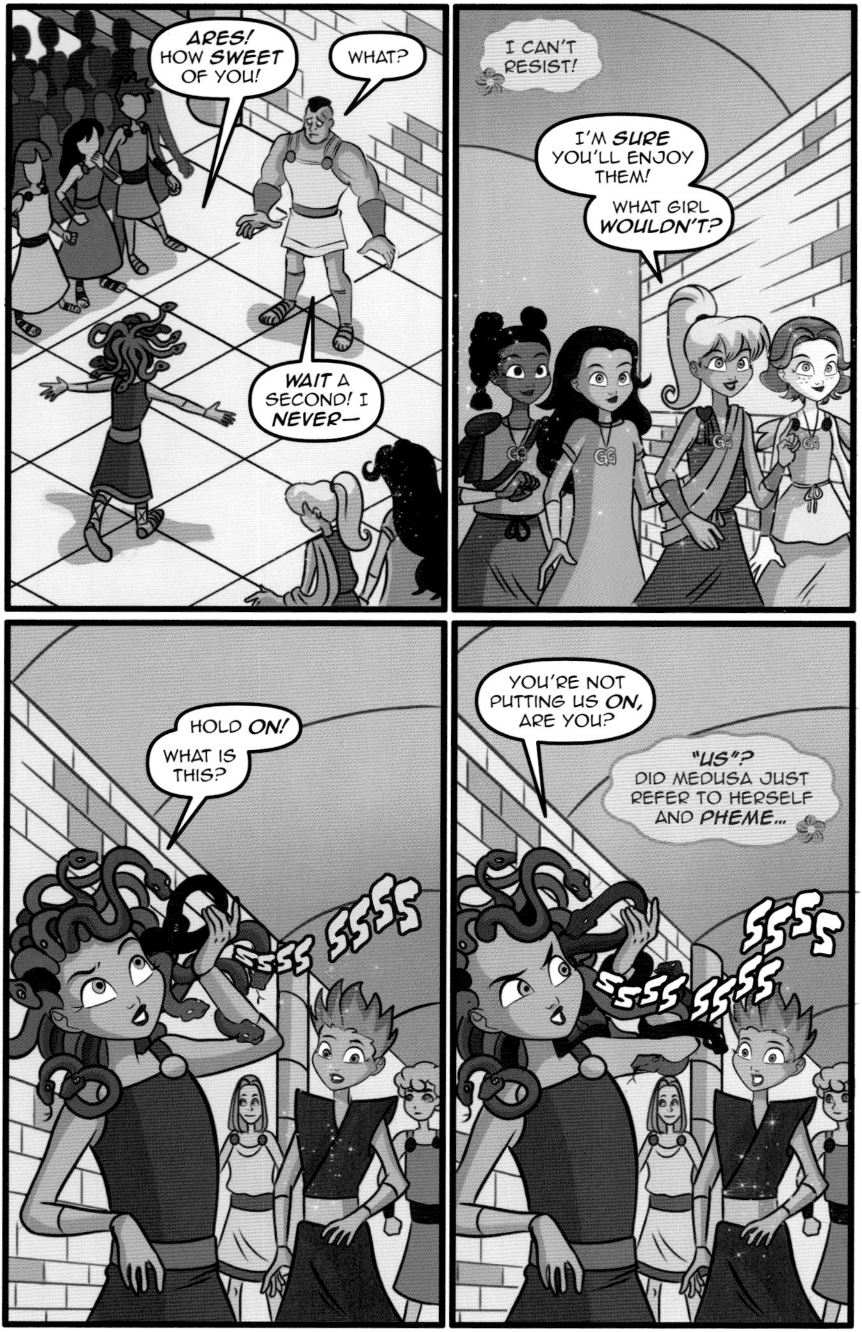
ARES! HOW SWEET OF YOU!
WHAT?
WAIT A SECOND! I NEVER—
I CAN'T RESIST!
I'M SURE YOU'LL ENJOY THEM!
WHAT GIRL WOULDN'T?
HOLD ON!
WHAT IS THIS?
SSSS SSSS
YOU'RE NOT PUTTING US ON, ARE YOU?
"US"? DID MEDUSA JUST REFER TO HERSELF AND PHEME...
SSSS SSSS SSSS

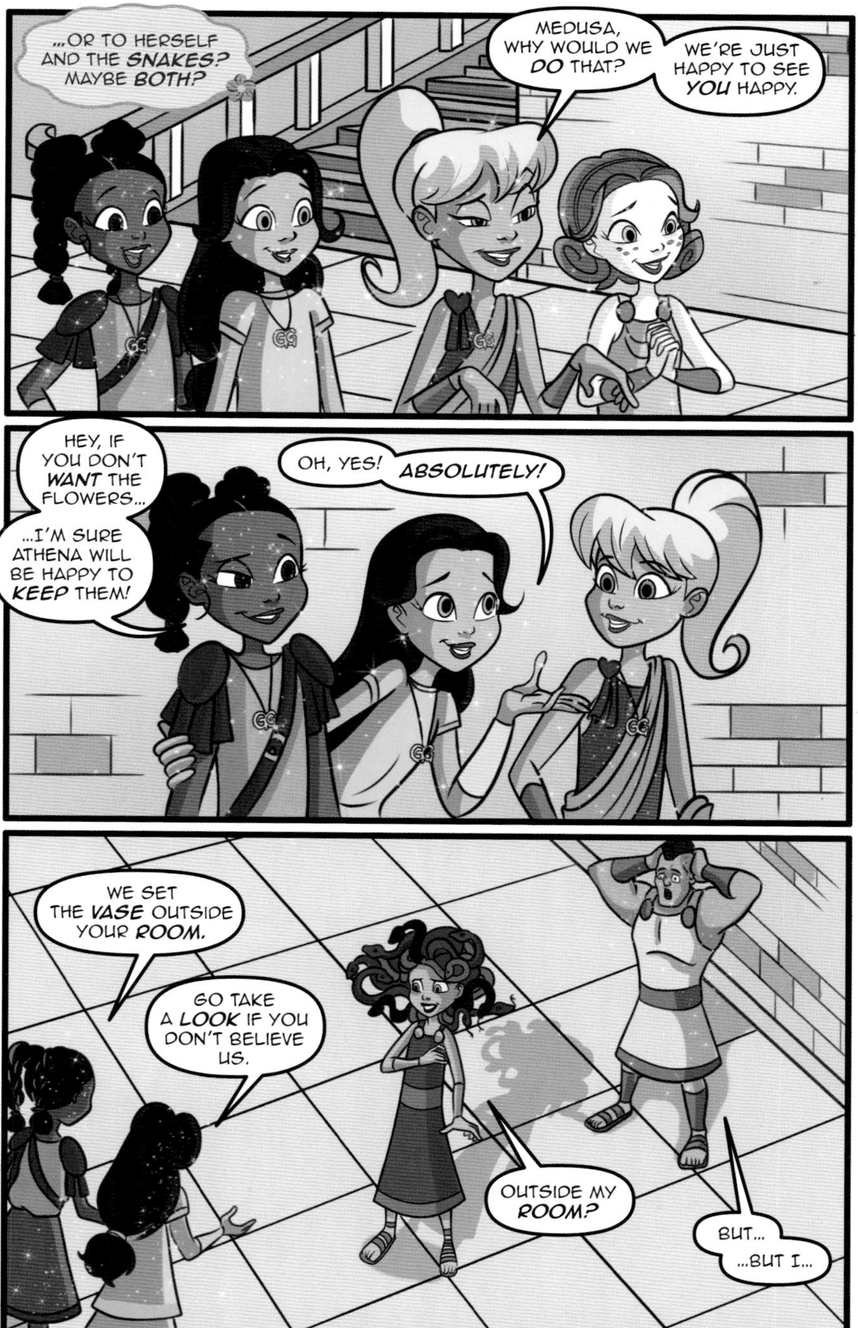
...OR TO HERSELF AND THE SNAKES? MAYBE BOTH?
MEDUSA, WHY WOULD WE DO THAT?
WE'RE JUST HAPPY TO SEE YOU HAPPY.
HEY, IF YOU DON'T WANT THE FLOWERS...
...I'M SURE ATHENA WILL BE HAPPY TO KEEP THEM!
OH, YES!
ABSOLUTELY!
WE SET THE VASE OUTSIDE YOUR ROOM.
GO TAKE A LOOK IF YOU DON'T BELIEVE US.
OUTSIDE MY ROOM?
BUT...
...BUT I...

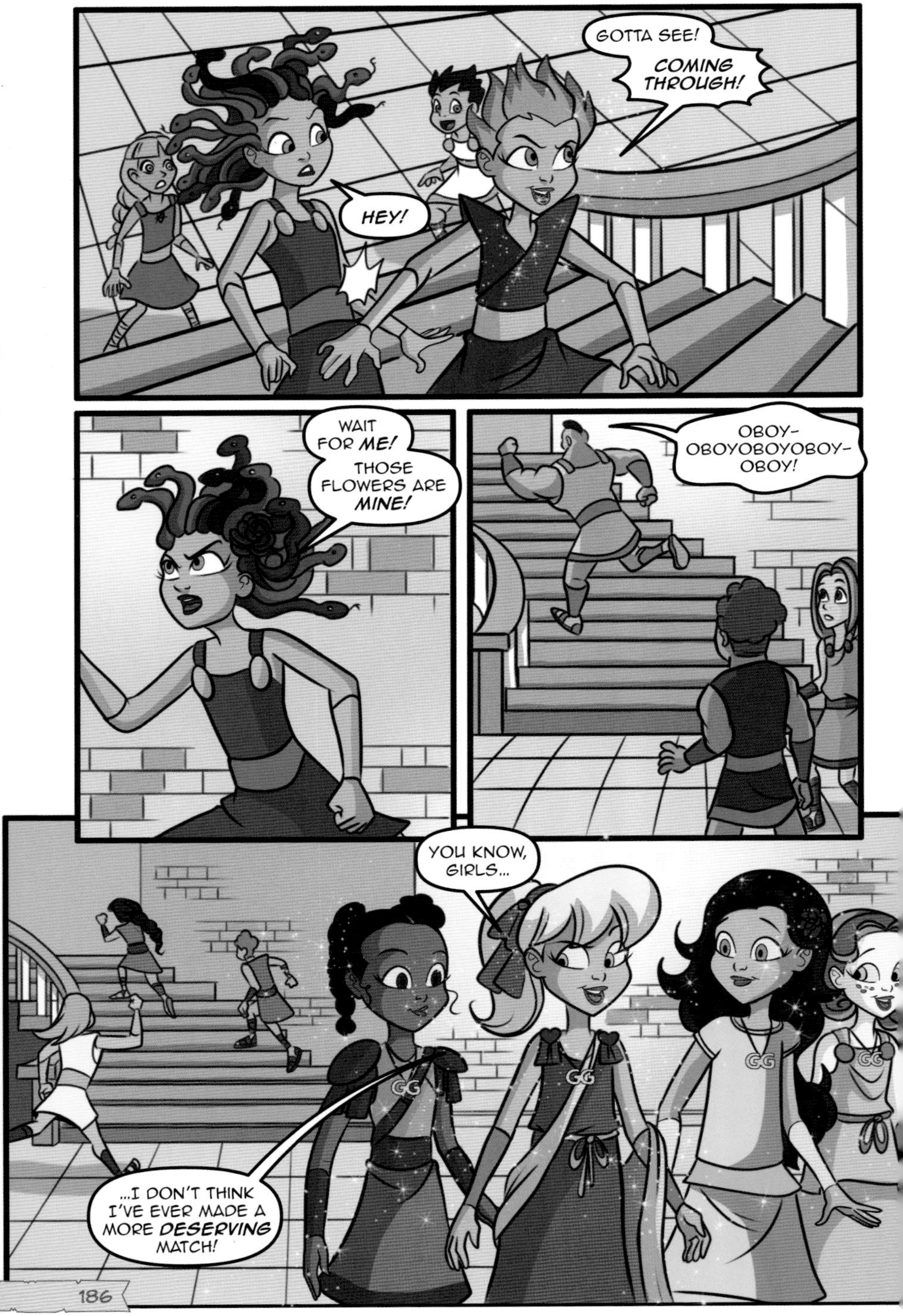
GOTTA SEE!
COMING THROUGH!
HEY!
WAIT FOR ME! THOSE FLOWERS ARE MINE!
OBOY-OBOYOBOYOBOYOBOY-OBOY!
YOU KNOW, GIRLS...
...I DON'T THINK I'VE EVER MADE A MORE DESERVING MATCH!

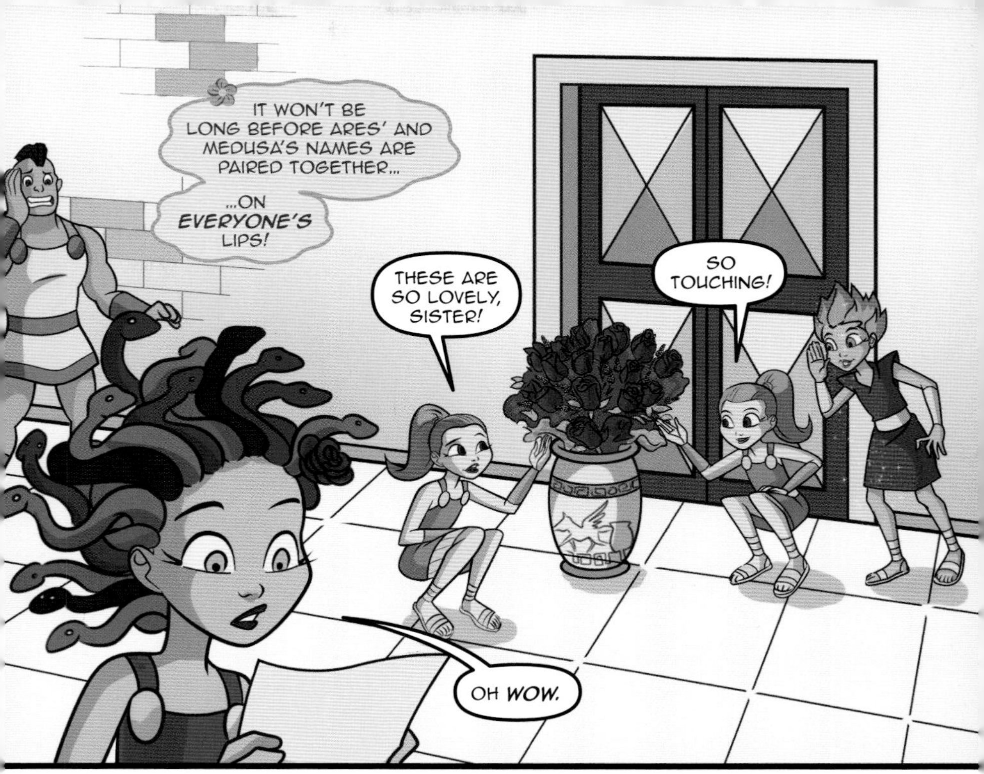
IT WON'T BE LONG BEFORE ARES' AND MEDUSA'S NAMES ARE PAIRED TOGETHER...
...ON *EVERYONE'S* LIPS!
THESE ARE SO LOVELY, SISTER!
SO TOUCHING!
OH *WOW.*

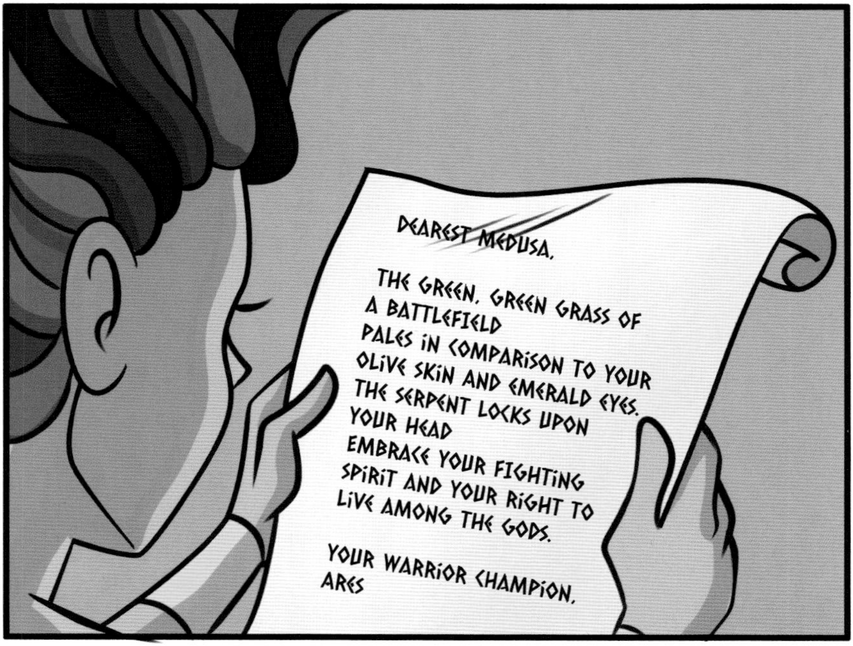
DEAREST MEDUSA,
THE GREEN, GREEN GRASS OF A BATTLEFIELD
PALES IN COMPARISON TO YOUR OLIVE SKIN AND EMERALD EYES.
THE SERPENT LOCKS UPON YOUR HEAD
EMBRACE YOUR FIGHTING SPIRIT AND YOUR RIGHT TO LIVE AMONG THE GODS.
YOUR WARRIOR CHAMPION,
ARES

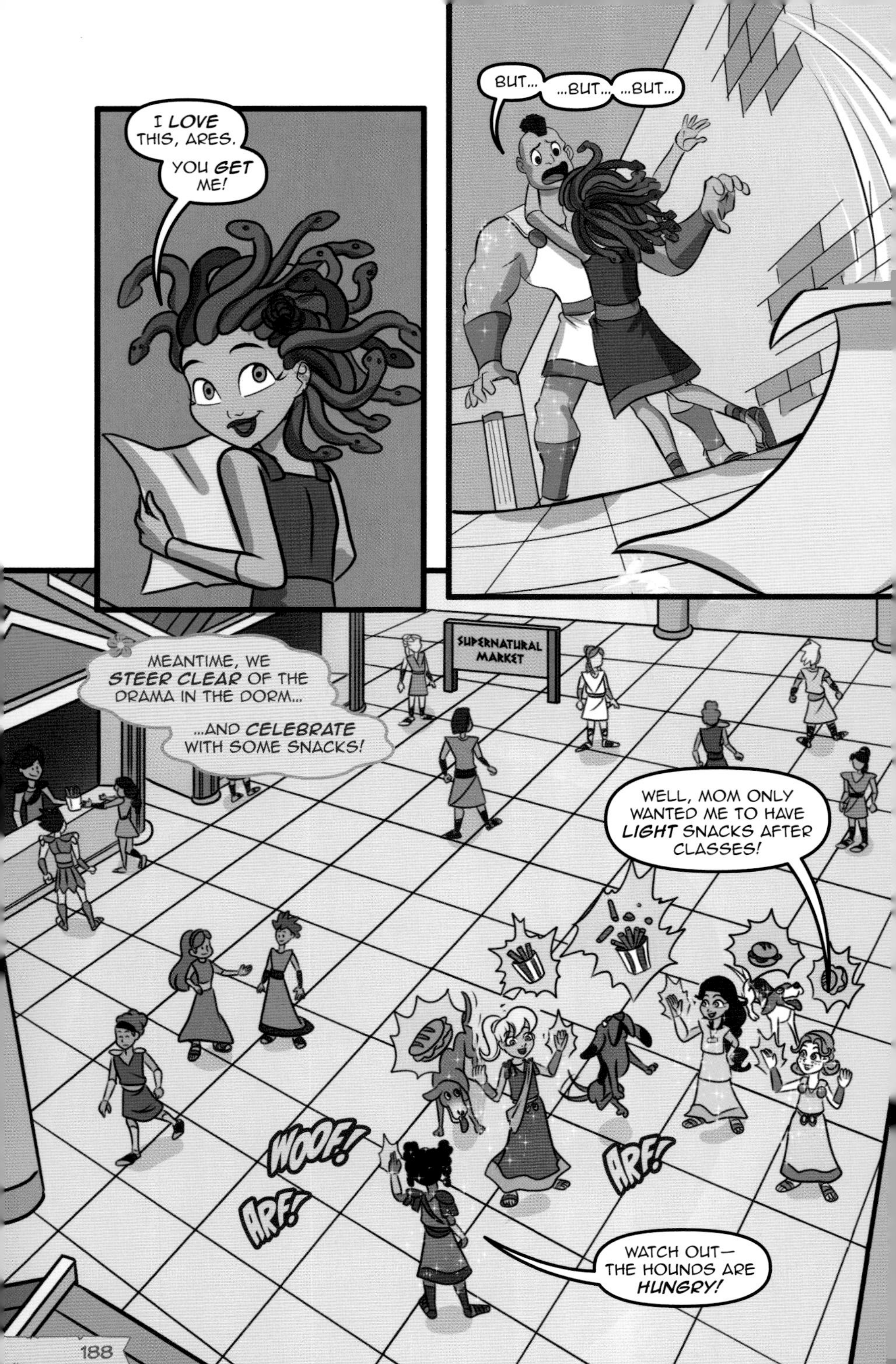
I LOVE THIS, ARES.
YOU GET ME!
BUT...
...BUT...
...BUT...
SUPERNATURAL MARKET
MEANTIME, WE STEER CLEAR OF THE DRAMA IN THE DORM...
...AND CELEBRATE WITH SOME SNACKS!
WELL, MOM ONLY WANTED ME TO HAVE LIGHT SNACKS AFTER CLASSES!
WOOF!
ARF!
ARF!
WATCH OUT— THE HOUNDS ARE HUNGRY!

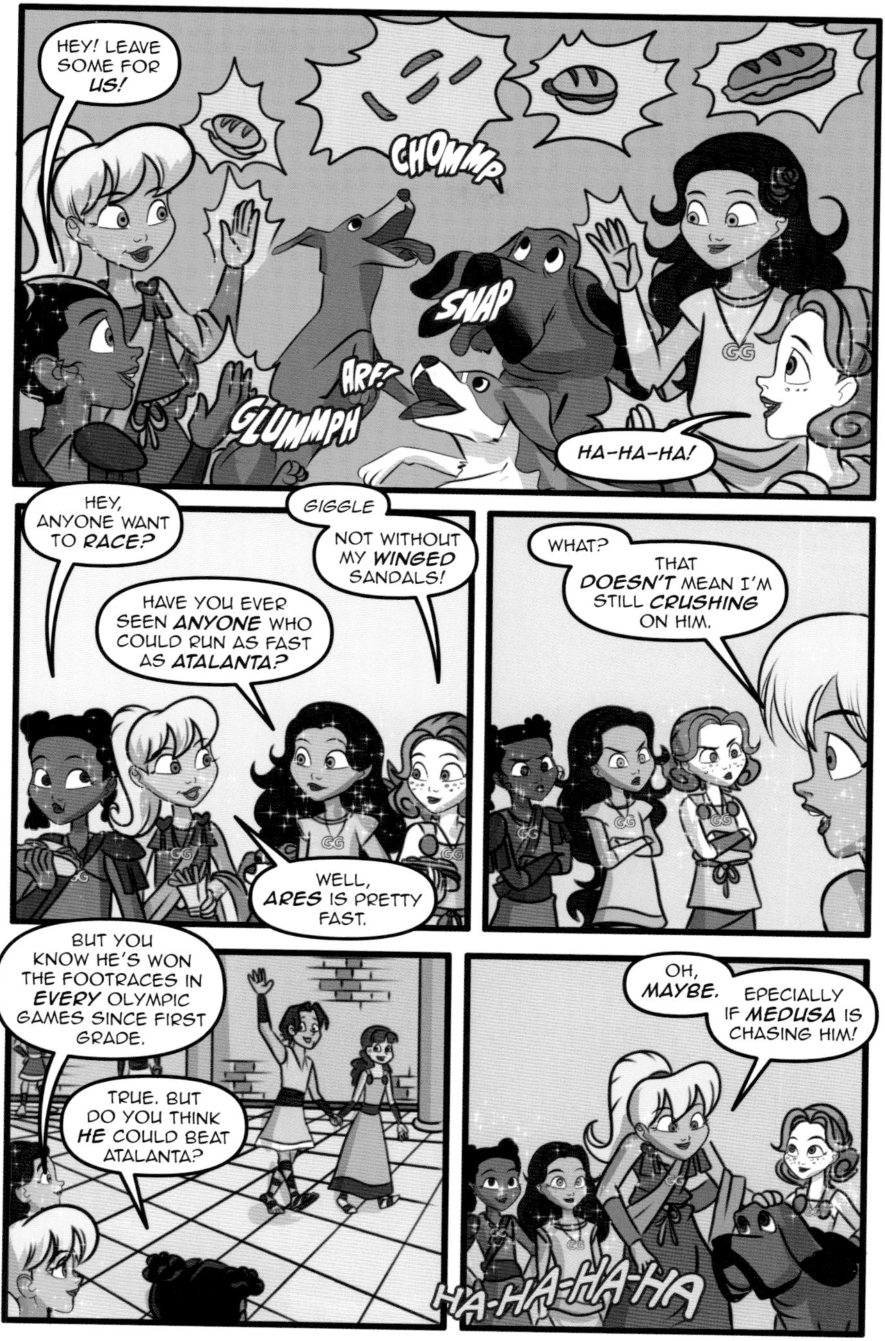
HEY! LEAVE SOME FOR US!
CHOMMP
SNAP
ARF!
GLUMMPH
HA-HA-HA!
HEY, ANYONE WANT TO RACE?
GIGGLE
NOT WITHOUT MY WINGED SANDALS!
HAVE YOU EVER SEEN ANYONE WHO COULD RUN AS FAST AS ATALANTA?
WELL, ARES IS PRETTY FAST.
WHAT?
THAT DOESN'T MEAN I'M STILL CRUSHING ON HIM.
BUT YOU KNOW HE'S WON THE FOOTRACES IN EVERY OLYMPIC GAMES SINCE FIRST GRADE.
TRUE. BUT DO YOU THINK HE COULD BEAT ATALANTA?
OH, MAYBE.
EPECIALLY IF MEDUSA IS CHASING HIM!
HA-HA-HA-HA-HA

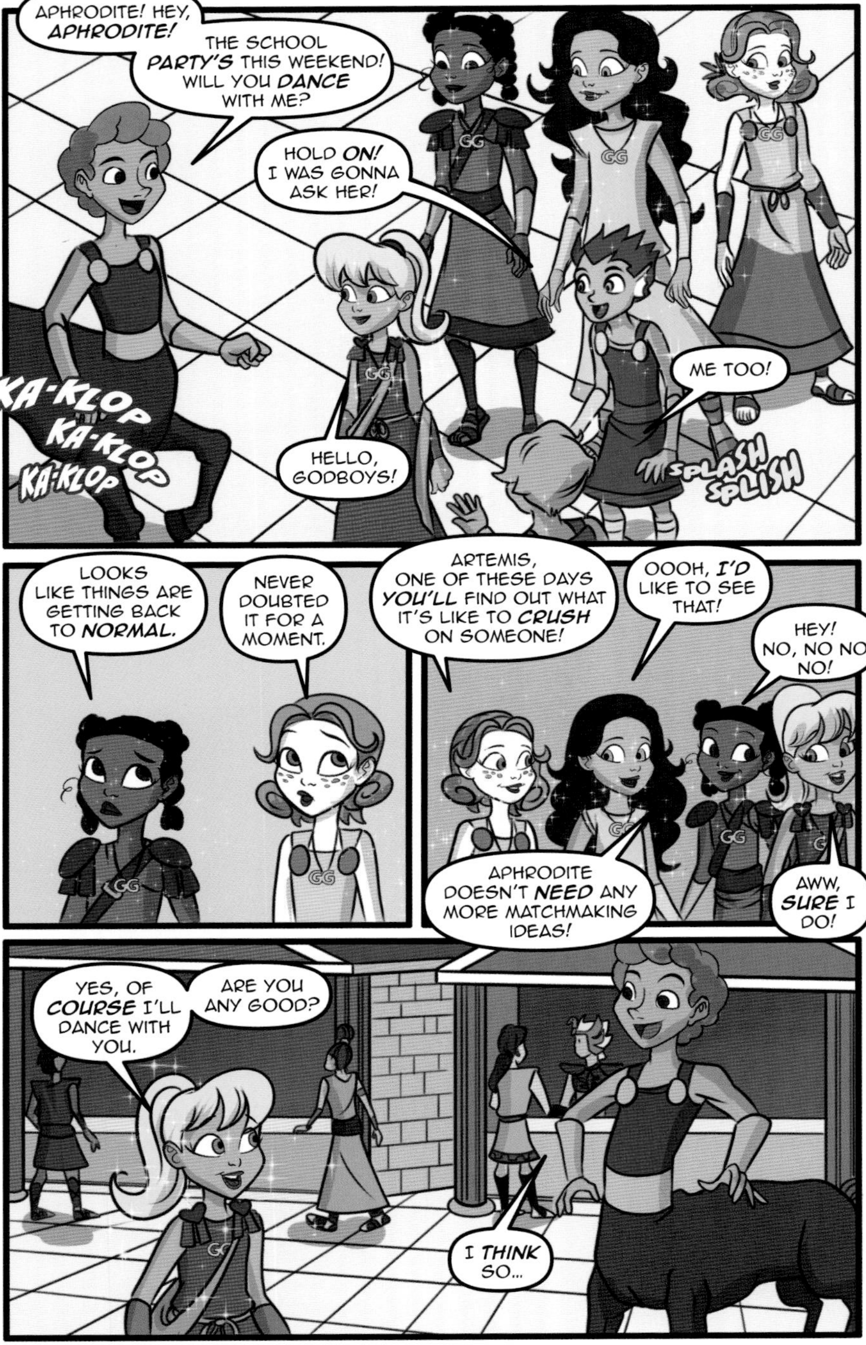
APHRODITE! HEY, APHRODITE!
THE SCHOOL PARTY'S THIS WEEKEND! WILL YOU DANCE WITH ME?
HOLD ON! I WAS GONNA ASK HER!
ME TOO!
HELLO, GODBOYS!
KA-KLOP KA-KLOP KA-KLOP
SPLASH SPLISH
LOOKS LIKE THINGS ARE GETTING BACK TO NORMAL.
NEVER DOUBTED IT FOR A MOMENT.
ARTEMIS, ONE OF THESE DAYS YOU'LL FIND OUT WHAT IT'S LIKE TO CRUSH ON SOMEONE!
OOOH, I'D LIKE TO SEE THAT!
HEY! NO, NO NO NO!
APHRODITE DOESN'T NEED ANY MORE MATCHMAKING IDEAS!
AWW, SURE I DO!
YES, OF COURSE I'LL DANCE WITH YOU.
ARE YOU ANY GOOD?
I THINK SO...

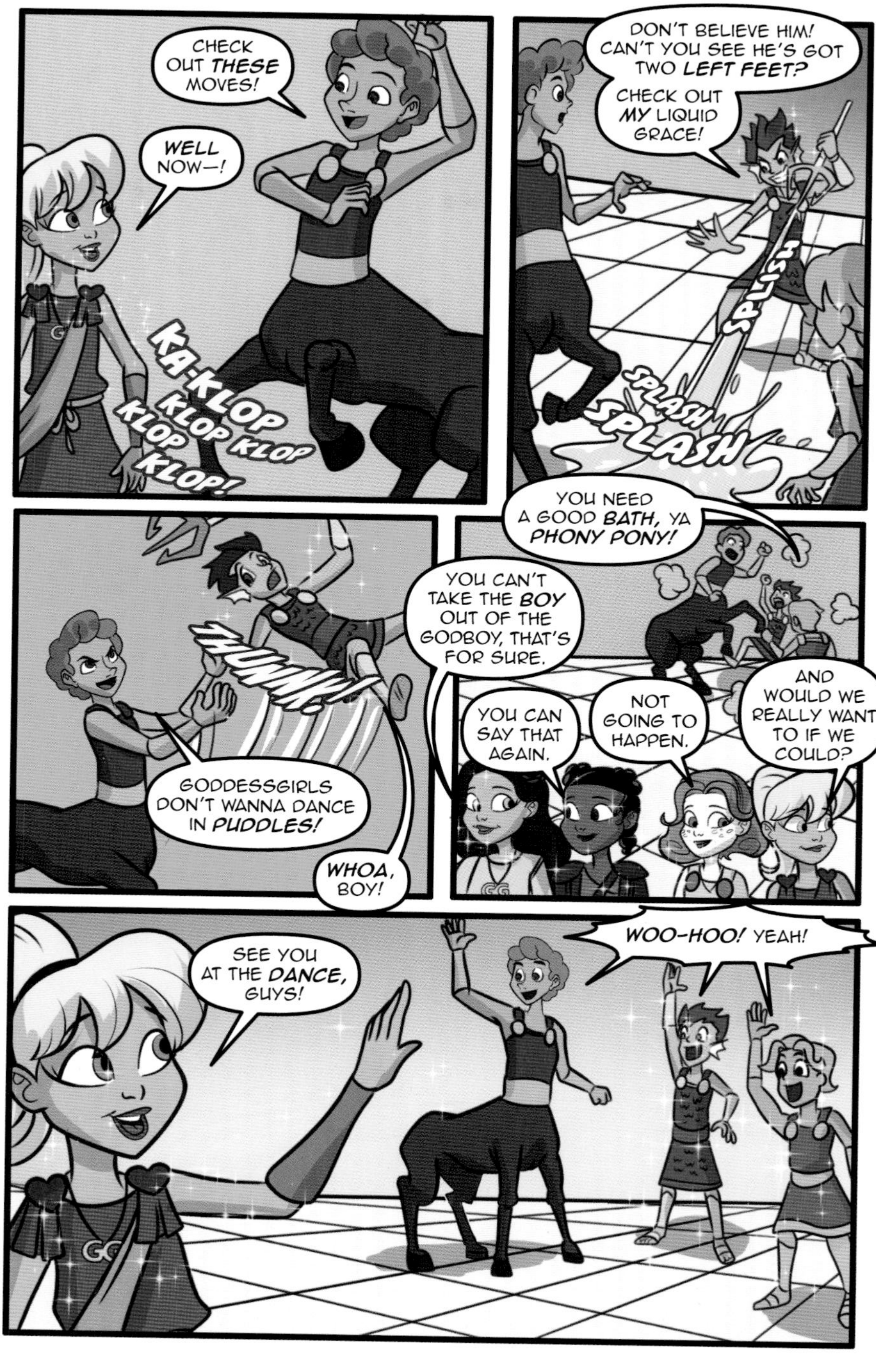
CHECK OUT THESE MOVES!
WELL NOW—!
KA-KLOP KLOP KLOP KLOP KLOP!
DON'T BELIEVE HIM! CAN'T YOU SEE HE'S GOT TWO LEFT FEET?
CHECK OUT MY LIQUID GRACE!
SPLISH
SPLASH
SPLASH
THUNK!
GODDESSGIRLS DON'T WANNA DANCE IN PUDDLES!
WHOA, BOY!
YOU NEED A GOOD BATH, YA PHONY PONY!
YOU CAN'T TAKE THE BOY OUT OF THE GODBOY, THAT'S FOR SURE.
YOU CAN SAY THAT AGAIN.
NOT GOING TO HAPPEN.
AND WOULD WE REALLY WANT TO IF WE COULD?
SEE YOU AT THE DANCE, GUYS!
WOO-HOO! YEAH!

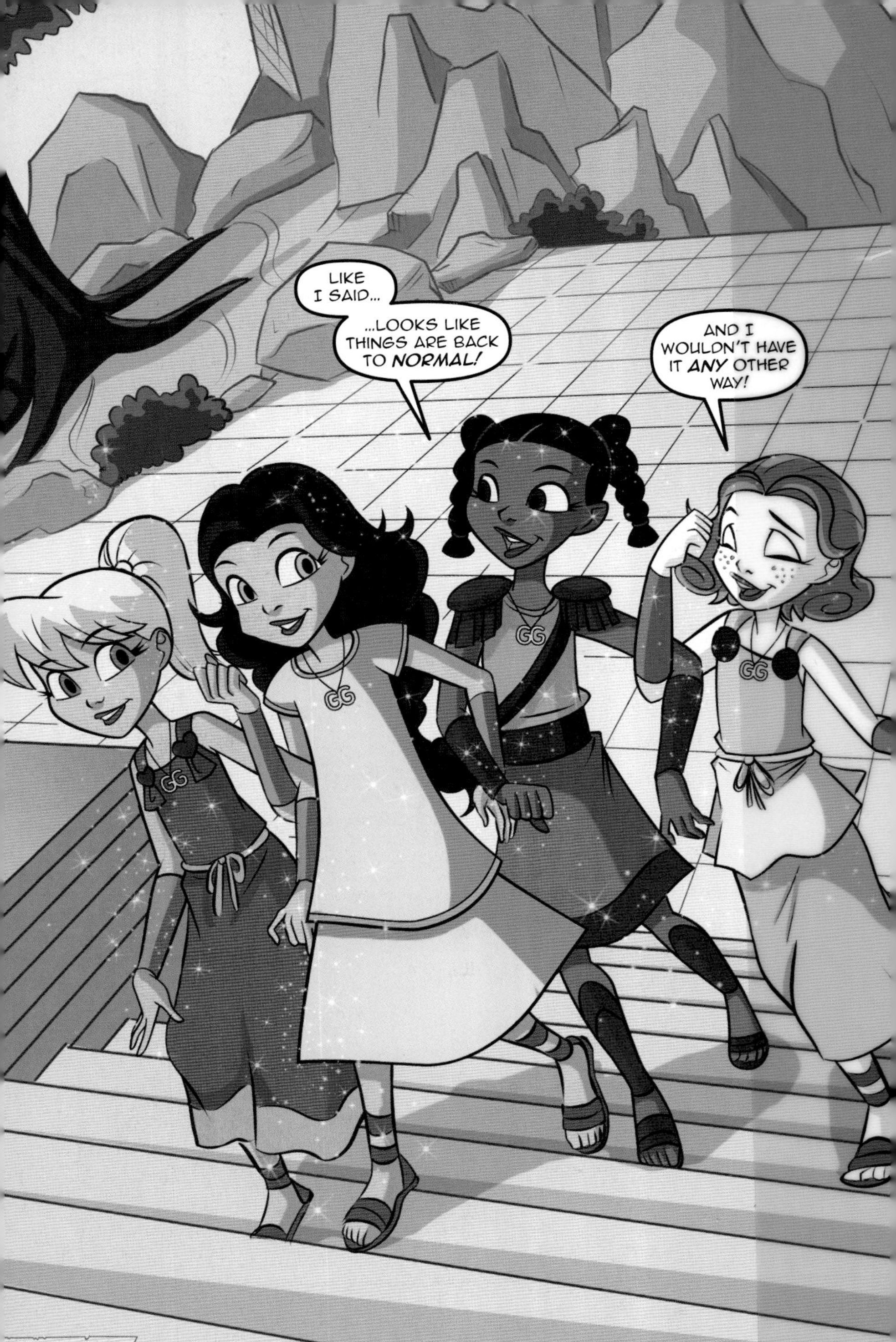
LIKE I SAID...
...LOOKS LIKE THINGS ARE BACK TO NORMAL!
AND I WOULDN'T HAVE IT ANY OTHER WAY!